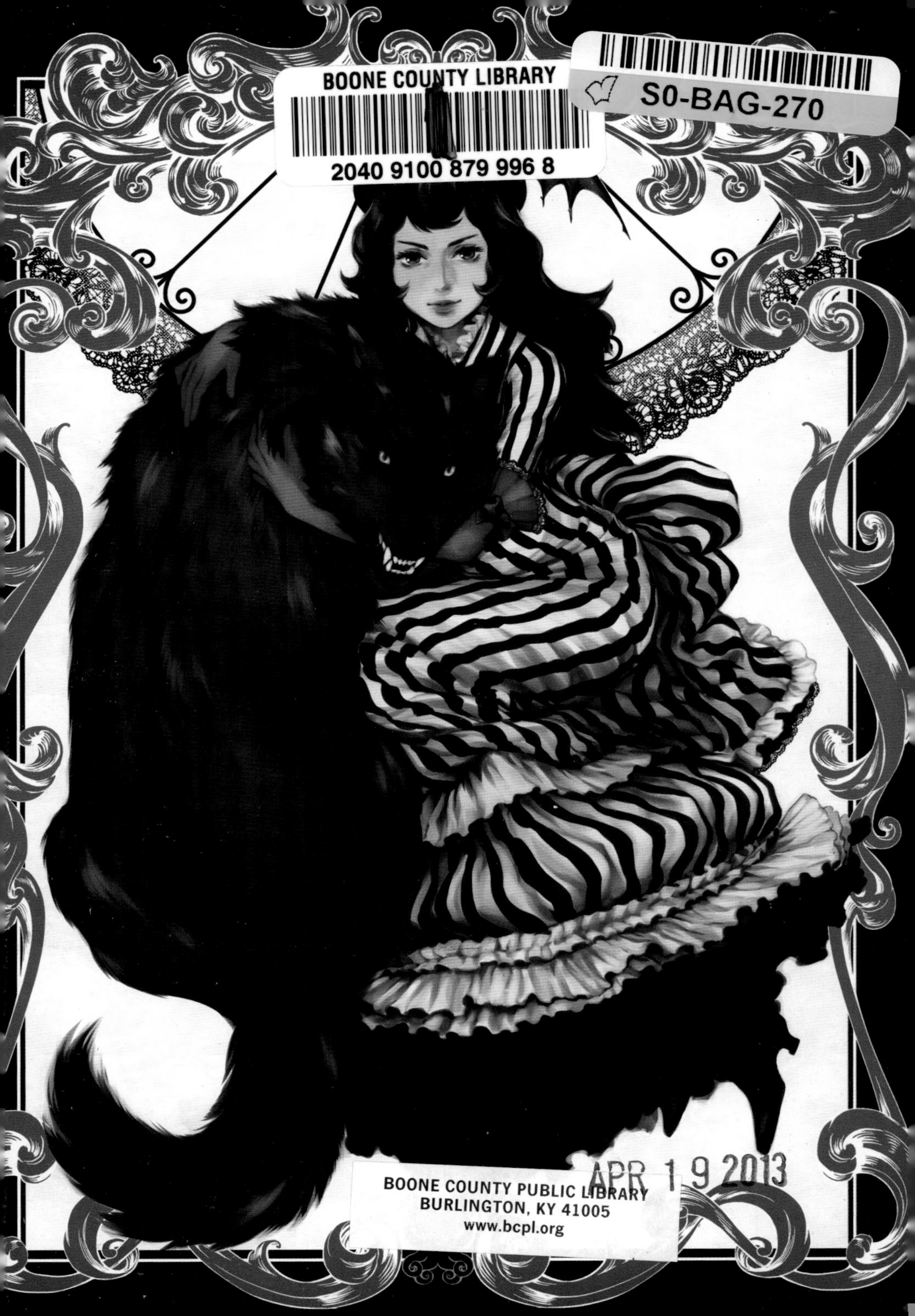

SOULLESS

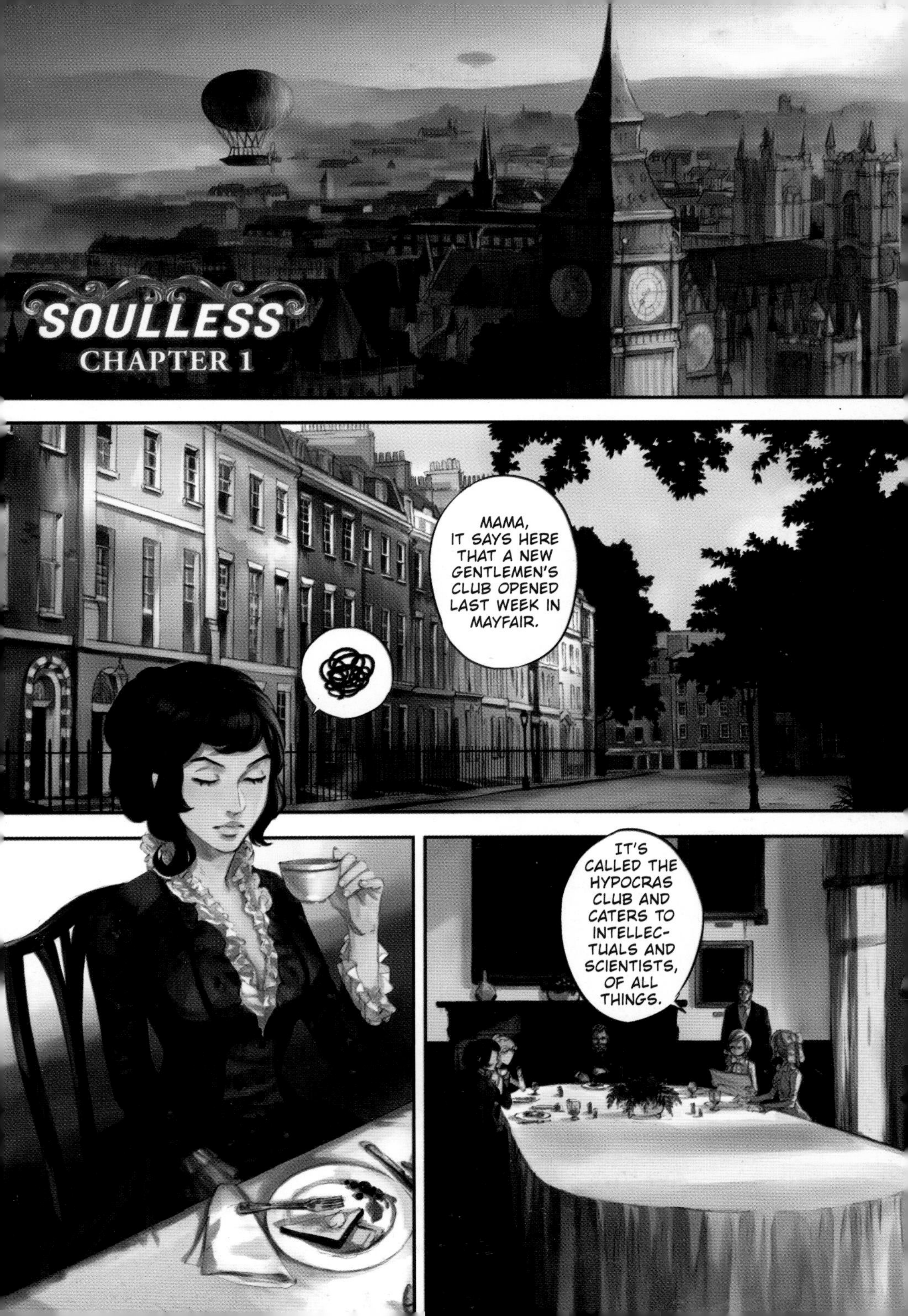
SOULLESS
CHAPTER 1
MAMA, IT SAYS HERE THAT A NEW GENTLEMEN'S CLUB OPENED LAST WEEK IN MAYFAIR.
IT'S CALLED THE HYPOCRAS CLUB AND CATERS TO INTELLEC-TUALS AND SCIENTISTS, OF ALL THINGS.

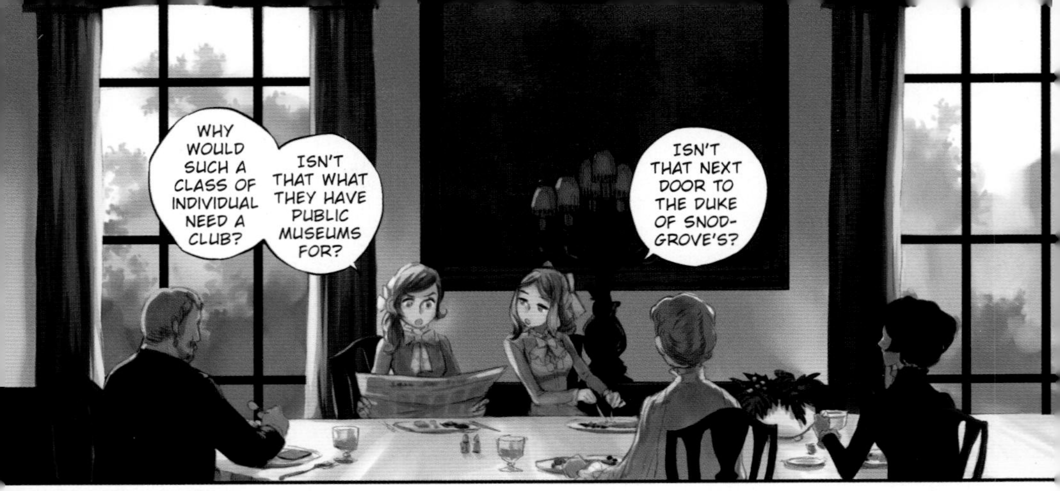
WHY WOULD SUCH A CLASS OF INDIVIDUAL NEED A CLUB?
ISN'T THAT WHAT THEY HAVE PUBLIC MUSEUMS FOR?
ISN'T THAT NEXT DOOR TO THE DUKE OF SNOD-GROVE'S?

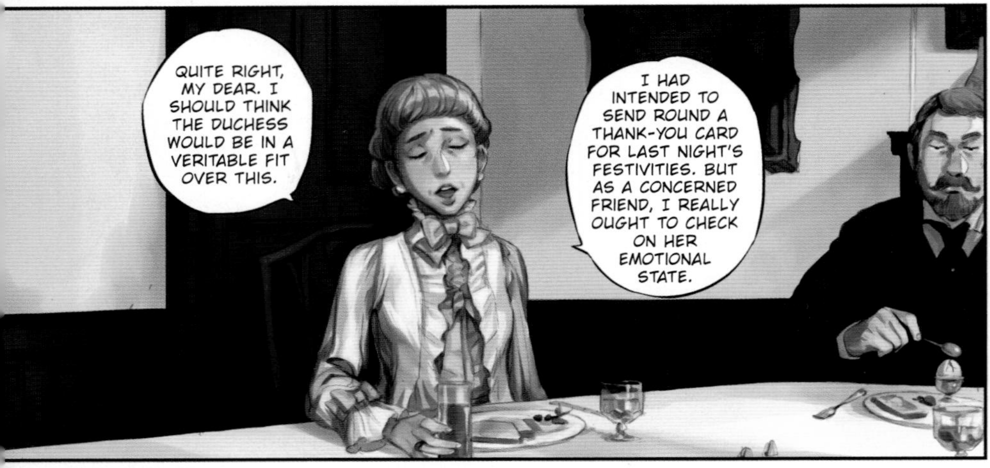
QUITE RIGHT, MY DEAR. I SHOULD THINK THE DUCHESS WOULD BE IN A VERITABLE FIT OVER THIS.
I HAD INTENDED TO SEND ROUND A THANK-YOU CARD FOR LAST NIGHT'S FESTIVITIES. BUT AS A CONCERNED FRIEND, I REALLY OUGHT TO CHECK ON HER EMOTIONAL STATE.

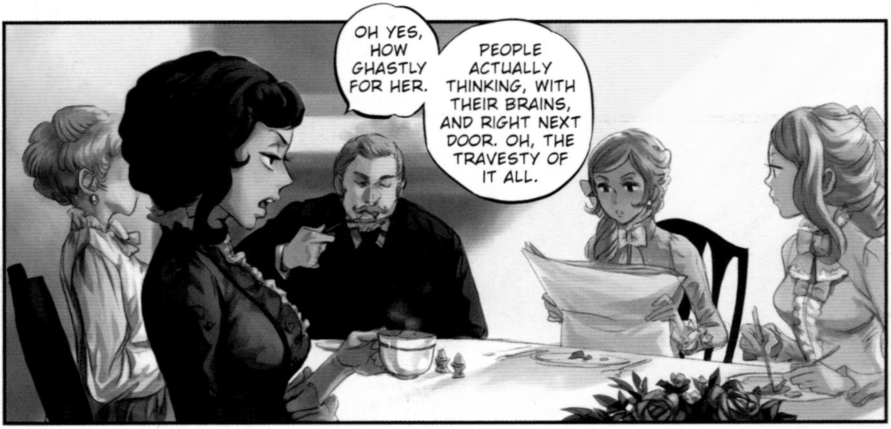
OH YES, HOW GHASTLY FOR HER.
PEOPLE ACTUALLY THINKING, WITH THEIR BRAINS, AND RIGHT NEXT DOOR. OH, THE TRAVESTY OF IT ALL.

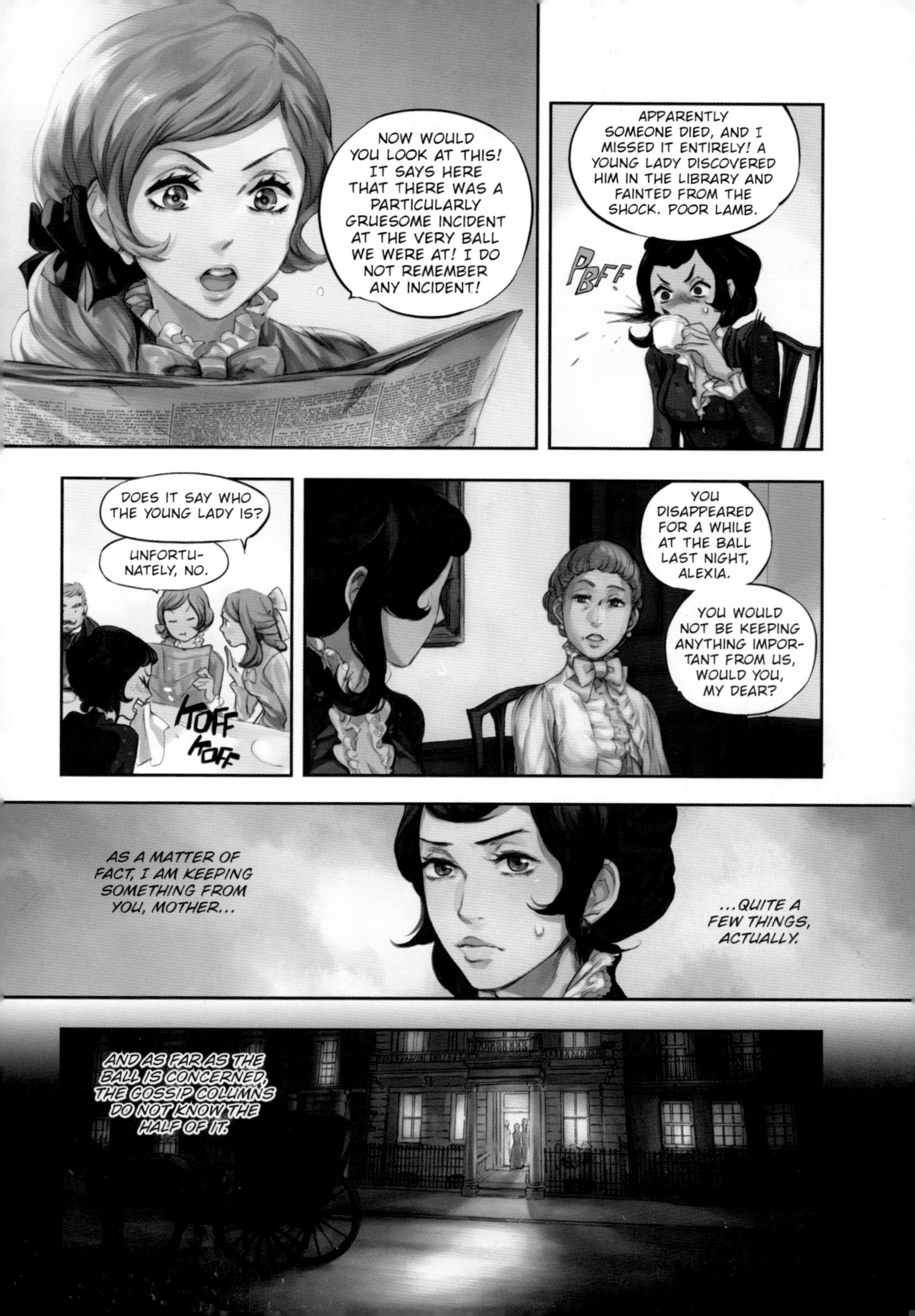
NOW WOULD YOU LOOK AT THIS! IT SAYS HERE THAT THERE WAS A PARTICULARLY GRUESOME INCIDENT AT THE VERY BALL WE WERE AT! I DO NOT REMEMBER ANY INCIDENT!
APPARENTLY SOMEONE DIED, AND I MISSED IT ENTIRELY! A YOUNG LADY DISCOVERED HIM IN THE LIBRARY AND FAINTED FROM THE SHOCK. POOR LAMB.
PBFF
DOES IT SAY WHO THE YOUNG LADY IS?
UNFORTU-NATELY, NO.
KOFF KOFF
YOU DISAPPEARED FOR A WHILE AT THE BALL LAST NIGHT, ALEXIA.
YOU WOULD NOT BE KEEPING ANYTHING IMPOR-TANT FROM US, WOULD YOU, MY DEAR?
AS A MATTER OF FACT, I AM KEEPING SOMETHING FROM YOU, MOTHER...
...QUITE A FEW THINGS, ACTUALLY.
AND AS FAR AS THE BALL IS CONCERNED, THE GOSSIP COLUMNS DO NOT KNOW THE HALF OF IT.

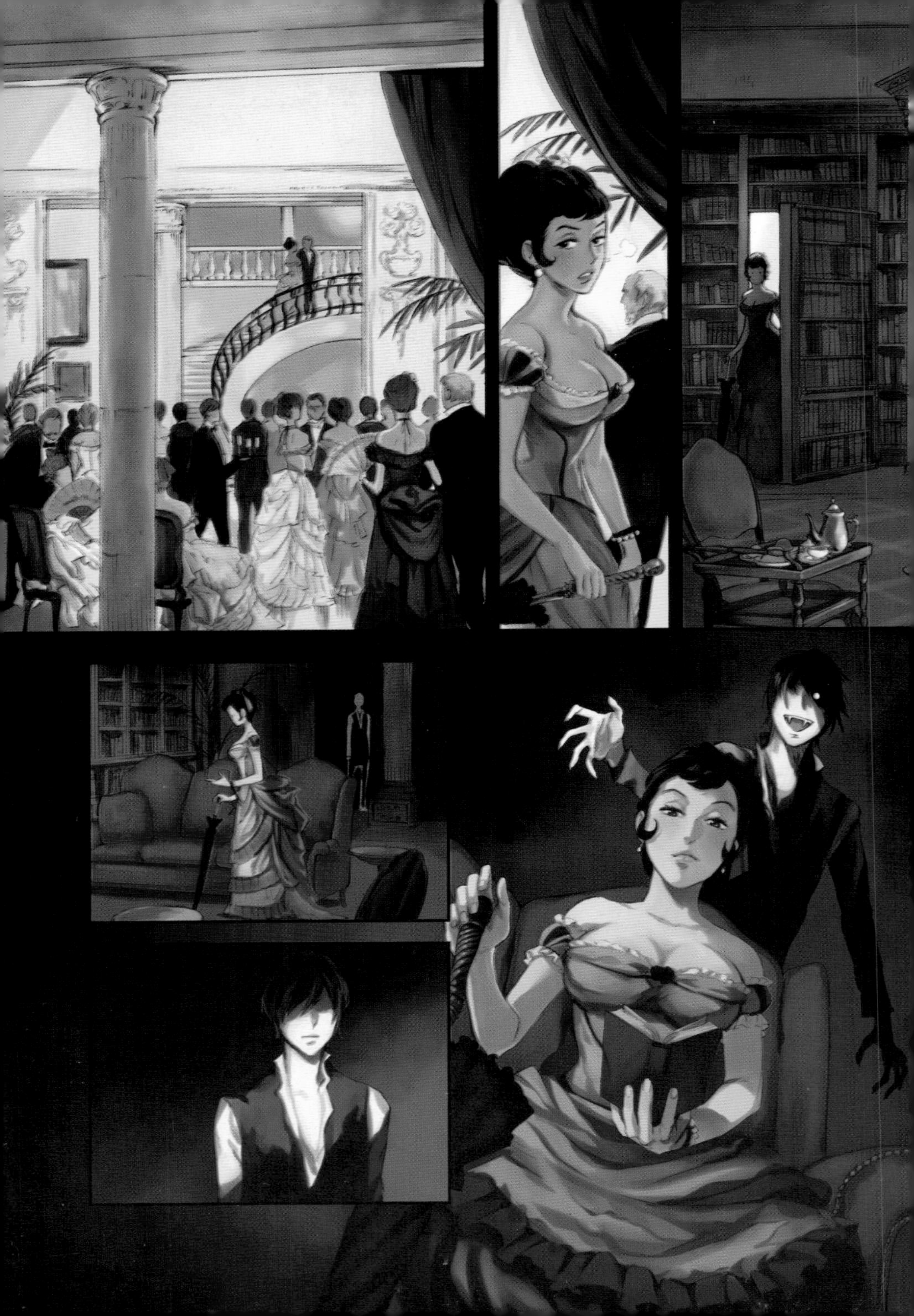

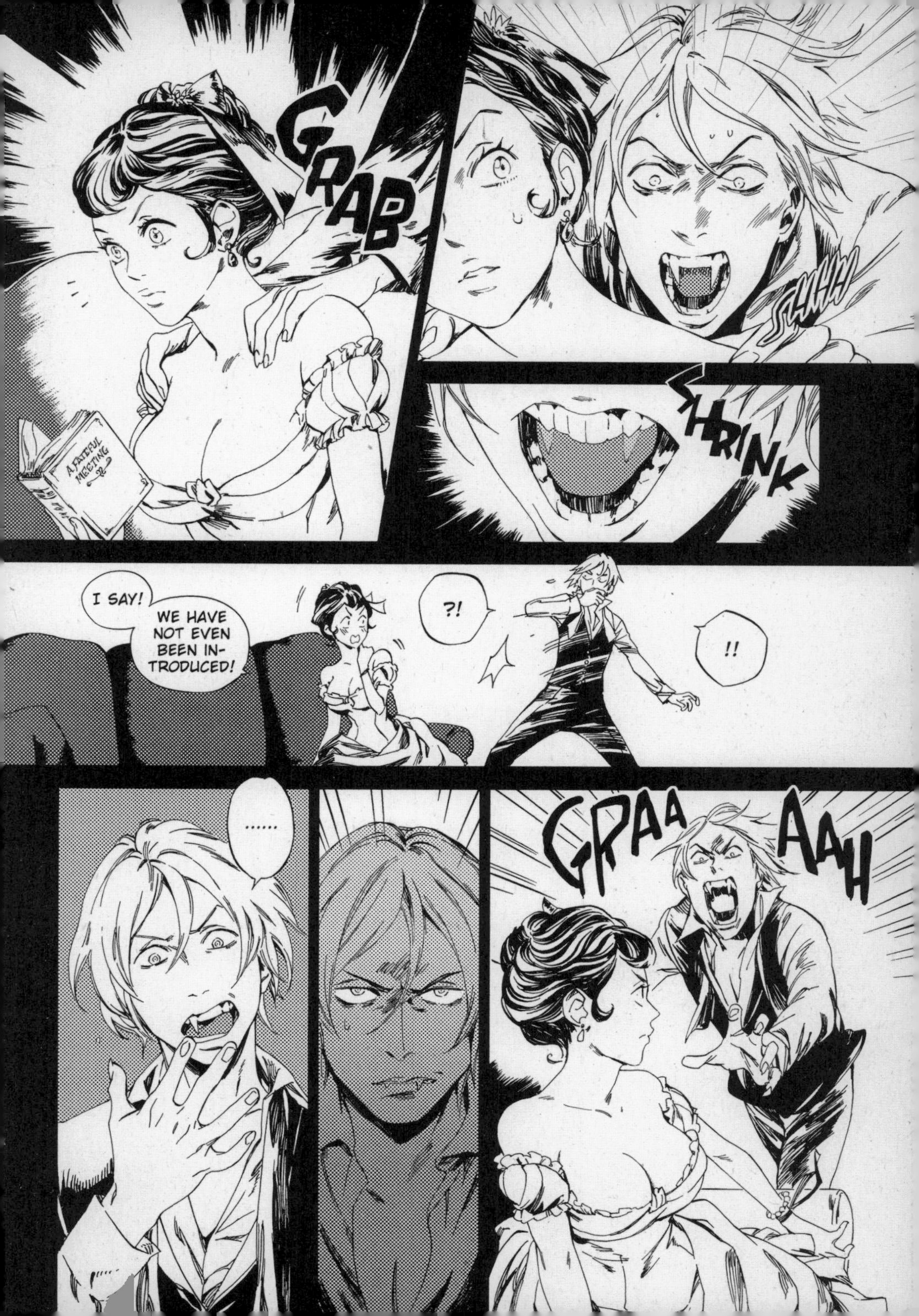
GRAB
A FATEFUL MEETING
SHHH
SHRINK
I SAY!
WE HAVE NOT EVEN BEEN IN-TRODUCED!
?!
!!
......
GRAA AAH

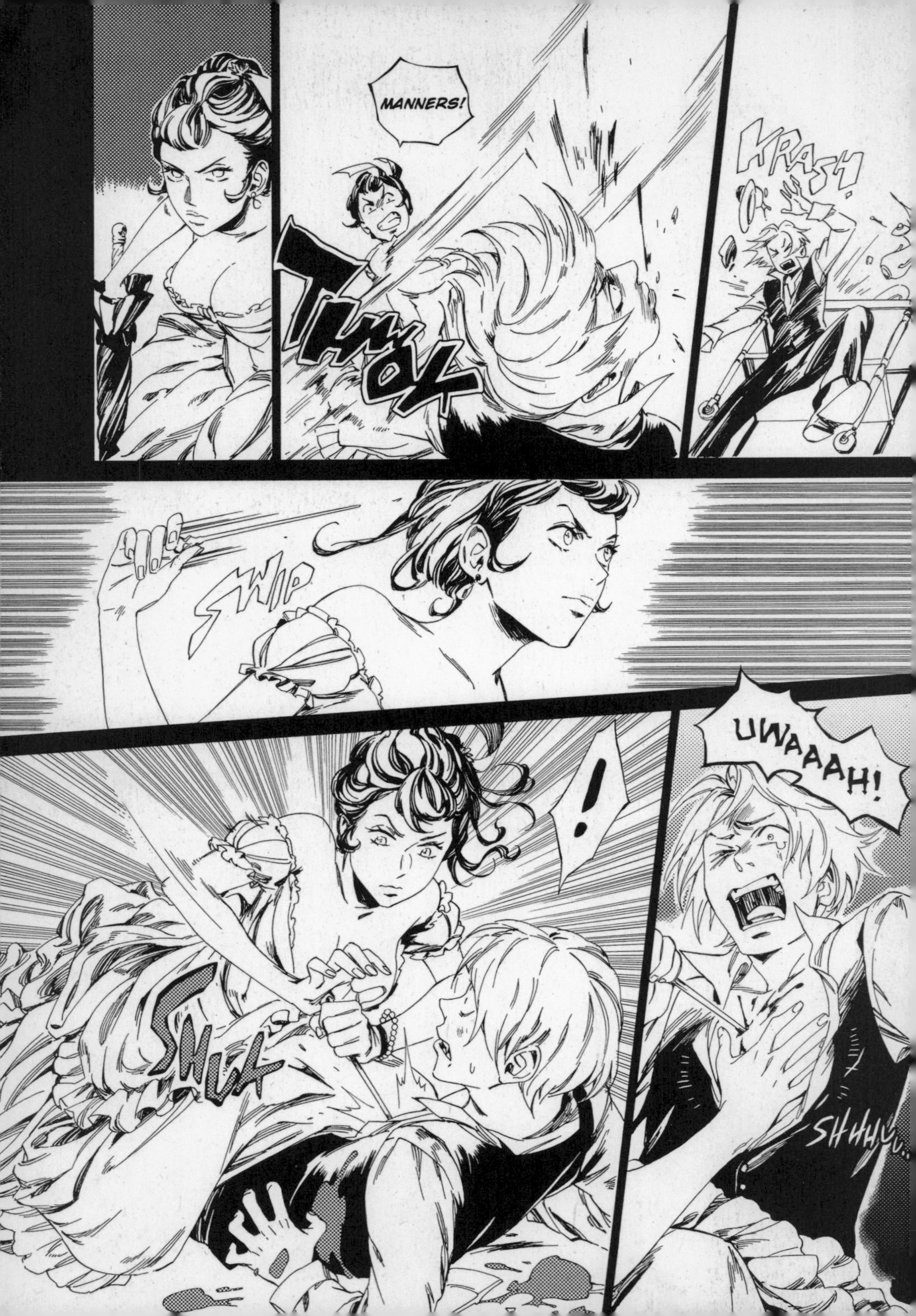
MANNERS!
THWOK
KRASH!
SWIP
!
SHUK
UWAAAH!
SHUUU...

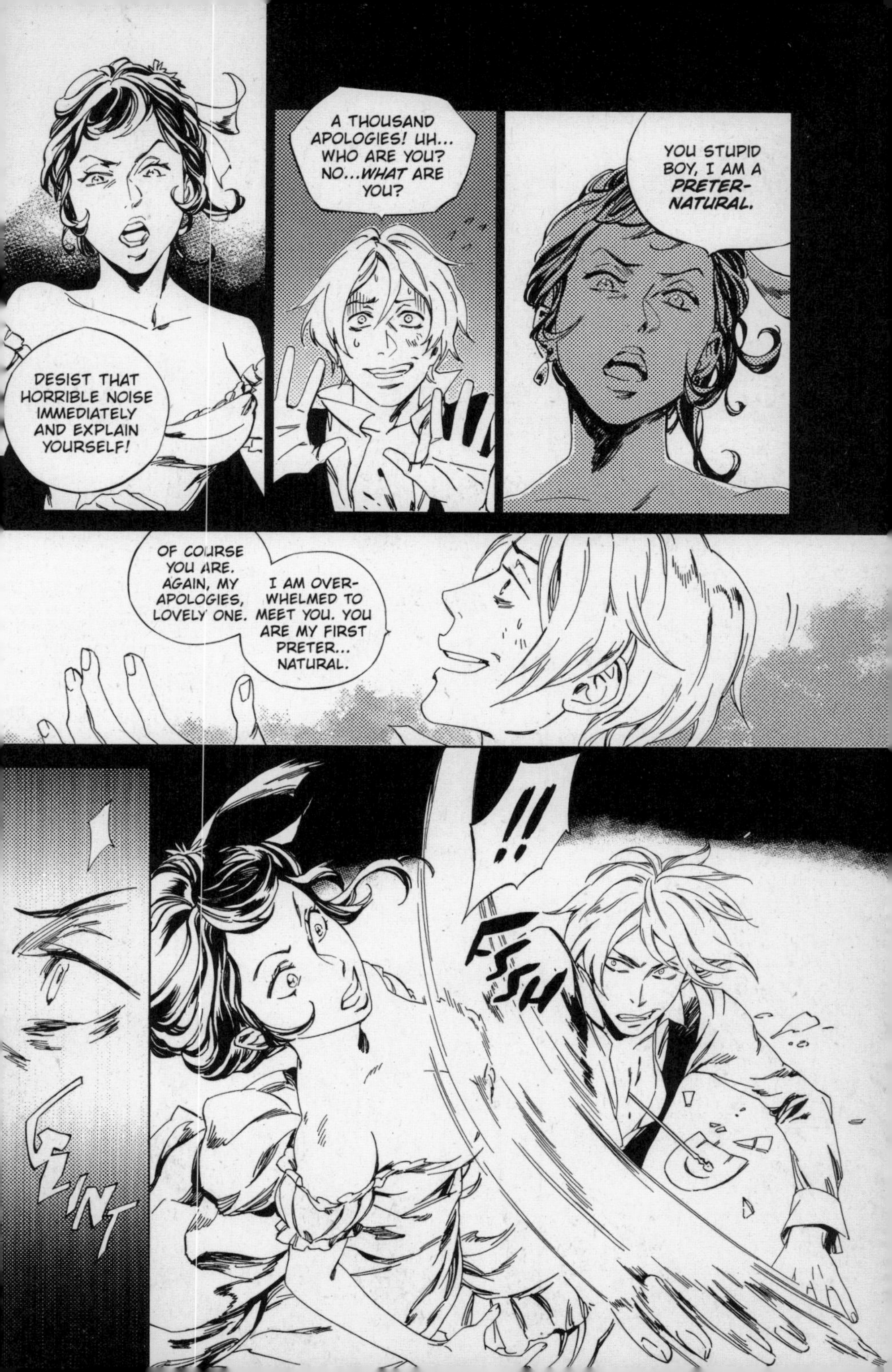
DESIST THAT HORRIBLE NOISE IMMEDIATELY AND EXPLAIN YOURSELF!
A THOUSAND APOLOGIES! UH... WHO ARE YOU? NO...*WHAT* ARE YOU?
YOU STUPID BOY, I AM A *PRETER-NATURAL.*
OF COURSE YOU ARE. AGAIN, MY APOLOGIES, LOVELY ONE.
I AM OVER-WHELMED TO MEET YOU. YOU ARE MY FIRST PRETER... NATURAL.
GLINT
!!
FSSH

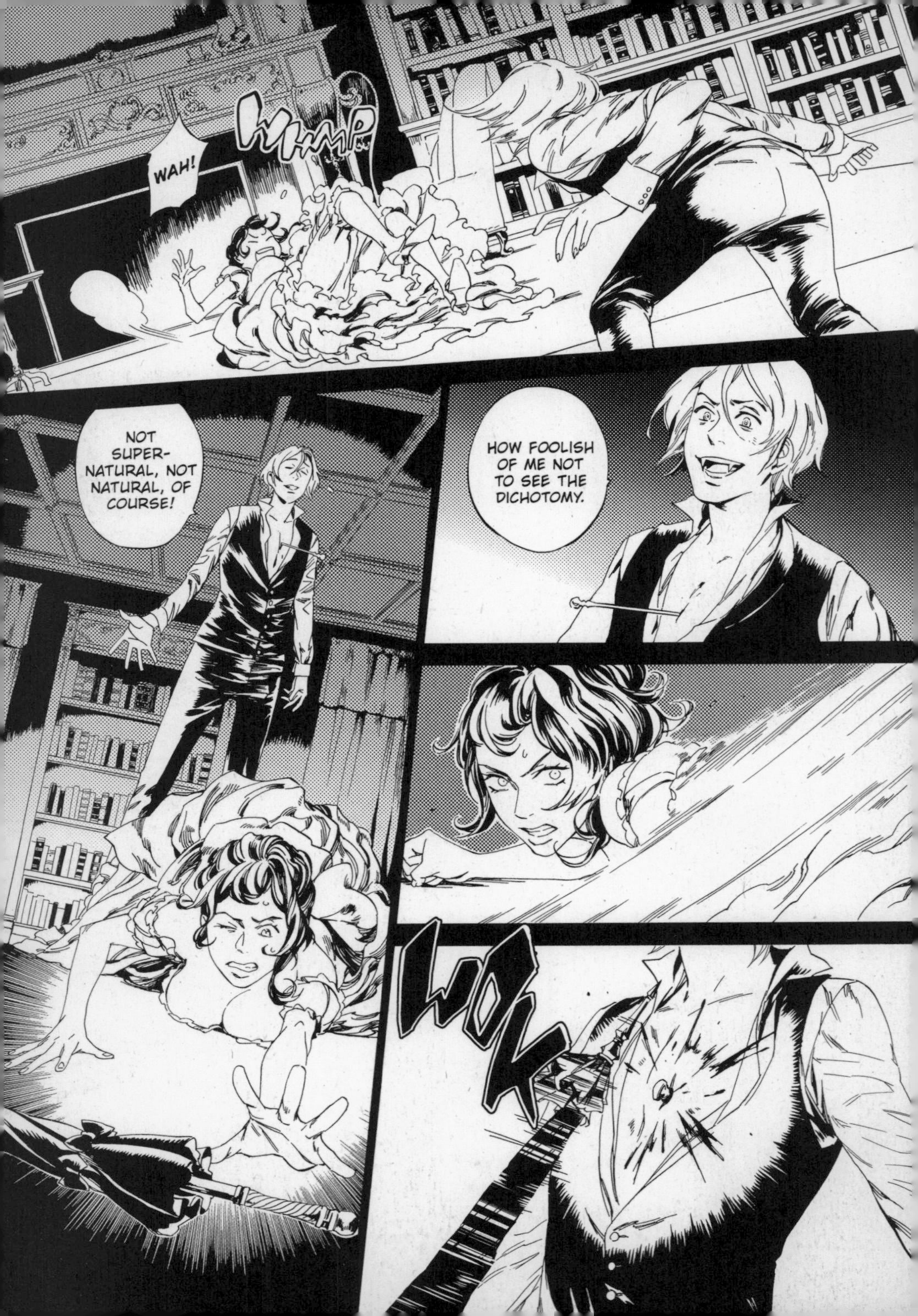
WHUMP
WAH!
NOT SUPER-NATURAL, NOT NATURAL, OF COURSE!
HOW FOOLISH OF ME NOT TO SEE THE DICHOTOMY.
WOK

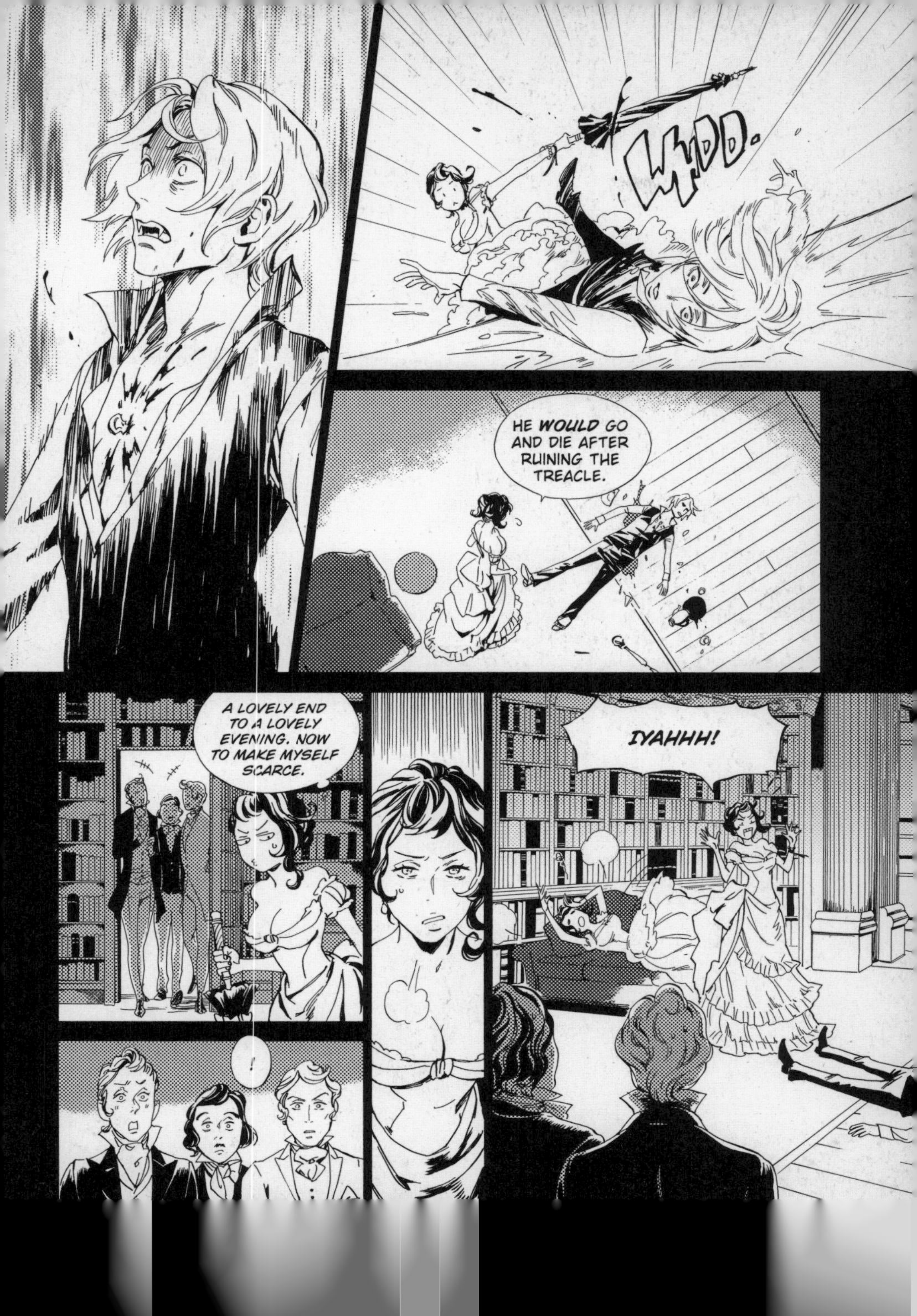
WHDD.
HE WOULD GO AND DIE AFTER RUINING THE TREACLE.
A LOVELY END TO A LOVELY EVENING. NOW TO MAKE MYSELF SCARCE.
!
IYAHHH!

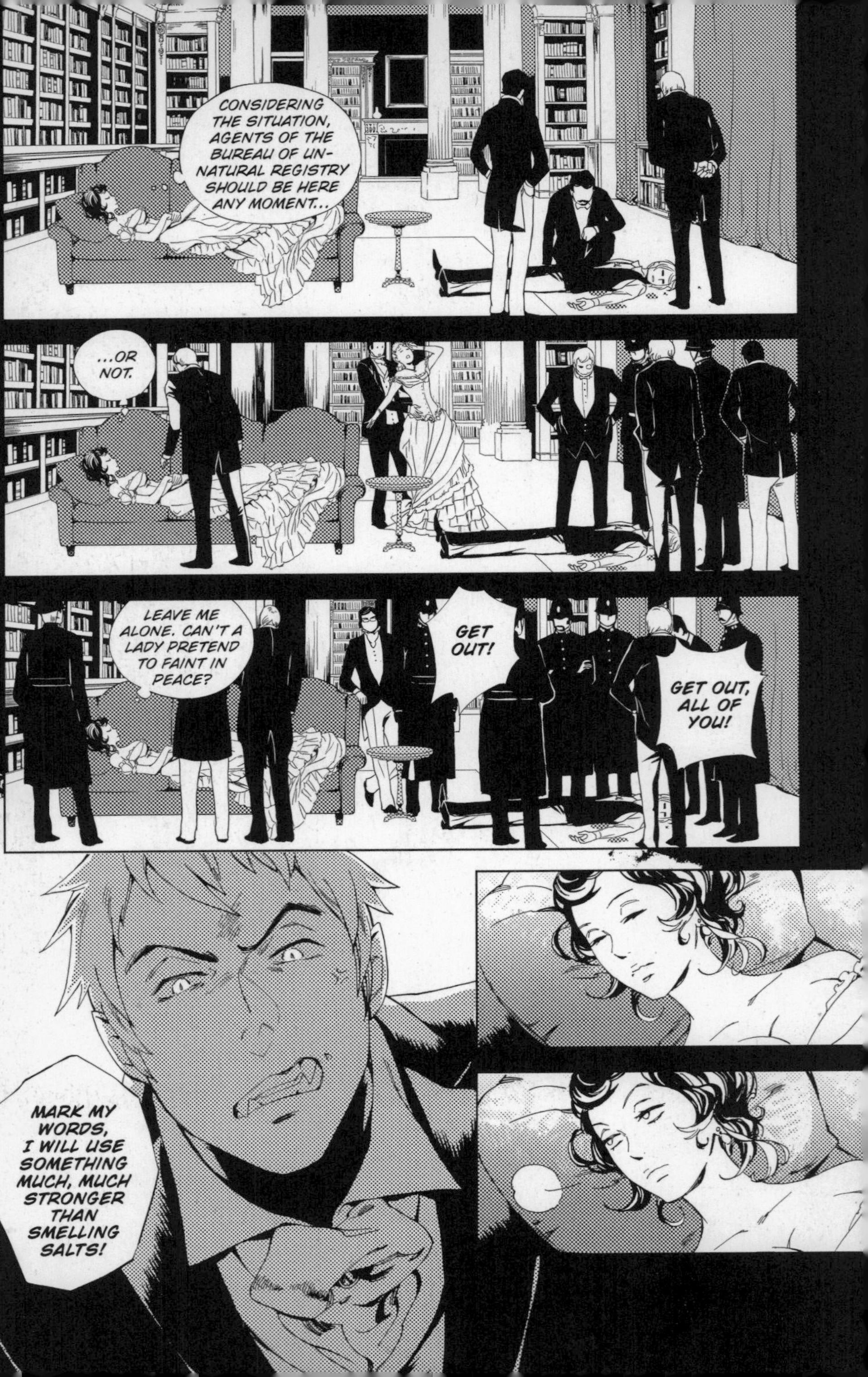
CONSIDERING THE SITUATION, AGENTS OF THE BUREAU OF UN-NATURAL REGISTRY SHOULD BE HERE ANY MOMENT...
...OR NOT.
LEAVE ME ALONE. CAN'T A LADY PRETEND TO FAINT IN PEACE?
GET OUT!
GET OUT, ALL OF YOU!
MARK MY WORDS, I WILL USE SOMETHING MUCH, MUCH STRONGER THAN SMELLING SALTS!

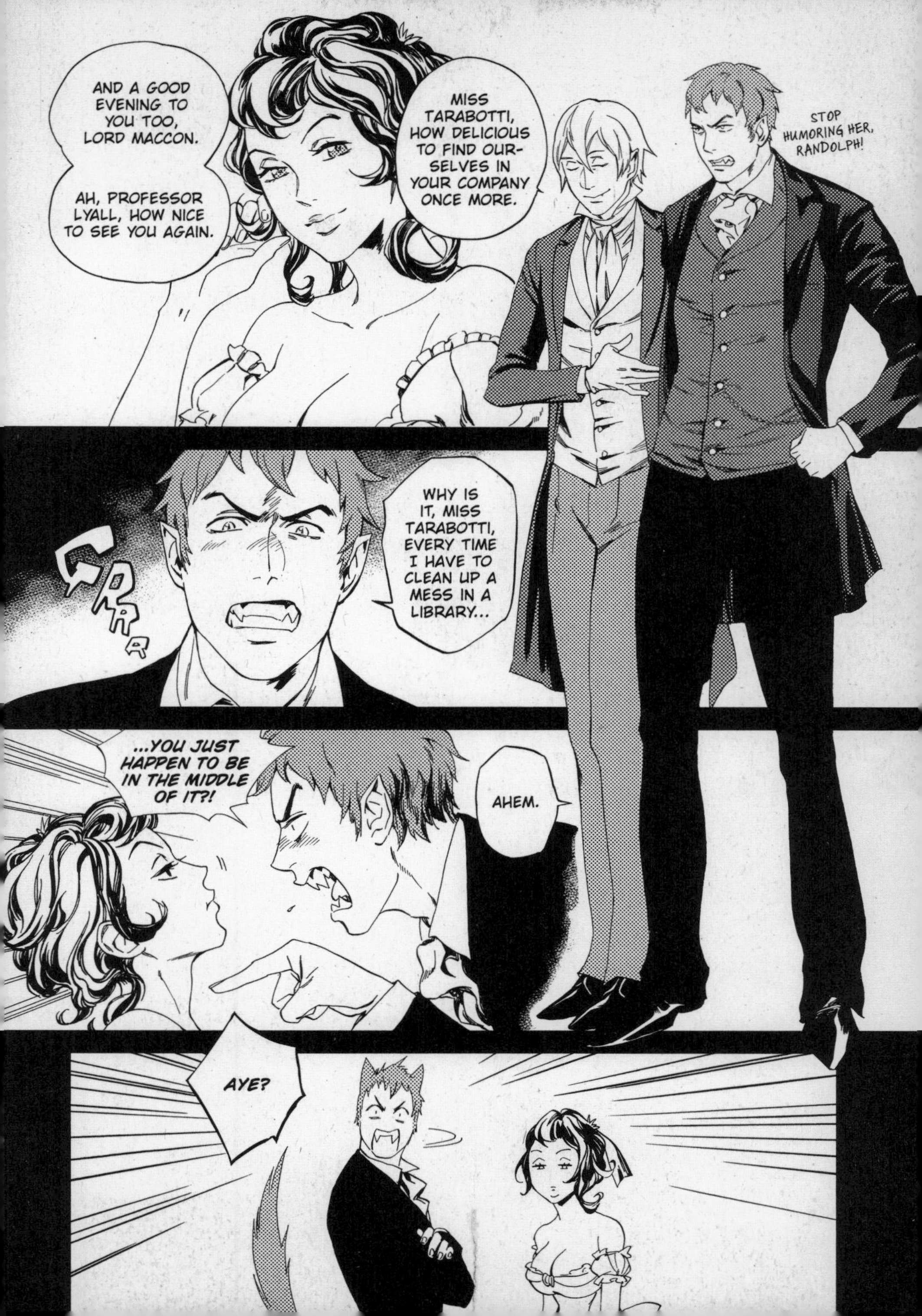
AND A GOOD EVENING TO YOU TOO, LORD MACCON.
AH, PROFESSOR LYALL, HOW NICE TO SEE YOU AGAIN.
MISS TARABOTTI, HOW DELICIOUS TO FIND OURSELVES IN YOUR COMPANY ONCE MORE.
STOP HUMORING HER, RANDOLPH!
GRRRR
WHY IS IT, MISS TARABOTTI, EVERY TIME I HAVE TO CLEAN UP A MESS IN A LIBRARY...
...YOU JUST HAPPEN TO BE IN THE MIDDLE OF IT?!
AHEM.
AYE?

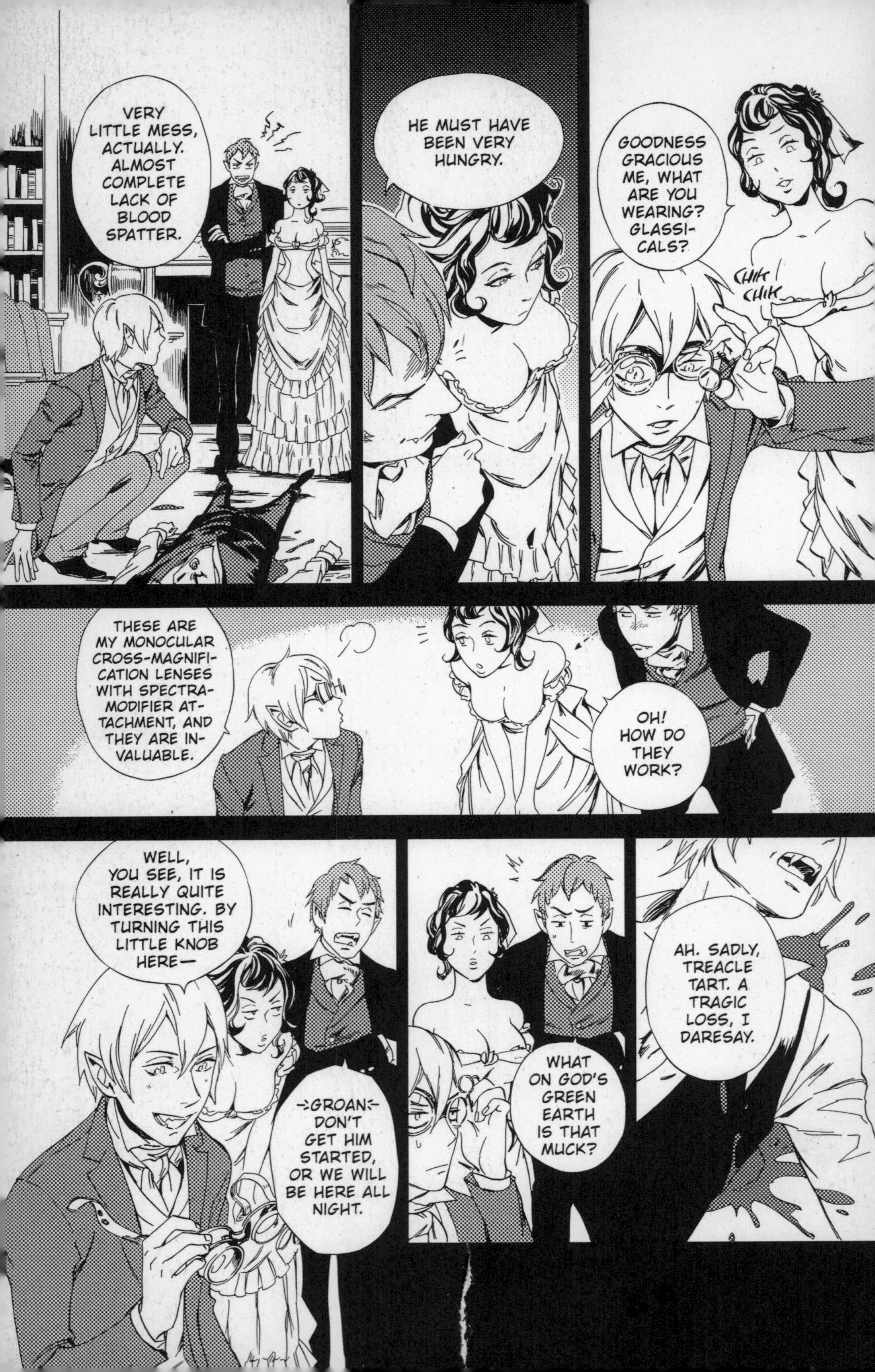
VERY LITTLE MESS, ACTUALLY. ALMOST COMPLETE LACK OF BLOOD SPATTER.
HE MUST HAVE BEEN VERY HUNGRY.
GOODNESS GRACIOUS ME, WHAT ARE YOU WEARING? GLASSI-CALS?
CHIK CHIK
THESE ARE MY MONOCULAR CROSS-MAGNIFI-CATION LENSES WITH SPECTRA-MODIFIER AT-TACHMENT, AND THEY ARE IN-VALUABLE.
OH! HOW DO THEY WORK?
WELL, YOU SEE, IT IS REALLY QUITE INTERESTING. BY TURNING THIS LITTLE KNOB HERE—
⇝GROAN⇜ DON'T GET HIM STARTED, OR WE WILL BE HERE ALL NIGHT.
WHAT ON GOD'S GREEN EARTH IS THAT MUCK?
AH. SADLY, TREACLE TART. A TRAGIC LOSS, I DARESAY.

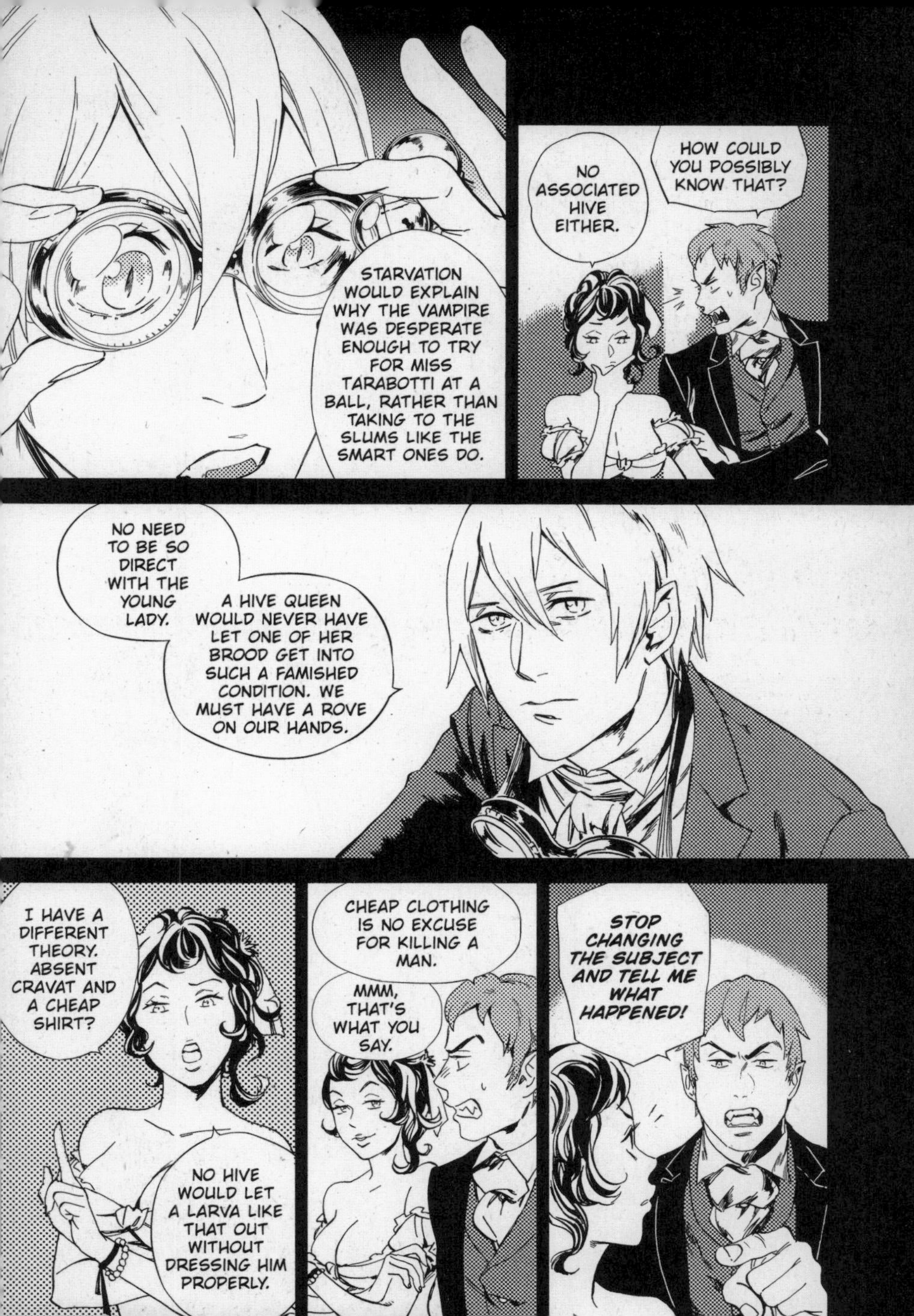
STARVATION WOULD EXPLAIN WHY THE VAMPIRE WAS DESPERATE ENOUGH TO TRY FOR MISS TARABOTTI AT A BALL, RATHER THAN TAKING TO THE SLUMS LIKE THE SMART ONES DO.
NO ASSOCIATED HIVE EITHER.
HOW COULD YOU POSSIBLY KNOW THAT?
NO NEED TO BE SO DIRECT WITH THE YOUNG LADY.
A HIVE QUEEN WOULD NEVER HAVE LET ONE OF HER BROOD GET INTO SUCH A FAMISHED CONDITION. WE MUST HAVE A ROVE ON OUR HANDS.
I HAVE A DIFFERENT THEORY. ABSENT CRAVAT AND A CHEAP SHIRT?
NO HIVE WOULD LET A LARVA LIKE THAT OUT WITHOUT DRESSING HIM PROPERLY.
CHEAP CLOTHING IS NO EXCUSE FOR KILLING A MAN.
MMM, THAT'S WHAT YOU SAY.
STOP CHANGING THE SUBJECT AND TELL ME WHAT HAPPENED!

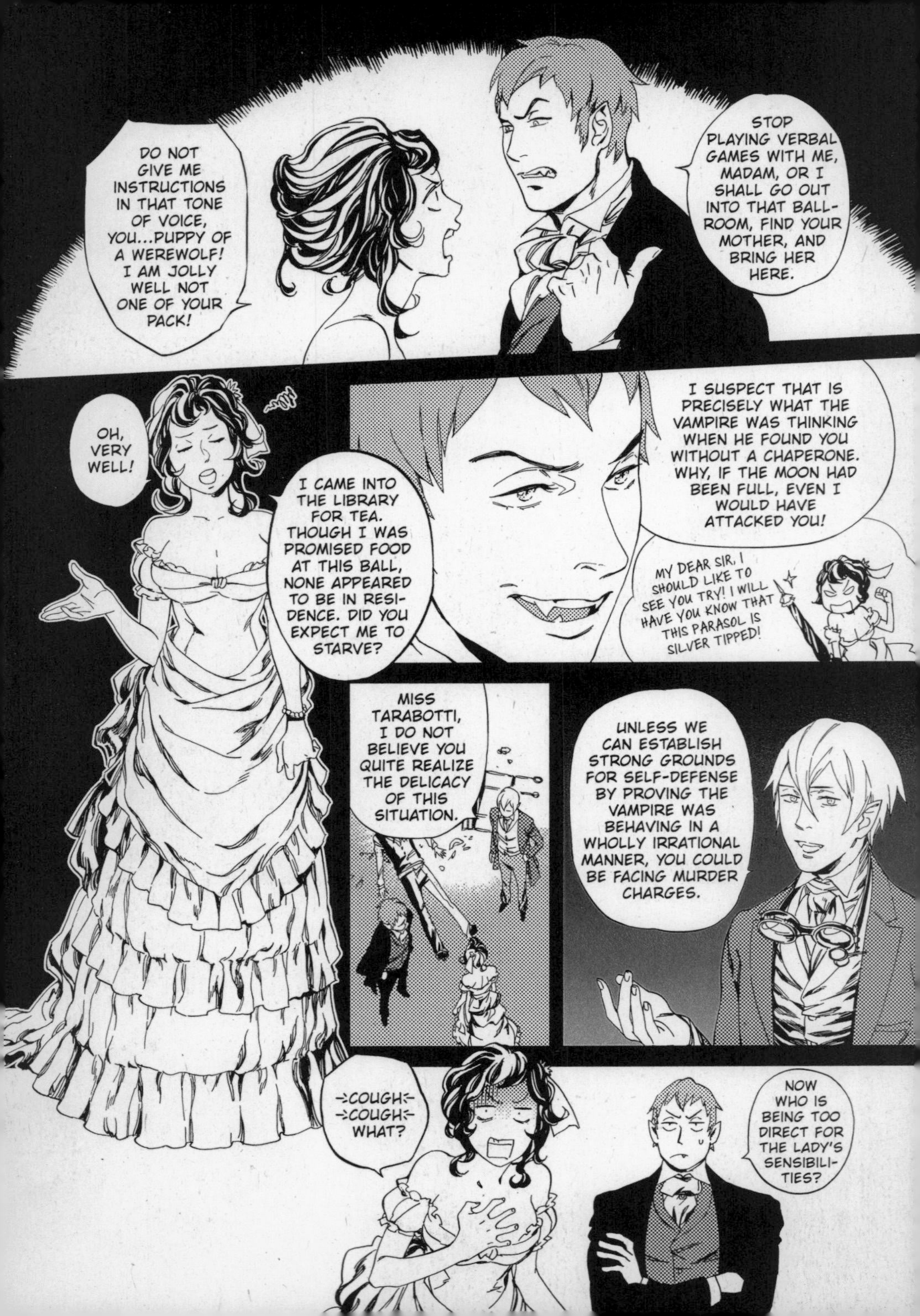
DO NOT GIVE ME INSTRUCTIONS IN THAT TONE OF VOICE, YOU...PUPPY OF A WEREWOLF! I AM JOLLY WELL NOT ONE OF YOUR PACK!
STOP PLAYING VERBAL GAMES WITH ME, MADAM, OR I SHALL GO OUT INTO THAT BALL-ROOM, FIND YOUR MOTHER, AND BRING HER HERE.
OH, VERY WELL!
I CAME INTO THE LIBRARY FOR TEA. THOUGH I WAS PROMISED FOOD AT THIS BALL, NONE APPEARED TO BE IN RESI-DENCE. DID YOU EXPECT ME TO STARVE?
I SUSPECT THAT IS PRECISELY WHAT THE VAMPIRE WAS THINKING WHEN HE FOUND YOU WITHOUT A CHAPERONE. WHY, IF THE MOON HAD BEEN FULL, EVEN I WOULD HAVE ATTACKED YOU!
MY DEAR SIR, I SHOULD LIKE TO SEE YOU TRY! I WILL HAVE YOU KNOW THAT THIS PARASOL IS SILVER TIPPED!
MISS TARABOTTI, I DO NOT BELIEVE YOU QUITE REALIZE THE DELICACY OF THIS SITUATION.
UNLESS WE CAN ESTABLISH STRONG GROUNDS FOR SELF-DEFENSE BY PROVING THE VAMPIRE WAS BEHAVING IN A WHOLLY IRRATIONAL MANNER, YOU COULD BE FACING MURDER CHARGES.
-COUGH- -COUGH- WHAT?
NOW WHO IS BEING TOO DIRECT FOR THE LADY'S SENSIBILI-TIES?

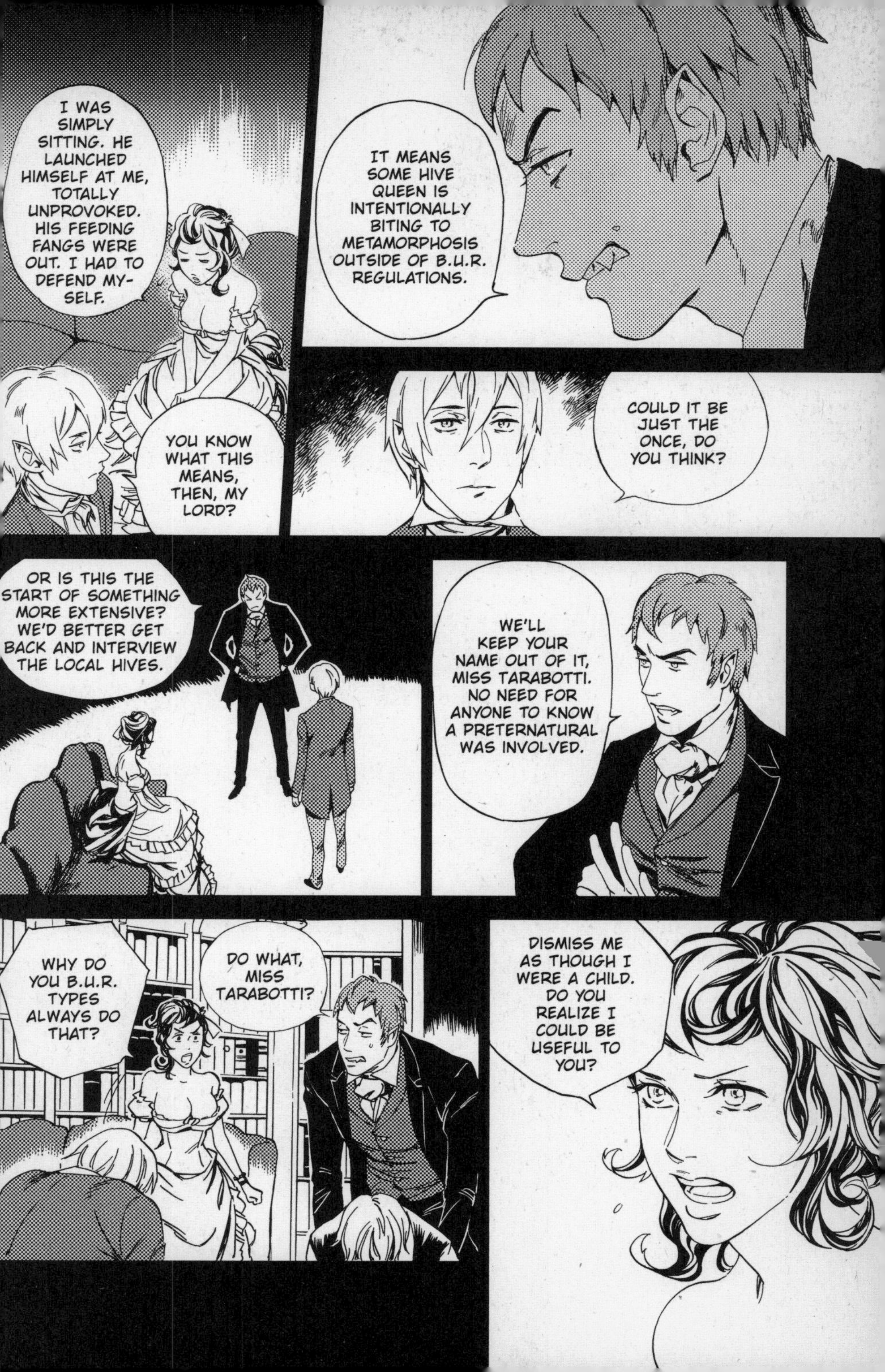
I WAS SIMPLY SITTING. HE LAUNCHED HIMSELF AT ME, TOTALLY UNPROVOKED. HIS FEEDING FANGS WERE OUT. I HAD TO DEFEND MY-SELF.
YOU KNOW WHAT THIS MEANS, THEN, MY LORD?
IT MEANS SOME HIVE QUEEN IS INTENTIONALLY BITING TO METAMORPHOSIS OUTSIDE OF B.U.R. REGULATIONS.
COULD IT BE JUST THE ONCE, DO YOU THINK?
OR IS THIS THE START OF SOMETHING MORE EXTENSIVE? WE'D BETTER GET BACK AND INTERVIEW THE LOCAL HIVES.
WE'LL KEEP YOUR NAME OUT OF IT, MISS TARABOTTI. NO NEED FOR ANYONE TO KNOW A PRETERNATURAL WAS INVOLVED.
WHY DO YOU B.U.R. TYPES ALWAYS DO THAT?
DO WHAT, MISS TARABOTTI?
DISMISS ME AS THOUGH I WERE A CHILD. DO YOU REALIZE I COULD BE USEFUL TO YOU?

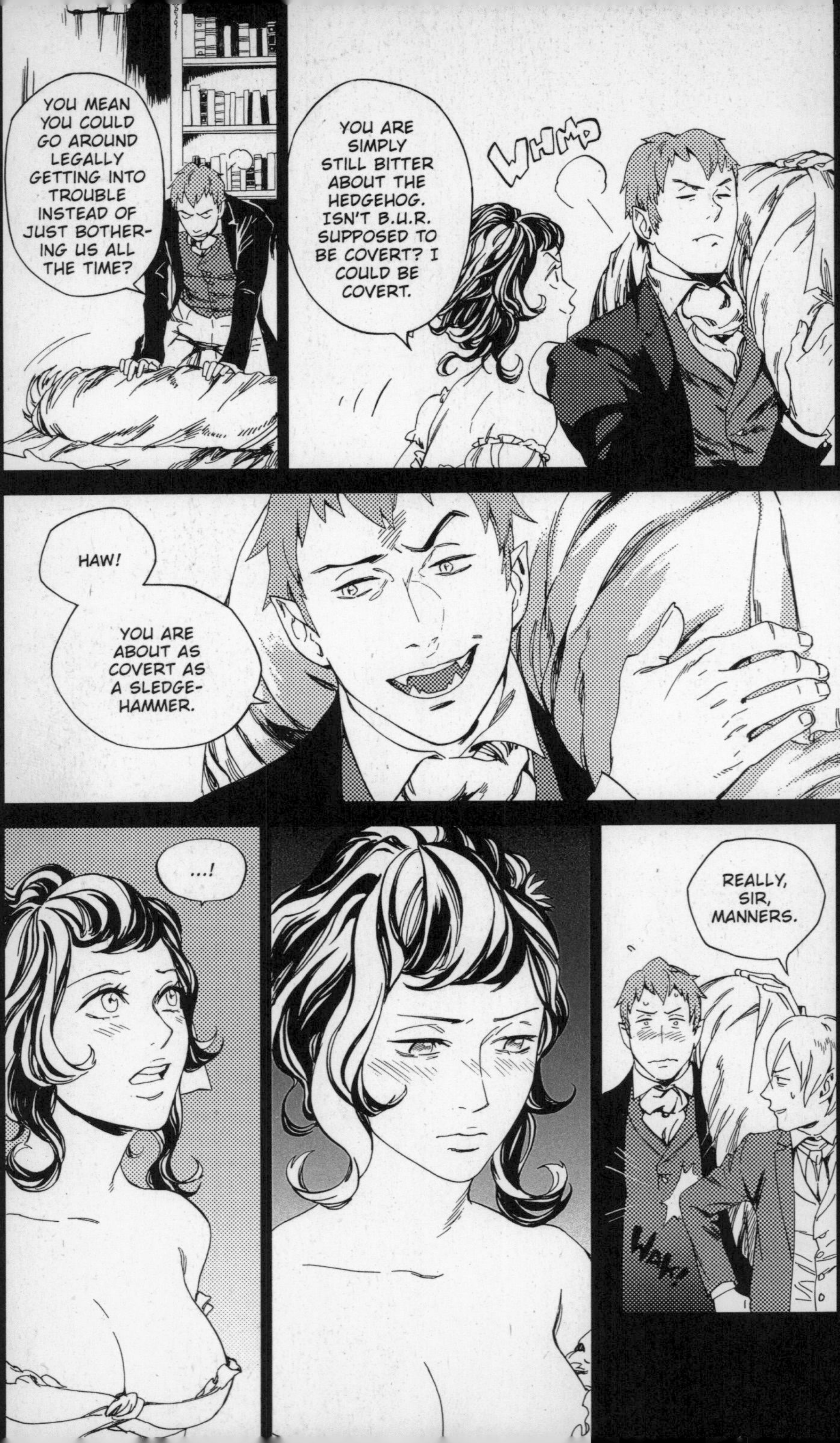
YOU MEAN YOU COULD GO AROUND LEGALLY GETTING INTO TROUBLE INSTEAD OF JUST BOTHERING US ALL THE TIME?
YOU ARE SIMPLY STILL BITTER ABOUT THE HEDGEHOG. ISN'T B.U.R. SUPPOSED TO BE COVERT? I COULD BE COVERT.
WHMP
HAW!
YOU ARE ABOUT AS COVERT AS A SLEDGEHAMMER.
...!
REALLY, SIR, MANNERS.
WAK!

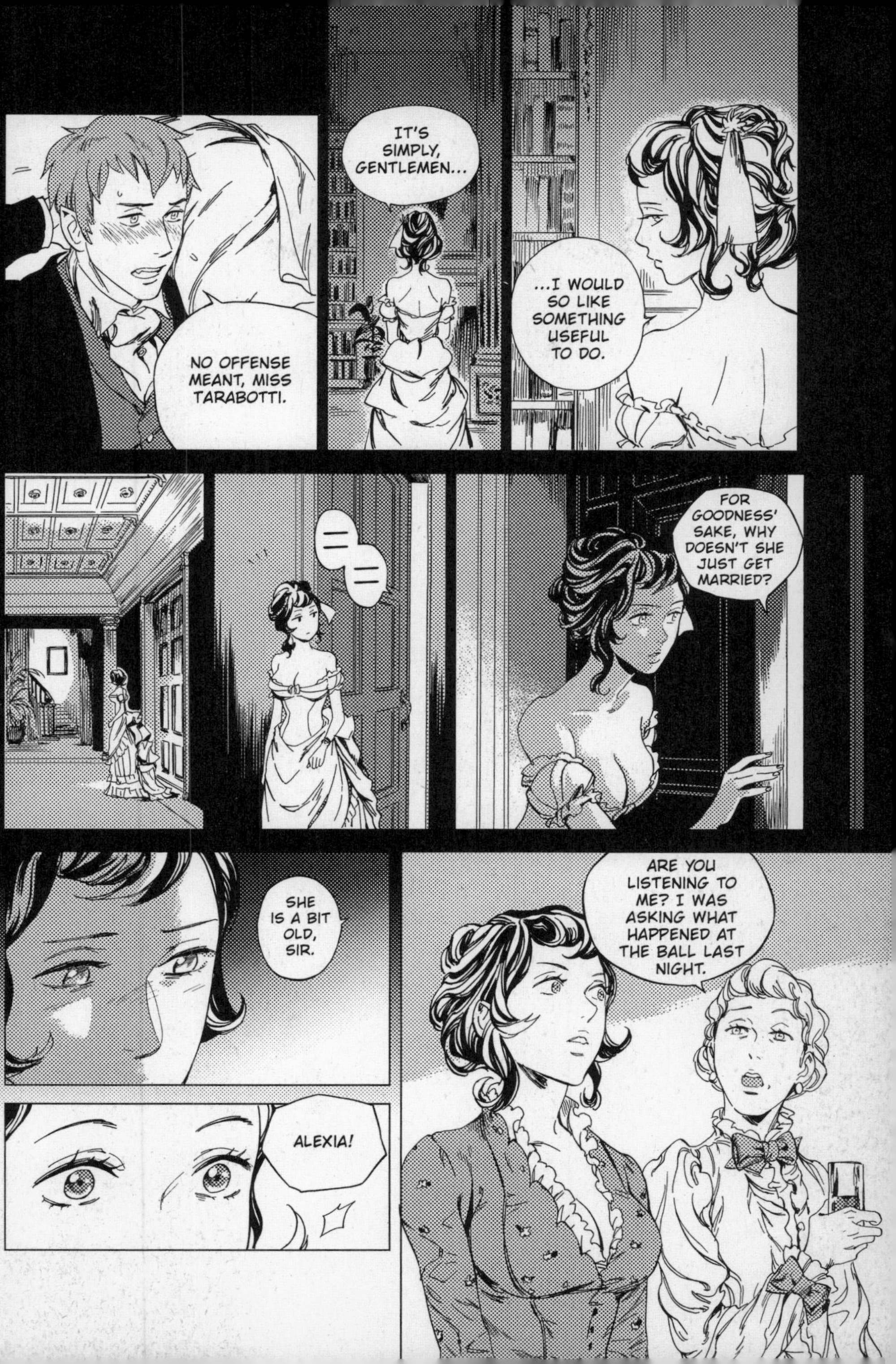
NO OFFENSE MEANT, MISS TARABOTTI.
IT'S SIMPLY, GENTLEMEN...
...I WOULD SO LIKE SOMETHING USEFUL TO DO.
FOR GOODNESS' SAKE, WHY DOESN'T SHE JUST GET MARRIED?
SHE IS A BIT OLD, SIR.
ALEXIA!
ARE YOU LISTENING TO ME? I WAS ASKING WHAT HAPPENED AT THE BALL LAST NIGHT.

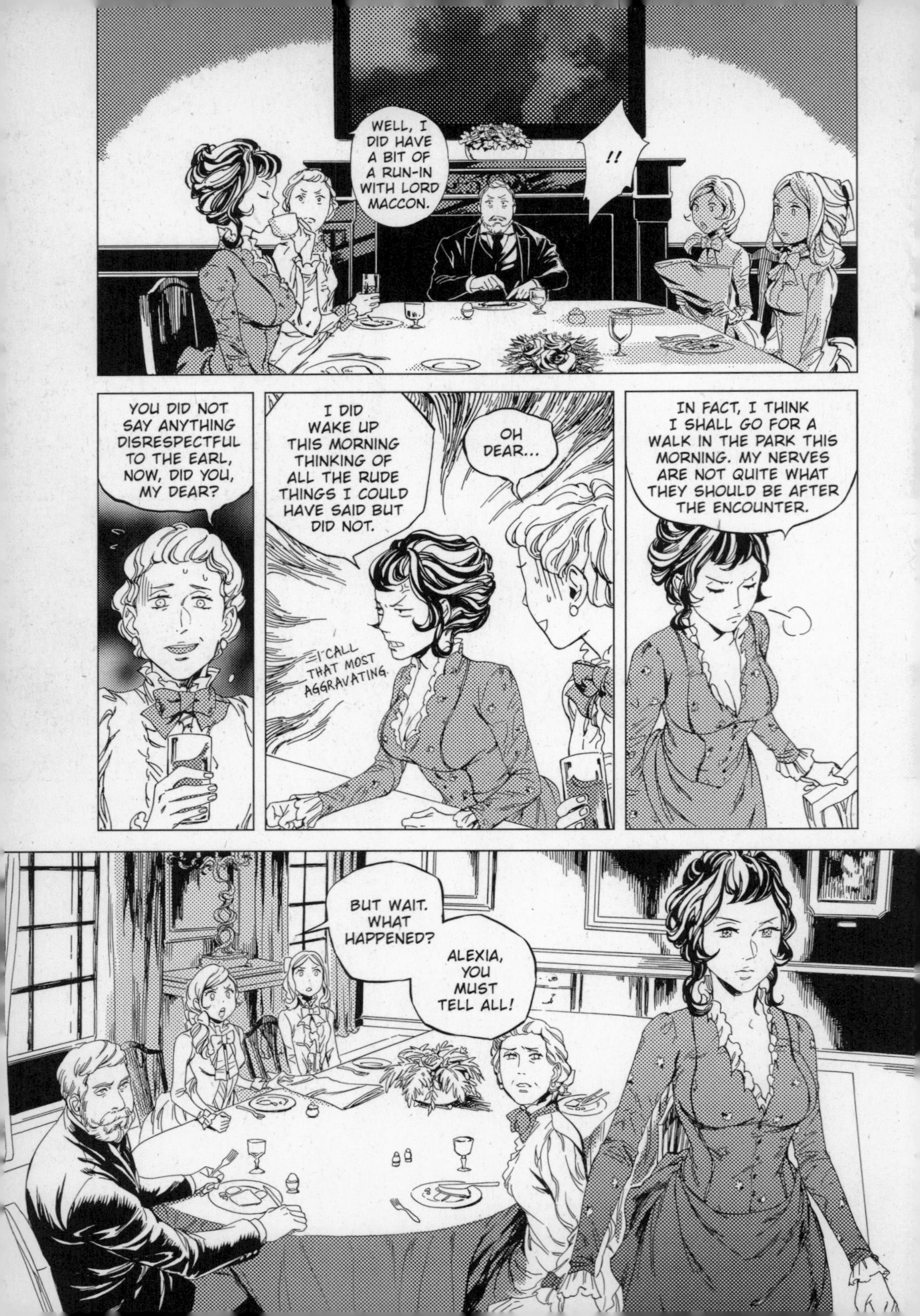
WELL, I DID HAVE A BIT OF A RUN-IN WITH LORD MACCON.
!!
YOU DID NOT SAY ANYTHING DISRESPECTFUL TO THE EARL, NOW, DID YOU, MY DEAR?
I DID WAKE UP THIS MORNING THINKING OF ALL THE RUDE THINGS I COULD HAVE SAID BUT DID NOT.
I CALL THAT MOST AGGRAVATING.
OH DEAR...
IN FACT, I THINK I SHALL GO FOR A WALK IN THE PARK THIS MORNING. MY NERVES ARE NOT QUITE WHAT THEY SHOULD BE AFTER THE ENCOUNTER.
BUT WAIT. WHAT HAPPENED?
ALEXIA, YOU MUST TELL ALL!

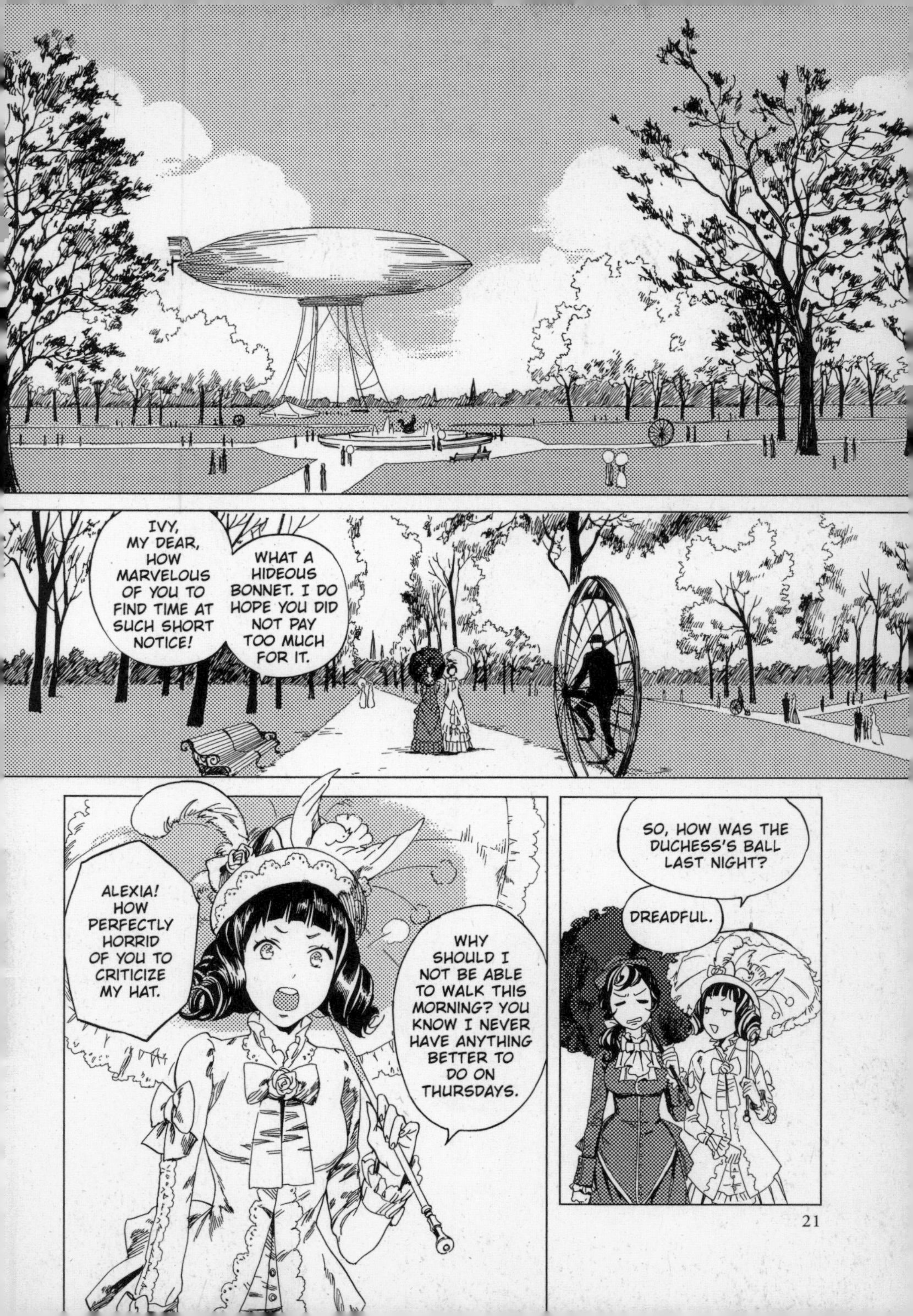
IVY, MY DEAR, HOW MARVELOUS OF YOU TO FIND TIME AT SUCH SHORT NOTICE!
WHAT A HIDEOUS BONNET. I DO HOPE YOU DID NOT PAY TOO MUCH FOR IT.
ALEXIA! HOW PERFECTLY HORRID OF YOU TO CRITICIZE MY HAT.
WHY SHOULD I NOT BE ABLE TO WALK THIS MORNING? YOU KNOW I NEVER HAVE ANYTHING BETTER TO DO ON THURSDAYS.
SO, HOW WAS THE DUCHESS'S BALL LAST NIGHT?
DREADFUL.

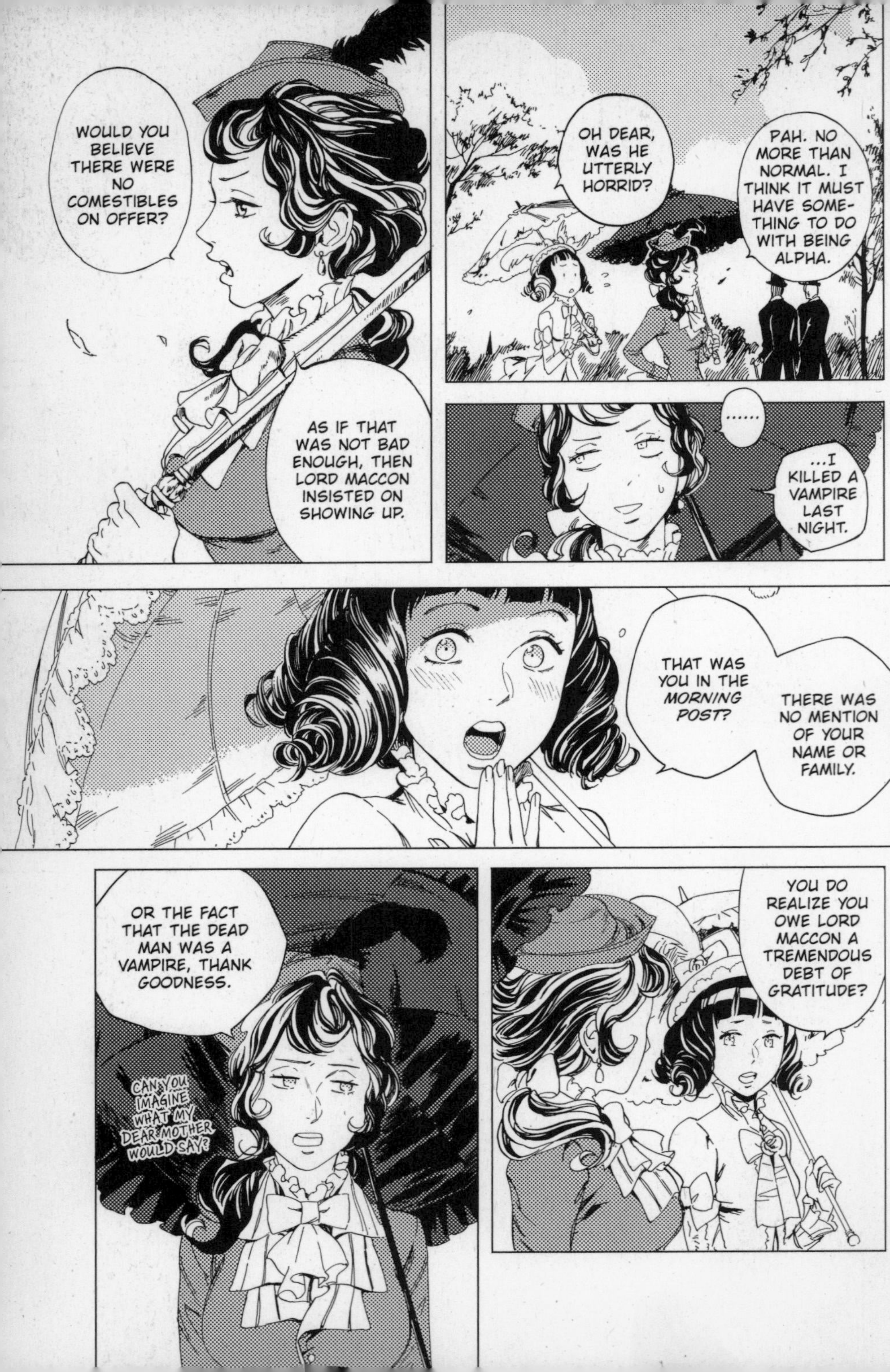
WOULD YOU BELIEVE THERE WERE NO COMESTIBLES ON OFFER?
AS IF THAT WAS NOT BAD ENOUGH, THEN LORD MACCON INSISTED ON SHOWING UP.
OH DEAR, WAS HE UTTERLY HORRID?
PAH. NO MORE THAN NORMAL. I THINK IT MUST HAVE SOME-THING TO DO WITH BEING ALPHA.
......
...I KILLED A VAMPIRE LAST NIGHT.
THAT WAS YOU IN THE *MORNING POST?*
THERE WAS NO MENTION OF YOUR NAME OR FAMILY.
OR THE FACT THAT THE DEAD MAN WAS A VAMPIRE, THANK GOODNESS.
CAN YOU IMAGINE WHAT MY DEAR MOTHER WOULD SAY?
YOU DO REALIZE YOU OWE LORD MACCON A TREMENDOUS DEBT OF GRATITUDE?

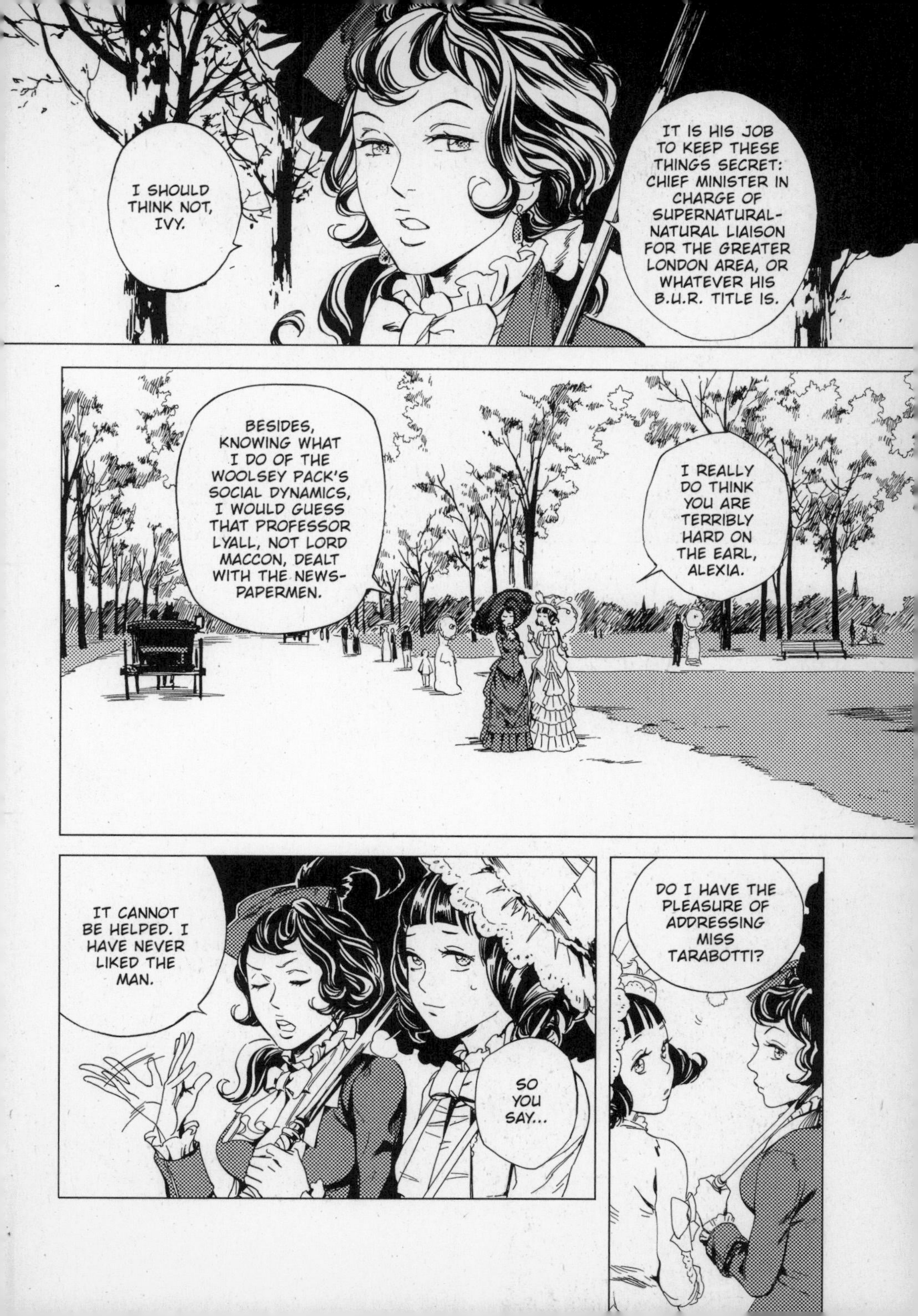
I SHOULD THINK NOT, IVY.
IT IS HIS JOB TO KEEP THESE THINGS SECRET: CHIEF MINISTER IN CHARGE OF SUPERNATURAL-NATURAL LIAISON FOR THE GREATER LONDON AREA, OR WHATEVER HIS B.U.R. TITLE IS.
BESIDES, KNOWING WHAT I DO OF THE WOOLSEY PACK'S SOCIAL DYNAMICS, I WOULD GUESS THAT PROFESSOR LYALL, NOT LORD MACCON, DEALT WITH THE NEWS-PAPERMEN.
I REALLY DO THINK YOU ARE TERRIBLY HARD ON THE EARL, ALEXIA.
IT CANNOT BE HELPED. I HAVE NEVER LIKED THE MAN.
SO YOU SAY...
DO I HAVE THE PLEASURE OF ADDRESSING MISS TARABOTTI?

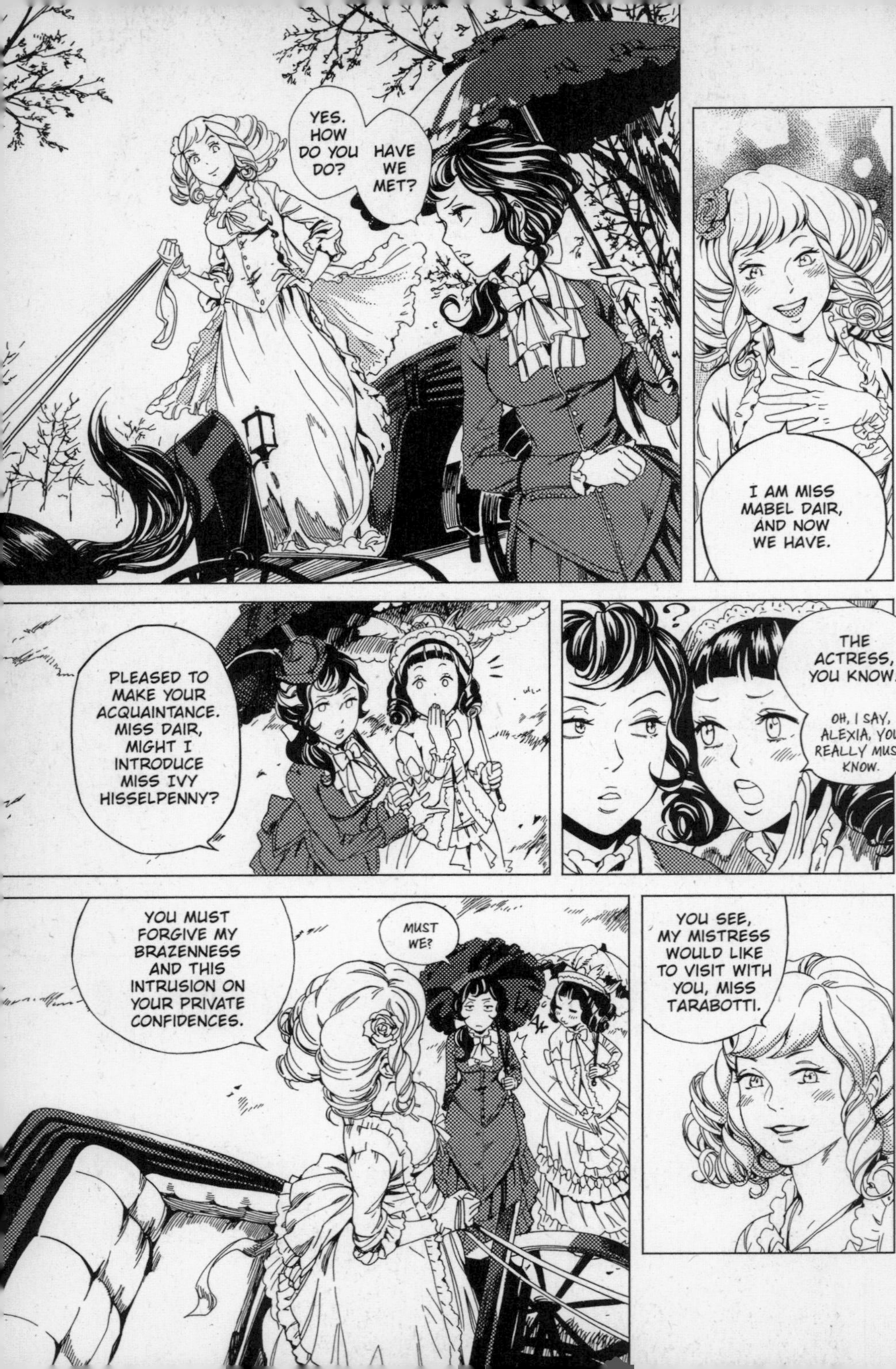
YES. HOW DO YOU DO?
HAVE WE MET?
I AM MISS MABEL DAIR, AND NOW WE HAVE.
PLEASED TO MAKE YOUR ACQUAINTANCE. MISS DAIR, MIGHT I INTRODUCE MISS IVY HISSELPENNY?
?
THE ACTRESS, YOU KNOW!
OH, I SAY, ALEXIA, YOU REALLY MUST KNOW.
YOU MUST FORGIVE MY BRAZENNESS AND THIS INTRUSION ON YOUR PRIVATE CONFIDENCES.
MUST WE?
YOU SEE, MY MISTRESS WOULD LIKE TO VISIT WITH YOU, MISS TARABOTTI.

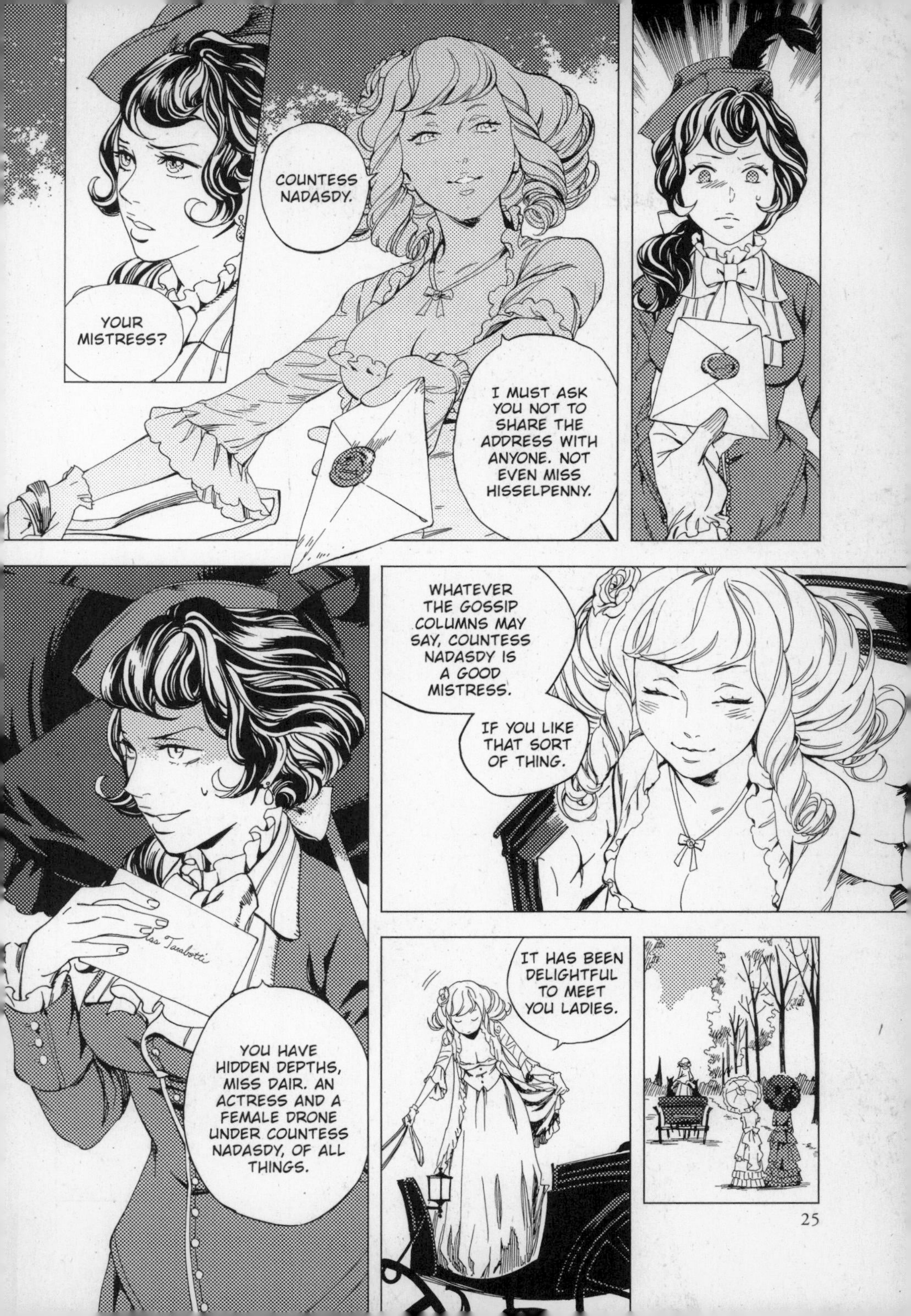
YOUR MISTRESS?
COUNTESS NADASDY.
I MUST ASK YOU NOT TO SHARE THE ADDRESS WITH ANYONE. NOT EVEN MISS HISSELPENNY.
YOU HAVE HIDDEN DEPTHS, MISS DAIR. AN ACTRESS AND A FEMALE DRONE UNDER COUNTESS NADASDY, OF ALL THINGS.
WHATEVER THE GOSSIP COLUMNS MAY SAY, COUNTESS NADASDY IS A GOOD MISTRESS.
IF YOU LIKE THAT SORT OF THING.
IT HAS BEEN DELIGHTFUL TO MEET YOU LADIES.

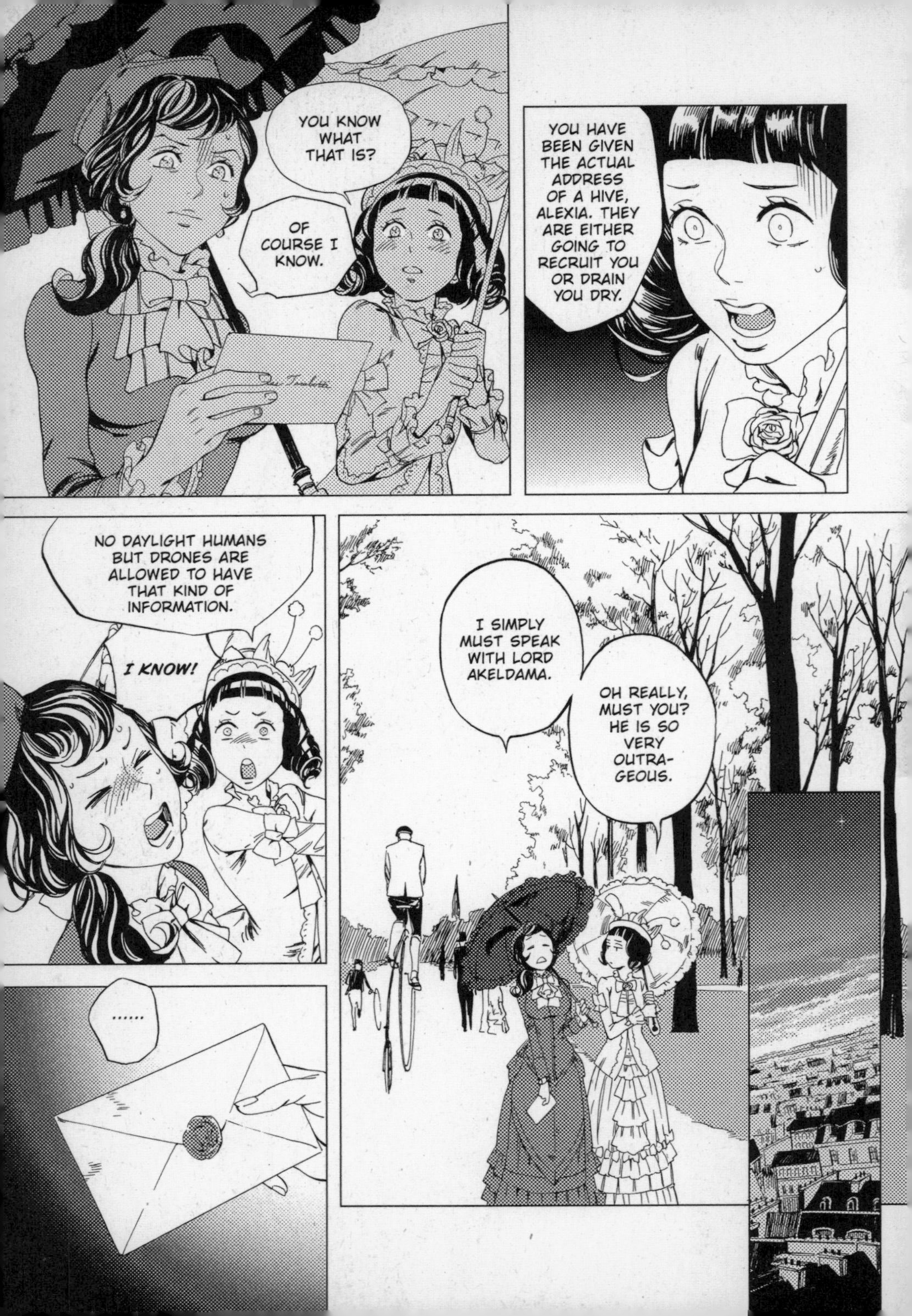
YOU KNOW WHAT THAT IS?
OF COURSE I KNOW.
YOU HAVE BEEN GIVEN THE ACTUAL ADDRESS OF A HIVE, ALEXIA. THEY ARE EITHER GOING TO RECRUIT YOU OR DRAIN YOU DRY.
NO DAYLIGHT HUMANS BUT DRONES ARE ALLOWED TO HAVE THAT KIND OF INFORMATION.
I KNOW!
......
I SIMPLY MUST SPEAK WITH LORD AKELDAMA.
OH REALLY, MUST YOU? HE IS SO VERY OUTRA-GEOUS.

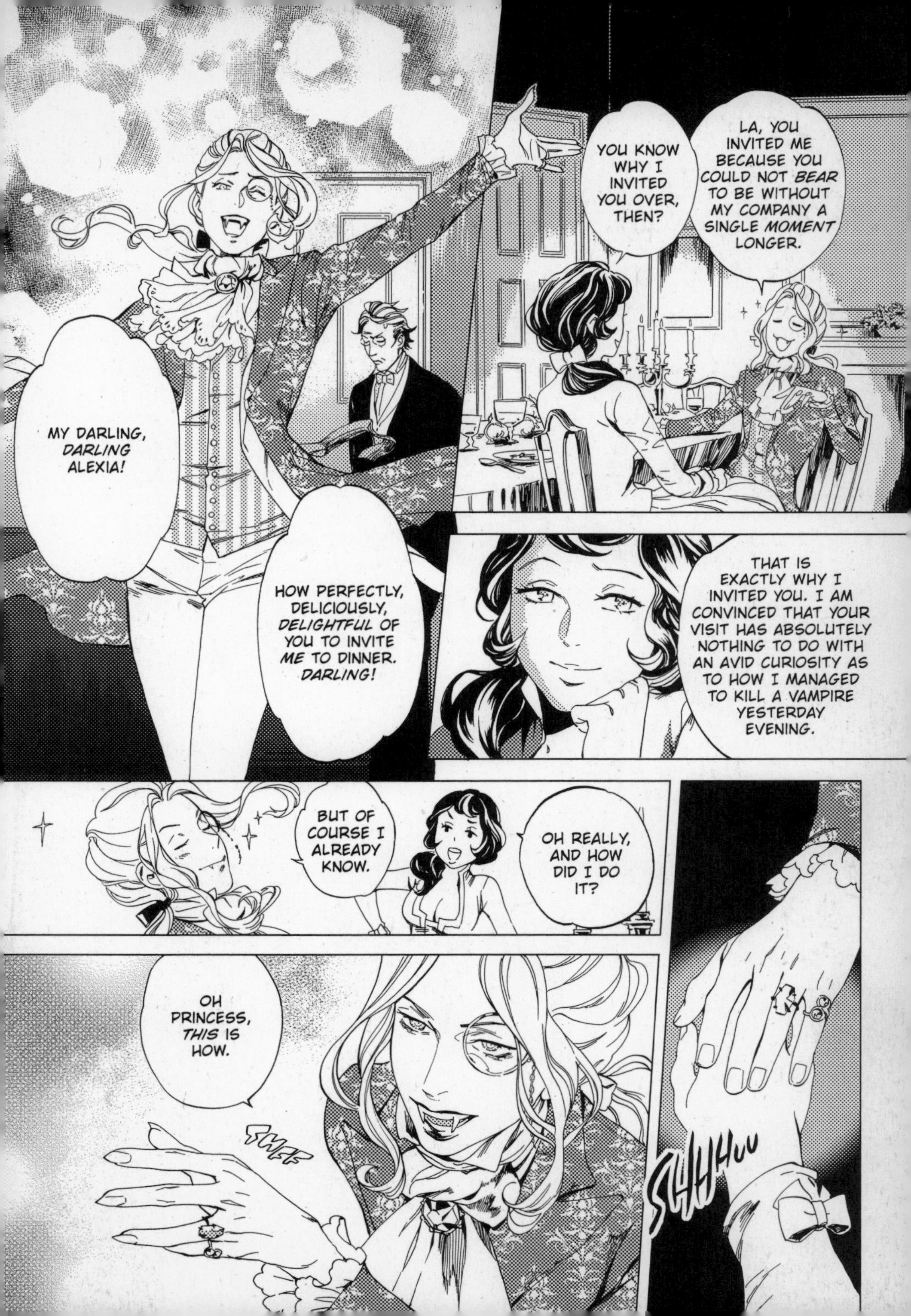
MY DARLING, *DARLING* ALEXIA!
HOW PERFECTLY, DELICIOUSLY, *DELIGHTFUL* OF YOU TO INVITE *ME* TO DINNER. *DARLING*!
YOU KNOW WHY I INVITED YOU OVER, THEN?
LA, YOU INVITED ME BECAUSE YOU COULD NOT *BEAR* TO BE WITHOUT MY COMPANY A SINGLE *MOMENT* LONGER.
THAT IS EXACTLY WHY I INVITED YOU. I AM CONVINCED THAT YOUR VISIT HAS ABSOLUTELY NOTHING TO DO WITH AN AVID CURIOSITY AS TO HOW I MANAGED TO KILL A VAMPIRE YESTERDAY EVENING.
BUT OF COURSE I ALREADY KNOW.
OH REALLY, AND HOW DID I DO IT?
OH PRINCESS, *THIS* IS HOW.

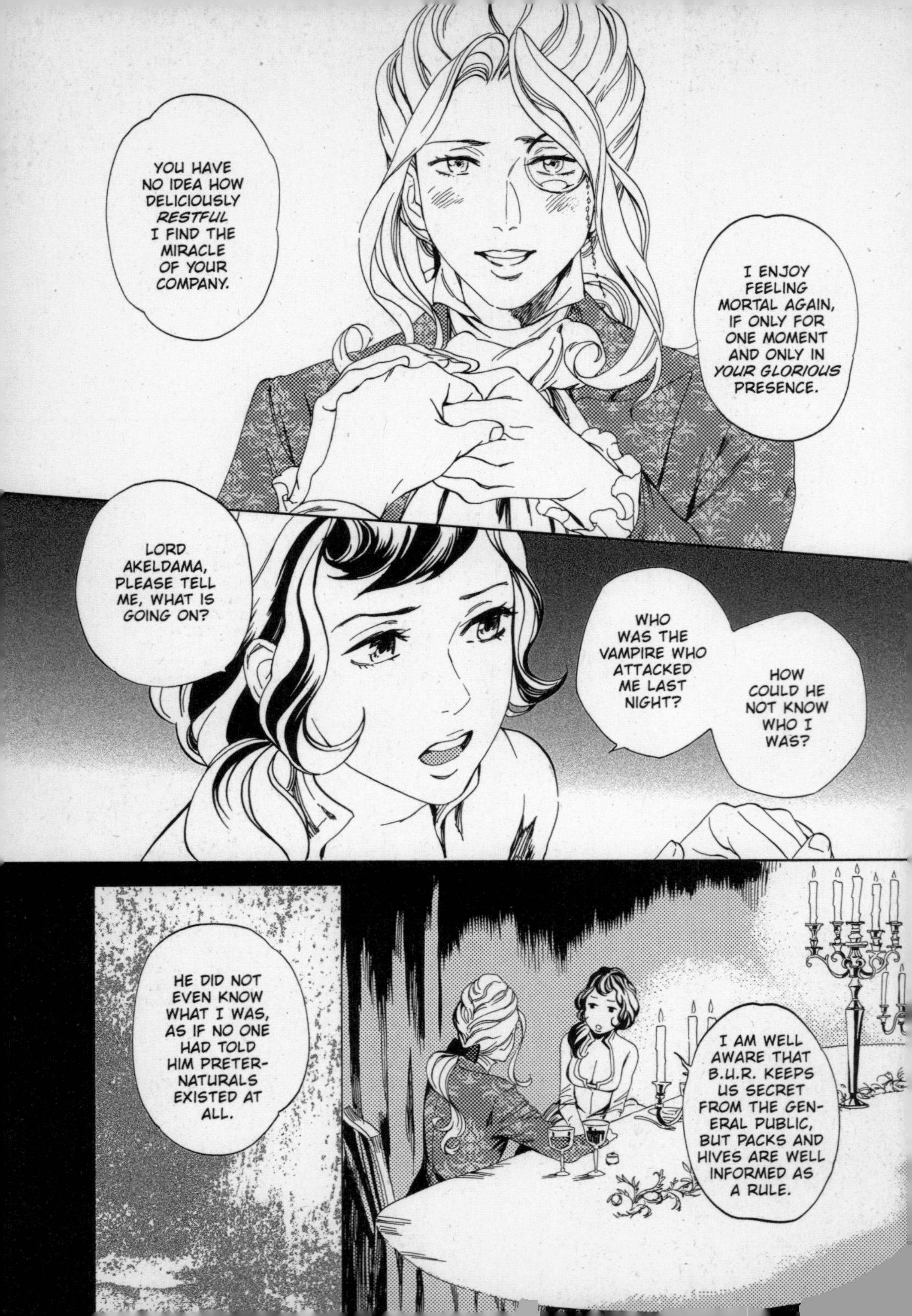
YOU HAVE NO IDEA HOW DELICIOUSLY *RESTFUL* I FIND THE MIRACLE OF YOUR COMPANY.
I ENJOY FEELING MORTAL AGAIN, IF ONLY FOR ONE MOMENT AND ONLY IN *YOUR GLORIOUS* PRESENCE.
LORD AKELDAMA, PLEASE TELL ME, WHAT IS GOING ON?
WHO WAS THE VAMPIRE WHO ATTACKED ME LAST NIGHT?
HOW COULD HE NOT KNOW WHO I WAS?
HE DID NOT EVEN KNOW WHAT I WAS, AS IF NO ONE HAD TOLD HIM PRETER-NATURALS EXISTED AT ALL.
I AM WELL AWARE THAT B.U.R. KEEPS US SECRET FROM THE GEN-ERAL PUBLIC, BUT PACKS AND HIVES ARE WELL INFORMED AS A RULE.

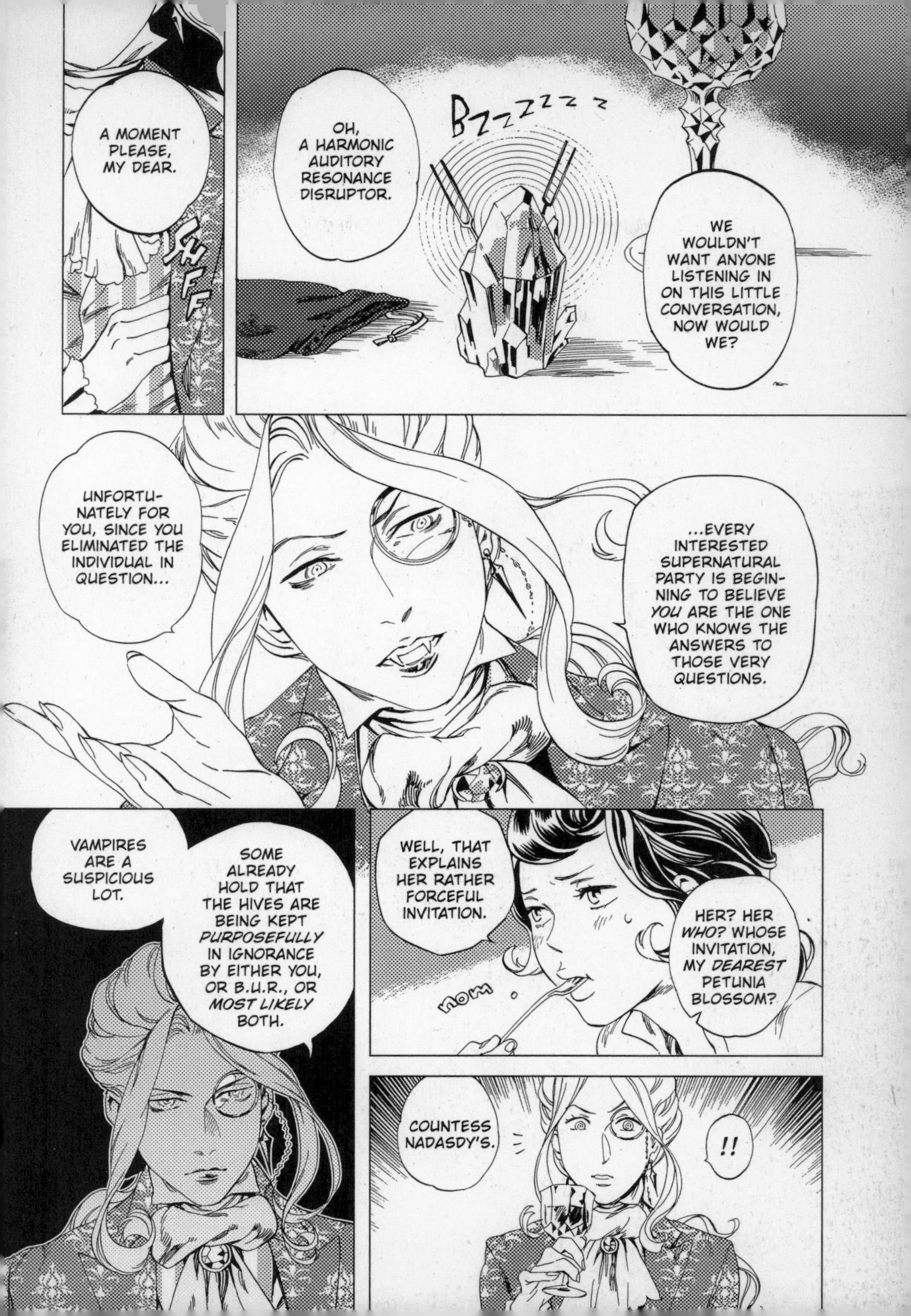
A MOMENT PLEASE, MY DEAR.
SHFF
OH, A HARMONIC AUDITORY RESONANCE DISRUPTOR.
BZZZZZZ
WE WOULDN'T WANT ANYONE LISTENING IN ON THIS LITTLE CONVERSATION, NOW WOULD WE?
UNFORTU-NATELY FOR YOU, SINCE YOU ELIMINATED THE INDIVIDUAL IN QUESTION...
...EVERY INTERESTED SUPERNATURAL PARTY IS BEGIN-NING TO BELIEVE *YOU* ARE THE ONE WHO KNOWS THE ANSWERS TO THOSE VERY QUESTIONS.
VAMPIRES ARE A SUSPICIOUS LOT.
SOME ALREADY HOLD THAT THE HIVES ARE BEING KEPT *PURPOSEFULLY* IN IGNORANCE BY EITHER YOU, OR B.U.R., OR *MOST LIKELY* BOTH.
WELL, THAT EXPLAINS HER RATHER FORCEFUL INVITATION.
nom
HER? HER *WHO?* WHOSE INVITATION, MY *DEAREST* PETUNIA BLOSSOM?
COUNTESS NADASDY'S.
!!

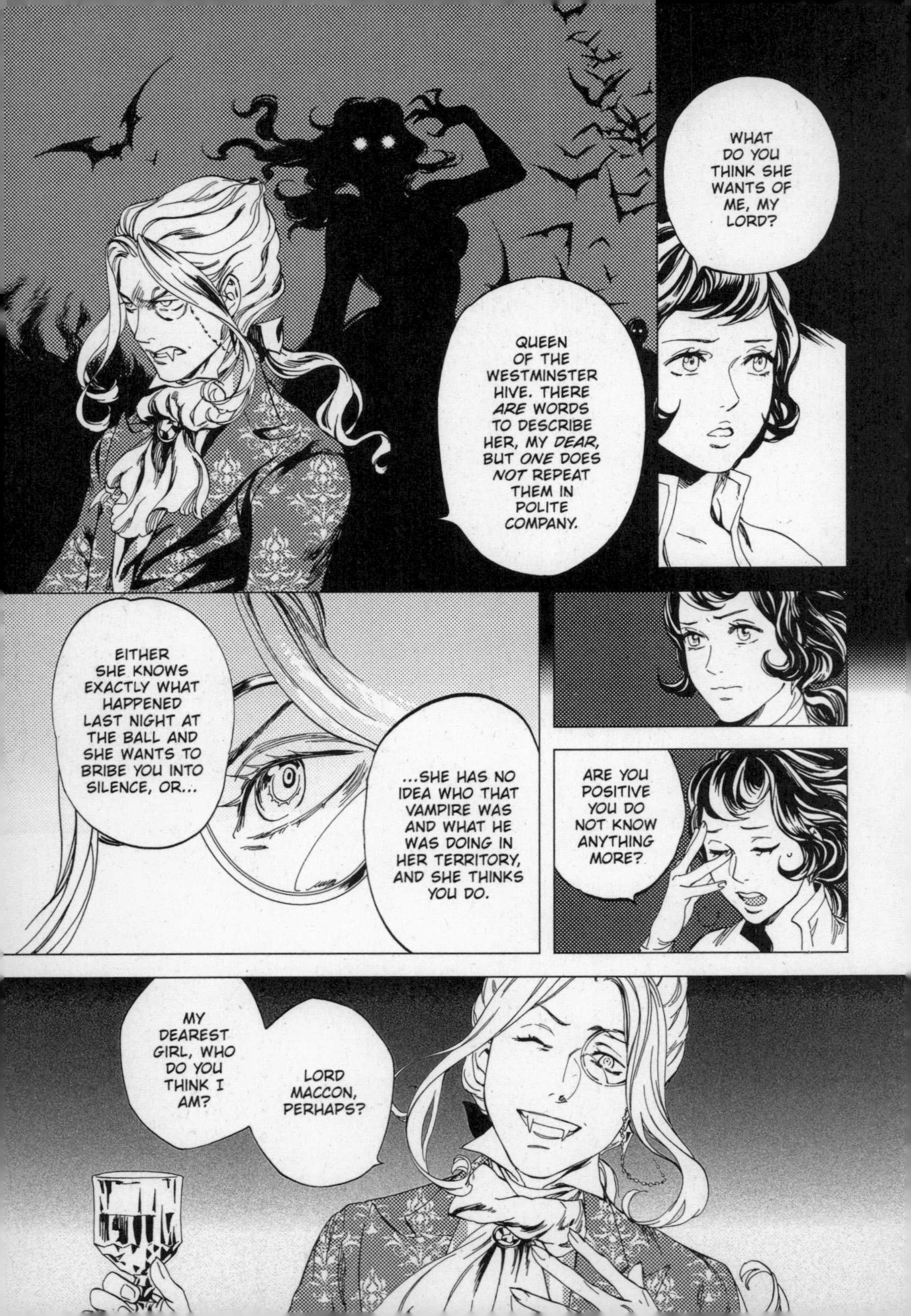
QUEEN OF THE WESTMINSTER HIVE. THERE *ARE* WORDS TO DESCRIBE HER, MY *DEAR*, BUT *ONE* DOES *NOT* REPEAT THEM IN POLITE COMPANY.
WHAT DO YOU THINK SHE WANTS OF ME, MY LORD?
EITHER SHE KNOWS EXACTLY WHAT HAPPENED LAST NIGHT AT THE BALL AND SHE WANTS TO BRIBE YOU INTO SILENCE, OR...
...SHE HAS NO IDEA WHO THAT VAMPIRE WAS AND WHAT HE WAS DOING IN HER TERRITORY, AND SHE THINKS YOU DO.
ARE YOU POSITIVE YOU DO NOT KNOW ANYTHING MORE?
MY DEAREST GIRL, WHO DO YOU THINK I AM?
LORD MACCON, PERHAPS?

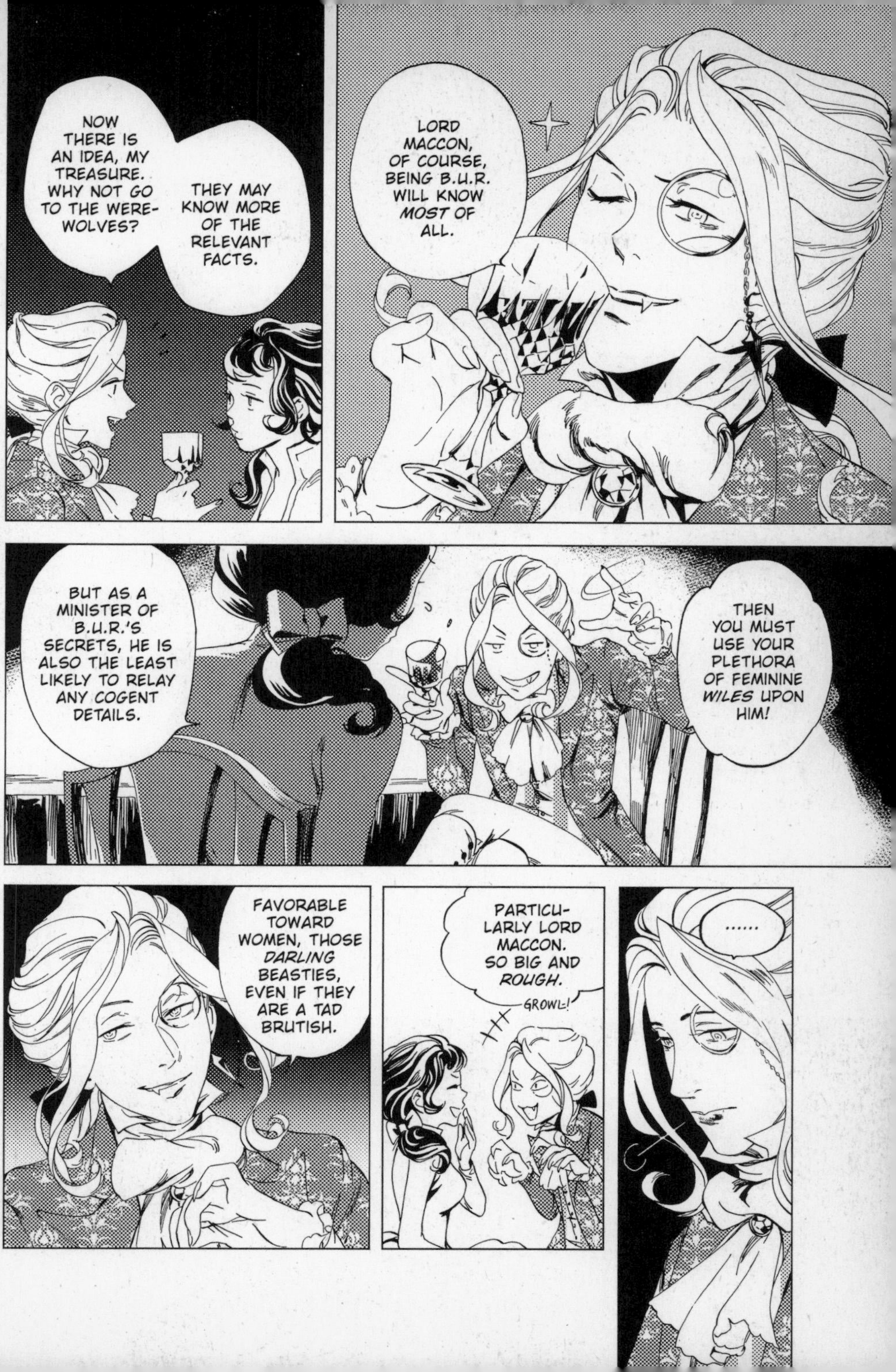
NOW THERE IS AN IDEA, MY TREASURE. WHY NOT GO TO THE WERE-WOLVES?
THEY MAY KNOW MORE OF THE RELEVANT FACTS.
LORD MACCON, OF COURSE, BEING B.U.R. WILL KNOW *MOST* OF ALL.
BUT AS A MINISTER OF B.U.R.'S SECRETS, HE IS ALSO THE LEAST LIKELY TO RELAY ANY COGENT DETAILS.
THEN YOU MUST USE YOUR PLETHORA OF FEMININE *WILES* UPON HIM!
FAVORABLE TOWARD WOMEN, THOSE *DARLING* BEASTIES, EVEN IF THEY ARE A TAD BRUTISH.
PARTICU-LARLY LORD MACCON. SO BIG AND *ROUGH*.
GROWL!
......

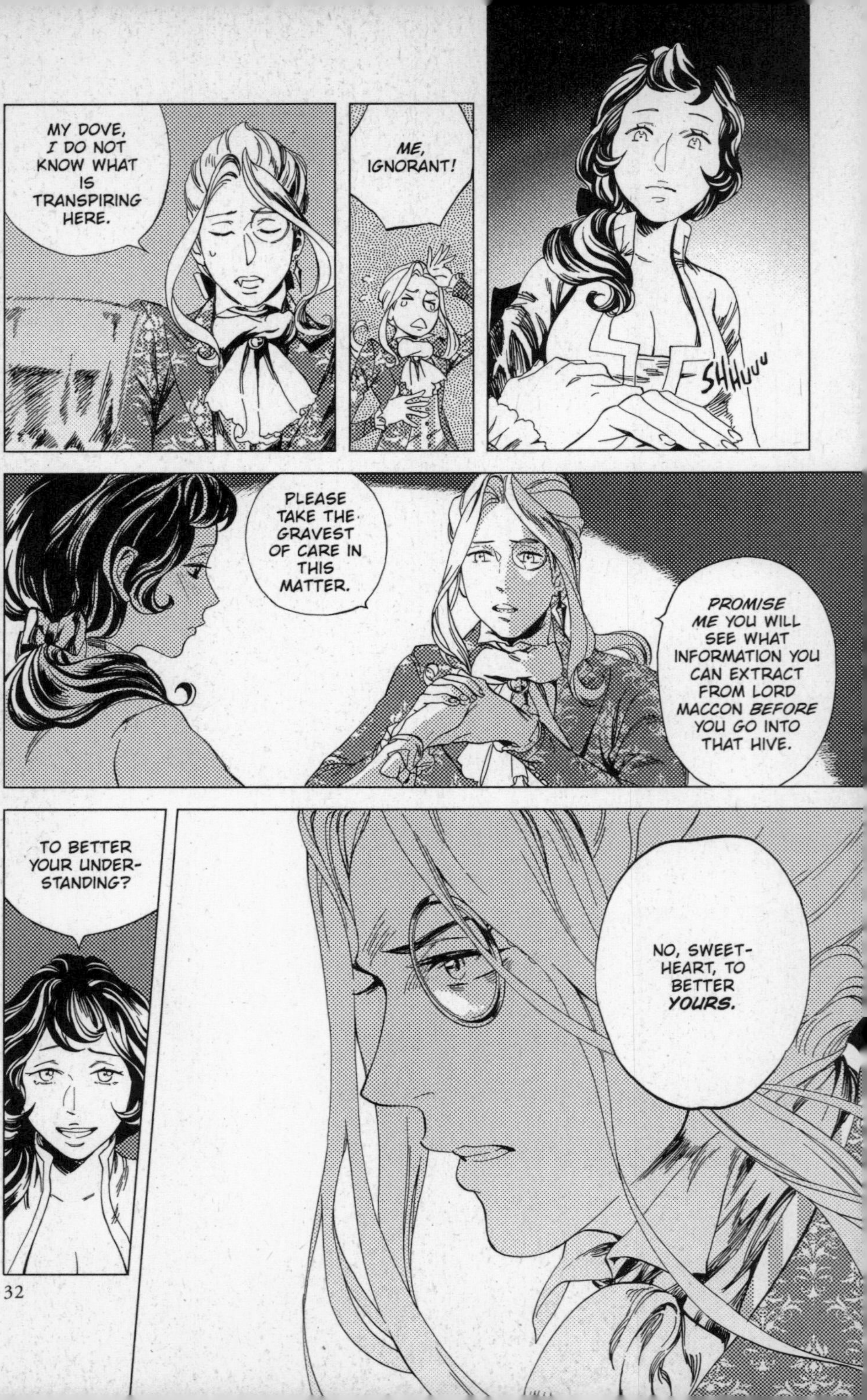
MY DOVE, *I* DO NOT KNOW WHAT IS TRANSPIRING HERE.
ME, IGNORANT!
SHHUUU
PLEASE TAKE THE GRAVEST OF CARE IN THIS MATTER.
PROMISE ME YOU WILL SEE WHAT INFORMATION YOU CAN EXTRACT FROM LORD MACCON *BEFORE* YOU GO INTO THAT HIVE.
TO BETTER YOUR UNDER-STANDING?
NO, SWEET-HEART, TO BETTER ***YOURS***.

SOULLESS

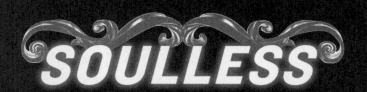

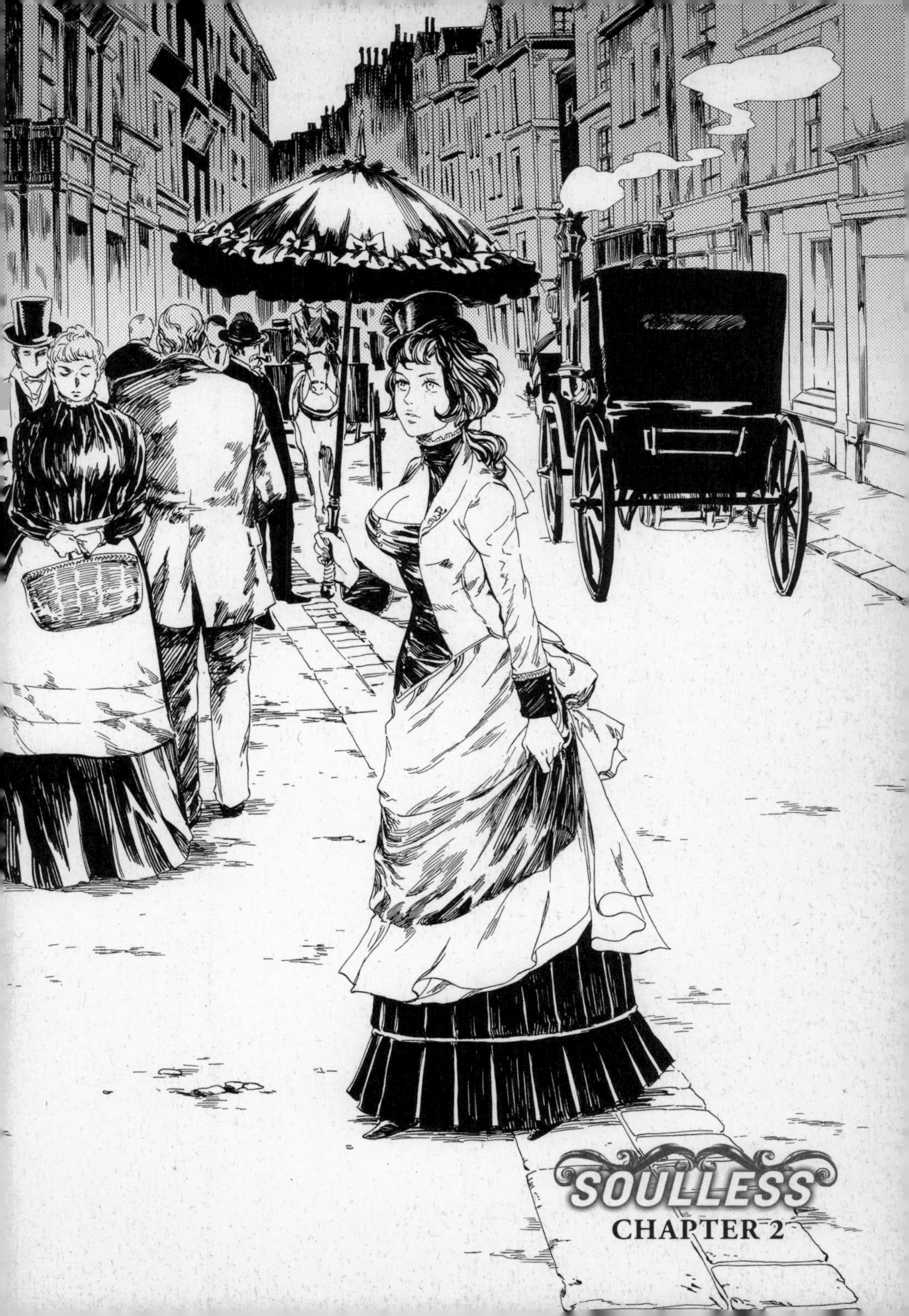
SOULLESS
CHAPTER 2

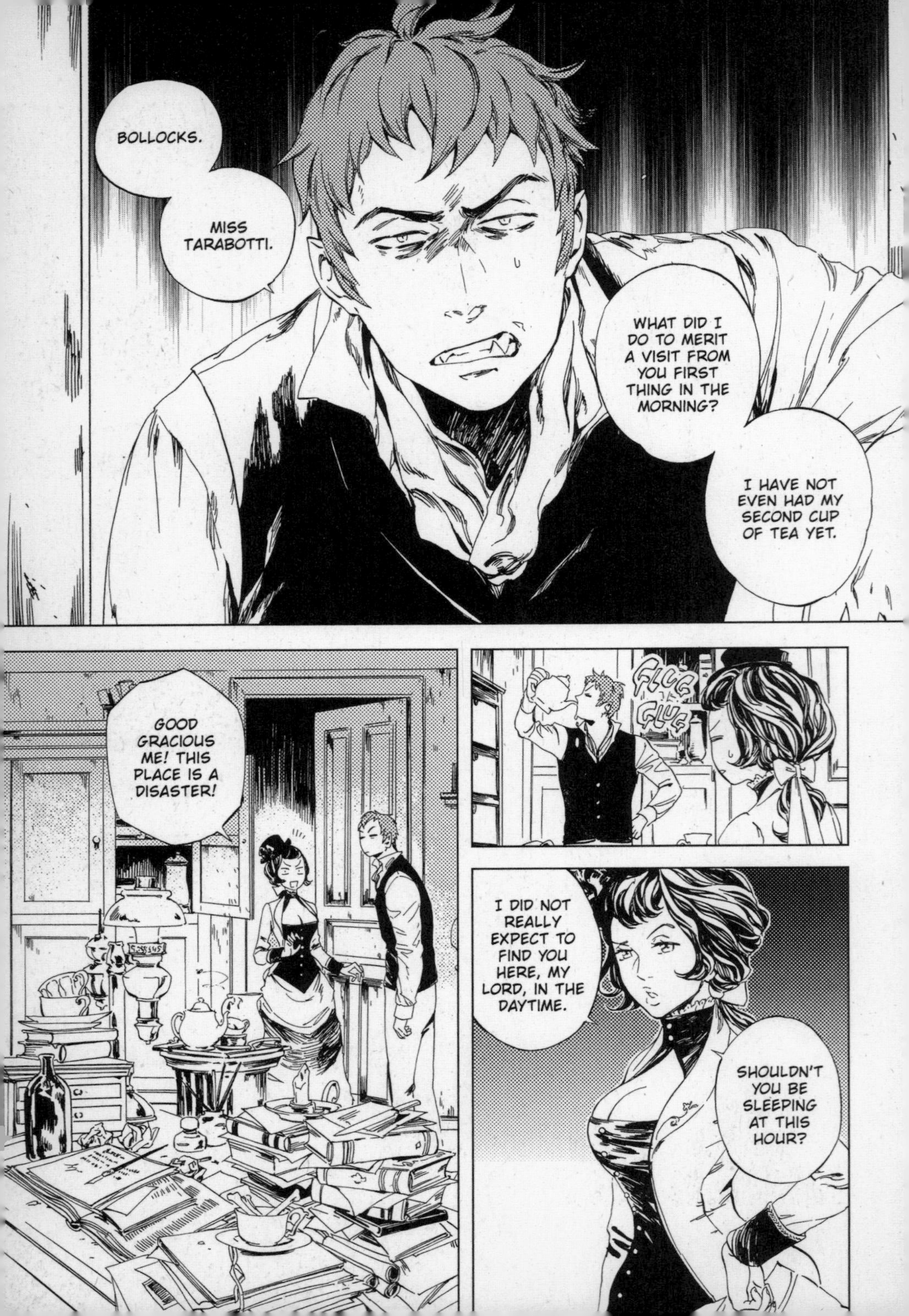
BOLLOCKS.
MISS TARABOTTI.
WHAT DID I DO TO MERIT A VISIT FROM YOU FIRST THING IN THE MORNING?
I HAVE NOT EVEN HAD MY SECOND CUP OF TEA YET.
GOOD GRACIOUS ME! THIS PLACE IS A DISASTER!
GLUG
GLUG
I DID NOT REALLY EXPECT TO FIND YOU HERE, MY LORD, IN THE DAYTIME.
SHOULDN'T YOU BE SLEEPING AT THIS HOUR?

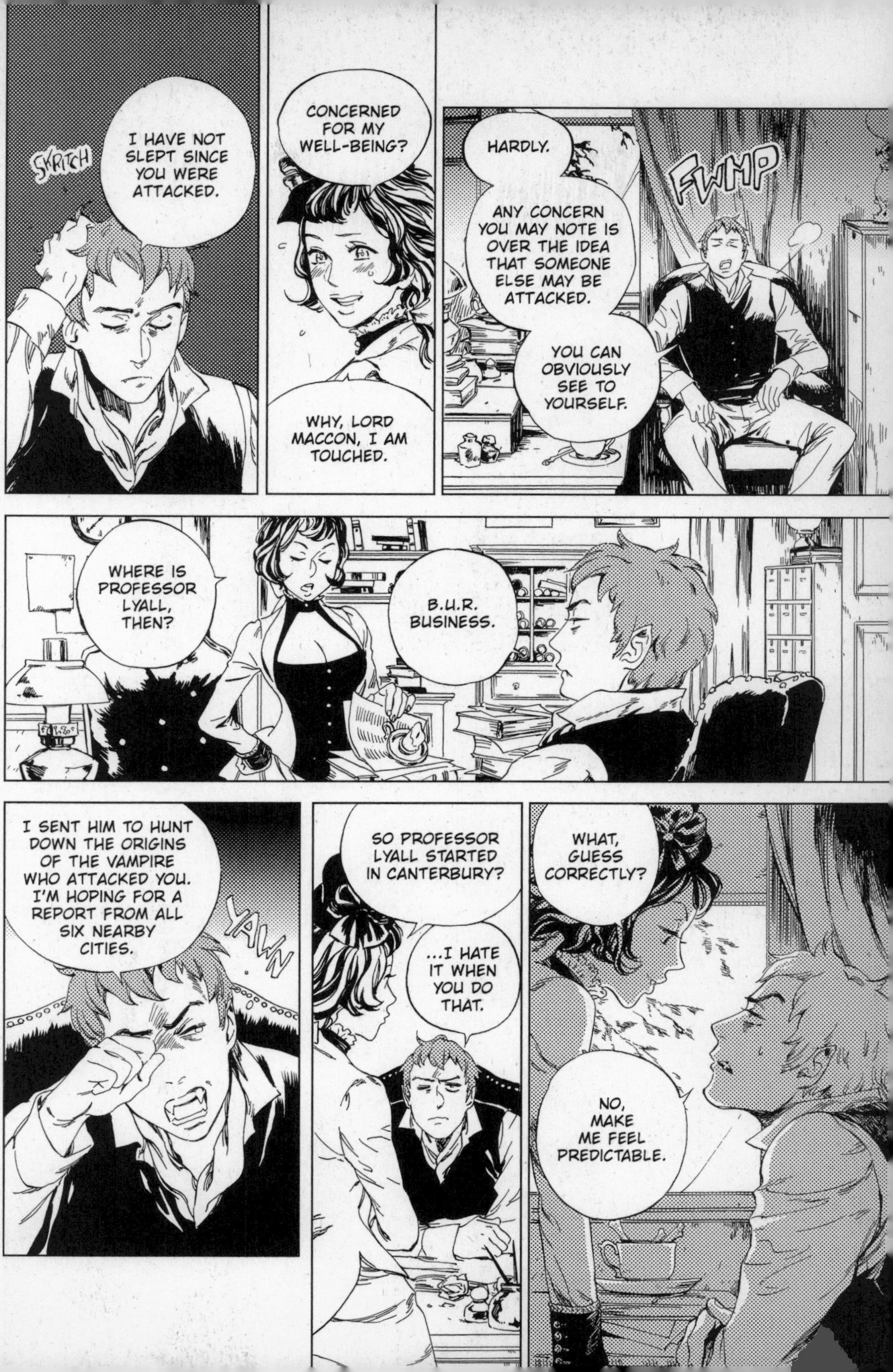
SKRITCH
I HAVE NOT SLEPT SINCE YOU WERE ATTACKED.
CONCERNED FOR MY WELL-BEING?
WHY, LORD MACCON, I AM TOUCHED.
HARDLY.
ANY CONCERN YOU MAY NOTE IS OVER THE IDEA THAT SOMEONE ELSE MAY BE ATTACKED.
YOU CAN OBVIOUSLY SEE TO YOURSELF.
FWMP
WHERE IS PROFESSOR LYALL, THEN?
B.U.R. BUSINESS.
I SENT HIM TO HUNT DOWN THE ORIGINS OF THE VAMPIRE WHO ATTACKED YOU. I'M HOPING FOR A REPORT FROM ALL SIX NEARBY CITIES.
YAWN
SO PROFESSOR LYALL STARTED IN CANTERBURY?
...I HATE IT WHEN YOU DO THAT.
WHAT, GUESS CORRECTLY?
NO, MAKE ME FEEL PREDICTABLE.

CANTERBURY IS A PORT CITY AND A CENTER FOR TRAVEL. IF HE CAME FROM ANYWHERE, IT WAS MOST LIKELY THERE.

BUT YOU DO NOT THINK HE CAME FROM OUTSIDE LONDON, DO YOU?

NO, THAT DOES NOT FEEL RIGHT.

HE SMELLED LOCAL, OF WESTMINSTER HIVE.

HOWEVER, I SPOKE TO COUNTESS NADASDY, AND SHE COMPLETELY DENIES ANY ASSOCIATION WITH YOUR ATTACKER.

SO YOU HAVE A GENUINE MYSTERY ON YOUR PLATE. ONLY A FEMALE VAMPIRE, A QUEEN, CAN METAMORPHOSE A NEW VAMPIRE.

YET HERE WE FIND OURSELVES WITH A NEW VAMPIRE AND NO MAKER.

EITHER YOUR NOSE OR HER TONGUE IS LYING.

INDEED.

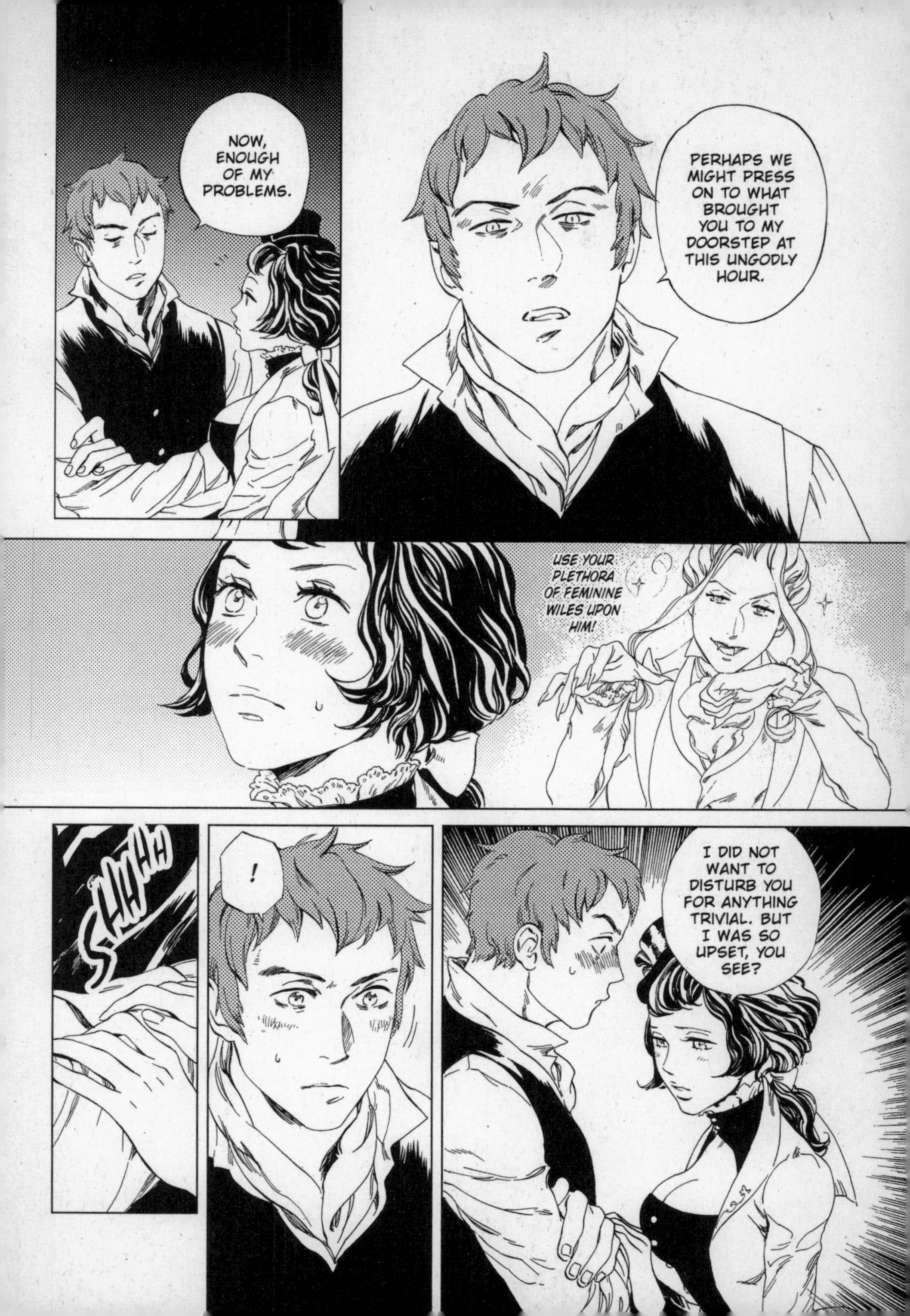
NOW, ENOUGH OF MY PROBLEMS.
PERHAPS WE MIGHT PRESS ON TO WHAT BROUGHT YOU TO MY DOORSTEP AT THIS UNGODLY HOUR.
USE YOUR PLETHORA OF FEMININE WILES UPON HIM!
!
I DID NOT WANT TO DISTURB YOU FOR ANYTHING TRIVIAL. BUT I WAS SO UPSET, YOU SEE?

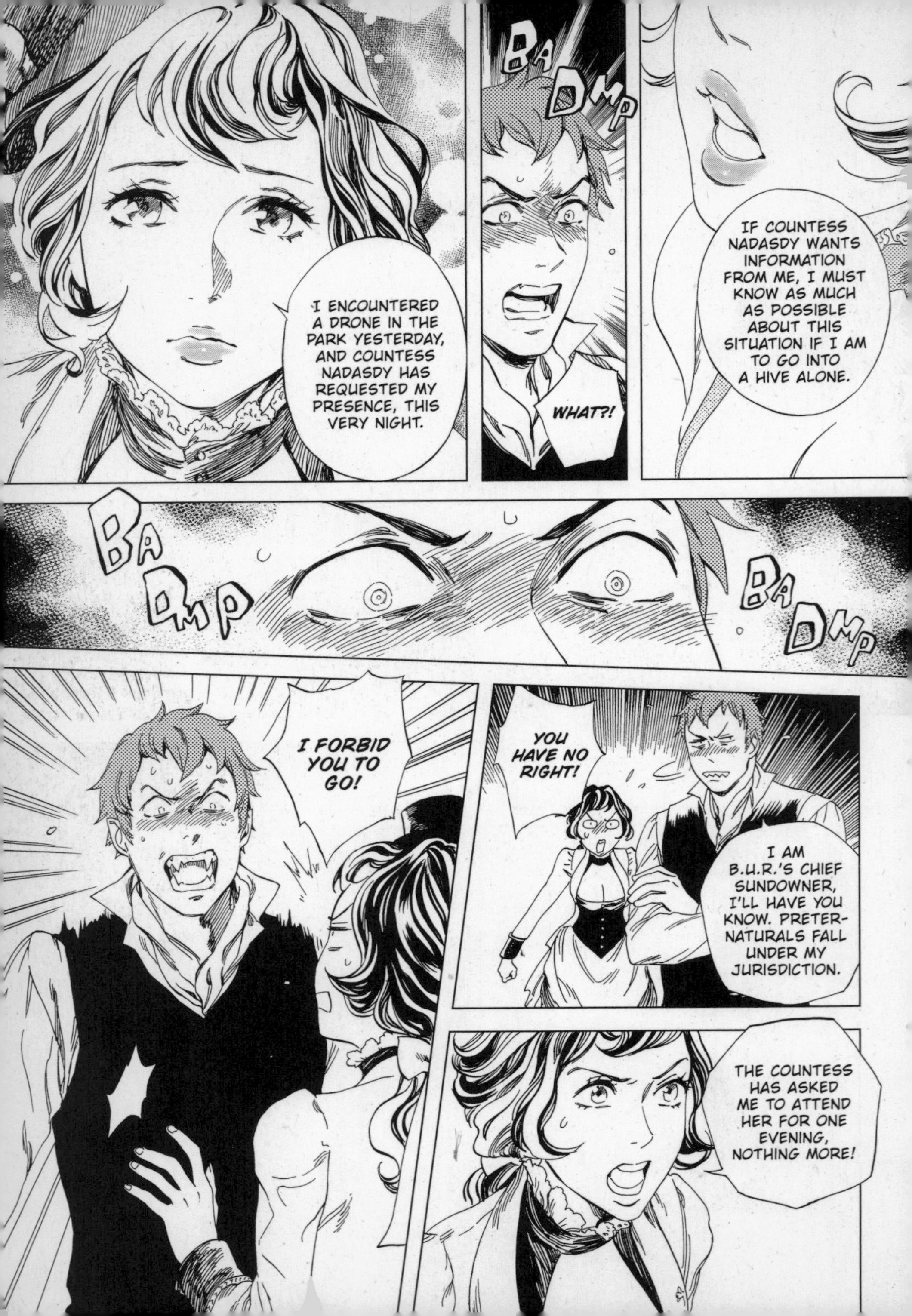
I ENCOUNTERED A DRONE IN THE PARK YESTERDAY, AND COUNTESS NADASDY HAS REQUESTED MY PRESENCE, THIS VERY NIGHT.
BADMP
WHAT?!
IF COUNTESS NADASDY WANTS INFORMATION FROM ME, I MUST KNOW AS MUCH AS POSSIBLE ABOUT THIS SITUATION IF I AM TO GO INTO A HIVE ALONE.
BADMP
BADMP
I FORBID YOU TO GO!
YOU HAVE NO RIGHT!
I AM B.U.R.'S CHIEF SUNDOWNER, I'LL HAVE YOU KNOW. PRETER-NATURALS FALL UNDER MY JURISDICTION.
THE COUNTESS HAS ASKED ME TO ATTEND HER FOR ONE EVENING, NOTHING MORE!

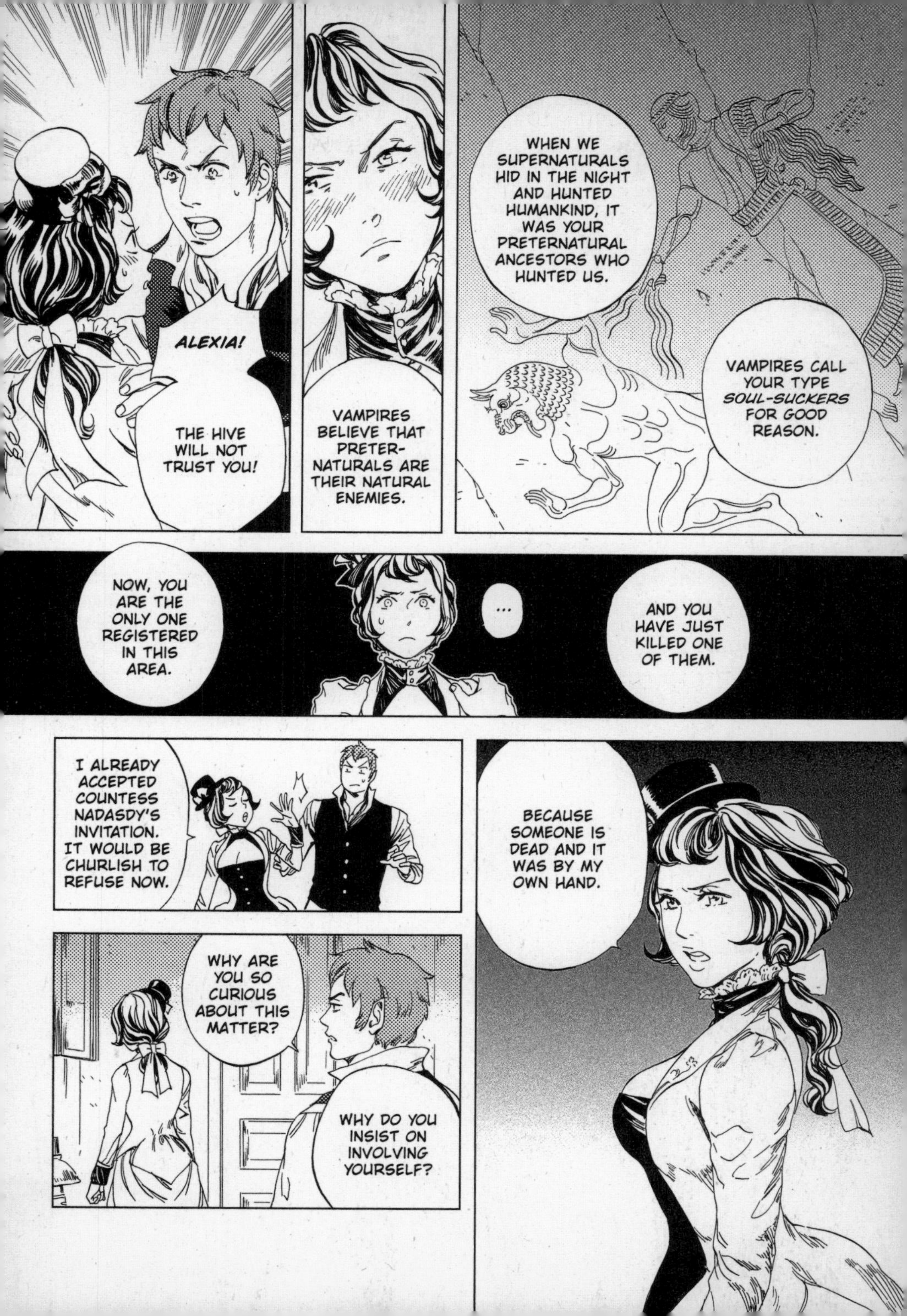
ALEXIA!
THE HIVE WILL NOT TRUST YOU!
VAMPIRES BELIEVE THAT PRETER-NATURALS ARE THEIR NATURAL ENEMIES.
WHEN WE SUPERNATURALS HID IN THE NIGHT AND HUNTED HUMANKIND, IT WAS YOUR PRETERNATURAL ANCESTORS WHO HUNTED US.
VAMPIRES CALL YOUR TYPE *SOUL-SUCKERS* FOR GOOD REASON.
NOW, YOU ARE THE ONLY ONE REGISTERED IN THIS AREA.
...
AND YOU HAVE JUST KILLED ONE OF THEM.
I ALREADY ACCEPTED COUNTESS NADASDY'S INVITATION. IT WOULD BE CHURLISH TO REFUSE NOW.
WHY ARE YOU SO CURIOUS ABOUT THIS MATTER?
WHY DO YOU INSIST ON INVOLVING YOURSELF?
BECAUSE SOMEONE IS DEAD AND IT WAS BY MY OWN HAND.

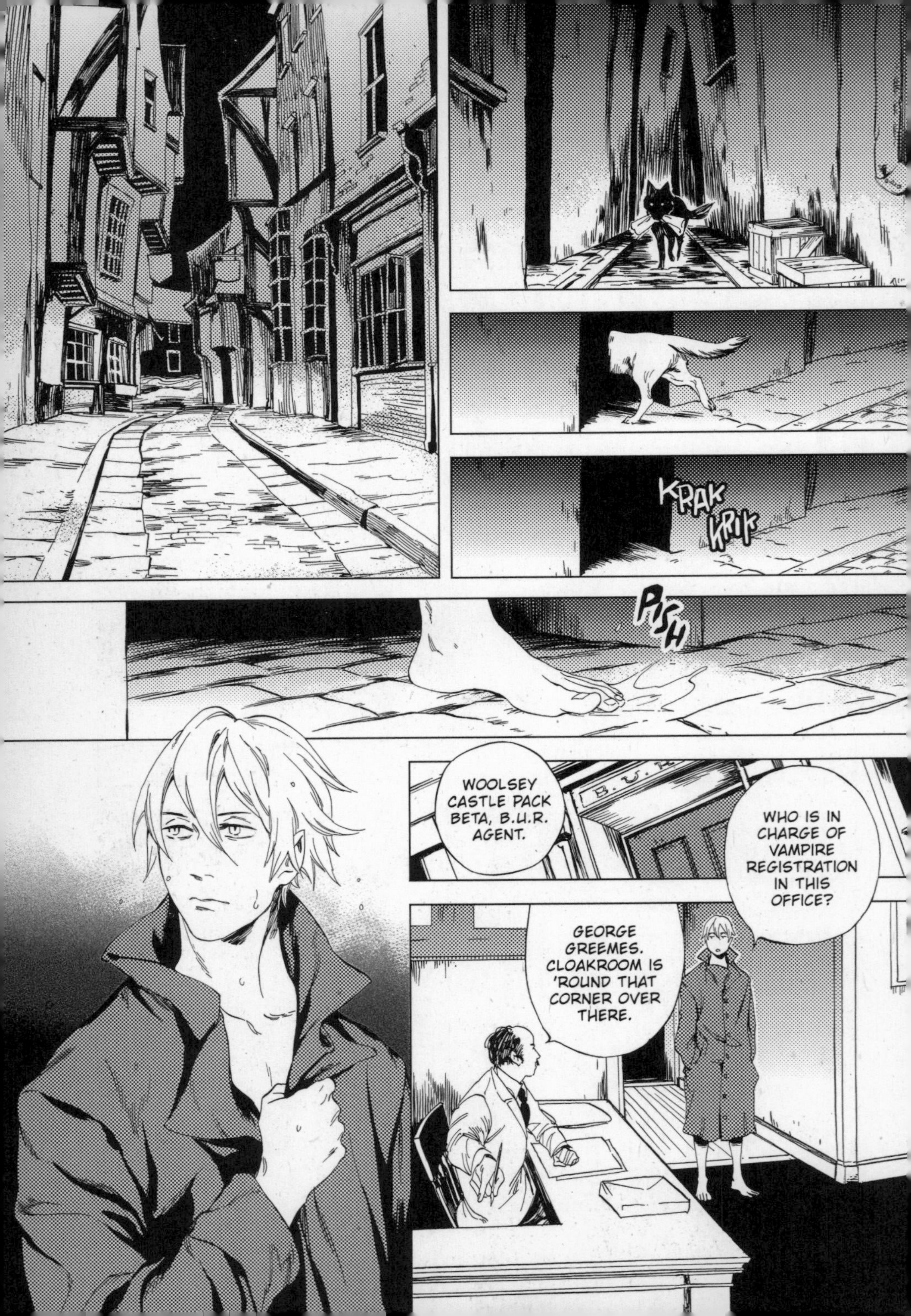
KRAK
KRIK
PISH
WOOLSEY CASTLE PACK BETA, B.U.R. AGENT.
WHO IS IN CHARGE OF VAMPIRE REGISTRATION IN THIS OFFICE?
GEORGE GREEMES. CLOAKROOM IS 'ROUND THAT CORNER OVER THERE.

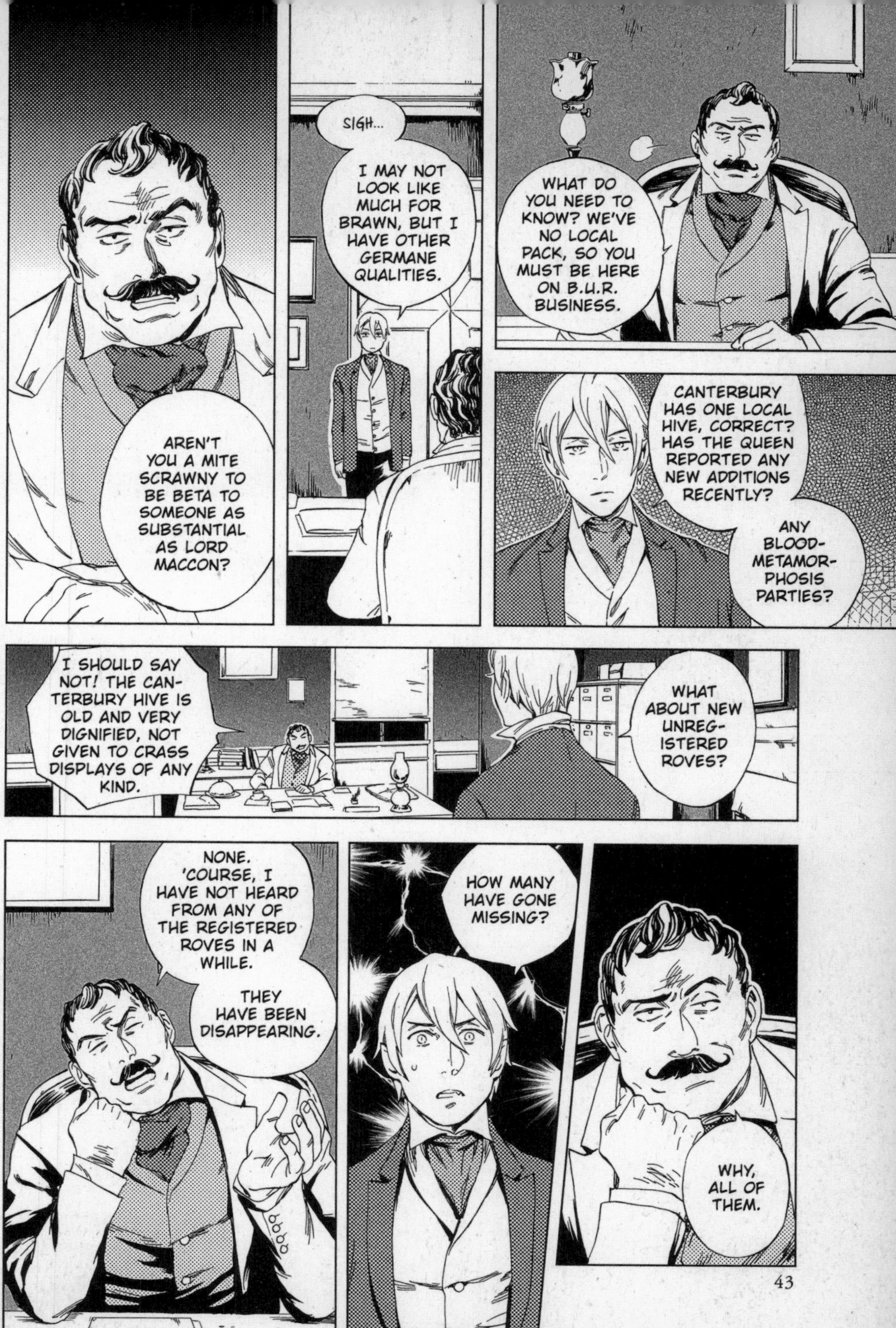
AREN'T YOU A MITE SCRAWNY TO BE BETA TO SOMEONE AS SUBSTANTIAL AS LORD MACCON?
SIGH...
I MAY NOT LOOK LIKE MUCH FOR BRAWN, BUT I HAVE OTHER GERMANE QUALITIES.
WHAT DO YOU NEED TO KNOW? WE'VE NO LOCAL PACK, SO YOU MUST BE HERE ON B.U.R. BUSINESS.
CANTERBURY HAS ONE LOCAL HIVE, CORRECT? HAS THE QUEEN REPORTED ANY NEW ADDITIONS RECENTLY?
ANY BLOOD-METAMORPHOSIS PARTIES?
I SHOULD SAY NOT! THE CANTERBURY HIVE IS OLD AND VERY DIGNIFIED, NOT GIVEN TO CRASS DISPLAYS OF ANY KIND.
WHAT ABOUT NEW UNREGISTERED ROVES?
NONE. 'COURSE, I HAVE NOT HEARD FROM ANY OF THE REGISTERED ROVES IN A WHILE.
THEY HAVE BEEN DISAPPEARING.
HOW MANY HAVE GONE MISSING?
WHY, ALL OF THEM.

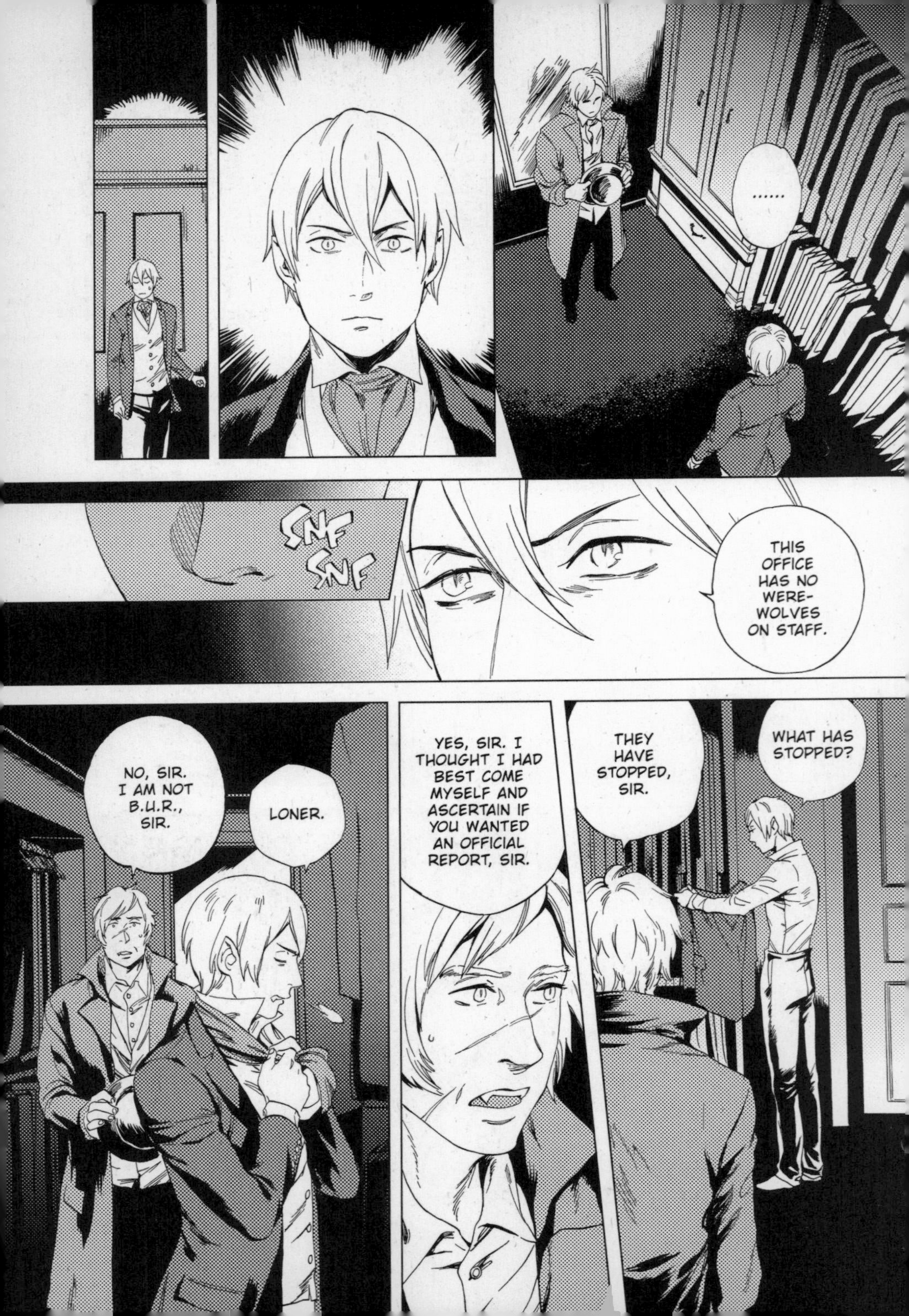
......
SNF
SNF
THIS OFFICE HAS NO WERE-WOLVES ON STAFF.
NO, SIR. I AM NOT B.U.R., SIR.
LONER.
YES, SIR. I THOUGHT I HAD BEST COME MYSELF AND ASCERTAIN IF YOU WANTED AN OFFICIAL REPORT, SIR.
THEY HAVE STOPPED, SIR.
WHAT HAS STOPPED?

THE DISAP-
PEARANCES
OF WEREWOLF
LONERS, SIR.

THOUGHT
YOU KNEW,
SIR. IT HAS
BEEN GOING
ON FOR
SEVERAL
MONTHS
NOW.

WELL,
I AM HERE
ON HIVE,
NOT PACK,
BUSINESS.

I HAVE
GOT
TO GET
MOVING.

IF THESE
DISAPPEAR-
ANCES START
UP AGAIN, YOU
WILL LET US
KNOW IMMEDI-
ATELY.

CANNOT DO
THAT, SIR. ALL
APOLOGIES,
SIR.

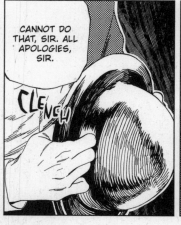

CLENCH

SORRY,
SIR, BUT
I AM THE
ONLY ONE
LEFT.

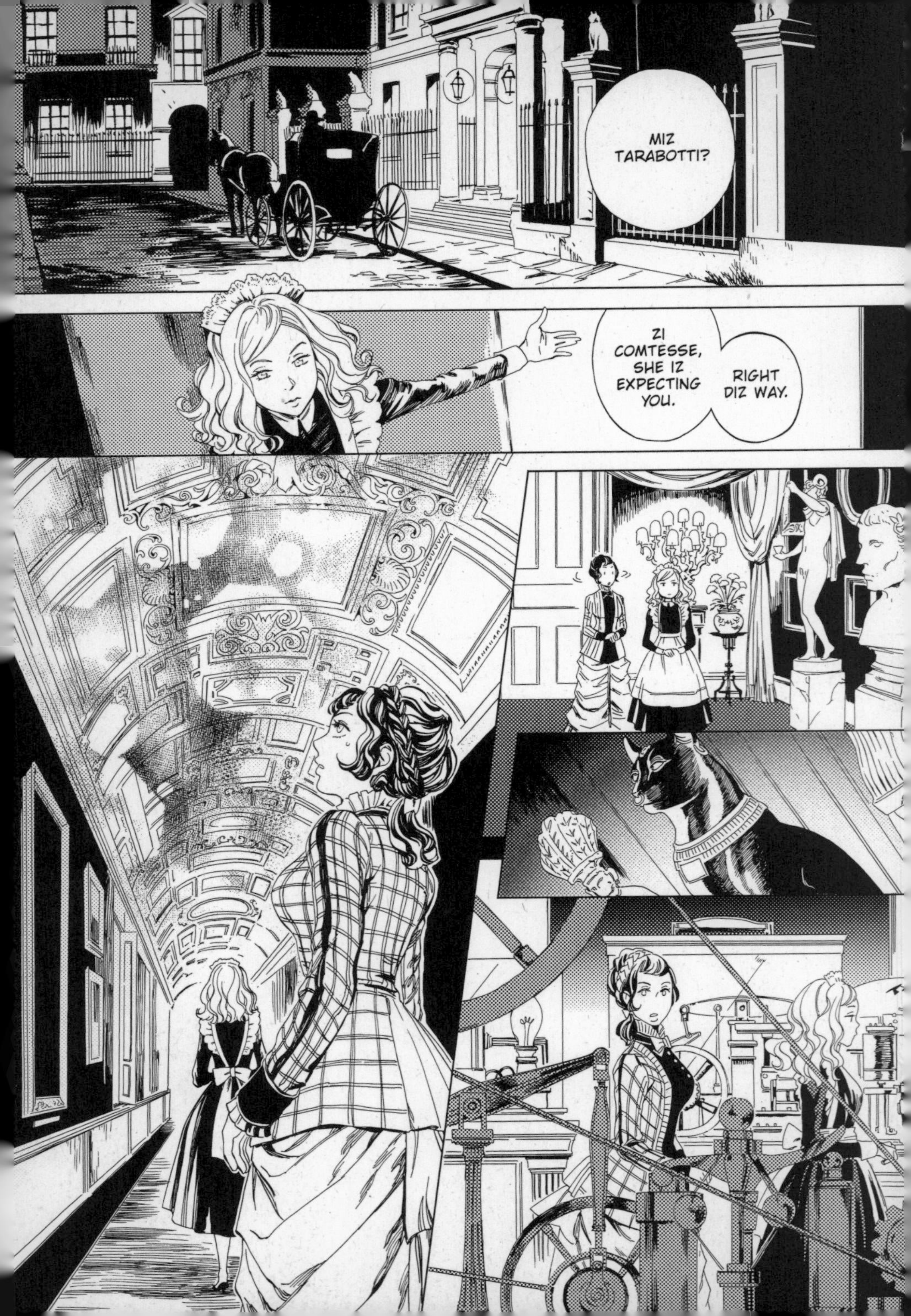
MIZ TARABOTTI?
ZI COMTESSE, SHE IZ EXPECTING YOU.
RIGHT DIZ WAY.

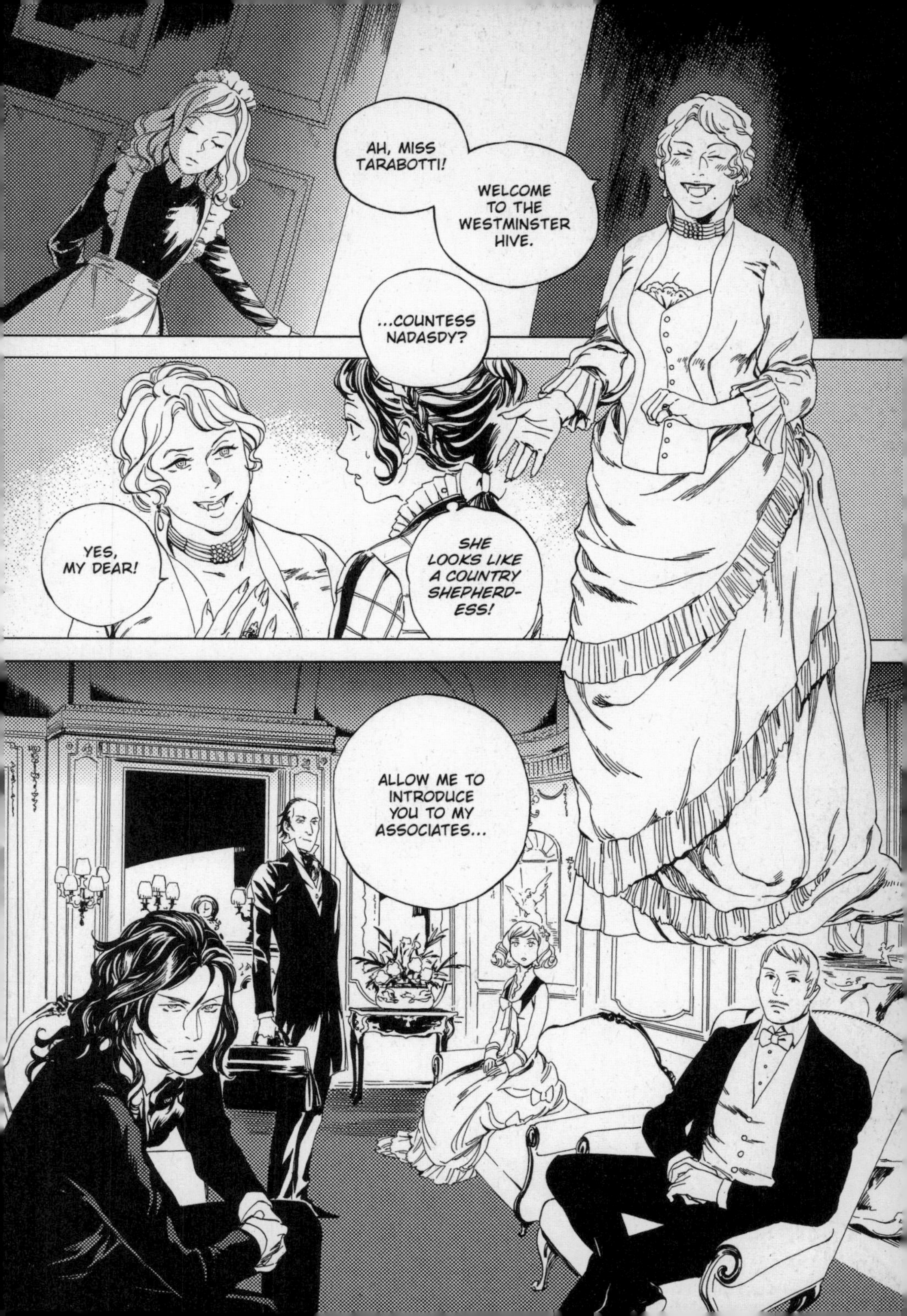
AH, MISS TARABOTTI!
WELCOME TO THE WESTMINSTER HIVE.
...COUNTESS NADASDY?
YES, MY DEAR!
SHE LOOKS LIKE A COUNTRY SHEPHERD-ESS!
ALLOW ME TO INTRODUCE YOU TO MY ASSOCIATES...

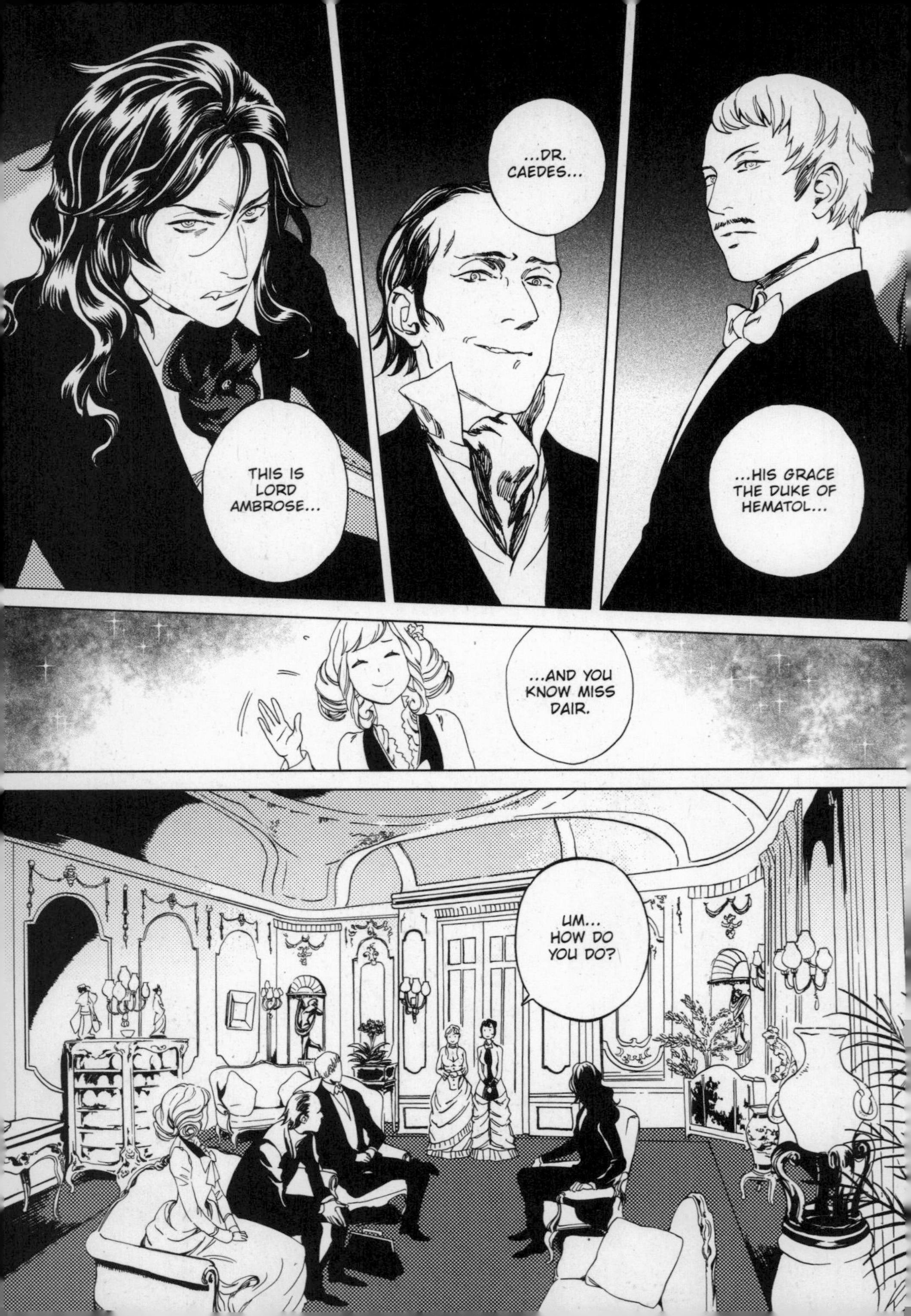
THIS IS LORD AMBROSE...
...DR. CAEDES...
...HIS GRACE THE DUKE OF HEMATOL...
...AND YOU KNOW MISS DAIR.
UM... HOW DO YOU DO?

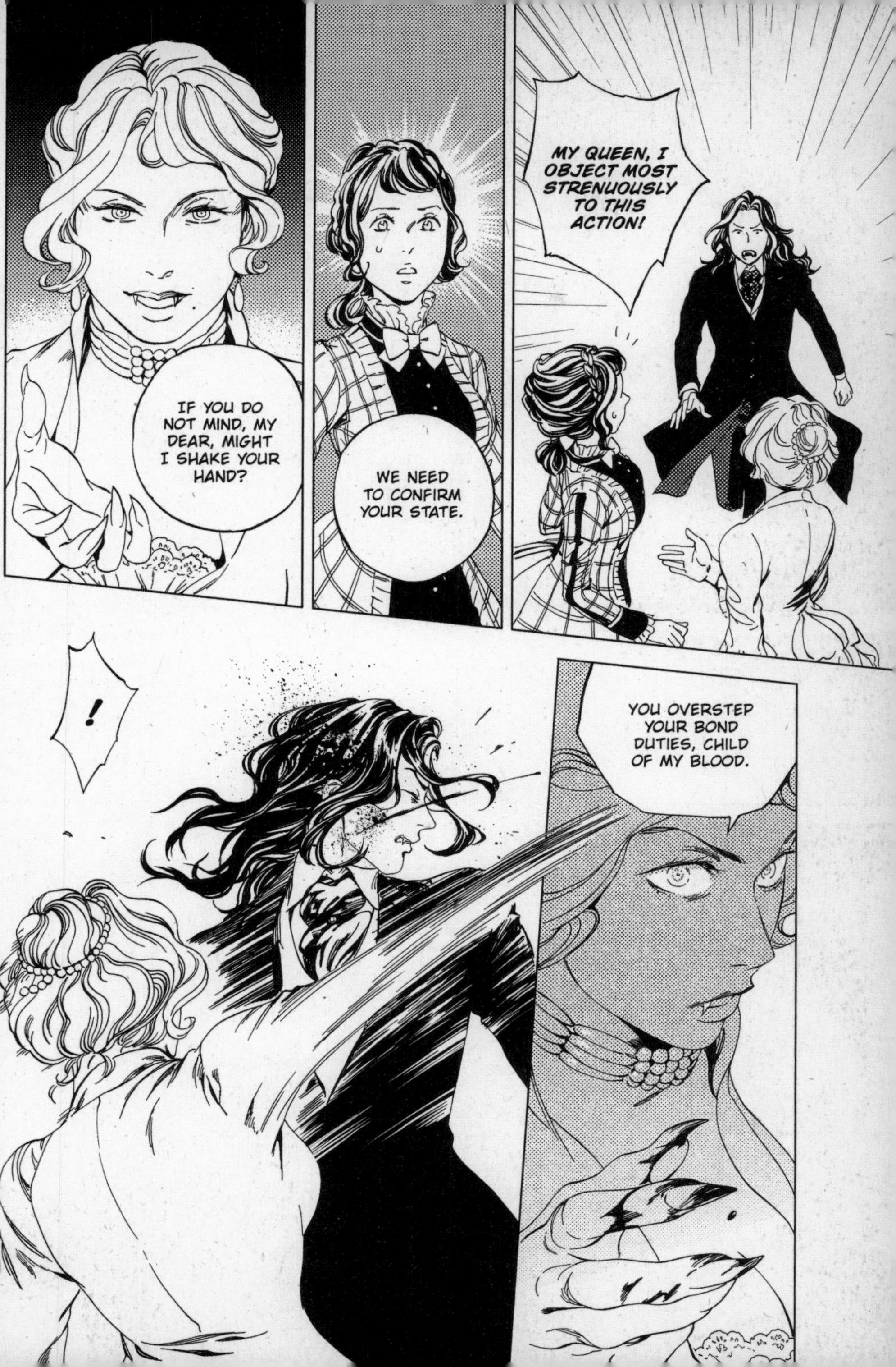
IF YOU DO NOT MIND, MY DEAR, MIGHT I SHAKE YOUR HAND?
WE NEED TO CONFIRM YOUR STATE.
MY QUEEN, I OBJECT MOST STRENUOUSLY TO THIS ACTION!
!
YOU OVERSTEP YOUR BOND DUTIES, CHILD OF MY BLOOD.

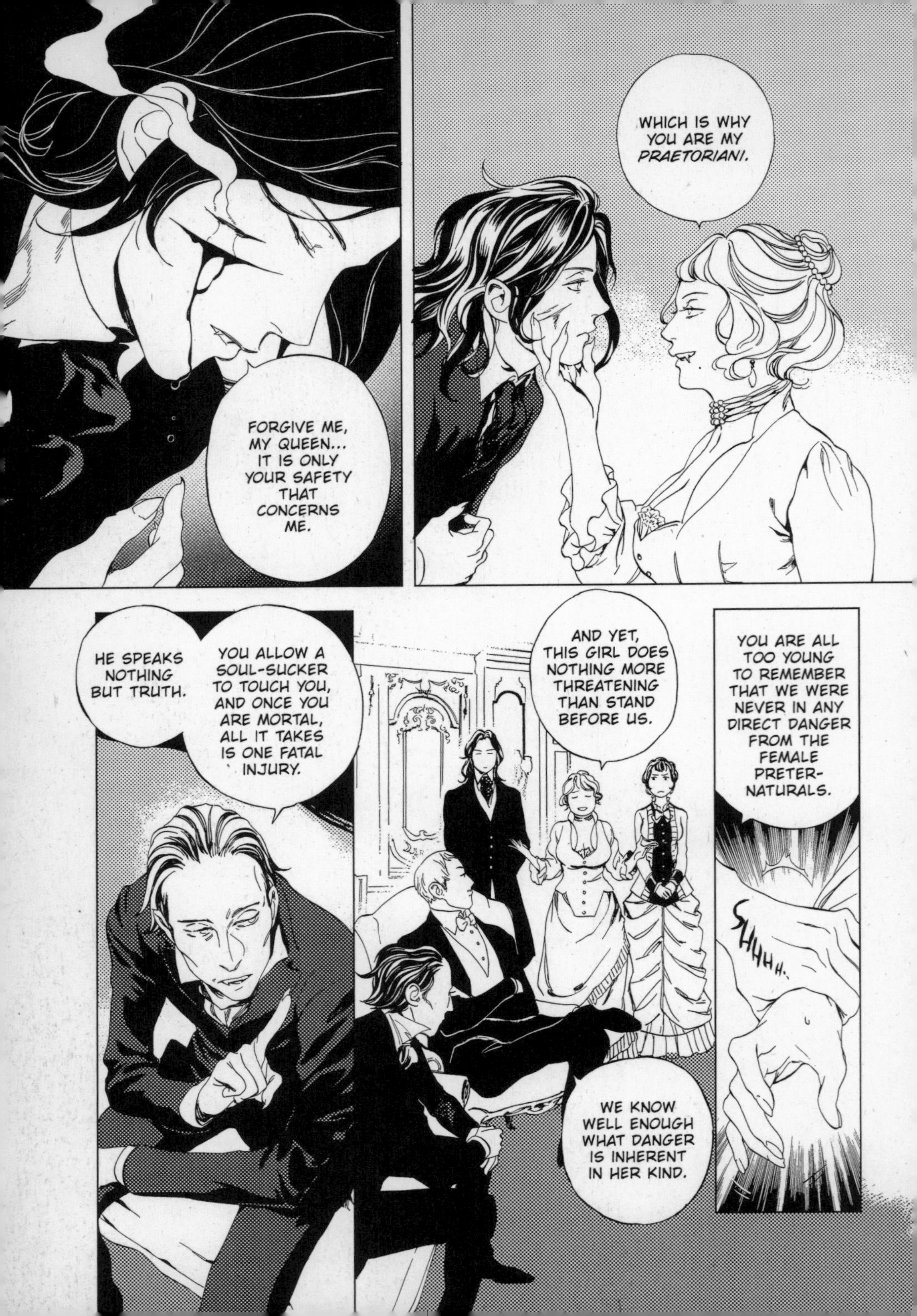
FORGIVE ME, MY QUEEN... IT IS ONLY YOUR SAFETY THAT CONCERNS ME.
WHICH IS WHY YOU ARE MY PRAETORIANI.
HE SPEAKS NOTHING BUT TRUTH.
YOU ALLOW A SOUL-SUCKER TO TOUCH YOU, AND ONCE YOU ARE MORTAL, ALL IT TAKES IS ONE FATAL INJURY.
AND YET, THIS GIRL DOES NOTHING MORE THREATENING THAN STAND BEFORE US.
WE KNOW WELL ENOUGH WHAT DANGER IS INHERENT IN HER KIND.
YOU ARE ALL TOO YOUNG TO REMEMBER THAT WE WERE NEVER IN ANY DIRECT DANGER FROM THE FEMALE PRETER-NATURALS.
SHHHH..

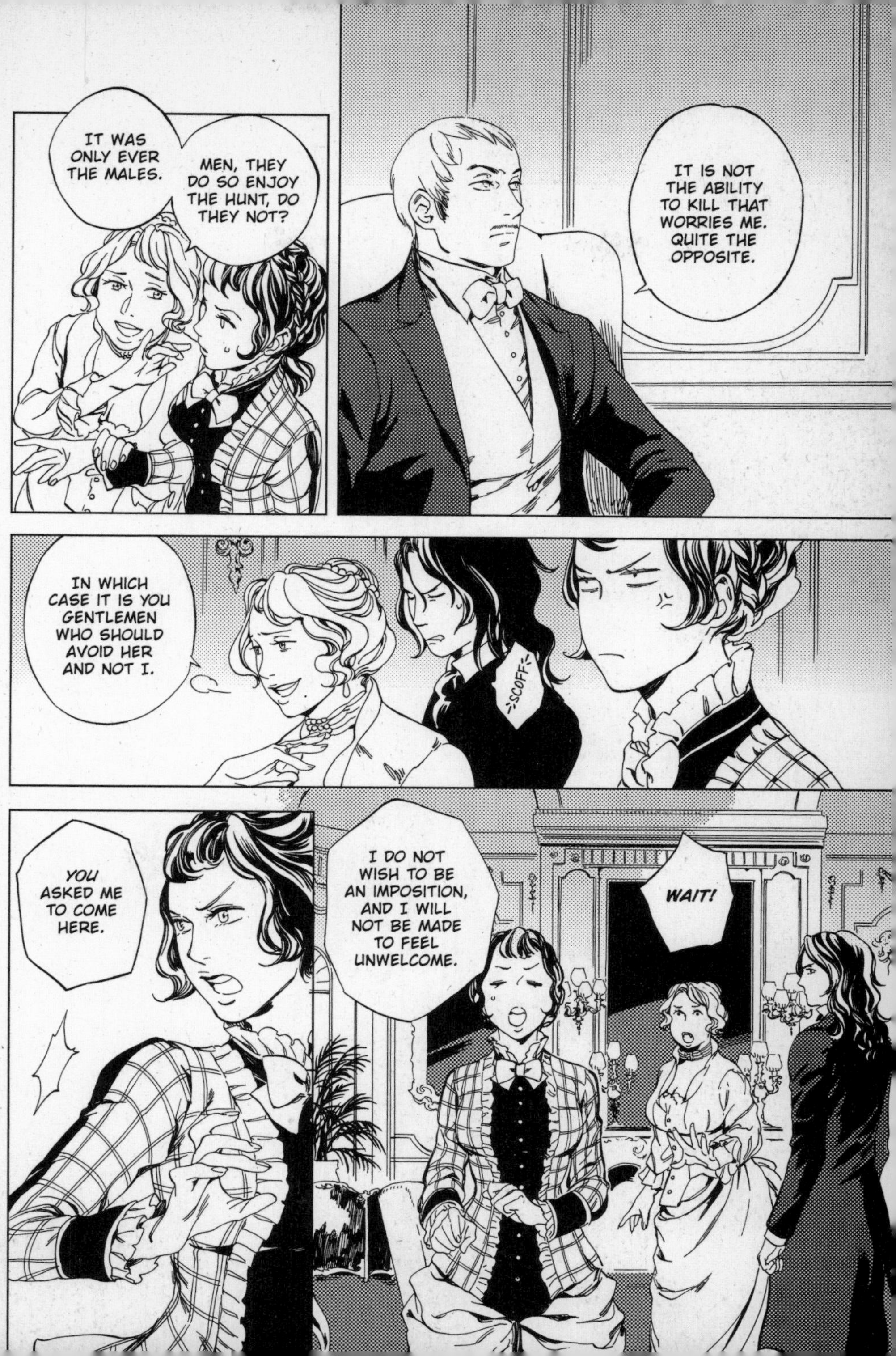
IT WAS ONLY EVER THE MALES.
MEN, THEY DO SO ENJOY THE HUNT, DO THEY NOT?
IT IS NOT THE ABILITY TO KILL THAT WORRIES ME. QUITE THE OPPOSITE.
IN WHICH CASE IT IS YOU GENTLEMEN WHO SHOULD AVOID HER AND NOT I.
SCOFF
YOU ASKED ME TO COME HERE.
I DO NOT WISH TO BE AN IMPOSITION, AND I WILL NOT BE MADE TO FEEL UNWELCOME.
WAIT!

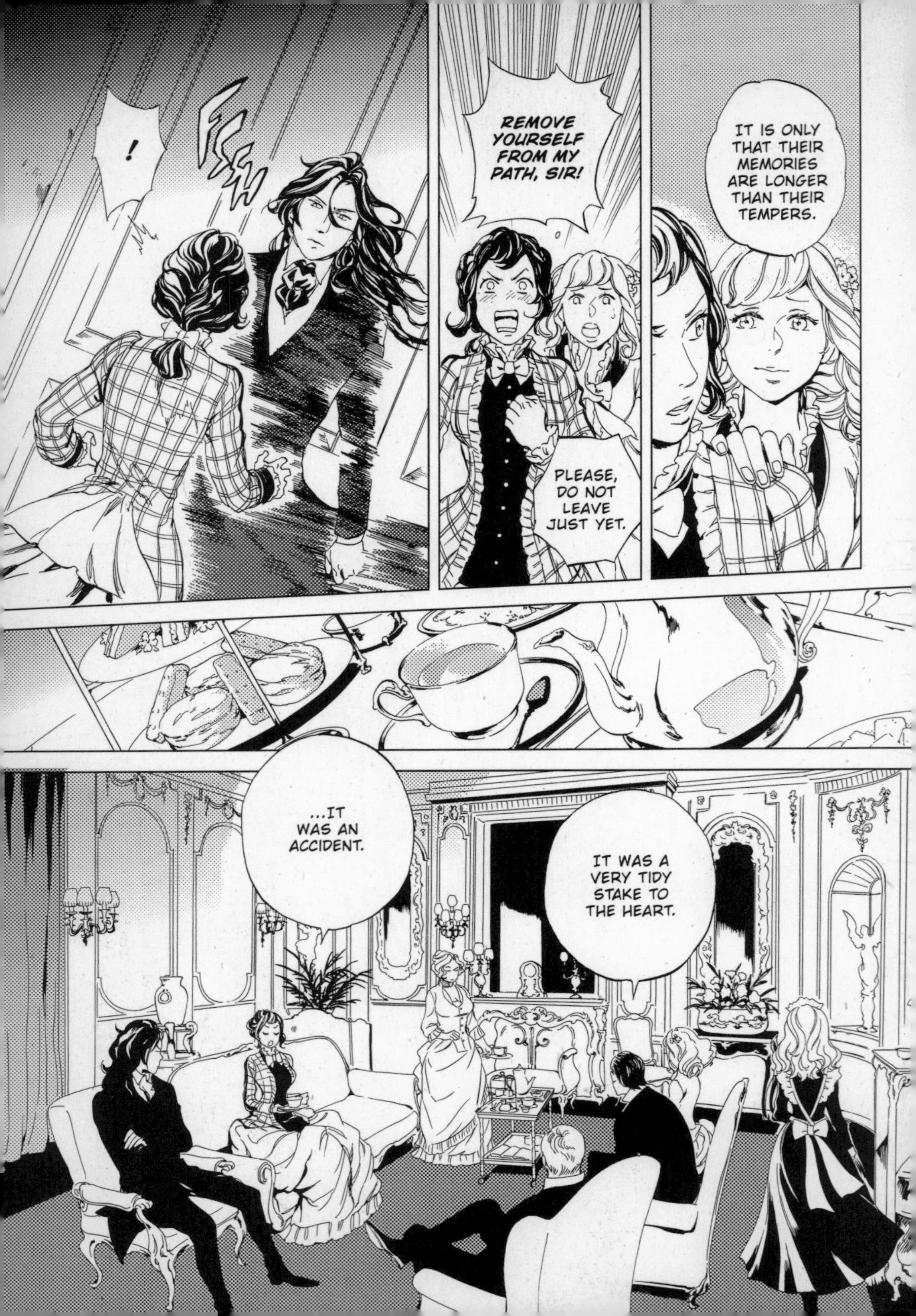
!
FSSH
REMOVE YOURSELF FROM MY PATH, SIR!
PLEASE, DO NOT LEAVE JUST YET.
IT IS ONLY THAT THEIR MEMORIES ARE LONGER THAN THEIR TEMPERS.
...IT WAS AN ACCIDENT.
IT WAS A VERY TIDY STAKE TO THE HEART.

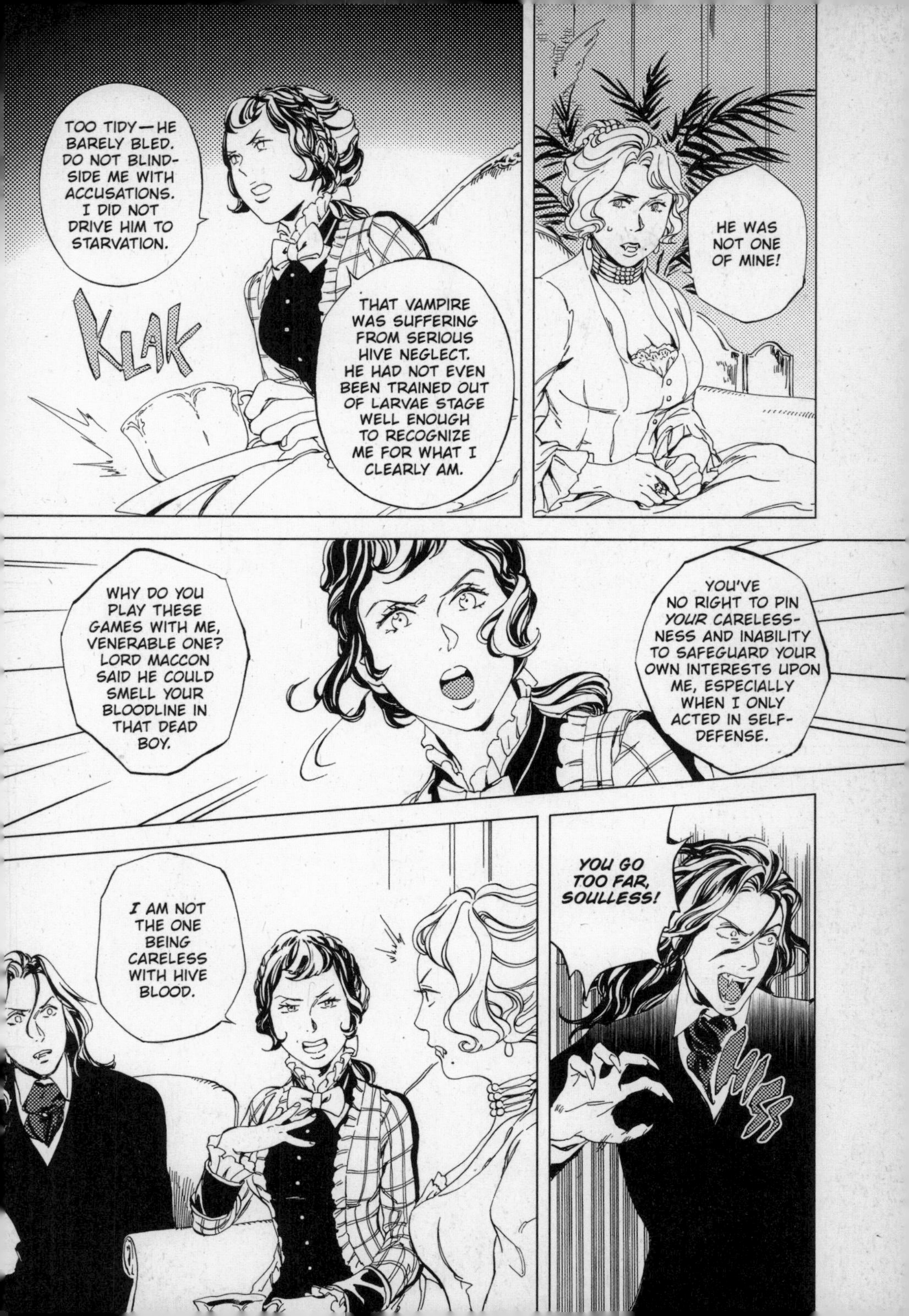
TOO TIDY—HE BARELY BLED. DO NOT BLIND-SIDE ME WITH ACCUSATIONS. I DID NOT DRIVE HIM TO STARVATION.
KLAK
THAT VAMPIRE WAS SUFFERING FROM SERIOUS HIVE NEGLECT. HE HAD NOT EVEN BEEN TRAINED OUT OF LARVAE STAGE WELL ENOUGH TO RECOGNIZE ME FOR WHAT I CLEARLY AM.
HE WAS NOT ONE OF MINE!
WHY DO YOU PLAY THESE GAMES WITH ME, VENERABLE ONE? LORD MACCON SAID HE COULD SMELL YOUR BLOODLINE IN THAT DEAD BOY.
YOU'VE NO RIGHT TO PIN YOUR CARELESS-NESS AND INABILITY TO SAFEGUARD YOUR OWN INTERESTS UPON ME, ESPECIALLY WHEN I ONLY ACTED IN SELF-DEFENSE.
I AM NOT THE ONE BEING CARELESS WITH HIVE BLOOD.
YOU GO TOO FAR, SOULLESS!

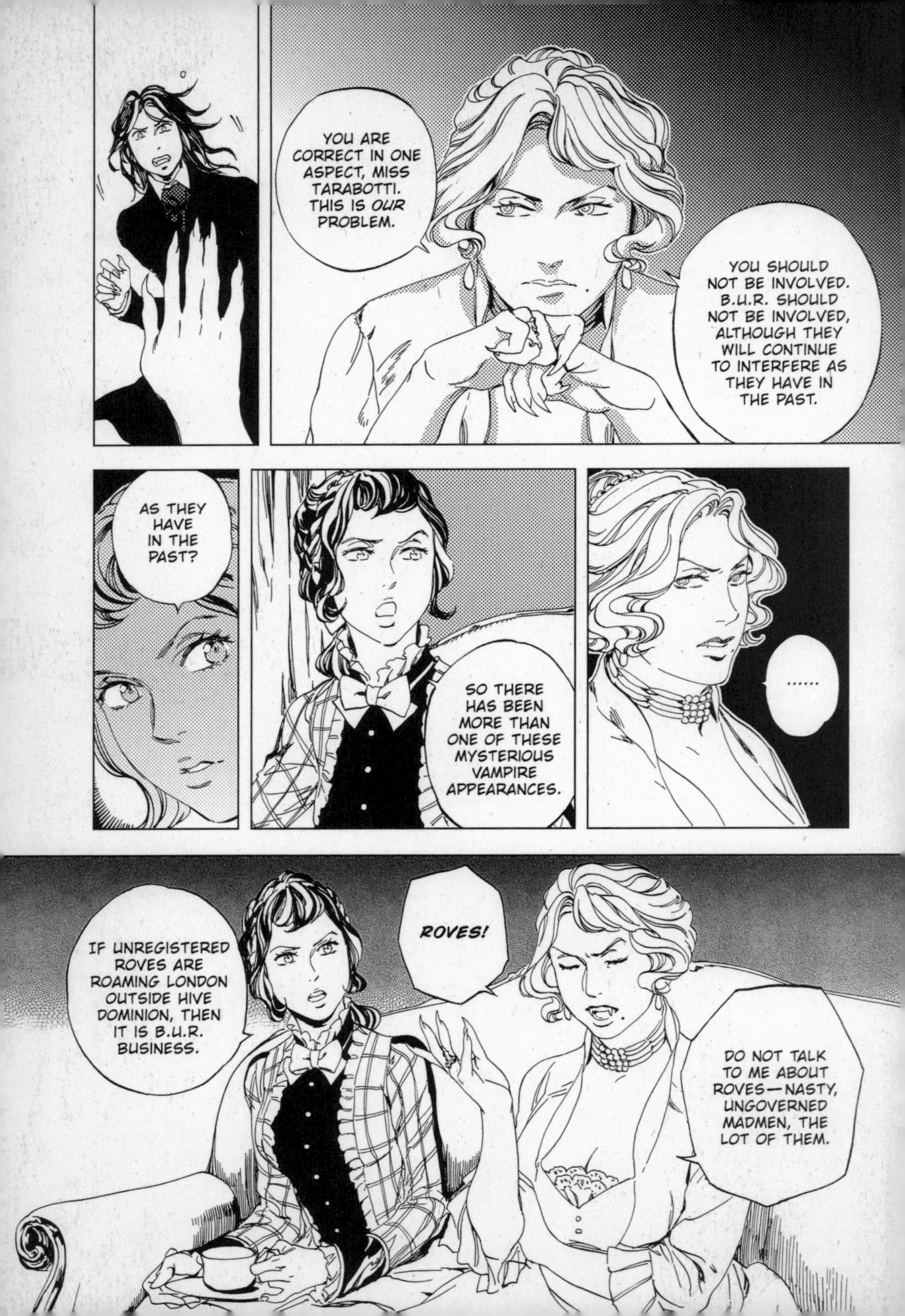
YOU ARE CORRECT IN ONE ASPECT, MISS TARABOTTI. THIS IS *OUR* PROBLEM.
YOU SHOULD NOT BE INVOLVED. B.U.R. SHOULD NOT BE INVOLVED, ALTHOUGH THEY WILL CONTINUE TO INTERFERE AS THEY HAVE IN THE PAST.
AS THEY HAVE IN THE PAST?
SO THERE HAS BEEN MORE THAN ONE OF THESE MYSTERIOUS VAMPIRE APPEARANCES.
......
IF UNREGISTERED ROVES ARE ROAMING LONDON OUTSIDE HIVE DOMINION, THEN IT IS B.U.R. BUSINESS.
ROVES!
DO NOT TALK TO ME ABOUT ROVES—NASTY, UNGOVERNED MADMEN, THE LOT OF THEM.

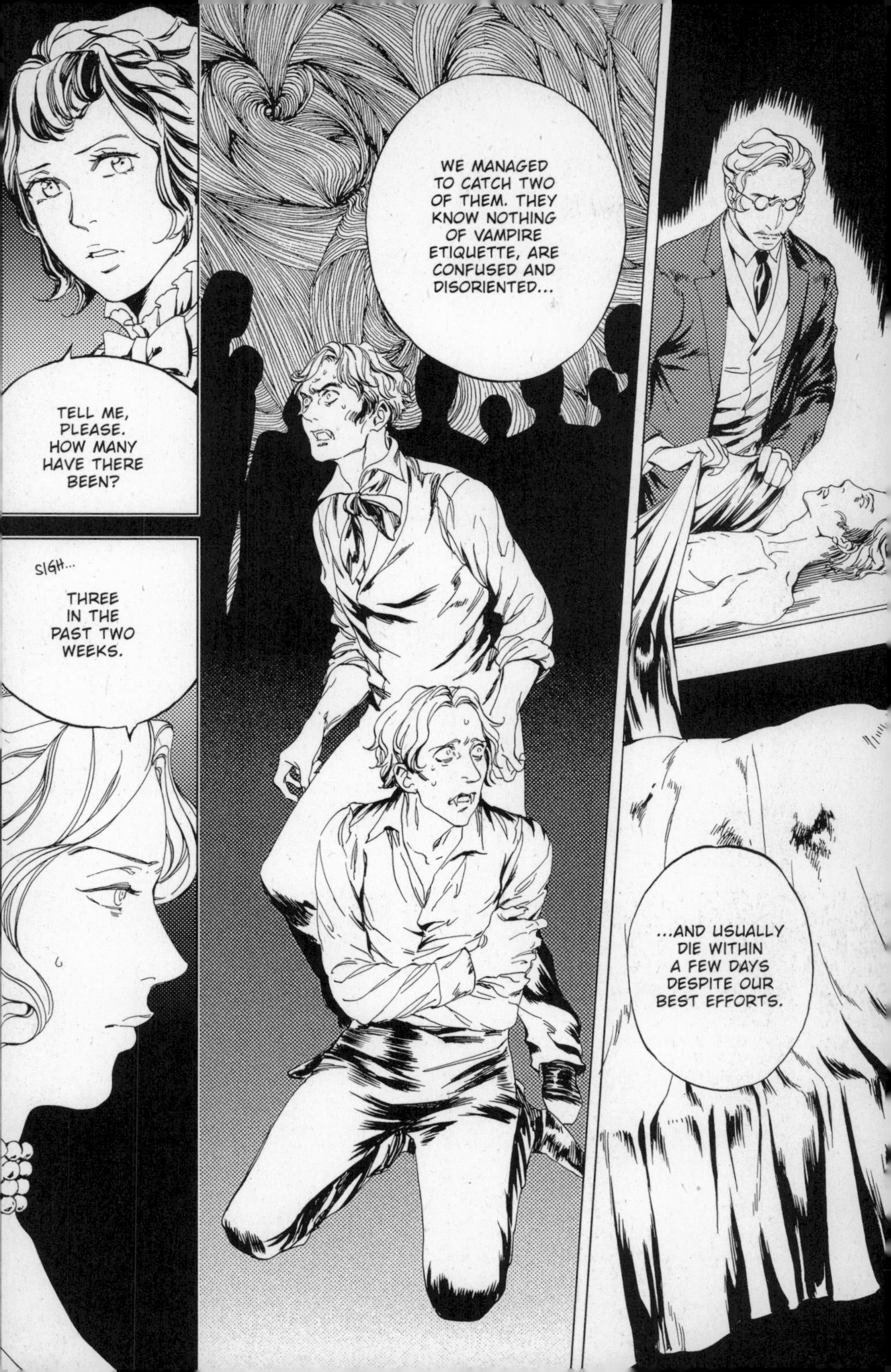
TELL ME, PLEASE. HOW MANY HAVE THERE BEEN?
SIGH...
THREE IN THE PAST TWO WEEKS.
WE MANAGED TO CATCH TWO OF THEM. THEY KNOW NOTHING OF VAMPIRE ETIQUETTE, ARE CONFUSED AND DISORIENTED...
...AND USUALLY DIE WITHIN A FEW DAYS DESPITE OUR BEST EFFORTS.

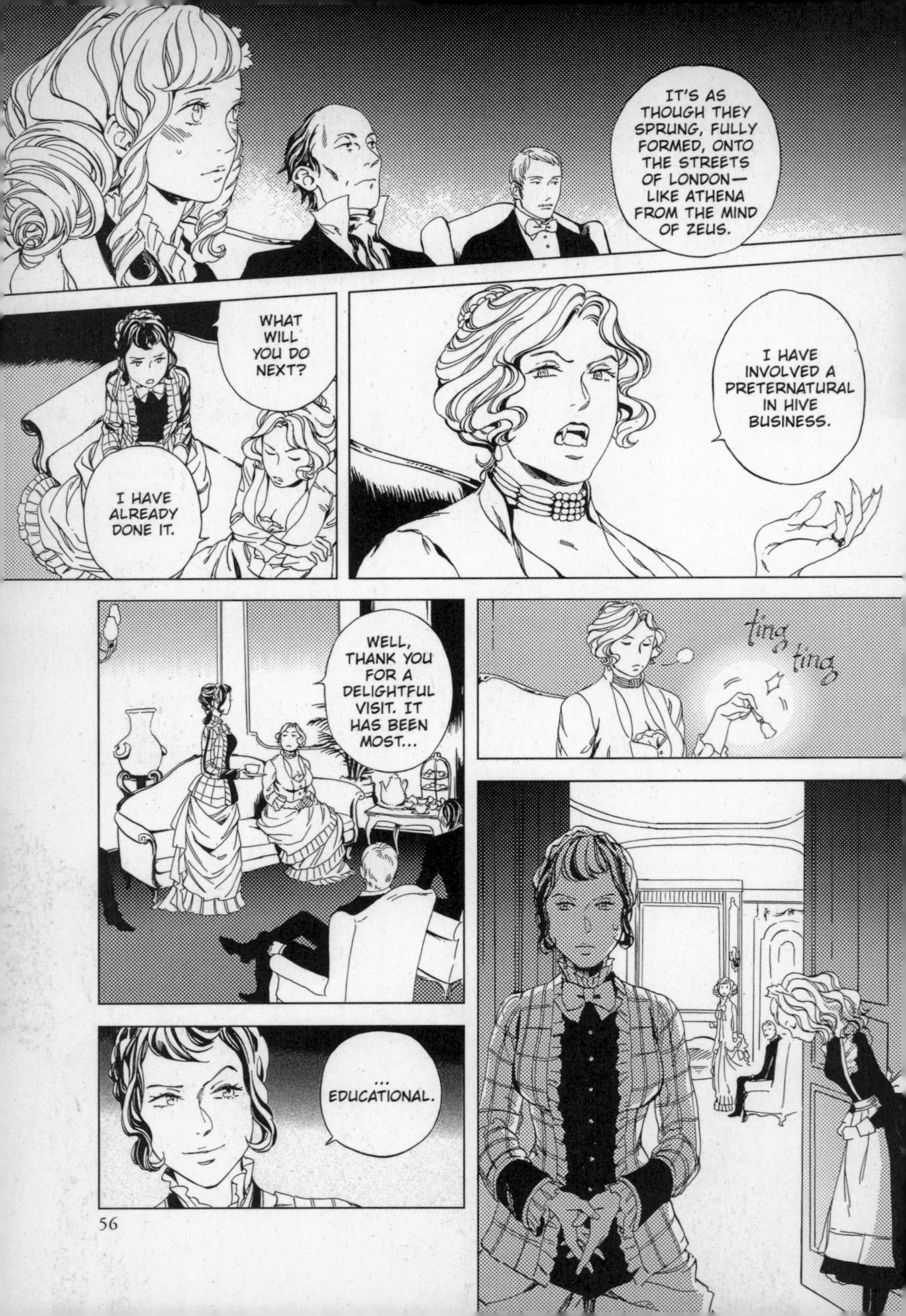
IT'S AS THOUGH THEY SPRUNG, FULLY FORMED, ONTO THE STREETS OF LONDON—LIKE ATHENA FROM THE MIND OF ZEUS.
WHAT WILL YOU DO NEXT?
I HAVE ALREADY DONE IT.
I HAVE INVOLVED A PRETERNATURAL IN HIVE BUSINESS.
WELL, THANK YOU FOR A DELIGHTFUL VISIT. IT HAS BEEN MOST...
ting ting
... EDUCATIONAL.

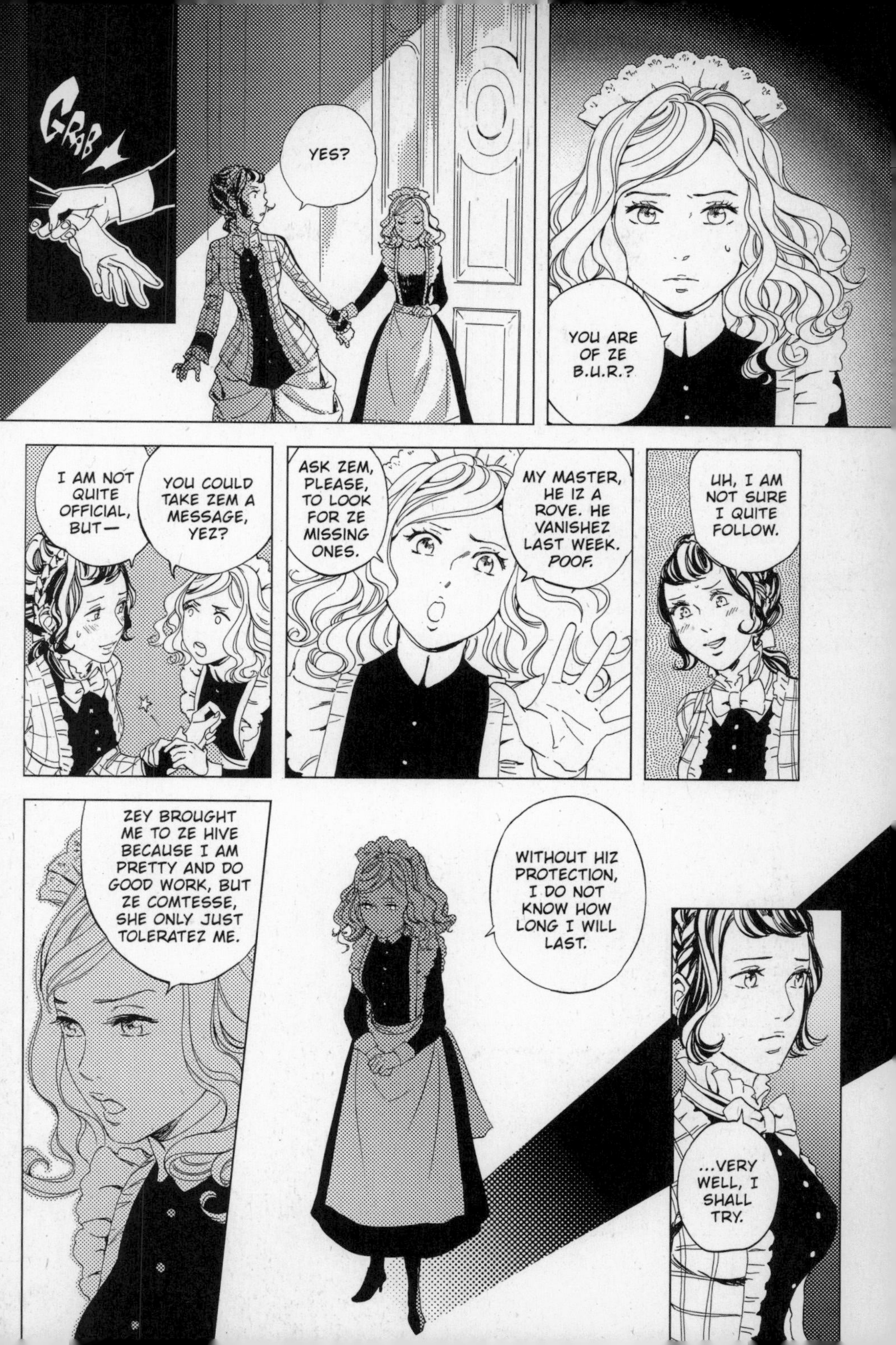
GRAB
YES?
YOU ARE OF ZE B.U.R.?
I AM NOT QUITE OFFICIAL, BUT—
YOU COULD TAKE ZEM A MESSAGE, YEZ?
ASK ZEM, PLEASE, TO LOOK FOR ZE MISSING ONES.
MY MASTER, HE IZ A ROVE. HE VANISHEZ LAST WEEK. *POOF.*
UH, I AM NOT SURE I QUITE FOLLOW.
ZEY BROUGHT ME TO ZE HIVE BECAUSE I AM PRETTY AND DO GOOD WORK, BUT ZE COMTESSE, SHE ONLY JUST TOLERATEZ ME.
WITHOUT HIZ PROTECTION, I DO NOT KNOW HOW LONG I WILL LAST.
...VERY WELL, I SHALL TRY.

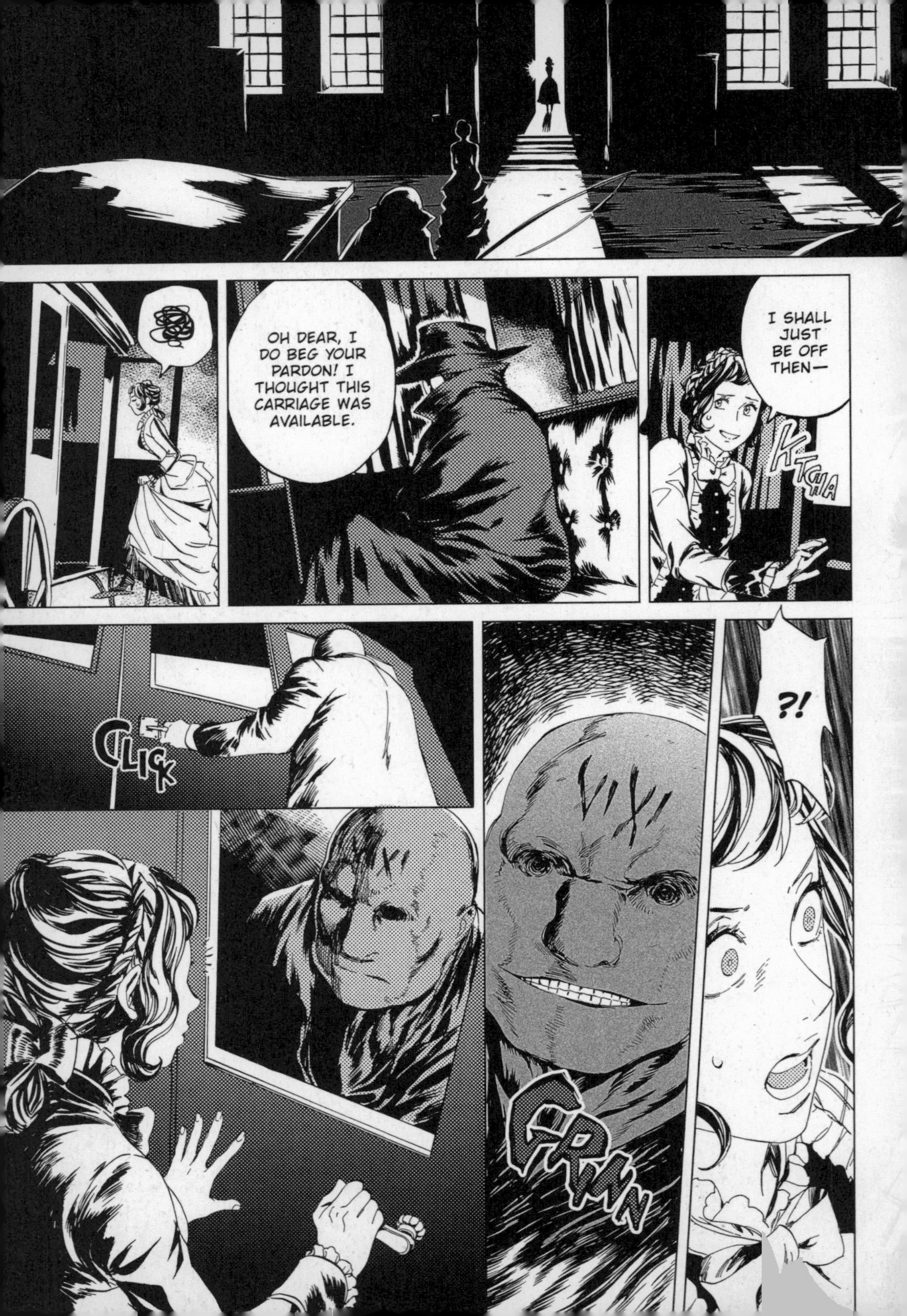
OH DEAR, I DO BEG YOUR PARDON! I THOUGHT THIS CARRIAGE WAS AVAILABLE.
I SHALL JUST BE OFF THEN—
KATCHA
CLICK
?!
GRIN

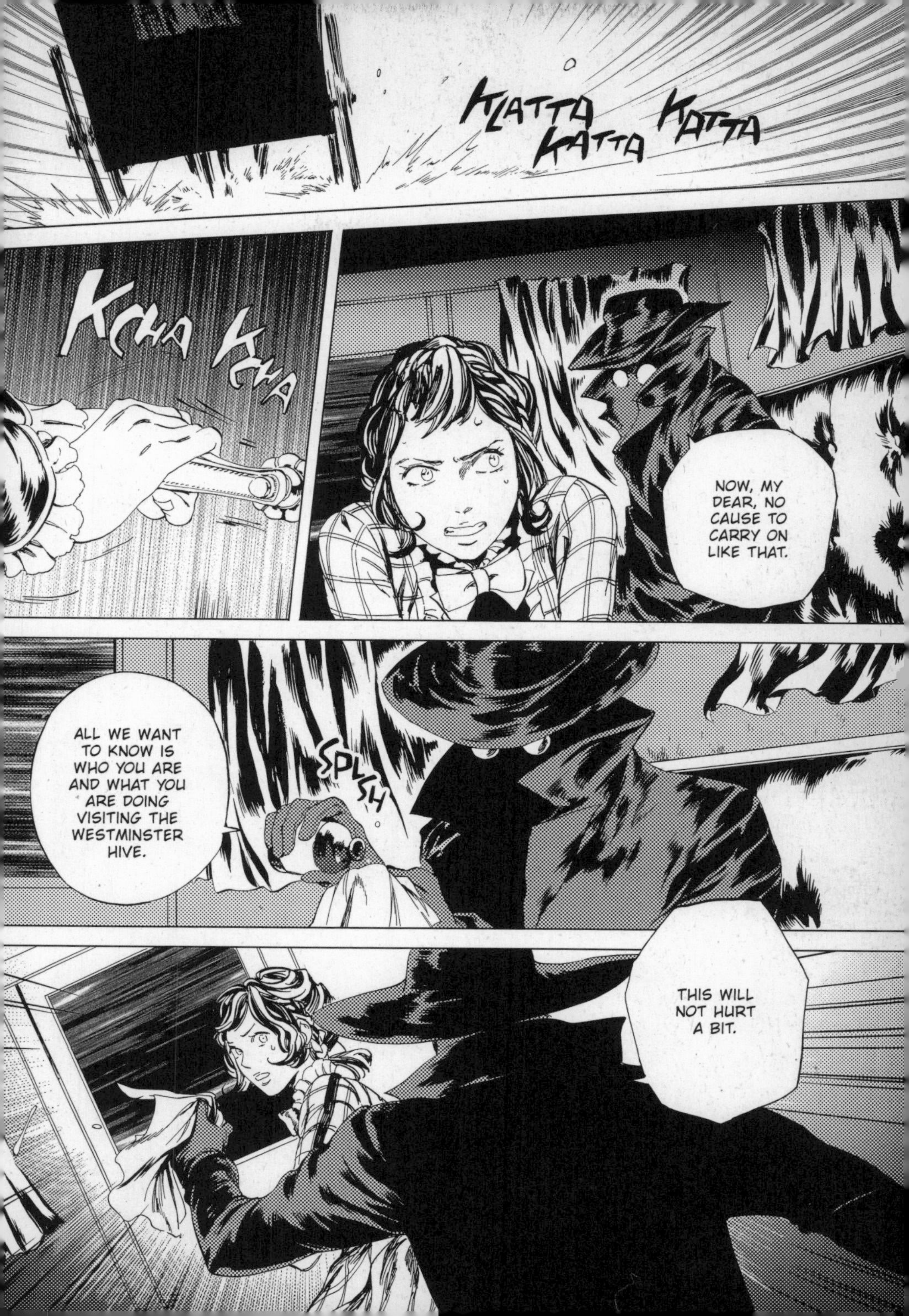
KLATTA KATTA KATTA KATTA
KCHA KCHA
NOW, MY DEAR, NO CAUSE TO CARRY ON LIKE THAT.
ALL WE WANT TO KNOW IS WHO YOU ARE AND WHAT YOU ARE DOING VISITING THE WESTMINSTER HIVE.
SPLSH
THIS WILL NOT HURT A BIT.

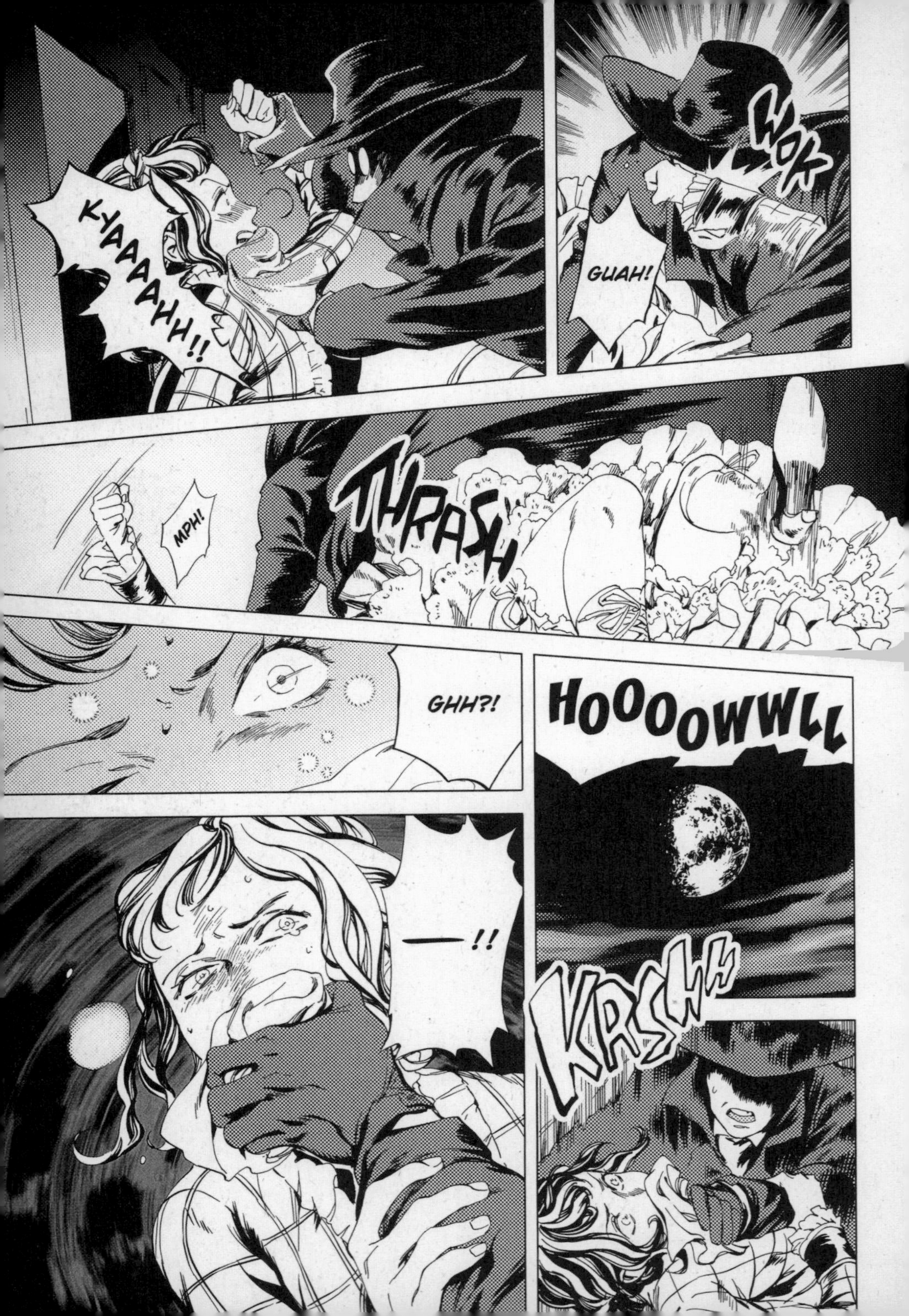
K-YAAAAAHH!!
WOK
GUAH!
MPH!
THRASH
GHH?!
HOOOOWLL
—!!
KRSHH

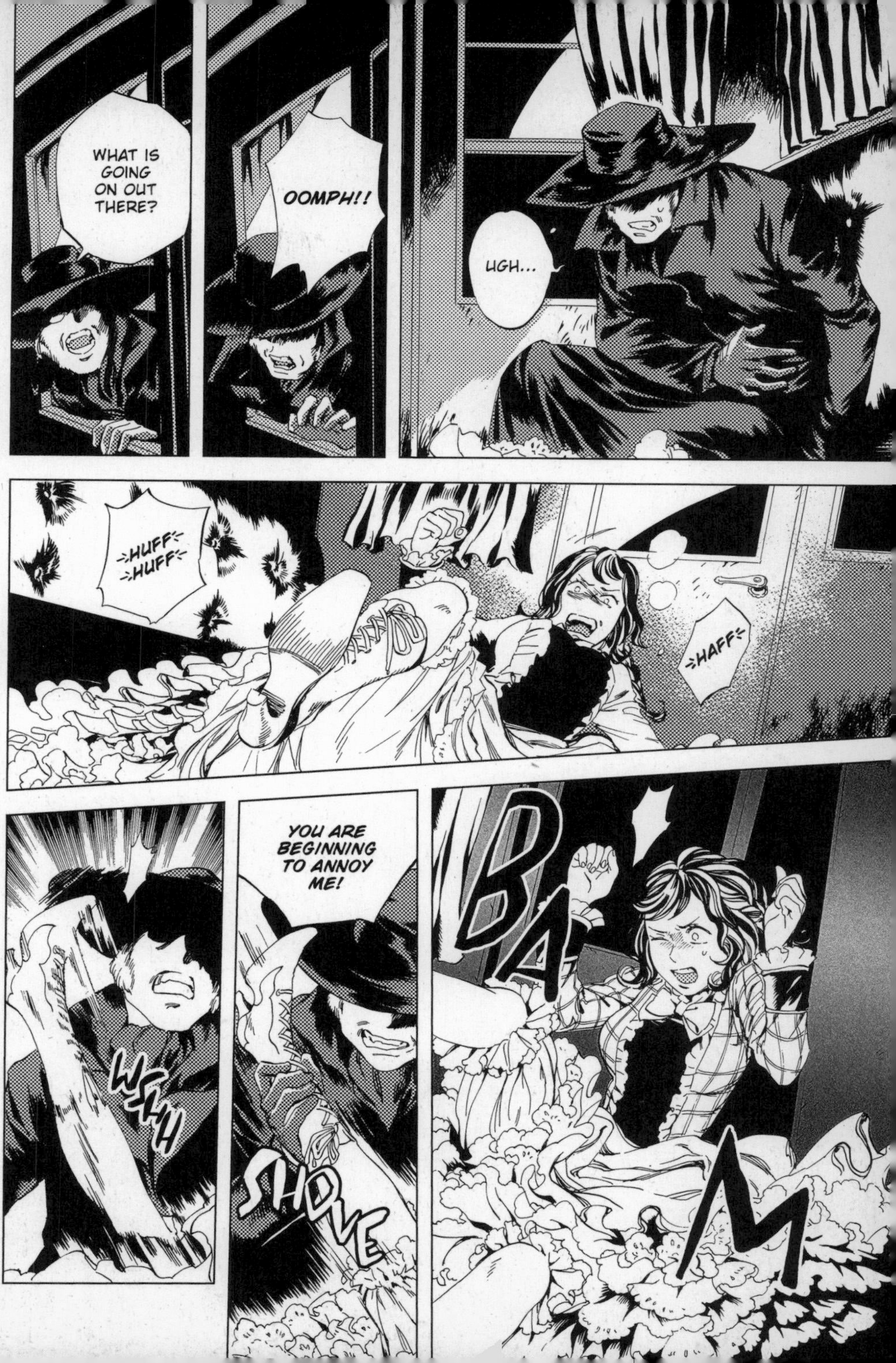
WHAT IS GOING ON OUT THERE?
OOMPH!!
UGH...
HUFF HUFF
HAFF
WSHH
YOU ARE BEGINNING TO ANNOY ME!
SHOVE
BAM

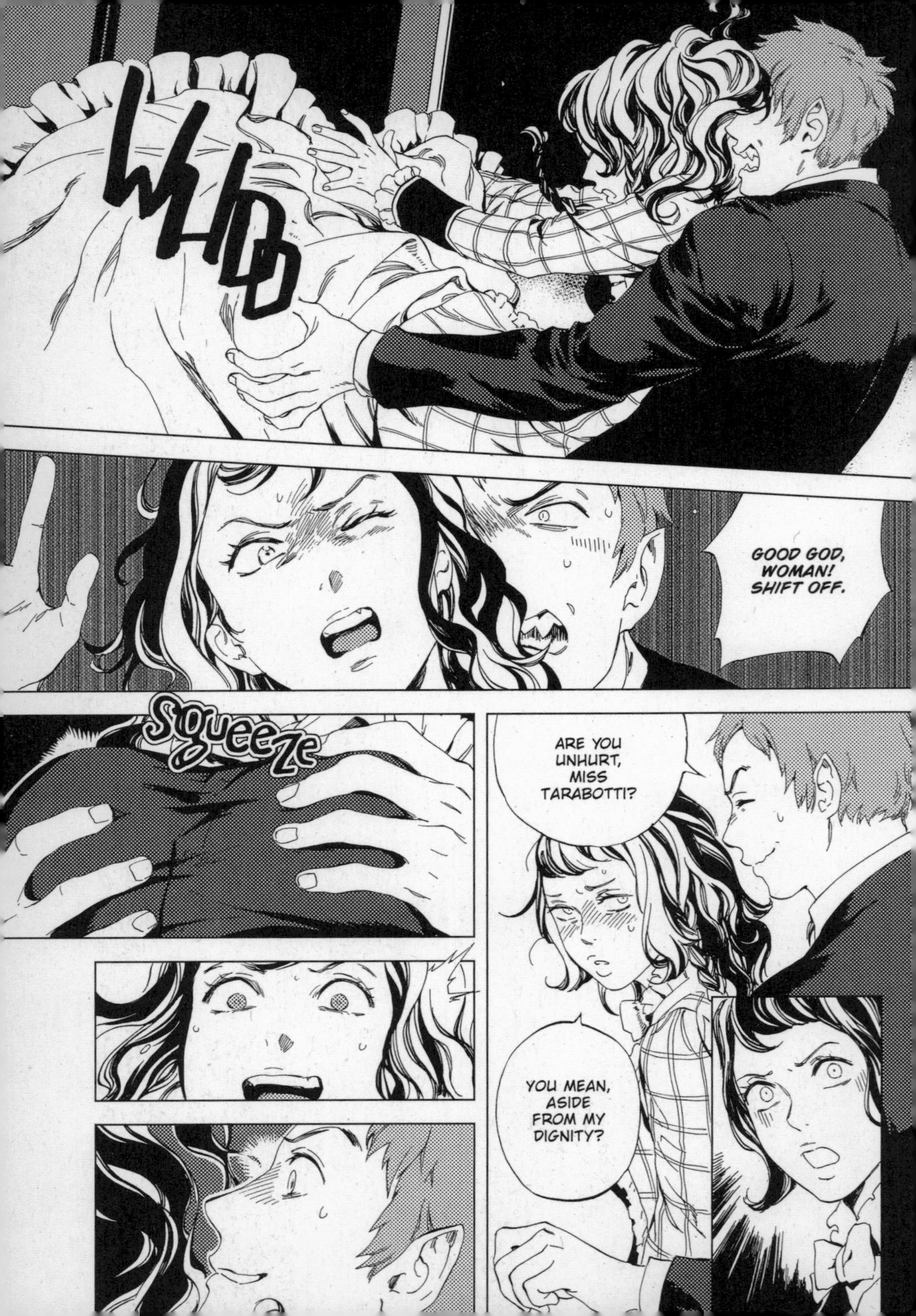
WHDD
GOOD GOD, WOMAN! SHIFT OFF.
SQUEEZE
ARE YOU UNHURT, MISS TARABOTTI?
YOU MEAN, ASIDE FROM MY DIGNITY?

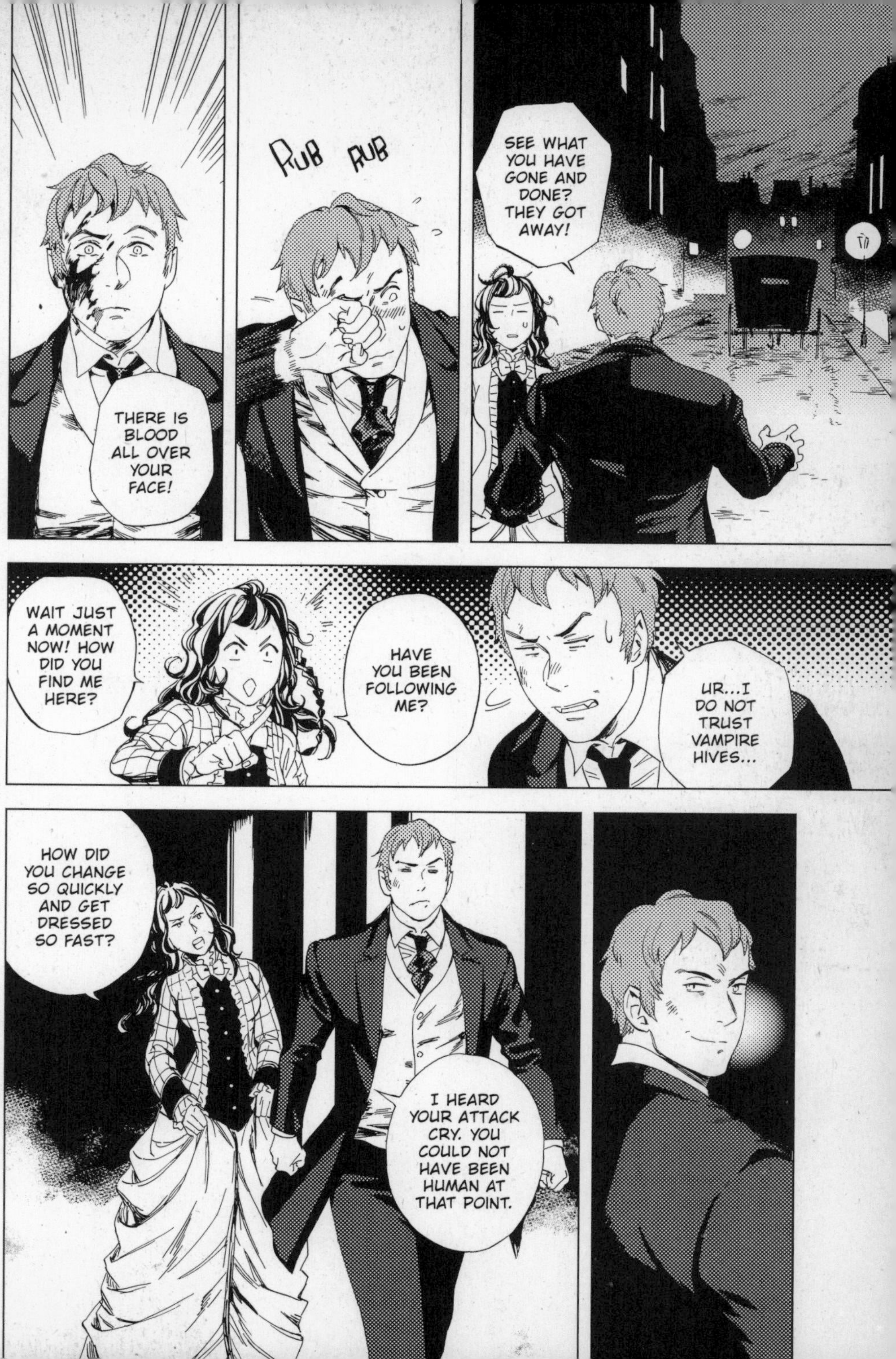
THERE IS BLOOD ALL OVER YOUR FACE!
RUB RUB
SEE WHAT YOU HAVE GONE AND DONE? THEY GOT AWAY!
WAIT JUST A MOMENT NOW! HOW DID YOU FIND ME HERE?
HAVE YOU BEEN FOLLOWING ME?
UR...I DO NOT TRUST VAMPIRE HIVES...
HOW DID YOU CHANGE SO QUICKLY AND GET DRESSED SO FAST?
I HEARD YOUR ATTACK CRY. YOU COULD NOT HAVE BEEN HUMAN AT THAT POINT.

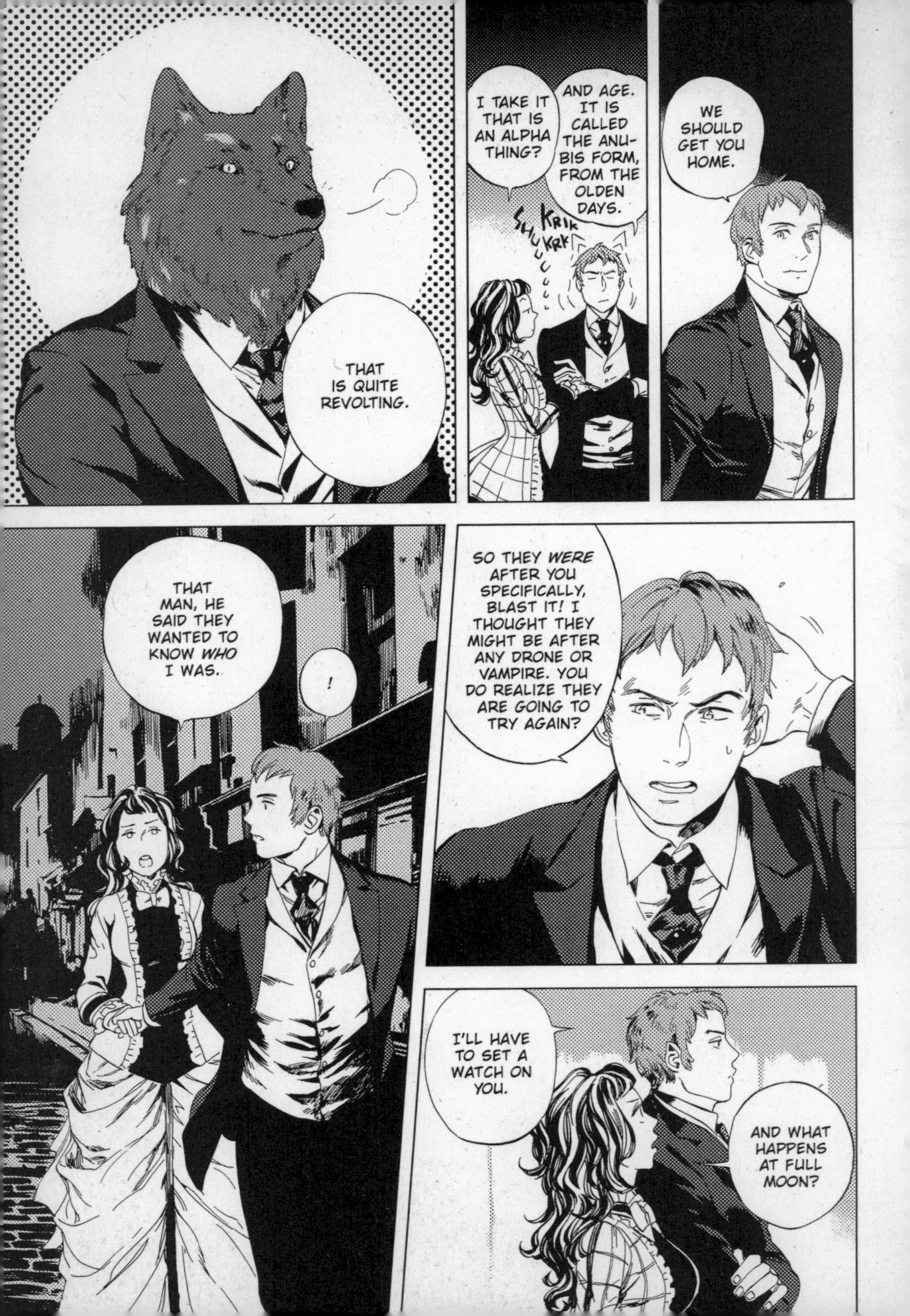
THAT IS QUITE REVOLTING.
I TAKE IT THAT IS AN ALPHA THING?
AND AGE. IT IS CALLED THE ANUBIS FORM, FROM THE OLDEN DAYS.
SHUUUUUU
KRIK KRK
WE SHOULD GET YOU HOME.
THAT MAN, HE SAID THEY WANTED TO KNOW *WHO* I WAS.
!
SO THEY *WERE* AFTER YOU SPECIFICALLY, BLAST IT! I THOUGHT THEY MIGHT BE AFTER ANY DRONE OR VAMPIRE. YOU DO REALIZE THEY ARE GOING TO TRY AGAIN?
I'LL HAVE TO SET A WATCH ON YOU.
AND WHAT HAPPENS AT FULL MOON?

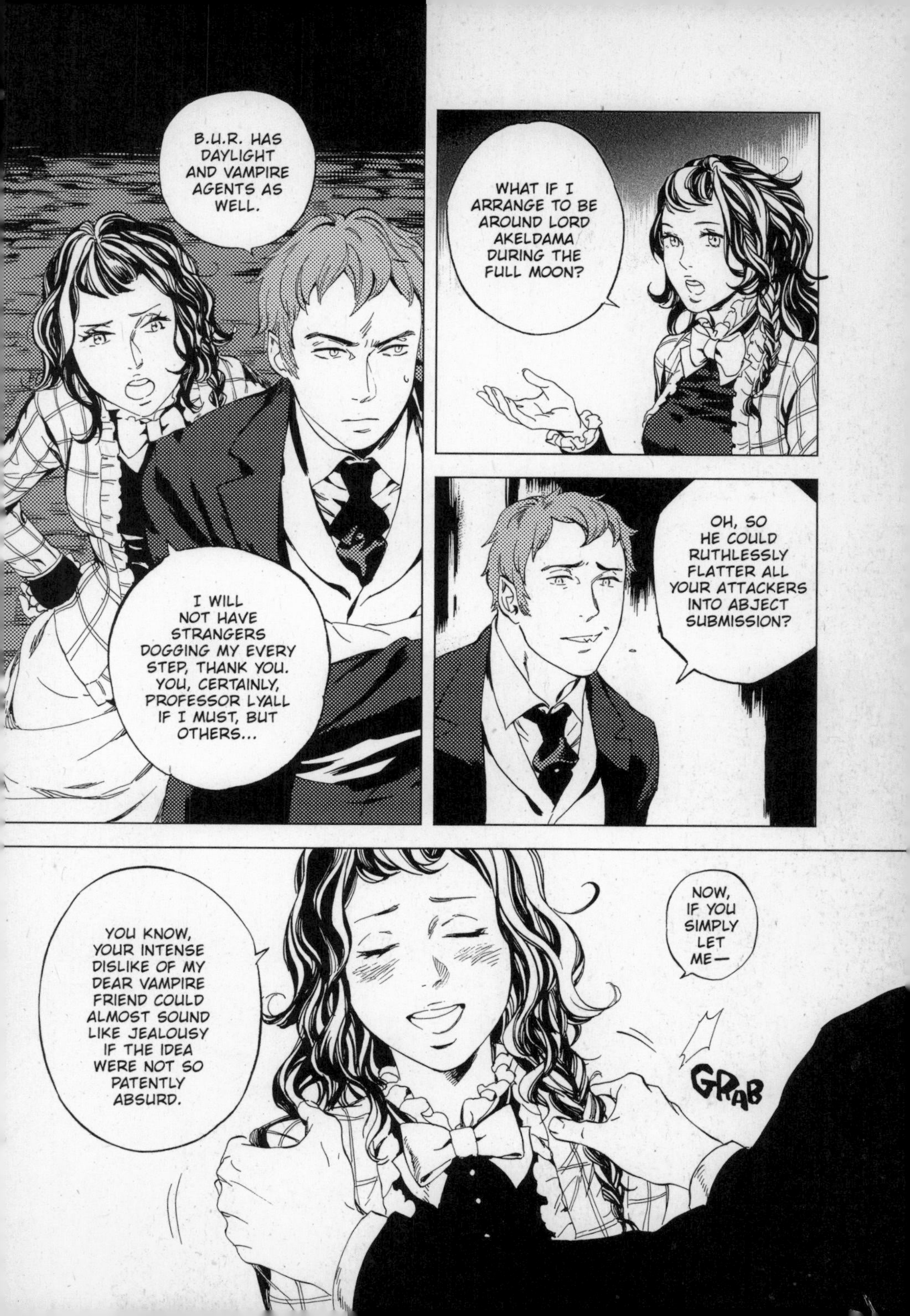
B.U.R. HAS DAYLIGHT AND VAMPIRE AGENTS AS WELL.
I WILL NOT HAVE STRANGERS DOGGING MY EVERY STEP, THANK YOU. YOU, CERTAINLY, PROFESSOR LYALL IF I MUST, BUT OTHERS...
WHAT IF I ARRANGE TO BE AROUND LORD AKELDAMA DURING THE FULL MOON?
OH, SO HE COULD RUTHLESSLY FLATTER ALL YOUR ATTACKERS INTO ABJECT SUBMISSION?
YOU KNOW, YOUR INTENSE DISLIKE OF MY DEAR VAMPIRE FRIEND COULD ALMOST SOUND LIKE JEALOUSY IF THE IDEA WERE NOT SO PATENTLY ABSURD.
NOW, IF YOU SIMPLY LET ME—
GRAB

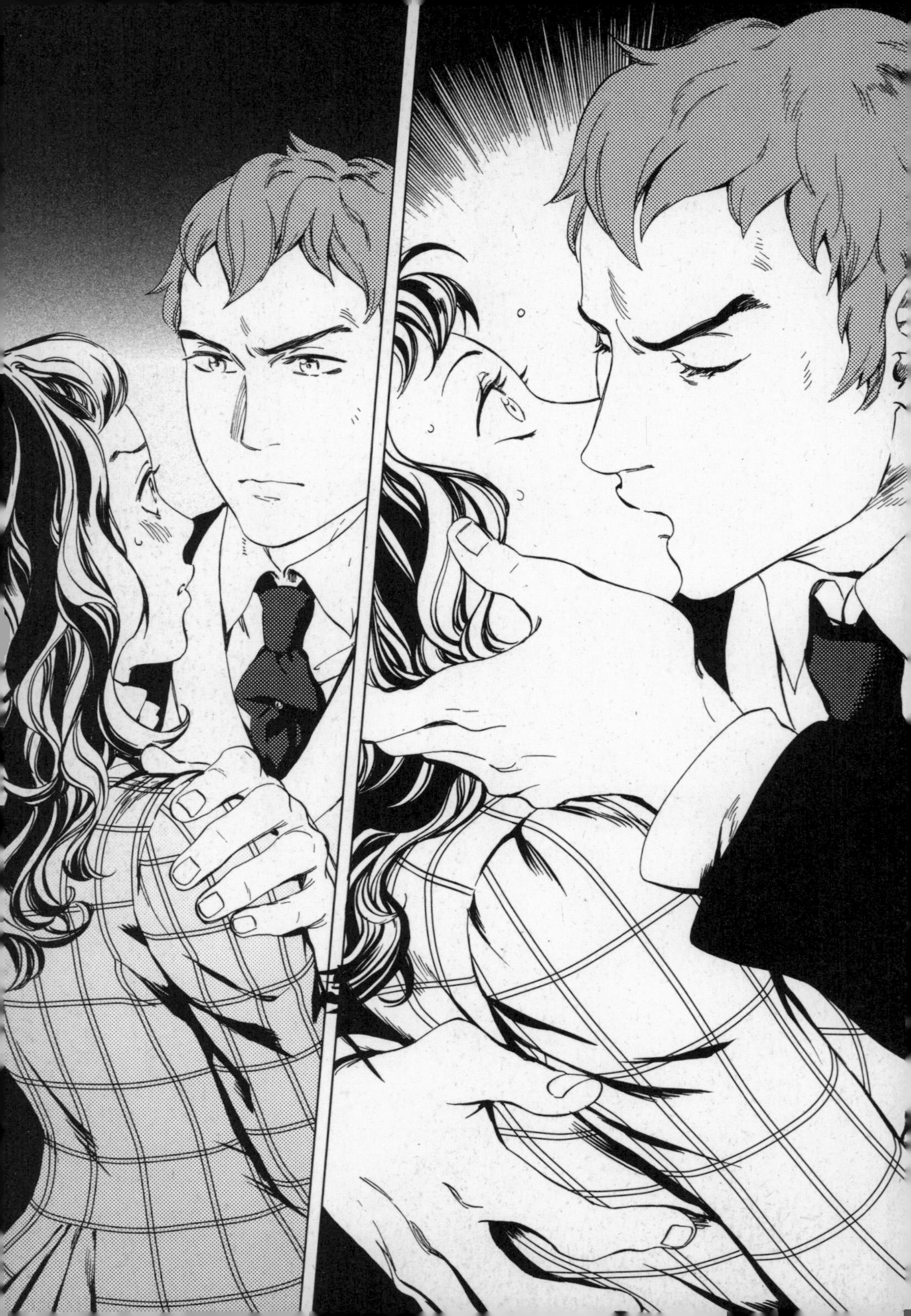

SOULLESS

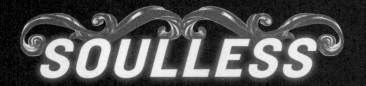

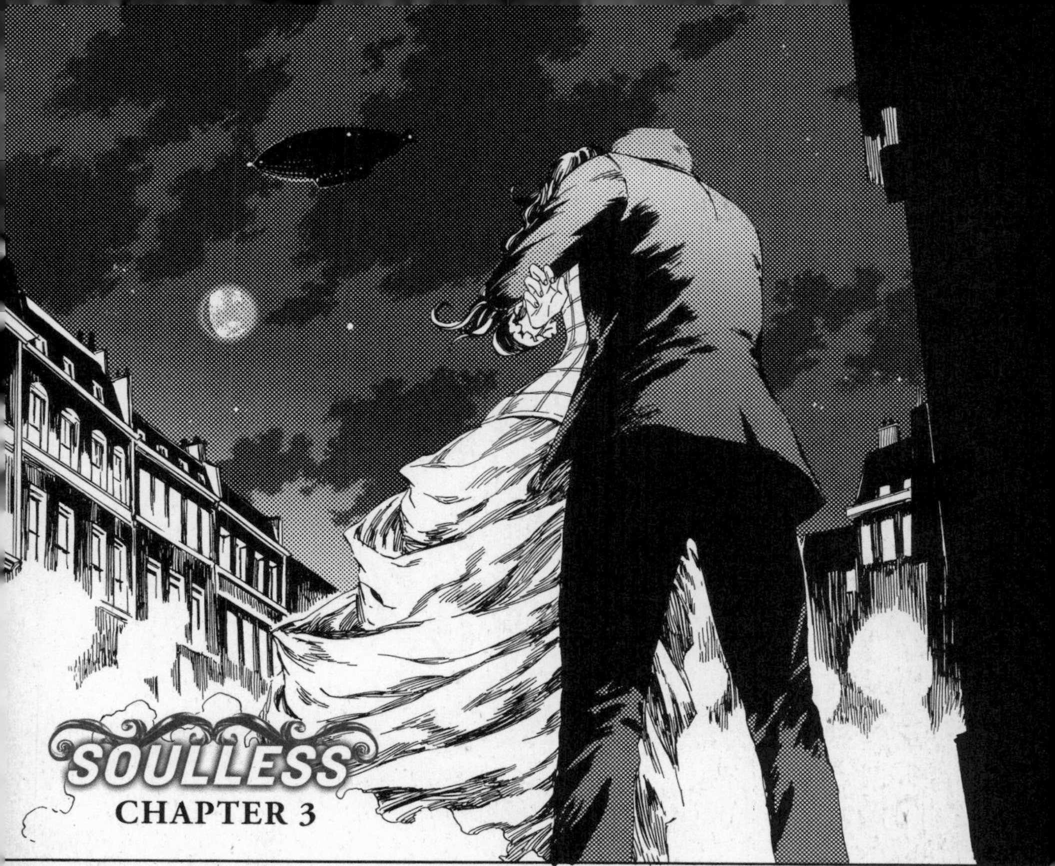
SOULLESS
CHAPTER 3

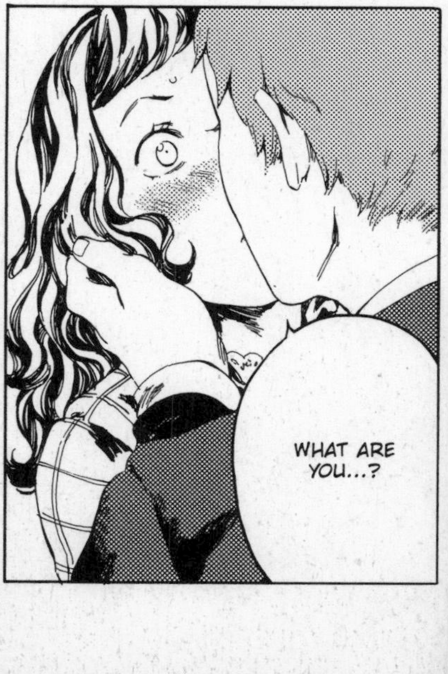
WHAT ARE YOU...?

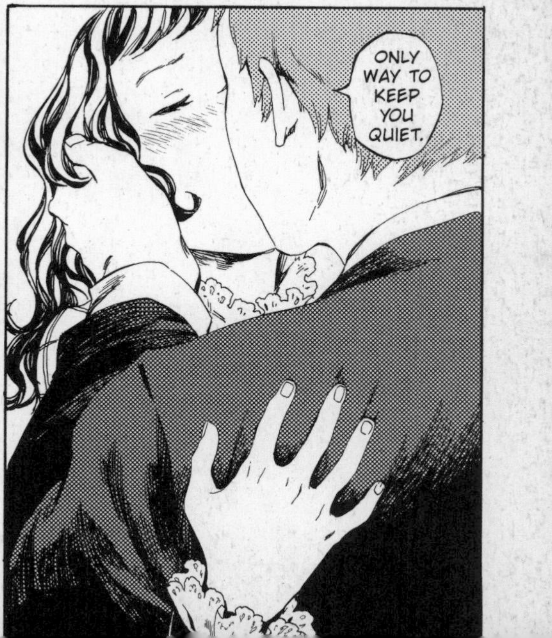
ONLY WAY TO KEEP YOU QUIET.

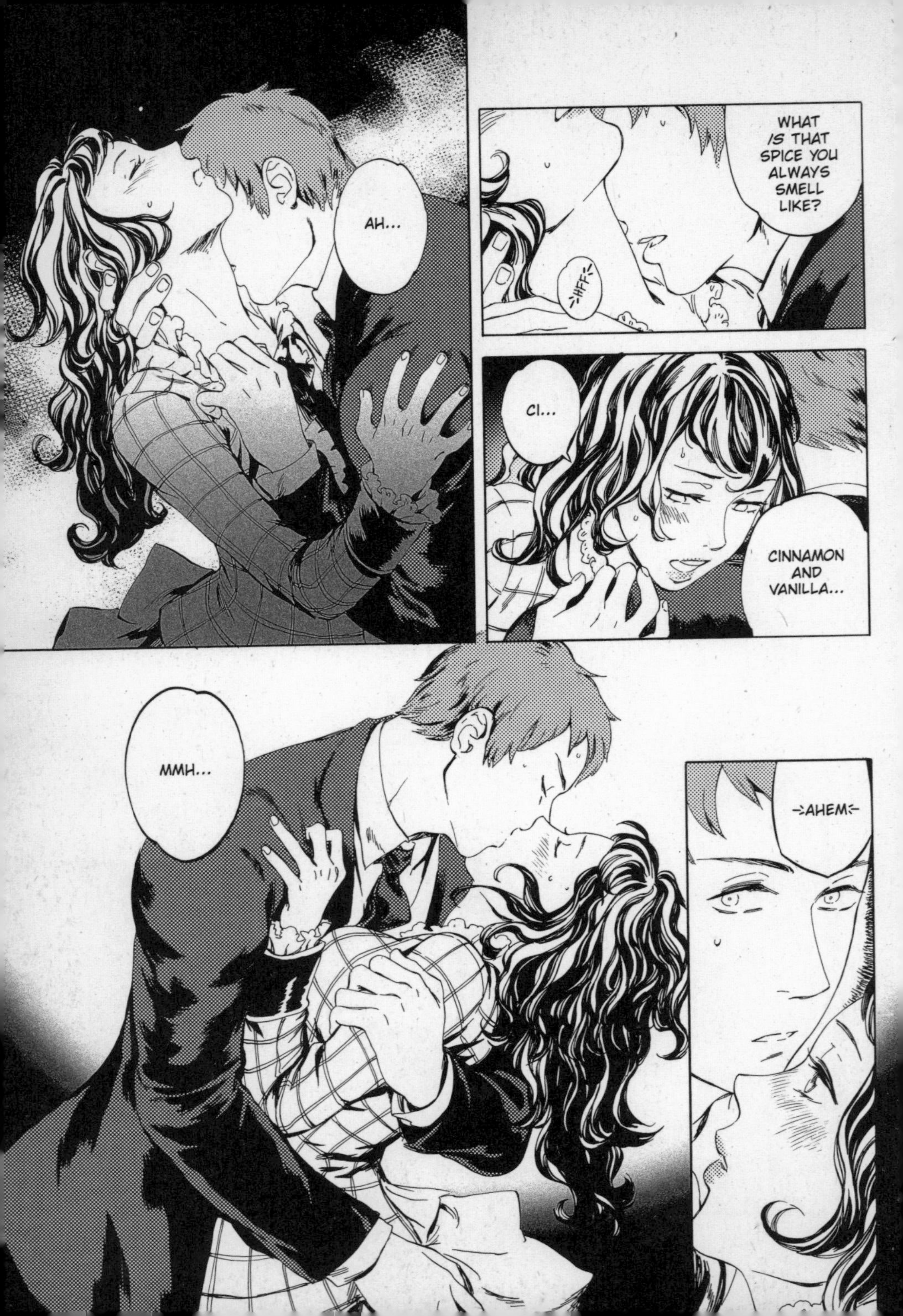
AH...
WHAT IS THAT SPICE YOU ALWAYS SMELL LIKE?
SNIFF
CI...
CINNAMON AND VANILLA...
MMH...
AHEM

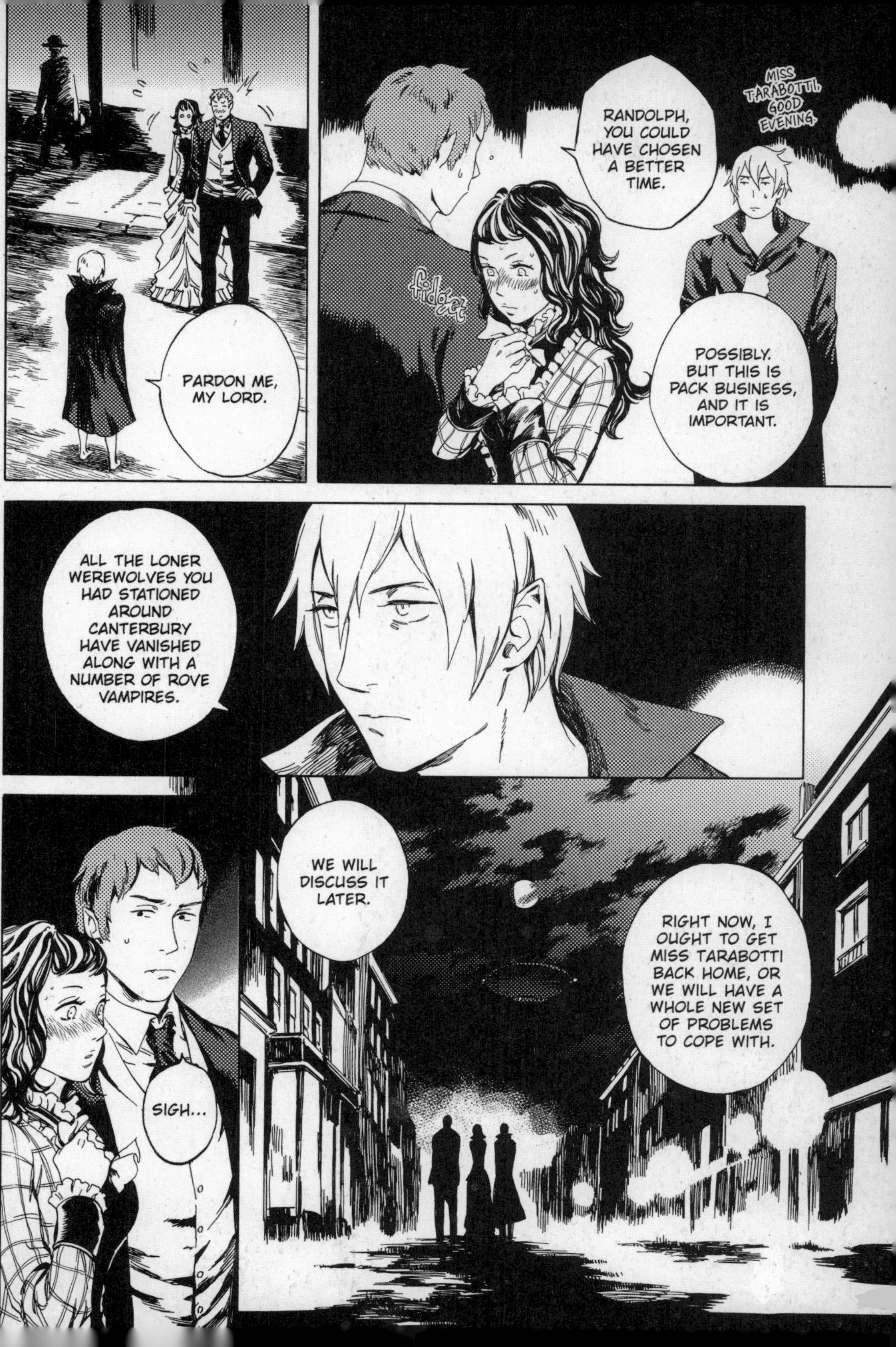
PARDON ME, MY LORD.
RANDOLPH, YOU COULD HAVE CHOSEN A BETTER TIME.
fidget
MISS TARABOTTI, GOOD EVENING.
POSSIBLY. BUT THIS IS PACK BUSINESS, AND IT IS IMPORTANT.
ALL THE LONER WEREWOLVES YOU HAD STATIONED AROUND CANTERBURY HAVE VANISHED ALONG WITH A NUMBER OF ROVE VAMPIRES.
SIGH...
WE WILL DISCUSS IT LATER.
RIGHT NOW, I OUGHT TO GET MISS TARABOTTI BACK HOME, OR WE WILL HAVE A WHOLE NEW SET OF PROBLEMS TO COPE WITH.

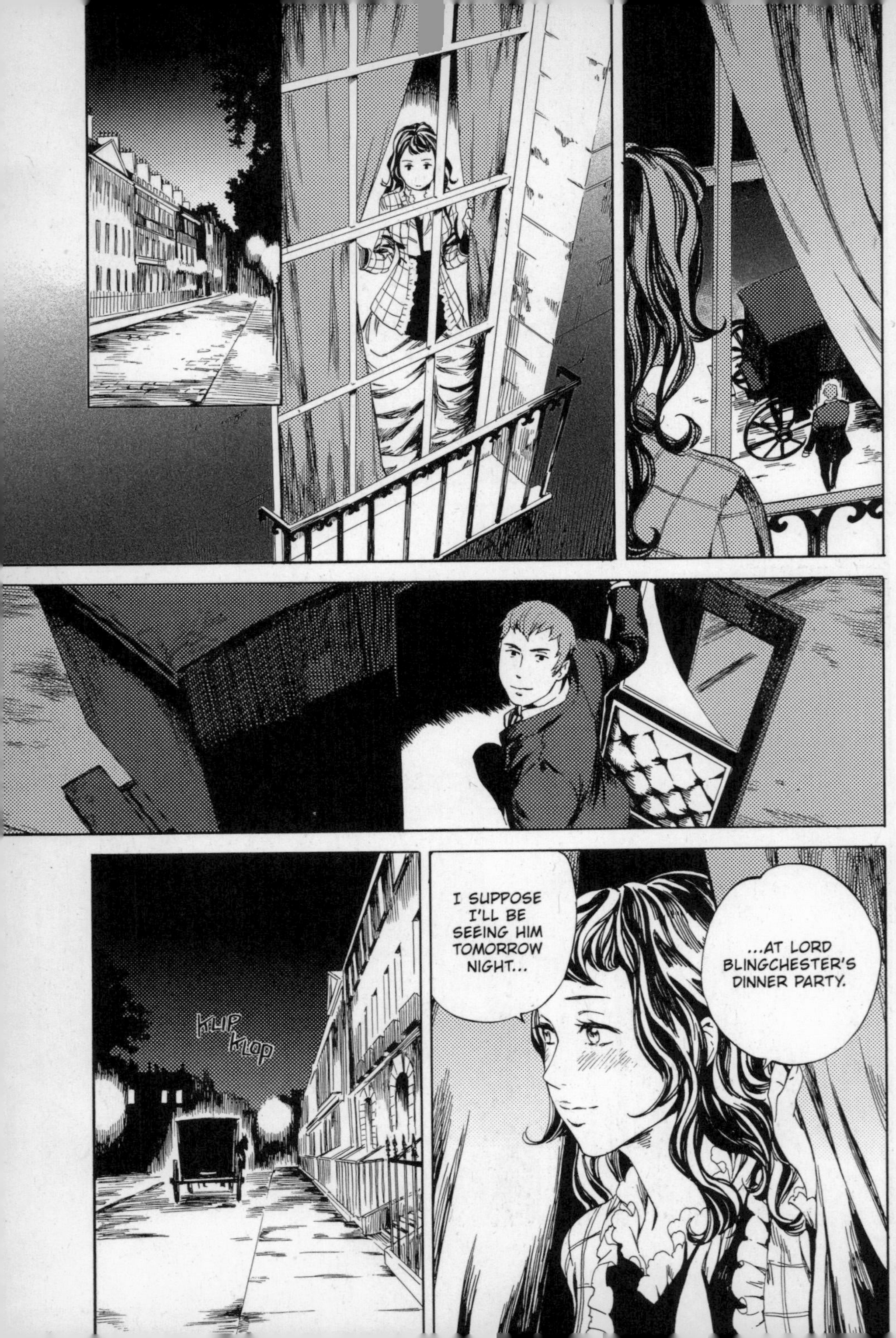
KLIP KLOP
I SUPPOSE I'LL BE SEEING HIM TOMORROW NIGHT...
...AT LORD BLINGCHESTER'S DINNER PARTY.

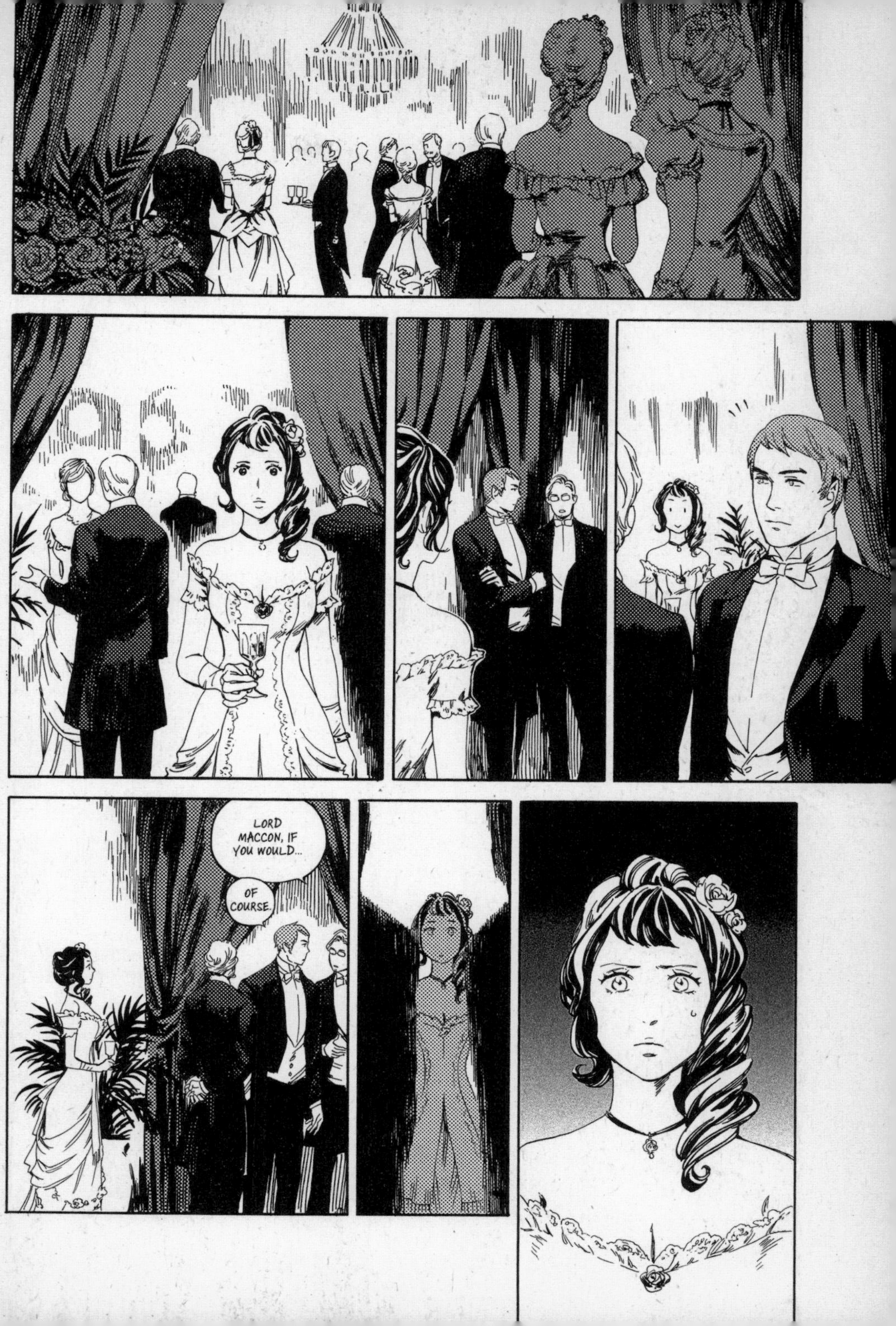
LORD MACCON, IF YOU WOULD...
OF COURSE.

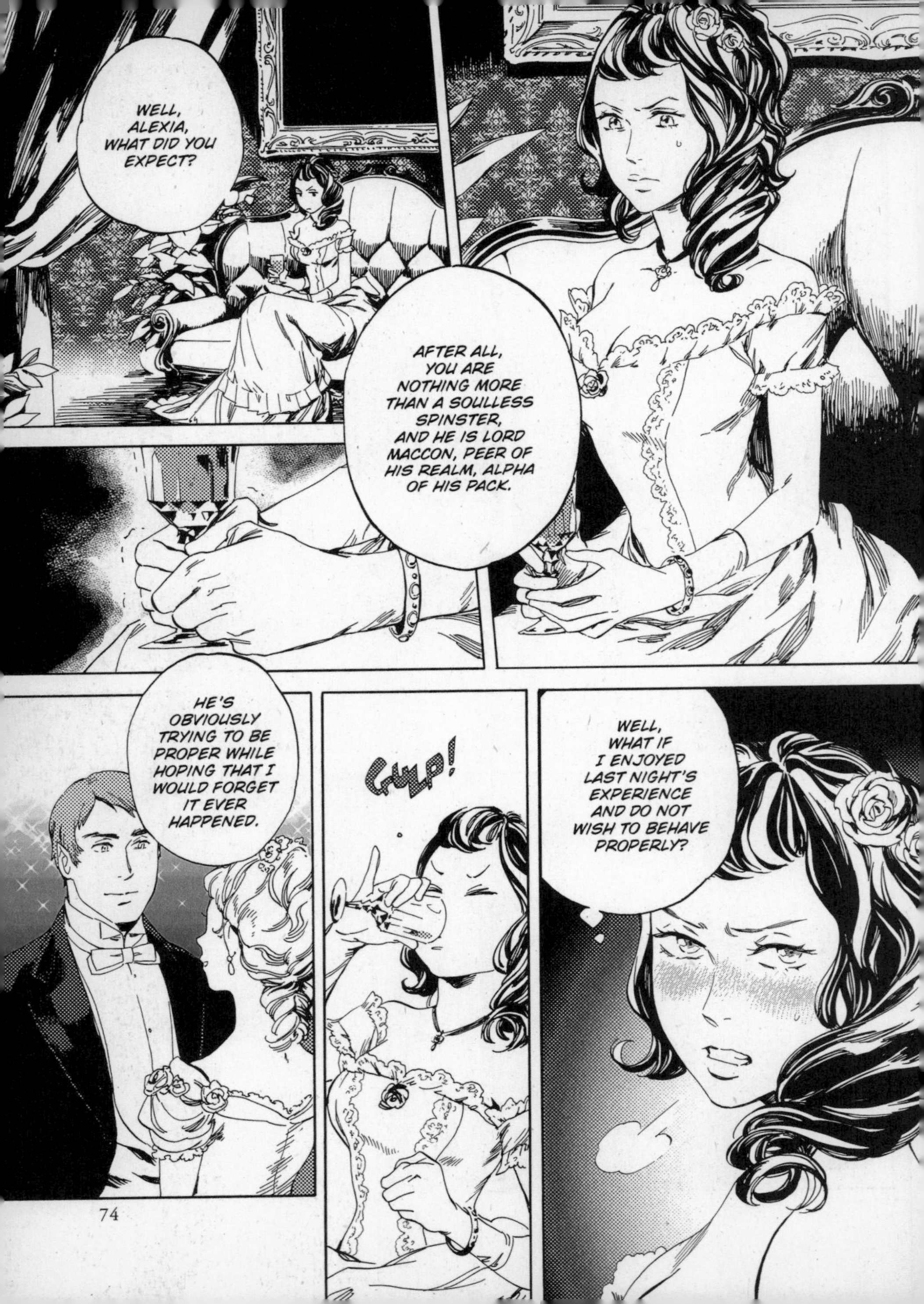
WELL, ALEXIA, WHAT DID YOU EXPECT?
AFTER ALL, YOU ARE NOTHING MORE THAN A SOULLESS SPINSTER, AND HE IS LORD MACCON, PEER OF HIS REALM, ALPHA OF HIS PACK.
HE'S OBVIOUSLY TRYING TO BE PROPER WHILE HOPING THAT I WOULD FORGET IT EVER HAPPENED.
GULP!
WELL, WHAT IF I ENJOYED LAST NIGHT'S EXPERIENCE AND DO NOT WISH TO BEHAVE PROPERLY?

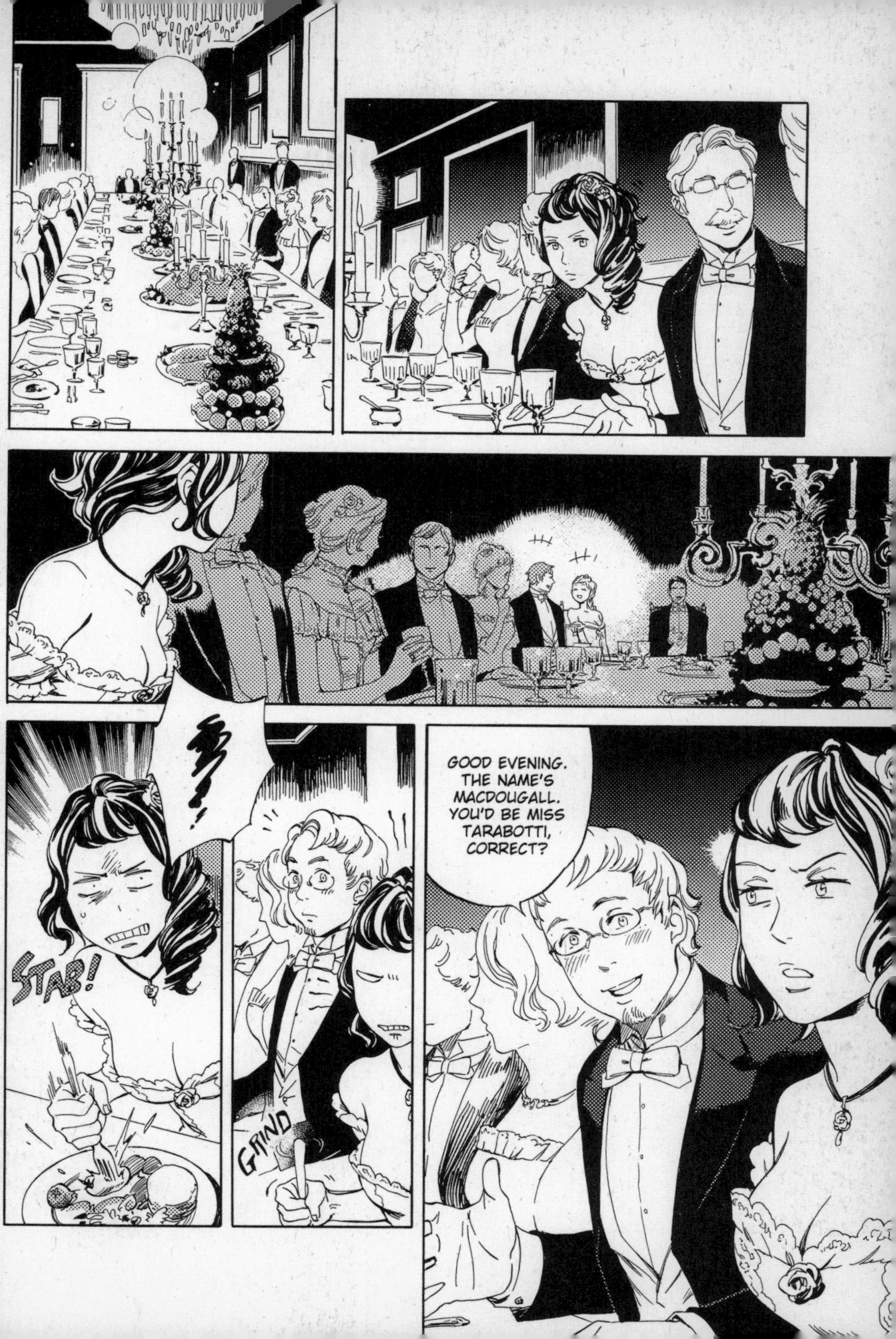
STAB!
GRIND
GOOD EVENING. THE NAME'S MACDOUGALL. YOU'D BE MISS TARABOTTI, CORRECT?

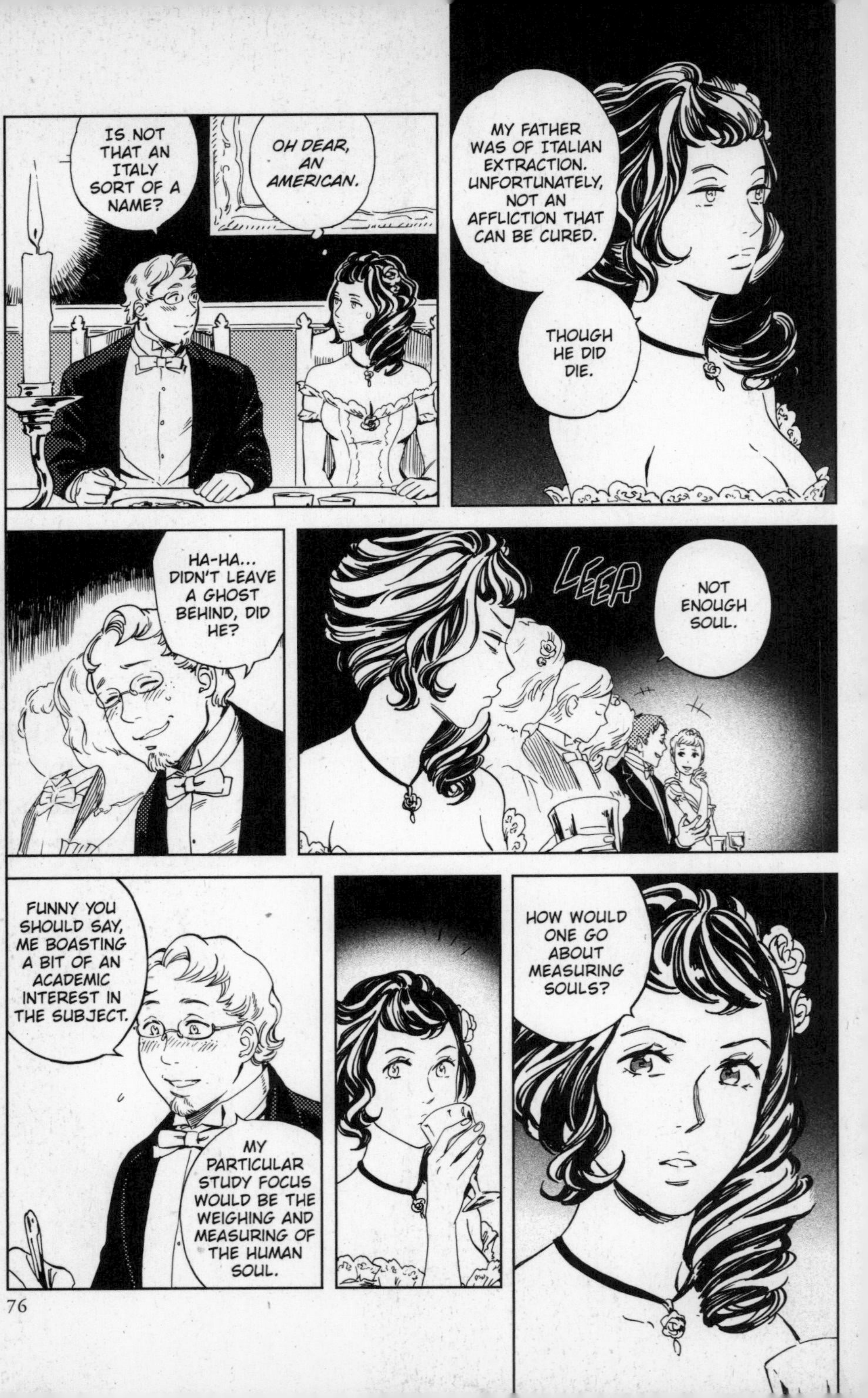
IS NOT THAT AN ITALY SORT OF A NAME?
OH DEAR, AN AMERICAN.
MY FATHER WAS OF ITALIAN EXTRACTION. UNFORTUNATELY, NOT AN AFFLICTION THAT CAN BE CURED.
THOUGH HE DID DIE.
HA-HA... DIDN'T LEAVE A GHOST BEHIND, DID HE?
LEER
NOT ENOUGH SOUL.
FUNNY YOU SHOULD SAY, ME BOASTING A BIT OF AN ACADEMIC INTEREST IN THE SUBJECT.
MY PARTICULAR STUDY FOCUS WOULD BE THE WEIGHING AND MEASURING OF THE HUMAN SOUL.
HOW WOULD ONE GO ABOUT MEASURING SOULS?

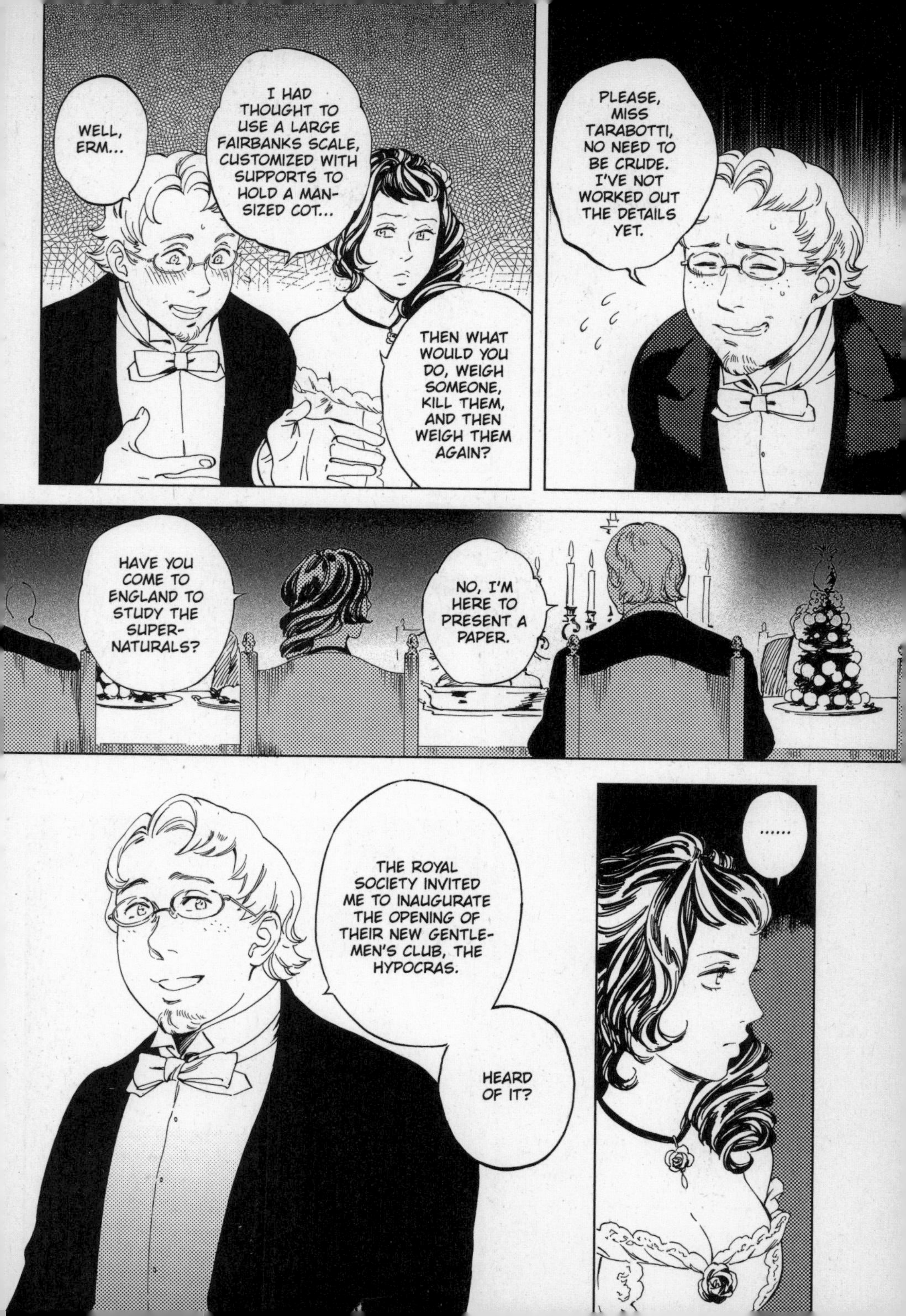
WELL, ERM...
I HAD THOUGHT TO USE A LARGE FAIRBANKS SCALE, CUSTOMIZED WITH SUPPORTS TO HOLD A MAN-SIZED COT...
THEN WHAT WOULD YOU DO, WEIGH SOMEONE, KILL THEM, AND THEN WEIGH THEM AGAIN?
PLEASE, MISS TARABOTTI, NO NEED TO BE CRUDE. I'VE NOT WORKED OUT THE DETAILS YET.
HAVE YOU COME TO ENGLAND TO STUDY THE SUPER-NATURALS?
NO, I'M HERE TO PRESENT A PAPER.
THE ROYAL SOCIETY INVITED ME TO INAUGURATE THE OPENING OF THEIR NEW GENTLE-MEN'S CLUB, THE HYPOCRAS.
HEARD OF IT?
......

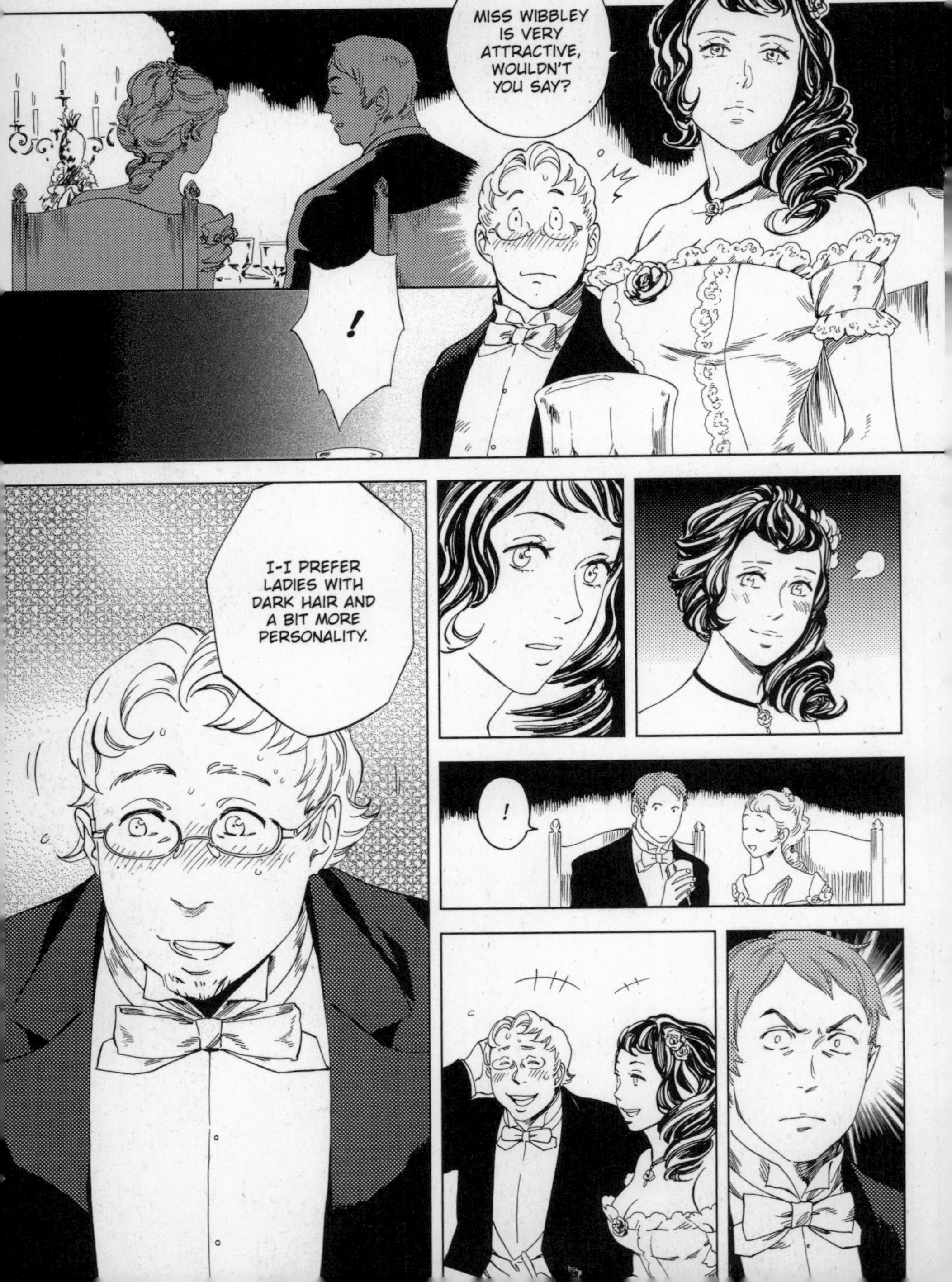
MISS WIBBLEY IS VERY ATTRACTIVE, WOULDN'T YOU SAY?
!
I-I PREFER LADIES WITH DARK HAIR AND A BIT MORE PERSONALITY.
!

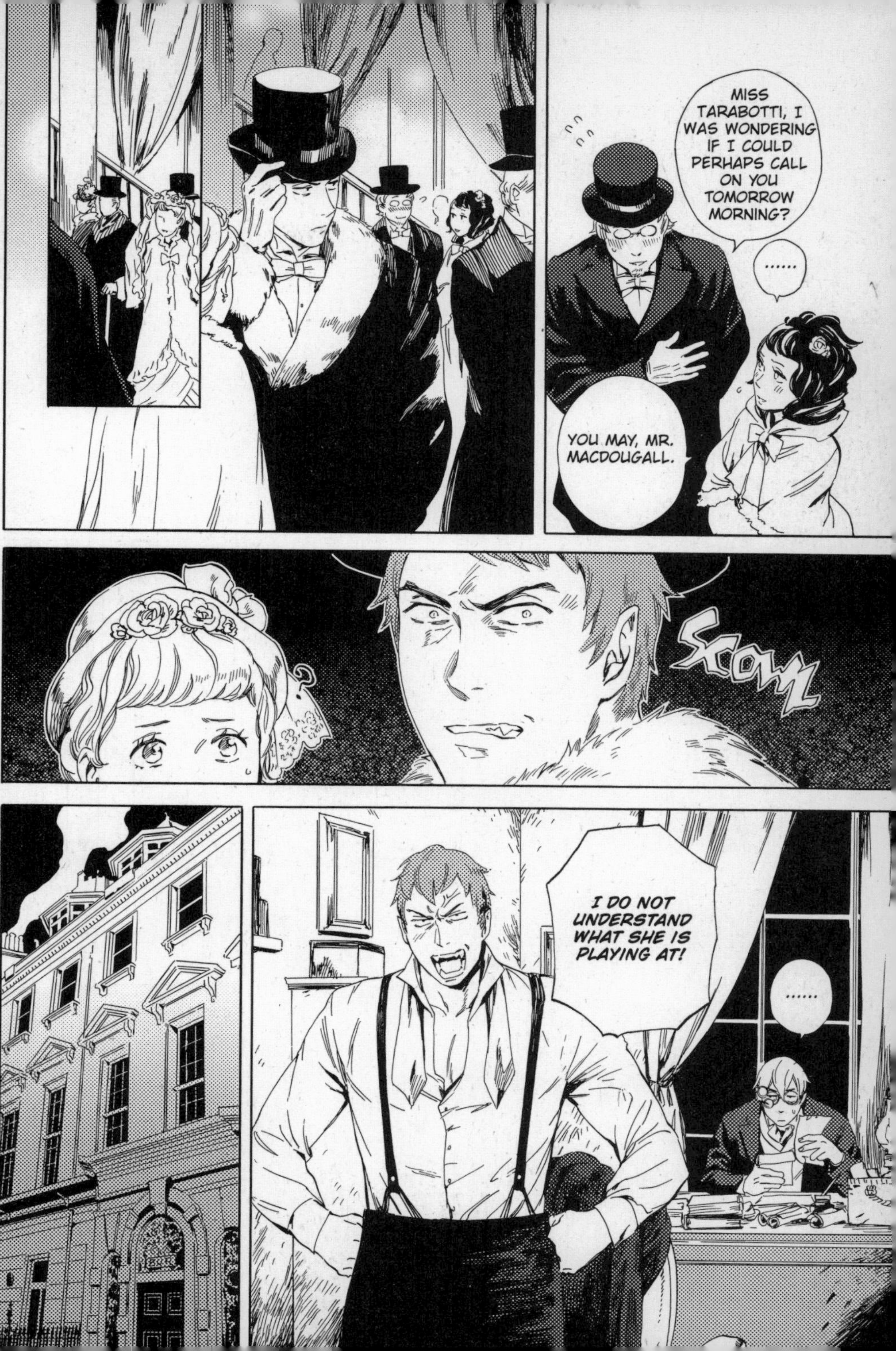
MISS TARABOTTI, I WAS WONDERING IF I COULD PERHAPS CALL ON YOU TOMORROW MORNING?
......
YOU MAY, MR. MACDOUGALL.
SCOWL
I DO NOT UNDERSTAND WHAT SHE IS PLAYING AT!
......

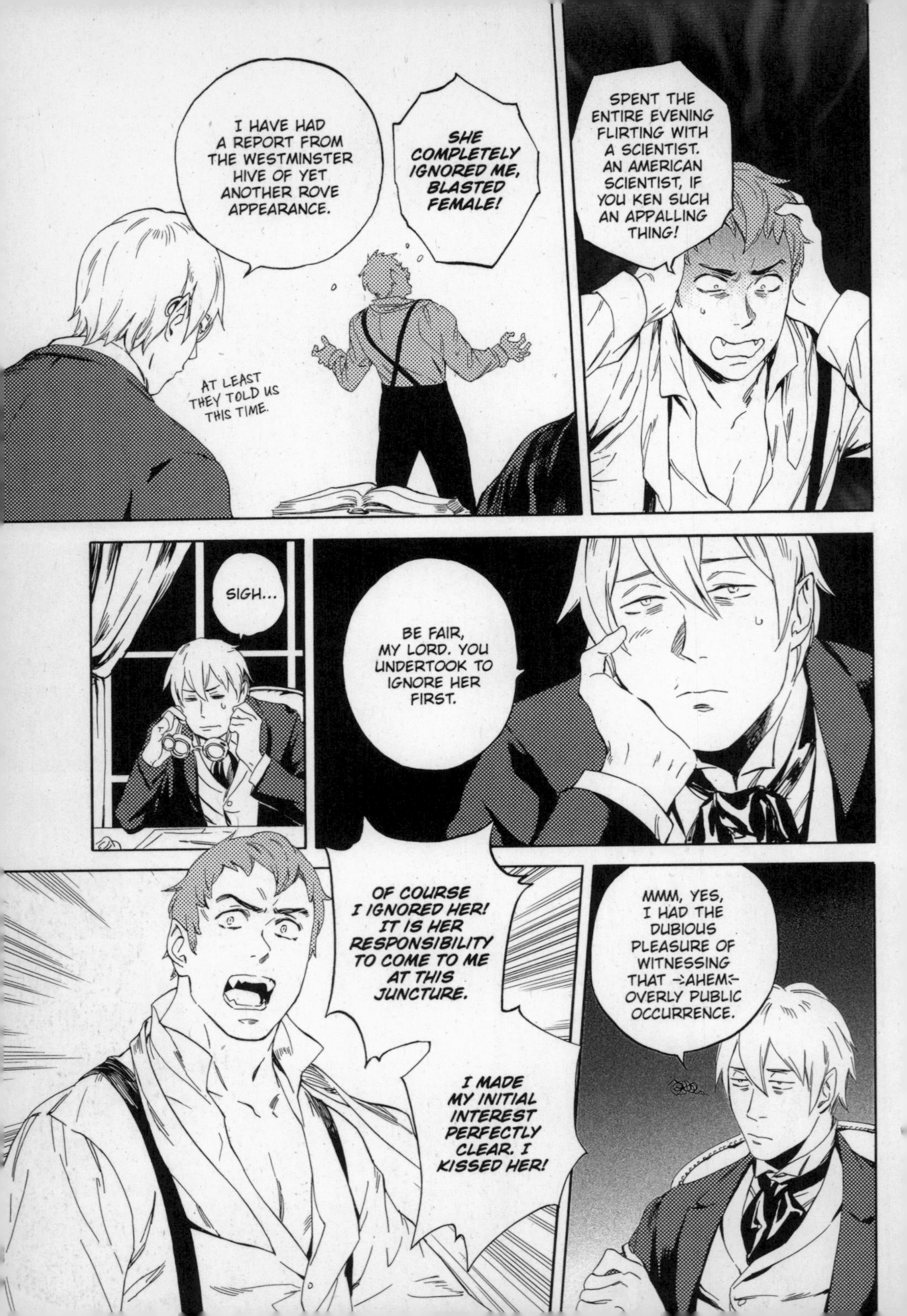
I HAVE HAD A REPORT FROM THE WESTMINSTER HIVE OF YET ANOTHER ROVE APPEARANCE.
AT LEAST THEY TOLD US THIS TIME.
SHE COMPLETELY IGNORED ME, BLASTED FEMALE!
SPENT THE ENTIRE EVENING FLIRTING WITH A SCIENTIST. AN AMERICAN SCIENTIST, IF YOU KEN SUCH AN APPALLING THING!
SIGH...
BE FAIR, MY LORD. YOU UNDERTOOK TO IGNORE HER FIRST.
OF COURSE I IGNORED HER! IT IS HER RESPONSIBILITY TO COME TO ME AT THIS JUNCTURE.
I MADE MY INITIAL INTEREST PERFECTLY CLEAR. I KISSED HER!
MMM, YES, I HAD THE DUBIOUS PLEASURE OF WITNESSING THAT —AHEM— OVERLY PUBLIC OCCURRENCE.

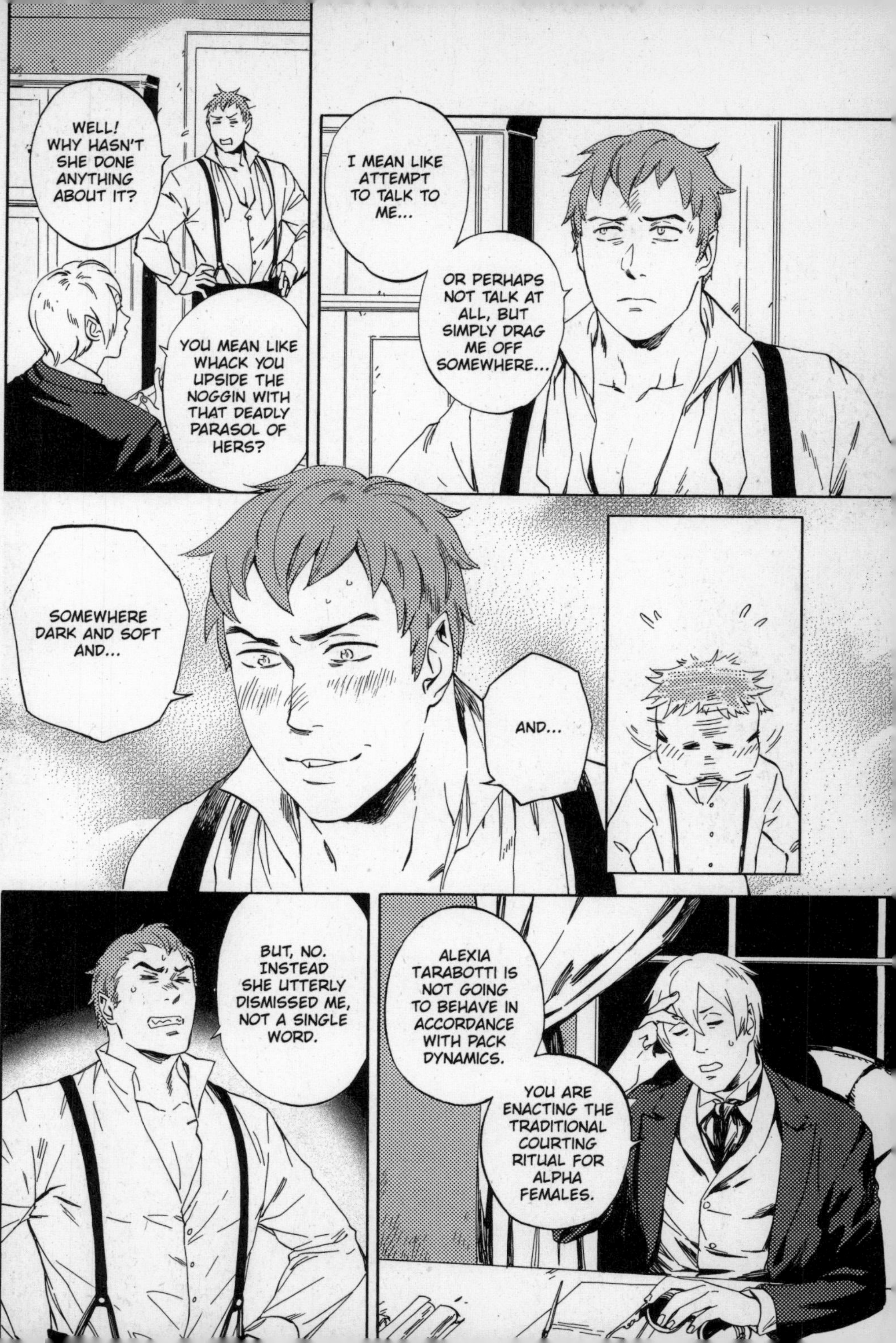
WELL! WHY HASN'T SHE DONE ANYTHING ABOUT IT?
YOU MEAN LIKE WHACK YOU UPSIDE THE NOGGIN WITH THAT DEADLY PARASOL OF HERS?
I MEAN LIKE ATTEMPT TO TALK TO ME...
OR PERHAPS NOT TALK AT ALL, BUT SIMPLY DRAG ME OFF SOMEWHERE...
SOMEWHERE DARK AND SOFT AND...
AND...
BUT, NO. INSTEAD SHE UTTERLY DISMISSED ME, NOT A SINGLE WORD.
ALEXIA TARABOTTI IS NOT GOING TO BEHAVE IN ACCORDANCE WITH PACK DYNAMICS.
YOU ARE ENACTING THE TRADITIONAL COURTING RITUAL FOR ALPHA FEMALES.

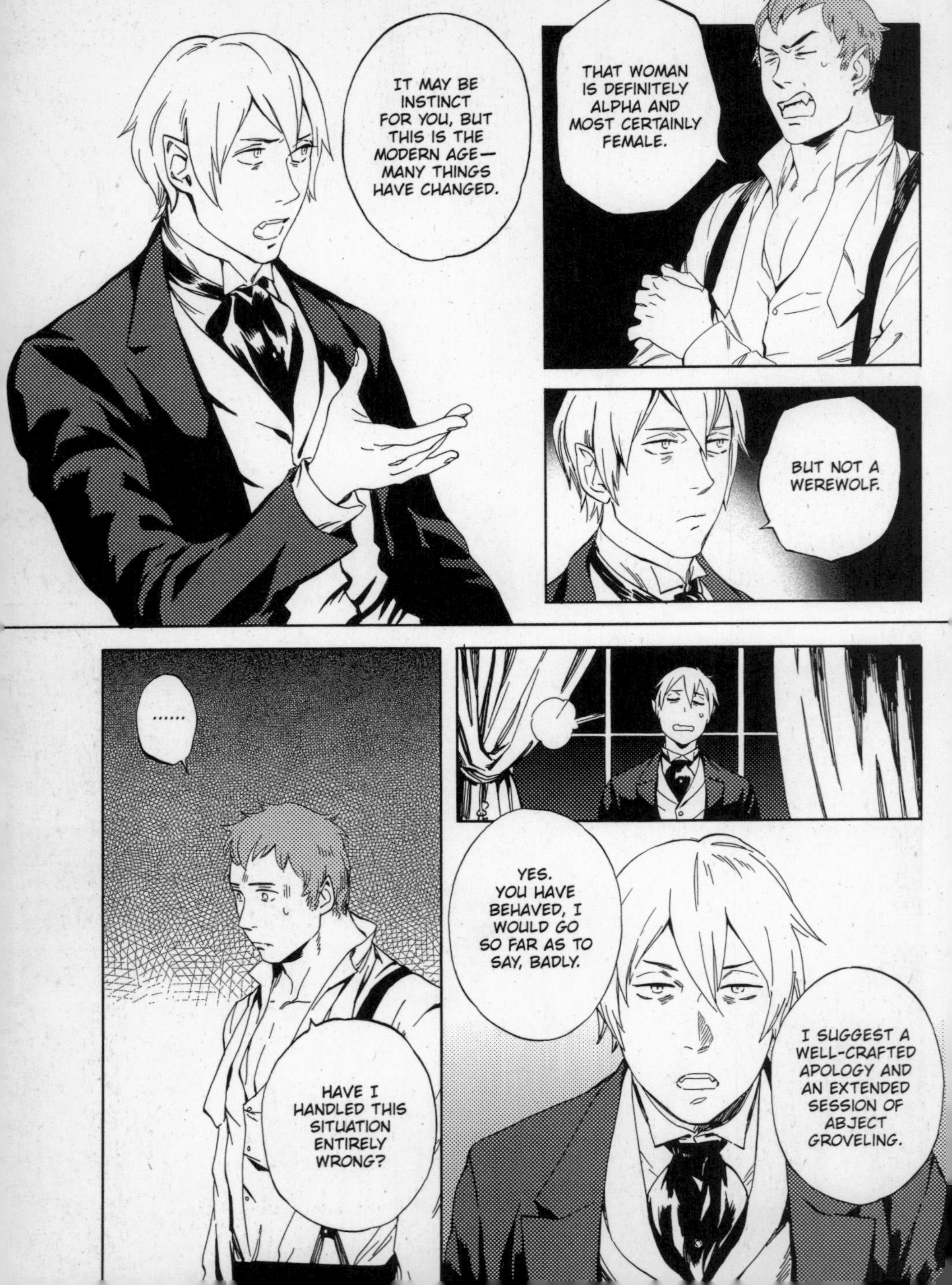
IT MAY BE INSTINCT FOR YOU, BUT THIS IS THE MODERN AGE— MANY THINGS HAVE CHANGED.
THAT WOMAN IS DEFINITELY ALPHA AND MOST CERTAINLY FEMALE.
BUT NOT A WEREWOLF.
......
HAVE I HANDLED THIS SITUATION ENTIRELY WRONG?
YES. YOU HAVE BEHAVED, I WOULD GO SO FAR AS TO SAY, BADLY.
I SUGGEST A WELL-CRAFTED APOLOGY AND AN EXTENDED SESSION OF ABJECT GROVELING.

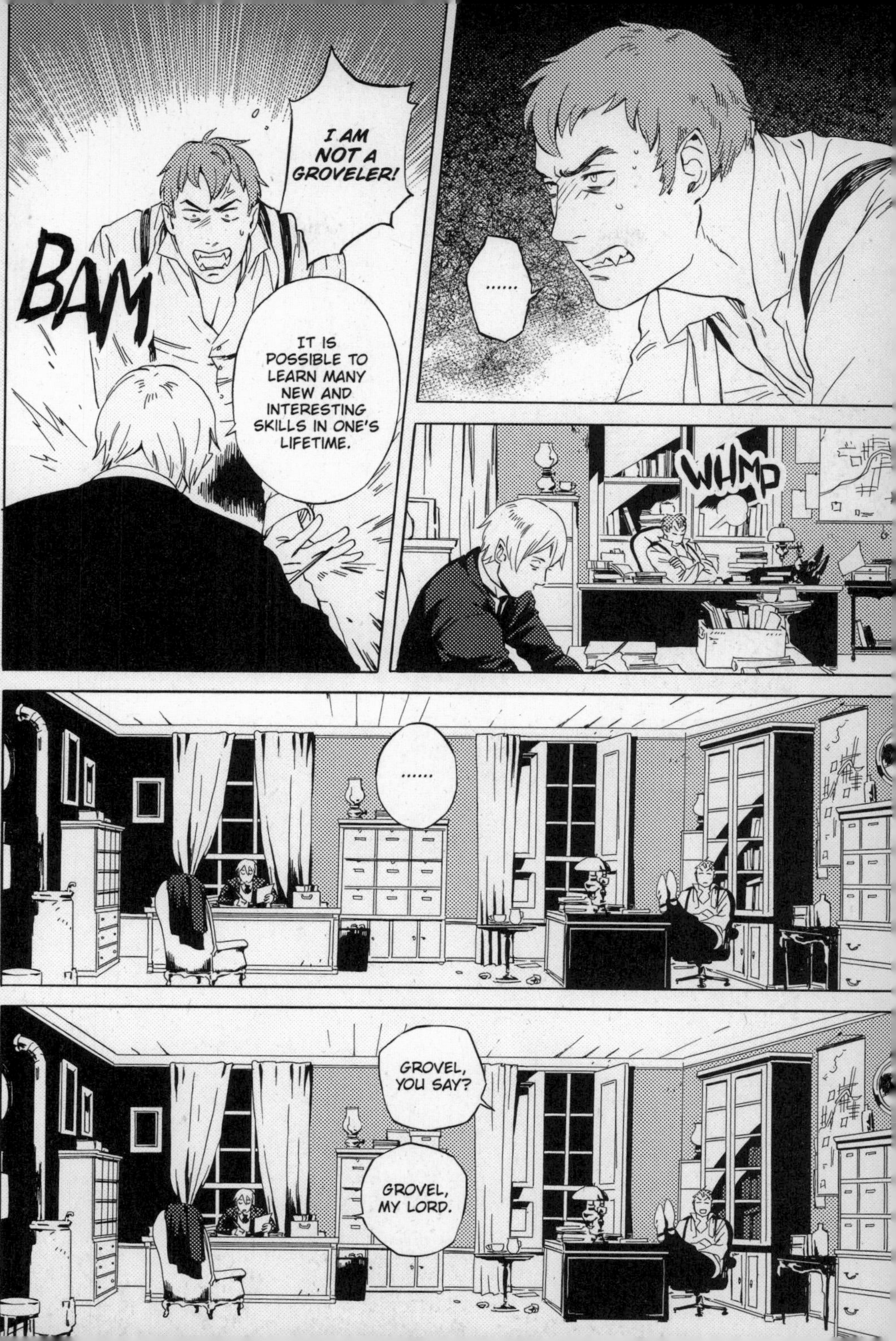
I AM NOT A GROVELER!
BAM
IT IS POSSIBLE TO LEARN MANY NEW AND INTERESTING SKILLS IN ONE'S LIFETIME.
......
WHMP
......
GROVEL, YOU SAY?
GROVEL, MY LORD.

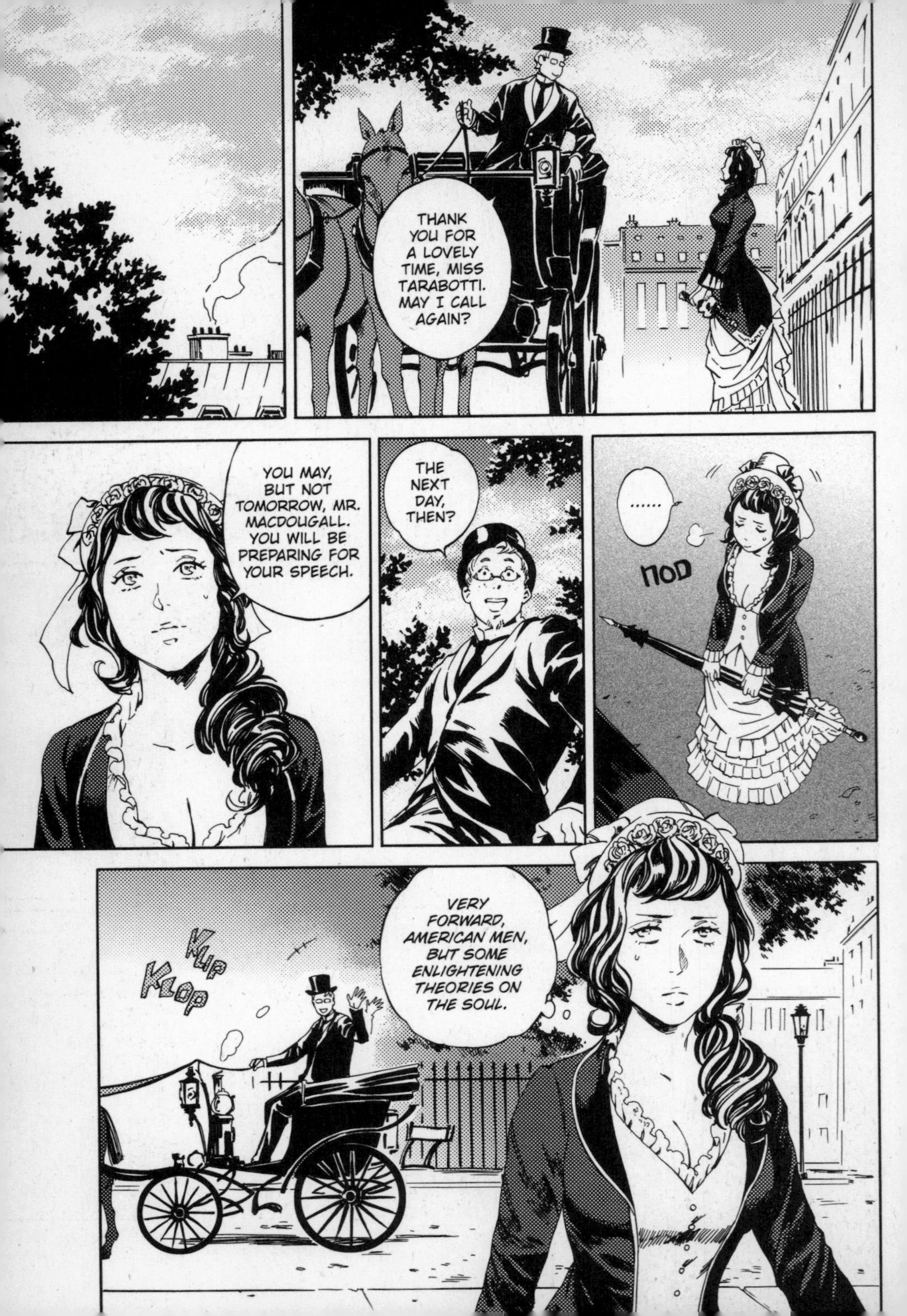
THANK YOU FOR A LOVELY TIME, MISS TARABOTTI. MAY I CALL AGAIN?
YOU MAY, BUT NOT TOMORROW, MR. MACDOUGALL. YOU WILL BE PREPARING FOR YOUR SPEECH.
THE NEXT DAY, THEN?
......
NOD
KLIP
KLOP
VERY FORWARD, AMERICAN MEN, BUT SOME ENLIGHTENING THEORIES ON THE SOUL.

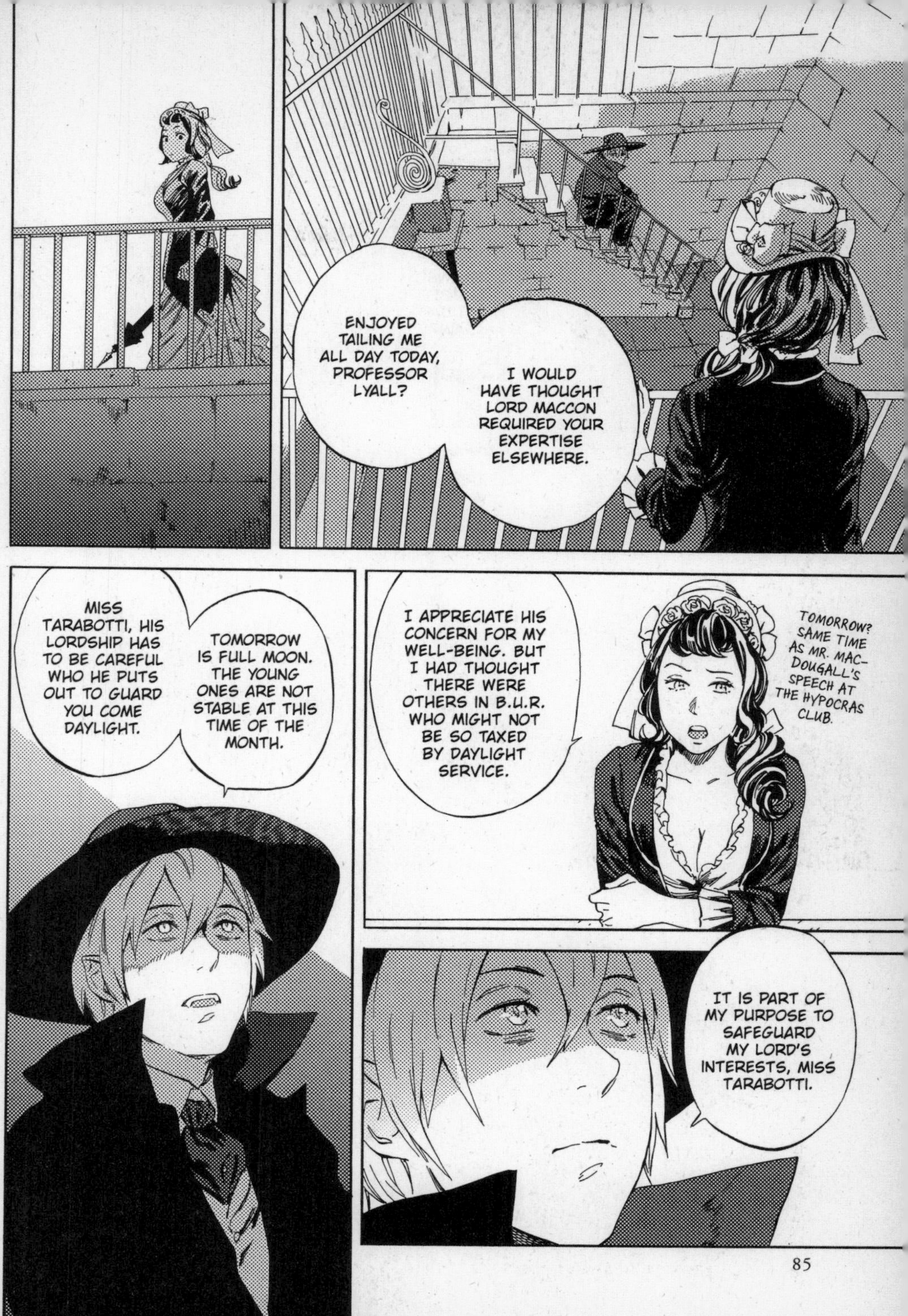

ENJOYED TAILING ME ALL DAY TODAY, PROFESSOR LYALL?
I WOULD HAVE THOUGHT LORD MACCON REQUIRED YOUR EXPERTISE ELSEWHERE.
MISS TARABOTTI, HIS LORDSHIP HAS TO BE CAREFUL WHO HE PUTS OUT TO GUARD YOU COME DAYLIGHT.
TOMORROW IS FULL MOON. THE YOUNG ONES ARE NOT STABLE AT THIS TIME OF THE MONTH.
I APPRECIATE HIS CONCERN FOR MY WELL-BEING. BUT I HAD THOUGHT THERE WERE OTHERS IN B.U.R. WHO MIGHT NOT BE SO TAXED BY DAYLIGHT SERVICE.
TOMORROW? SAME TIME AS MR. MACDOUGALL'S SPEECH AT THE HYPOCRAS CLUB.
IT IS PART OF MY PURPOSE TO SAFEGUARD MY LORD'S INTERESTS, MISS TARABOTTI.

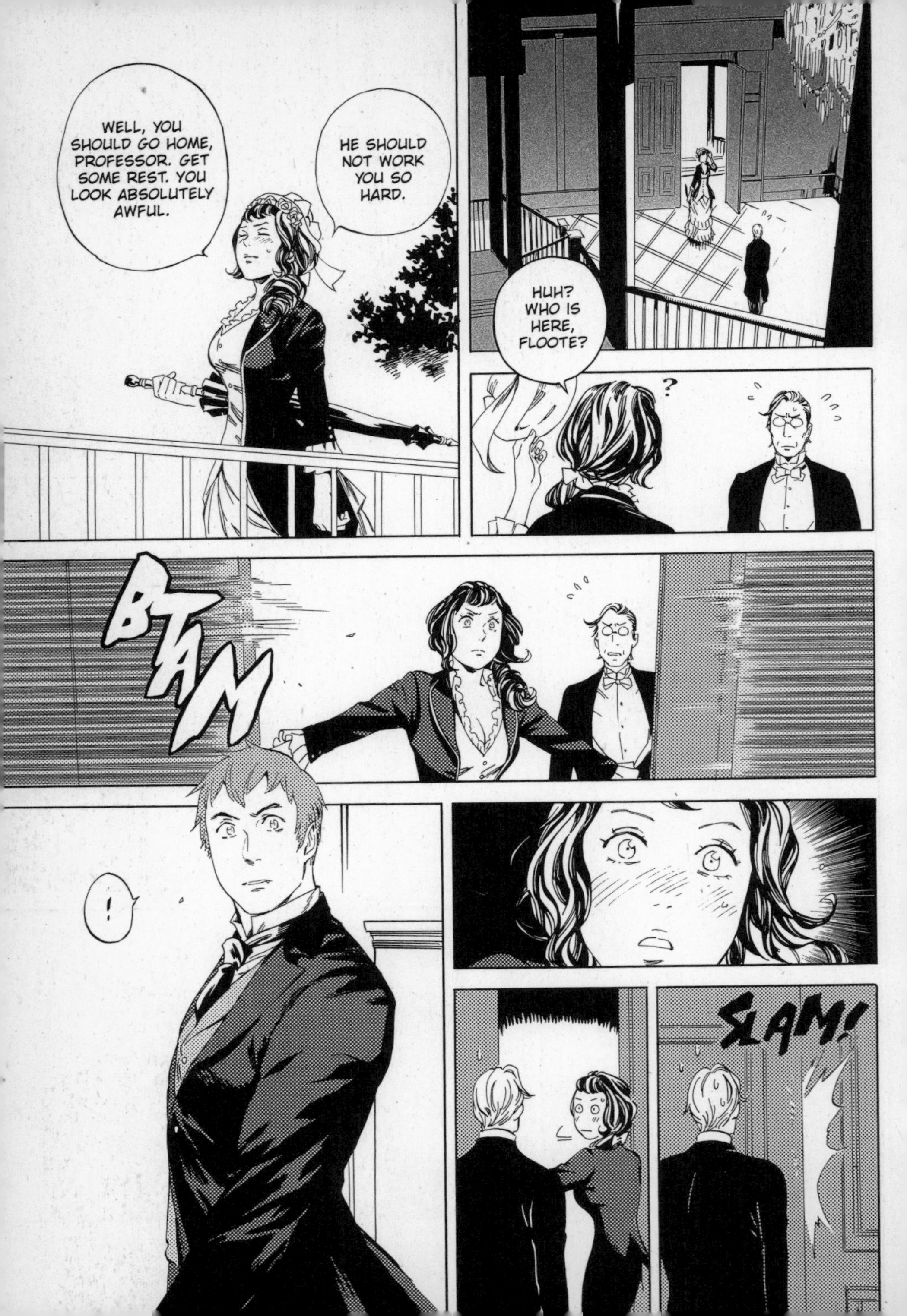
WELL, YOU SHOULD GO HOME, PROFESSOR. GET SOME REST. YOU LOOK ABSOLUTELY AWFUL.
HE SHOULD NOT WORK YOU SO HARD.
HUH? WHO IS HERE, FLOOTE?
?
BLAM
!
SLAM!

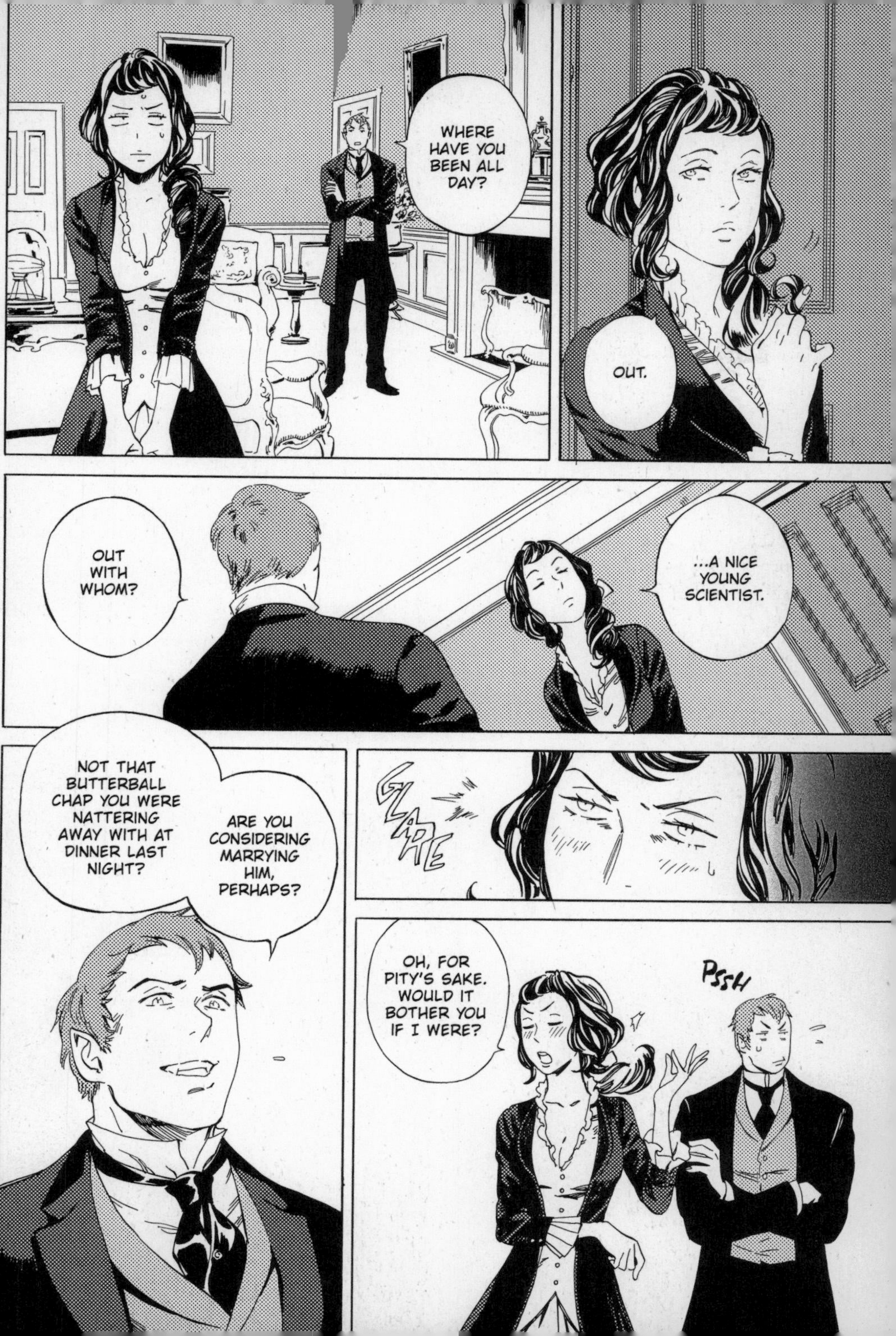
WHERE HAVE YOU BEEN ALL DAY?
OUT.
OUT WITH WHOM?
...A NICE YOUNG SCIENTIST.
NOT THAT BUTTERBALL CHAP YOU WERE NATTERING AWAY WITH AT DINNER LAST NIGHT?
ARE YOU CONSIDERING MARRYING HIM, PERHAPS?
GLARE
OH, FOR PITY'S SAKE. WOULD IT BOTHER YOU IF I WERE?
PSSH

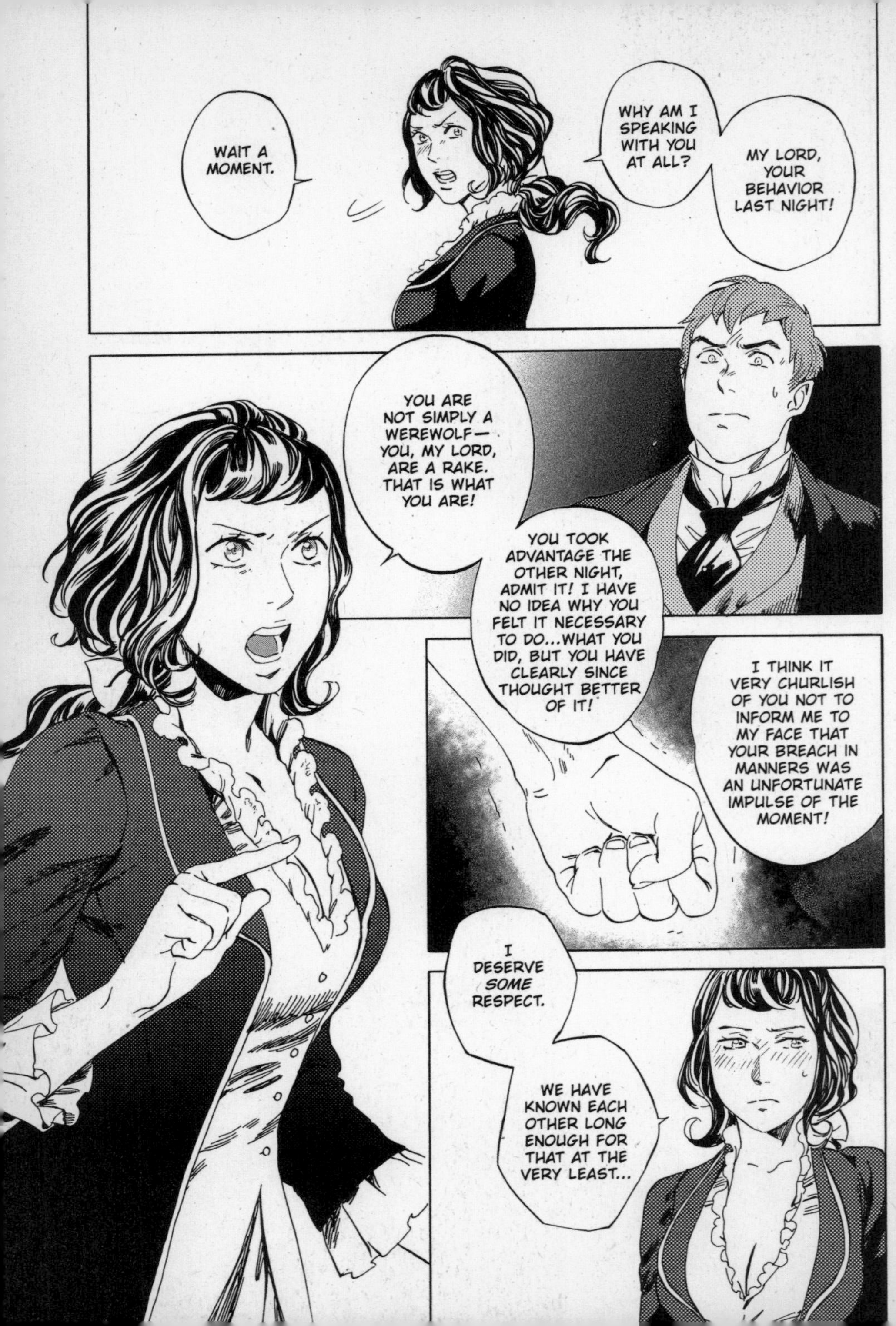
WAIT A MOMENT.
WHY AM I SPEAKING WITH YOU AT ALL?
MY LORD, YOUR BEHAVIOR LAST NIGHT!
YOU ARE NOT SIMPLY A WEREWOLF—YOU, MY LORD, ARE A RAKE. THAT IS WHAT YOU ARE!
YOU TOOK ADVANTAGE THE OTHER NIGHT, ADMIT IT! I HAVE NO IDEA WHY YOU FELT IT NECESSARY TO DO...WHAT YOU DID, BUT YOU HAVE CLEARLY SINCE THOUGHT BETTER OF IT!
I THINK IT VERY CHURLISH OF YOU NOT TO INFORM ME TO MY FACE THAT YOUR BREACH IN MANNERS WAS AN UNFORTUNATE IMPULSE OF THE MOMENT!
I DESERVE *SOME* RESPECT.
WE HAVE KNOWN EACH OTHER LONG ENOUGH FOR THAT AT THE VERY LEAST...

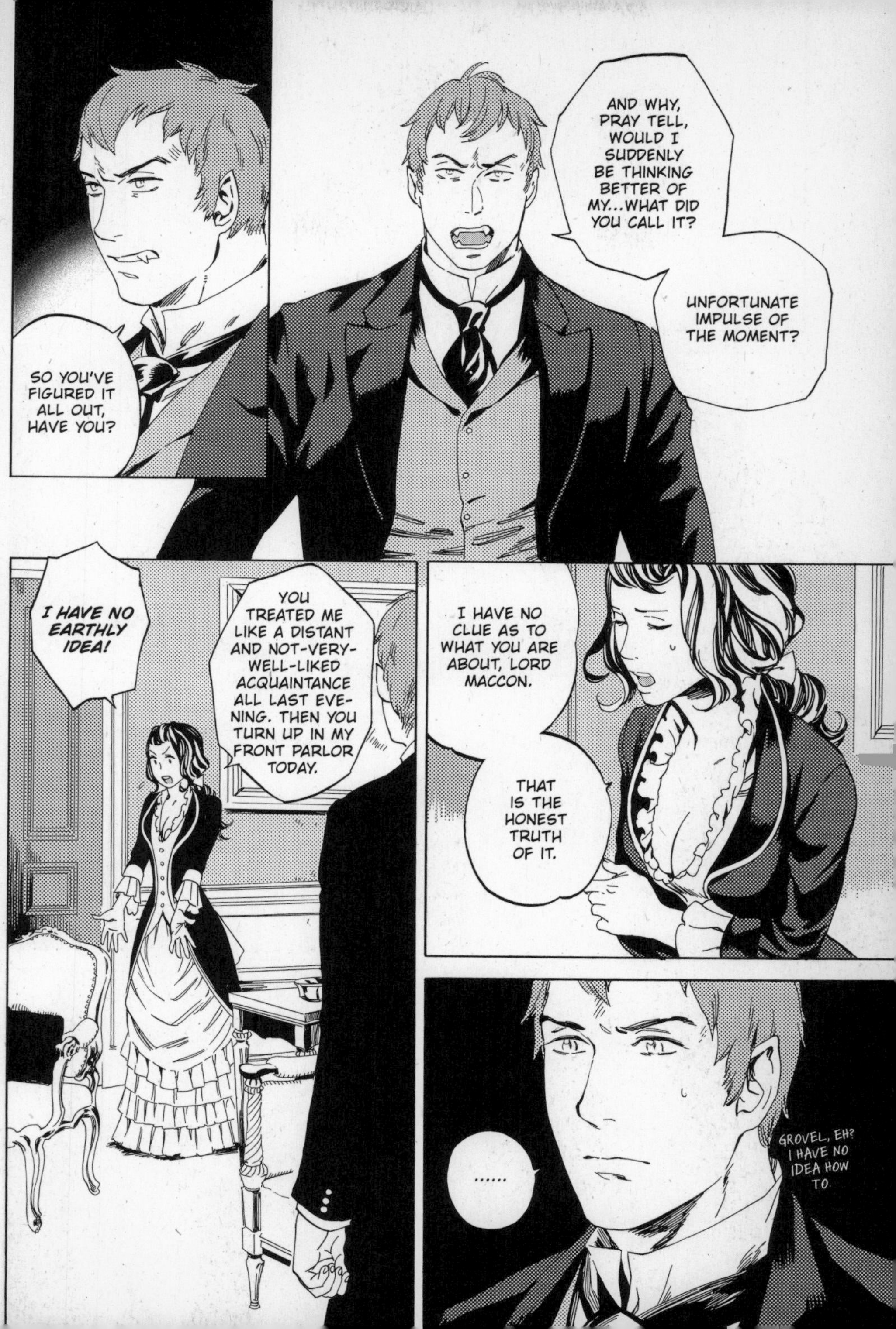
SO YOU'VE FIGURED IT ALL OUT, HAVE YOU?
AND WHY, PRAY TELL, WOULD I SUDDENLY BE THINKING BETTER OF MY...WHAT DID YOU CALL IT?
UNFORTUNATE IMPULSE OF THE MOMENT?
I HAVE NO EARTHLY IDEA!
YOU TREATED ME LIKE A DISTANT AND NOT-VERY-WELL-LIKED ACQUAINTANCE ALL LAST EVENING. THEN YOU TURN UP IN MY FRONT PARLOR TODAY.
I HAVE NO CLUE AS TO WHAT YOU ARE ABOUT, LORD MACCON.
THAT IS THE HONEST TRUTH OF IT.
......
GROVEL, EH? I HAVE NO IDEA HOW TO.

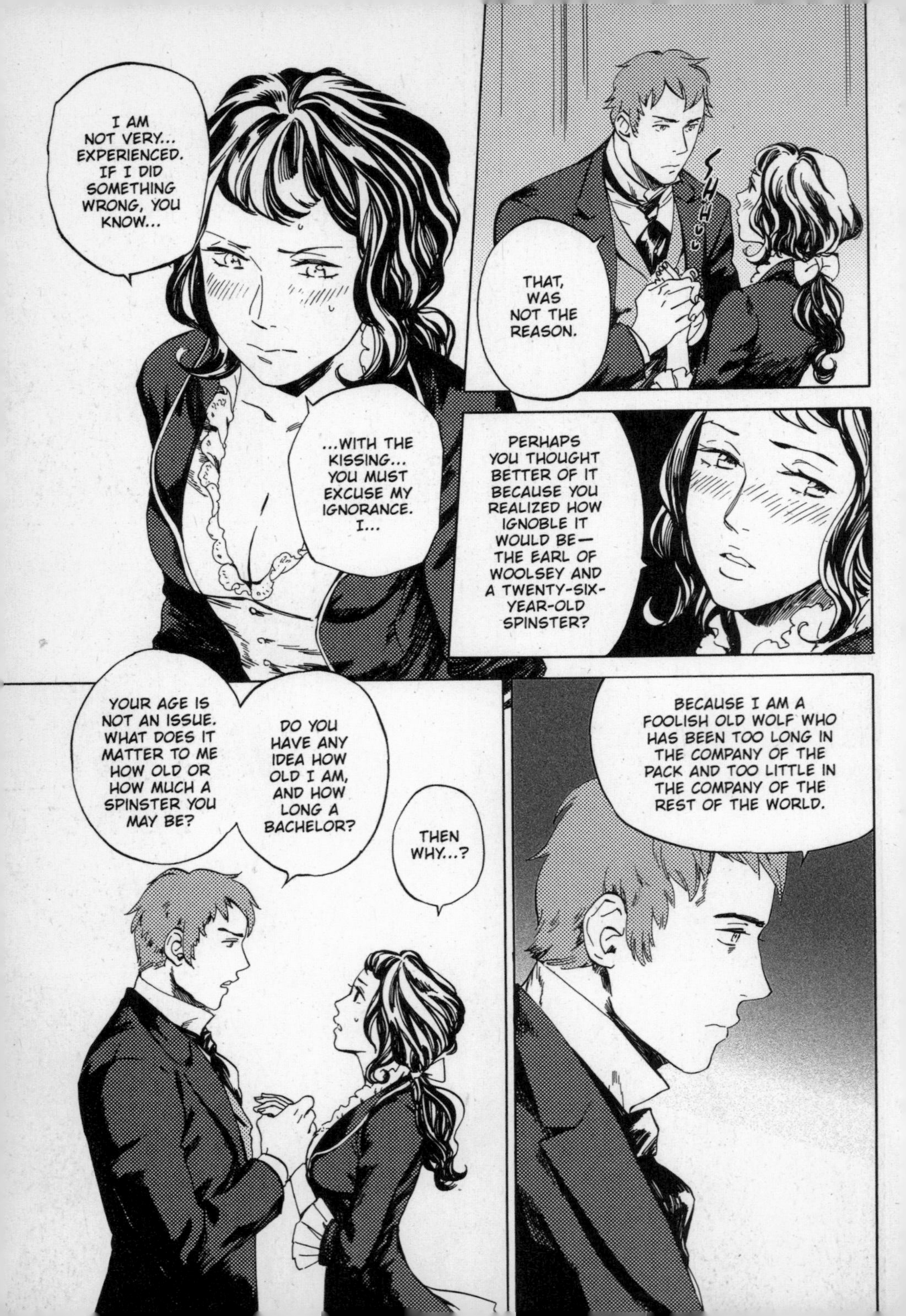
I AM NOT VERY... EXPERIENCED. IF I DID SOMETHING WRONG, YOU KNOW...
...WITH THE KISSING... YOU MUST EXCUSE MY IGNORANCE. I...
THAT, WAS NOT THE REASON.
PERHAPS YOU THOUGHT BETTER OF IT BECAUSE YOU REALIZED HOW IGNOBLE IT WOULD BE— THE EARL OF WOOLSEY AND A TWENTY-SIX-YEAR-OLD SPINSTER?
YOUR AGE IS NOT AN ISSUE. WHAT DOES IT MATTER TO ME HOW OLD OR HOW MUCH A SPINSTER YOU MAY BE?
DO YOU HAVE ANY IDEA HOW OLD I AM, AND HOW LONG A BACHELOR?
THEN WHY...?
BECAUSE I AM A FOOLISH OLD WOLF WHO HAS BEEN TOO LONG IN THE COMPANY OF THE PACK AND TOO LITTLE IN THE COMPANY OF THE REST OF THE WORLD.

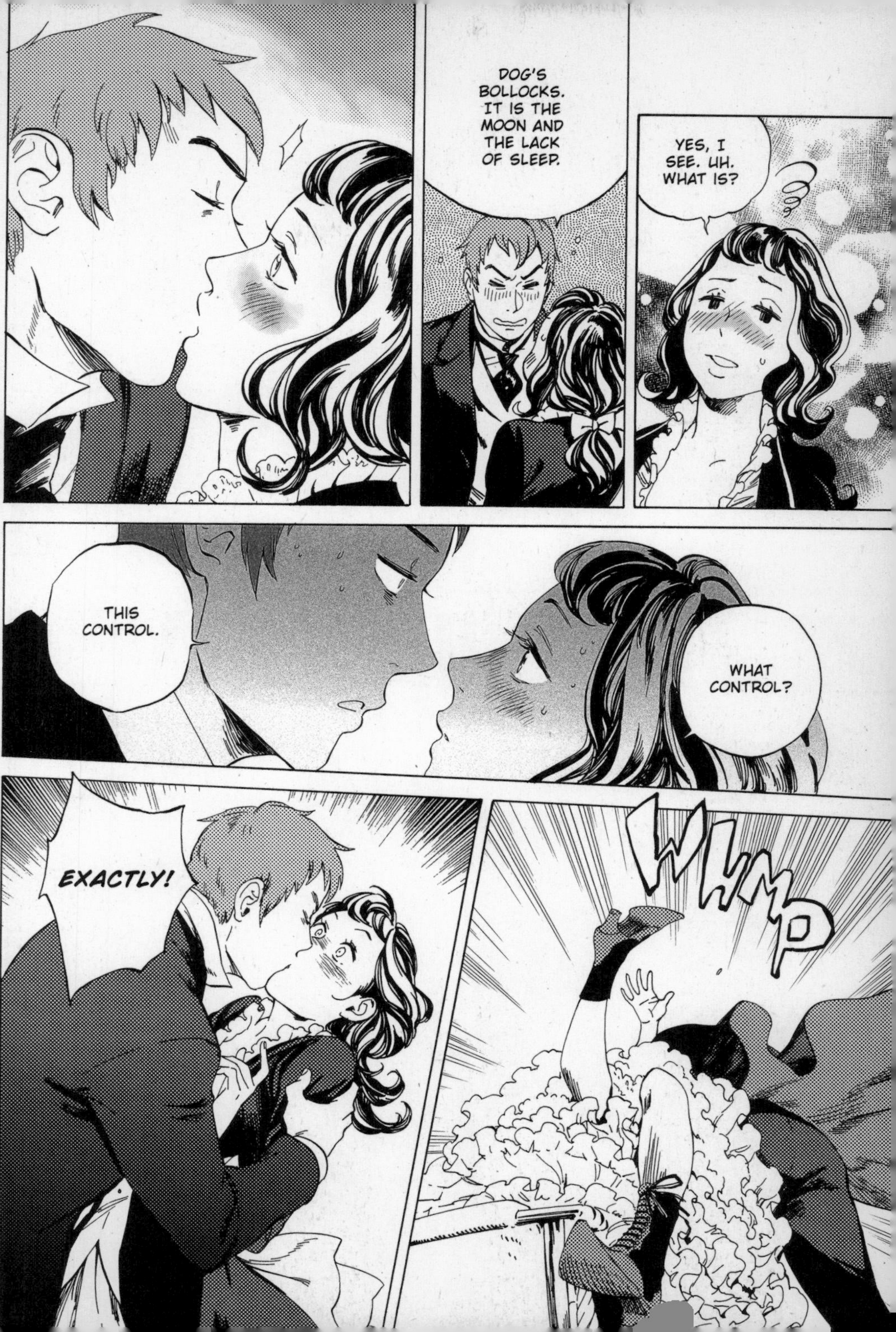
DOG'S BOLLOCKS. IT IS THE MOON AND THE LACK OF SLEEP.
YES, I SEE. UH. WHAT IS?
THIS CONTROL.
WHAT CONTROL?
EXACTLY!
WHMP

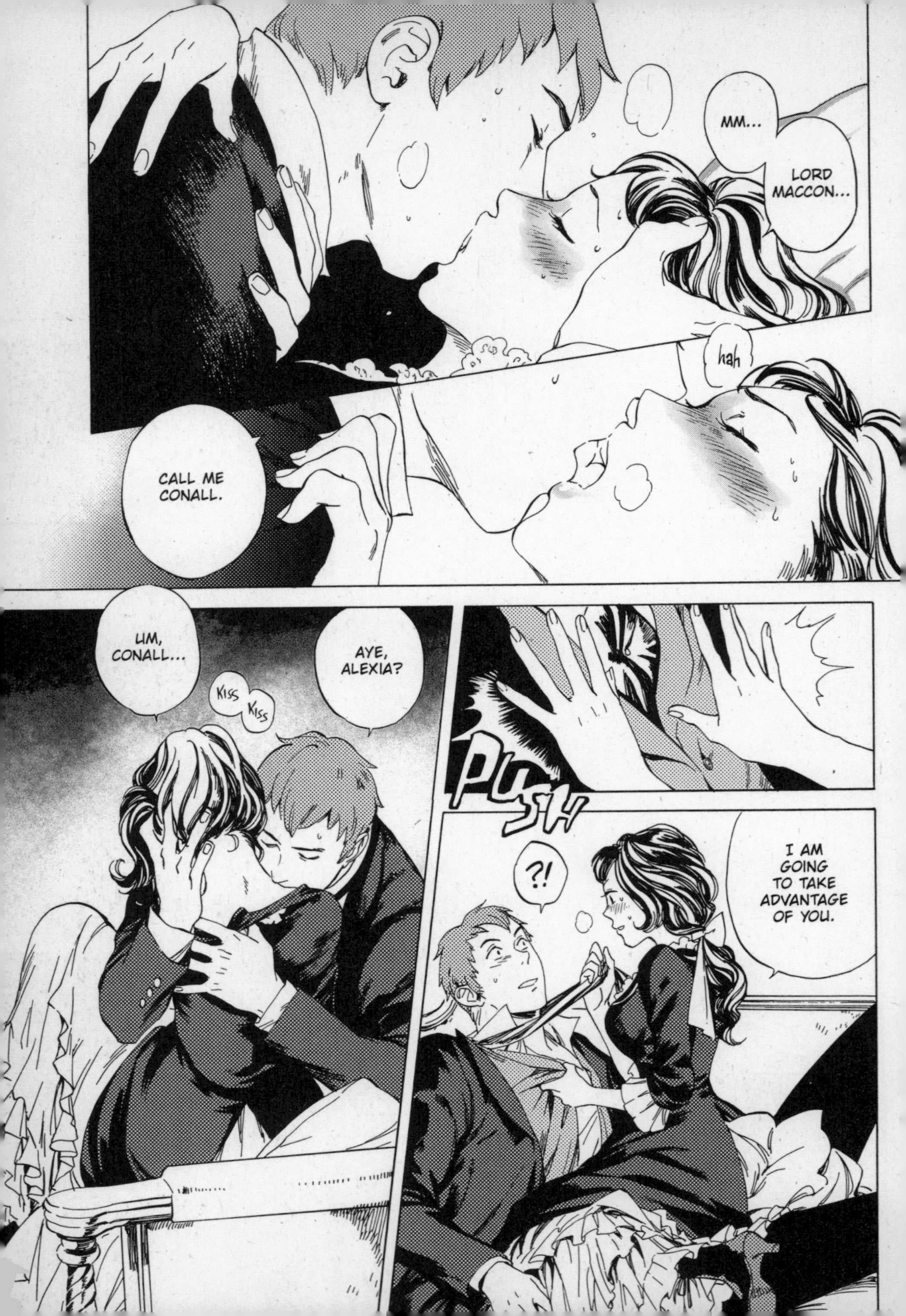
MM...
LORD MACCON...
hah
CALL ME CONALL.
UM, CONALL...
KISS KISS
AYE, ALEXIA?
PUSH
?!
I AM GOING TO TAKE ADVANTAGE OF YOU.

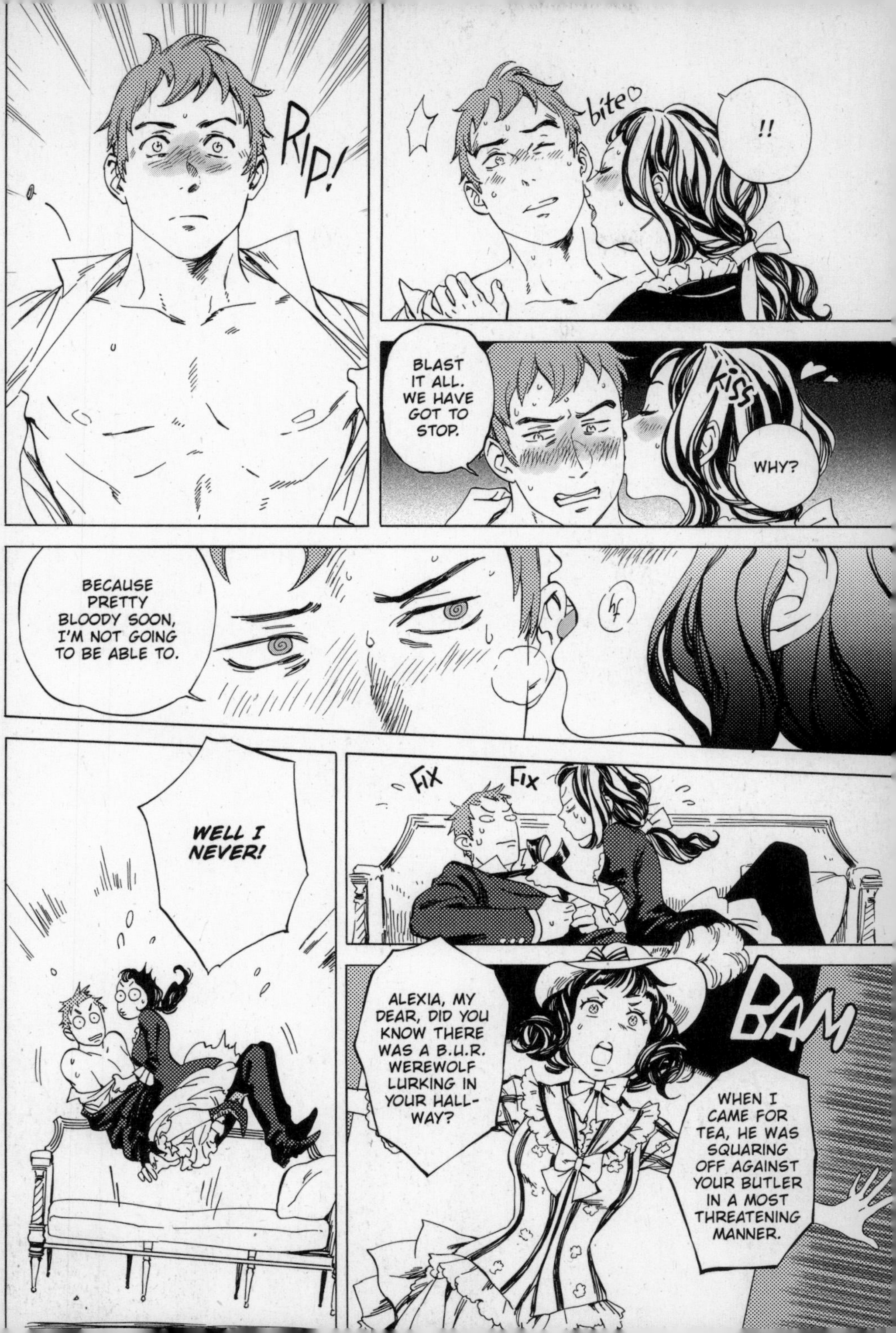
RIP!
bite♡
!!
BLAST IT ALL. WE HAVE GOT TO STOP.
KISS
WHY?
BECAUSE PRETTY BLOODY SOON, I'M NOT GOING TO BE ABLE TO.
FIX FIX
WELL I NEVER!
BAM
ALEXIA, MY DEAR, DID YOU KNOW THERE WAS A B.U.R. WEREWOLF LURKING IN YOUR HALL-WAY?
WHEN I CAME FOR TEA, HE WAS SQUARING OFF AGAINST YOUR BUTLER IN A MOST THREATENING MANNER.

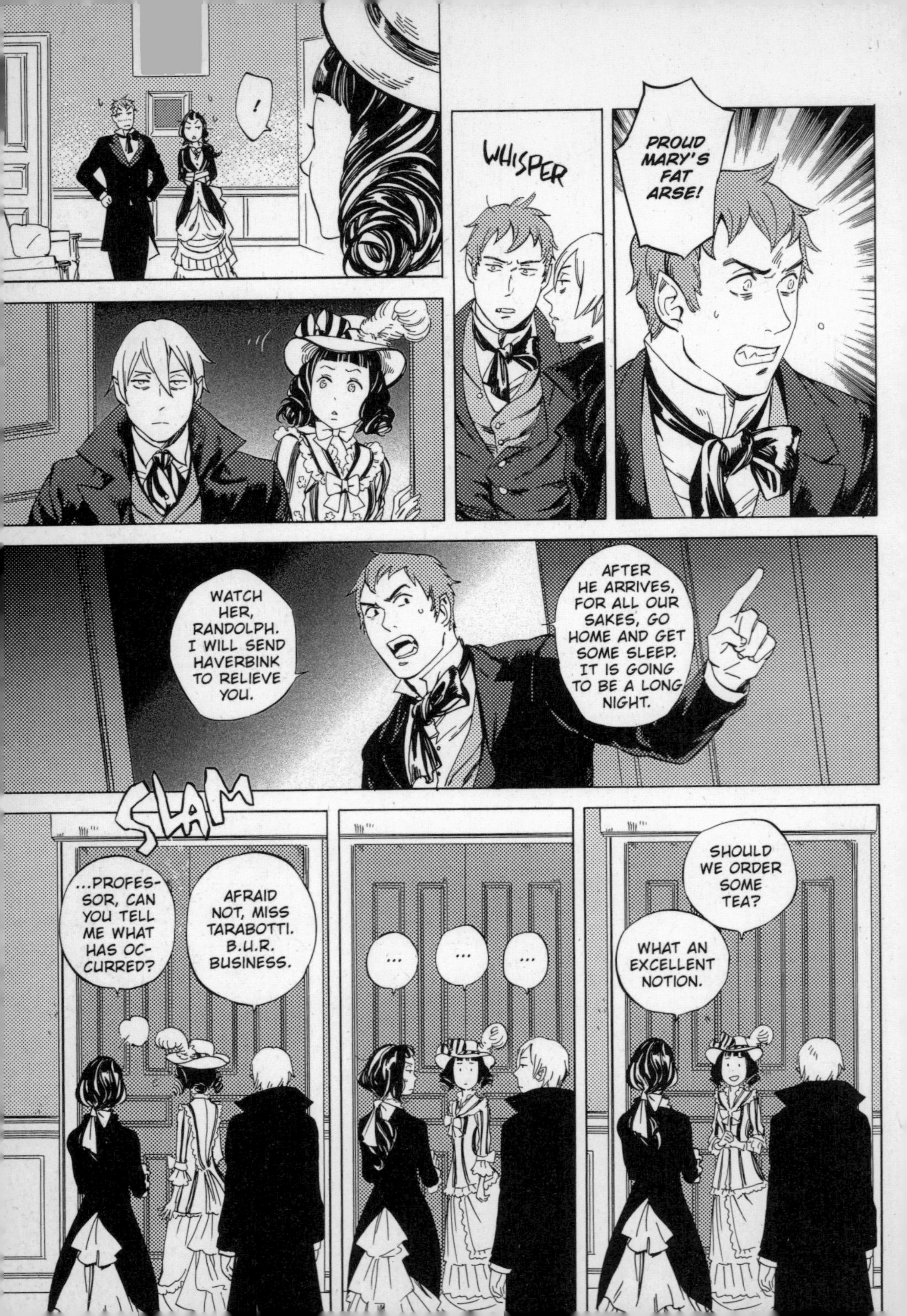
!
WHISPER
PROUD MARY'S FAT ARSE!
WATCH HER, RANDOLPH. I WILL SEND HAVERBINK TO RELIEVE YOU.
AFTER HE ARRIVES, FOR ALL OUR SAKES, GO HOME AND GET SOME SLEEP. IT IS GOING TO BE A LONG NIGHT.
SLAM
...PROFES-SOR, CAN YOU TELL ME WHAT HAS OC-CURRED?
AFRAID NOT, MISS TARABOTTI. B.U.R. BUSINESS.
...
...
...
SHOULD WE ORDER SOME TEA?
WHAT AN EXCELLENT NOTION.

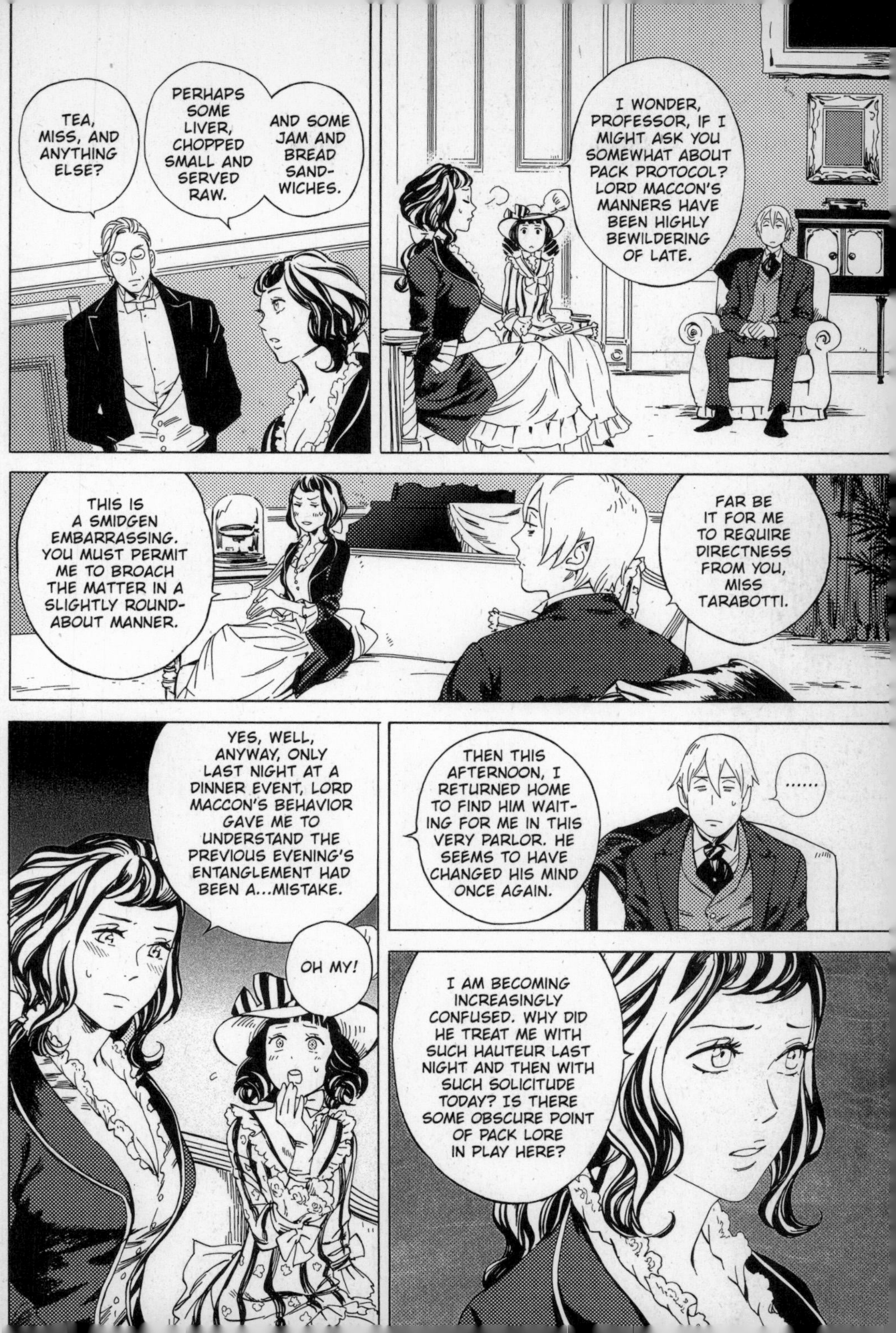
TEA, MISS, AND ANYTHING ELSE?
PERHAPS SOME LIVER, CHOPPED SMALL AND SERVED RAW.
AND SOME JAM AND BREAD SAND-WICHES.
I WONDER, PROFESSOR, IF I MIGHT ASK YOU SOMEWHAT ABOUT PACK PROTOCOL? LORD MACCON'S MANNERS HAVE BEEN HIGHLY BEWILDERING OF LATE.
THIS IS A SMIDGEN EMBARRASSING. YOU MUST PERMIT ME TO BROACH THE MATTER IN A SLIGHTLY ROUND-ABOUT MANNER.
FAR BE IT FOR ME TO REQUIRE DIRECTNESS FROM YOU, MISS TARABOTTI.
YES, WELL, ANYWAY, ONLY LAST NIGHT AT A DINNER EVENT, LORD MACCON'S BEHAVIOR GAVE ME TO UNDERSTAND THE PREVIOUS EVENING'S ENTANGLEMENT HAD BEEN A...MISTAKE.
OH MY!
THEN THIS AFTERNOON, I RETURNED HOME TO FIND HIM WAIT-ING FOR ME IN THIS VERY PARLOR. HE SEEMS TO HAVE CHANGED HIS MIND ONCE AGAIN.
......
I AM BECOMING INCREASINGLY CONFUSED. WHY DID HE TREAT ME WITH SUCH HAUTEUR LAST NIGHT AND THEN WITH SUCH SOLICITUDE TODAY? IS THERE SOME OBSCURE POINT OF PACK LORE IN PLAY HERE?

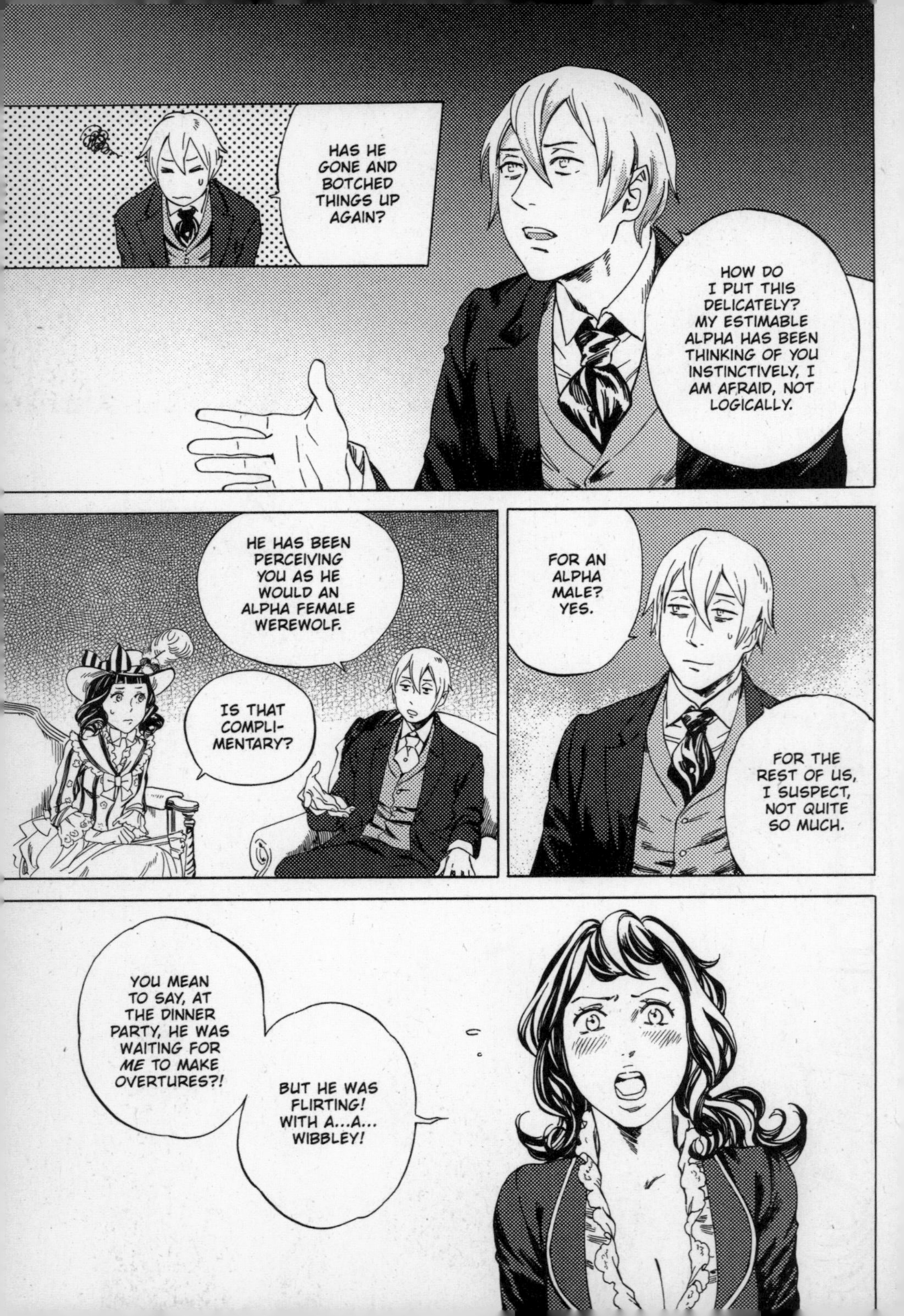
HAS HE GONE AND BOTCHED THINGS UP AGAIN?
HOW DO I PUT THIS DELICATELY? MY ESTIMABLE ALPHA HAS BEEN THINKING OF YOU INSTINCTIVELY, I AM AFRAID, NOT LOGICALLY.
HE HAS BEEN PERCEIVING YOU AS HE WOULD AN ALPHA FEMALE WEREWOLF.
IS THAT COMPLI-MENTARY?
FOR AN ALPHA MALE? YES.
FOR THE REST OF US, I SUSPECT, NOT QUITE SO MUCH.
YOU MEAN TO SAY, AT THE DINNER PARTY, HE WAS WAITING FOR *ME* TO MAKE OVERTURES?!
BUT HE WAS FLIRTING! WITH A...A... WIBBLEY!

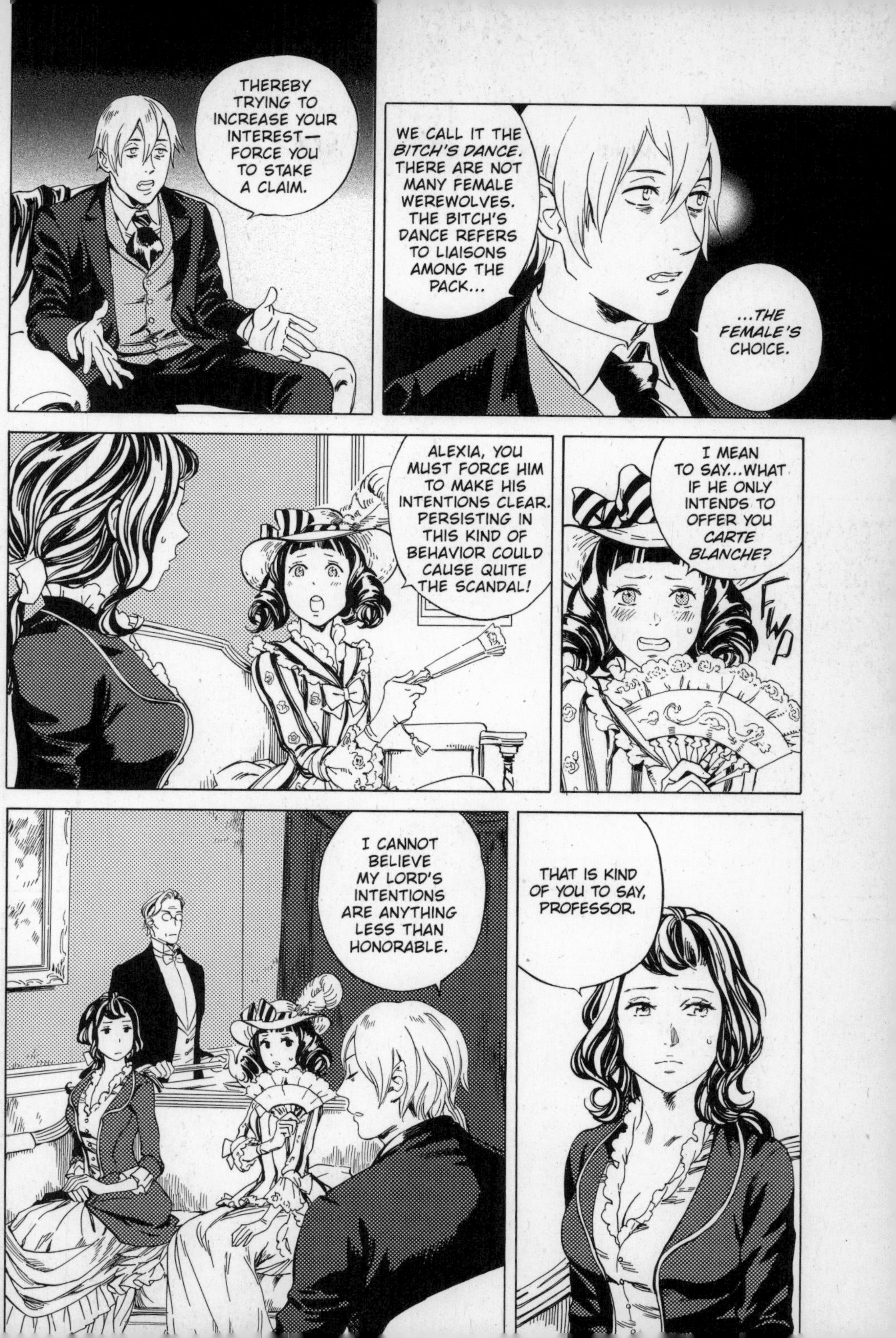
THEREBY TRYING TO INCREASE YOUR INTEREST— FORCE YOU TO STAKE A CLAIM.
WE CALL IT THE *BITCH'S DANCE.* THERE ARE NOT MANY FEMALE WEREWOLVES. THE BITCH'S DANCE REFERS TO LIAISONS AMONG THE PACK...
...THE FEMALE'S CHOICE.
ALEXIA, YOU MUST FORCE HIM TO MAKE HIS INTENTIONS CLEAR. PERSISTING IN THIS KIND OF BEHAVIOR COULD CAUSE QUITE THE SCANDAL!
I MEAN TO SAY...WHAT IF HE ONLY INTENDS TO OFFER YOU *CARTE BLANCHE?*
FWP
I CANNOT BELIEVE MY LORD'S INTENTIONS ARE ANYTHING LESS THAN HONORABLE.
THAT IS KIND OF YOU TO SAY, PROFESSOR.

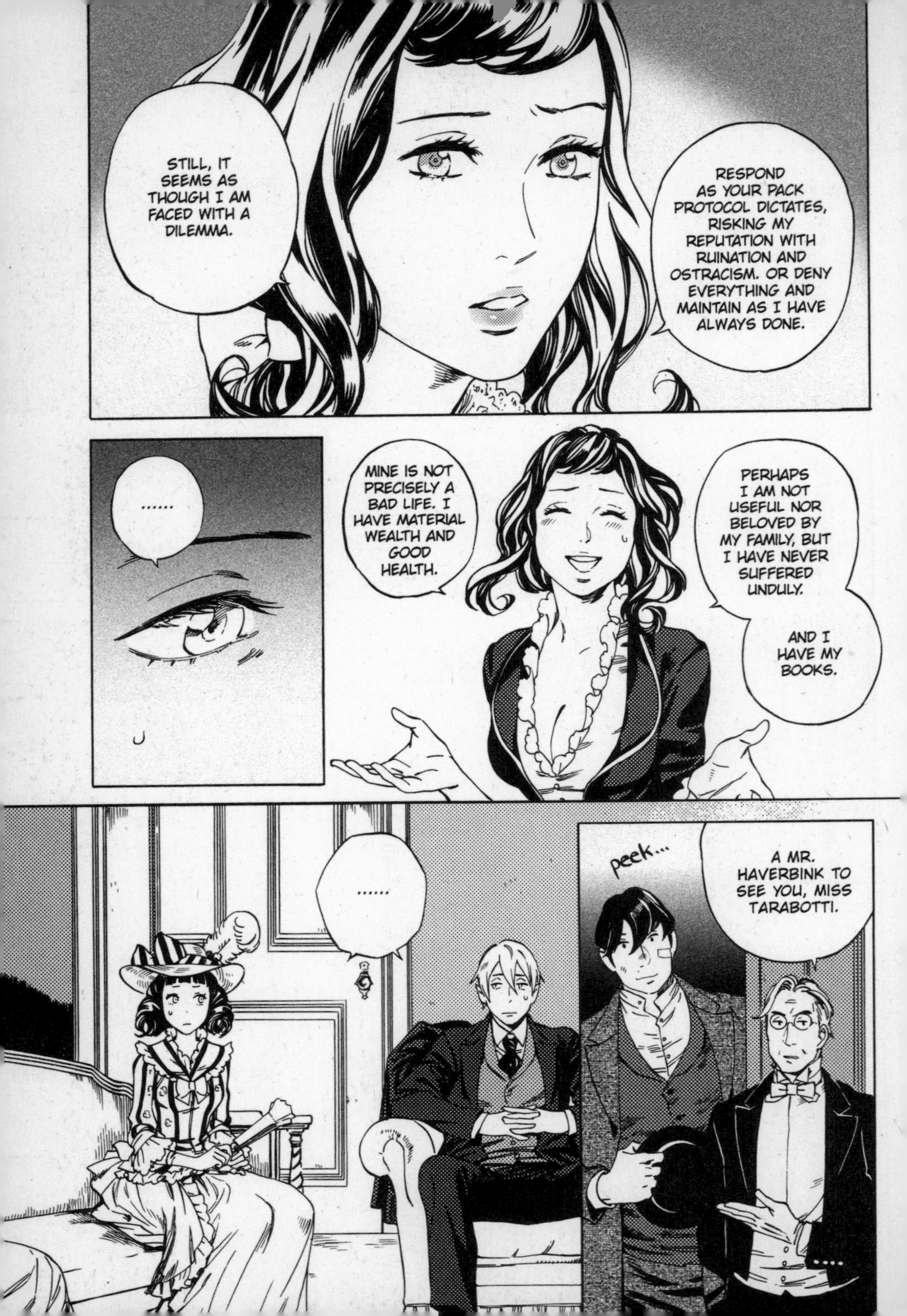

STILL, IT SEEMS AS THOUGH I AM FACED WITH A DILEMMA.
RESPOND AS YOUR PACK PROTOCOL DICTATES, RISKING MY REPUTATION WITH RUINATION AND OSTRACISM. OR DENY EVERYTHING AND MAINTAIN AS I HAVE ALWAYS DONE.
......
MINE IS NOT PRECISELY A BAD LIFE. I HAVE MATERIAL WEALTH AND GOOD HEALTH.
PERHAPS I AM NOT USEFUL NOR BELOVED BY MY FAMILY, BUT I HAVE NEVER SUFFERED UNDULY.
AND I HAVE MY BOOKS.
......
peek...
A MR. HAVERBINK TO SEE YOU, MISS TARABOTTI.

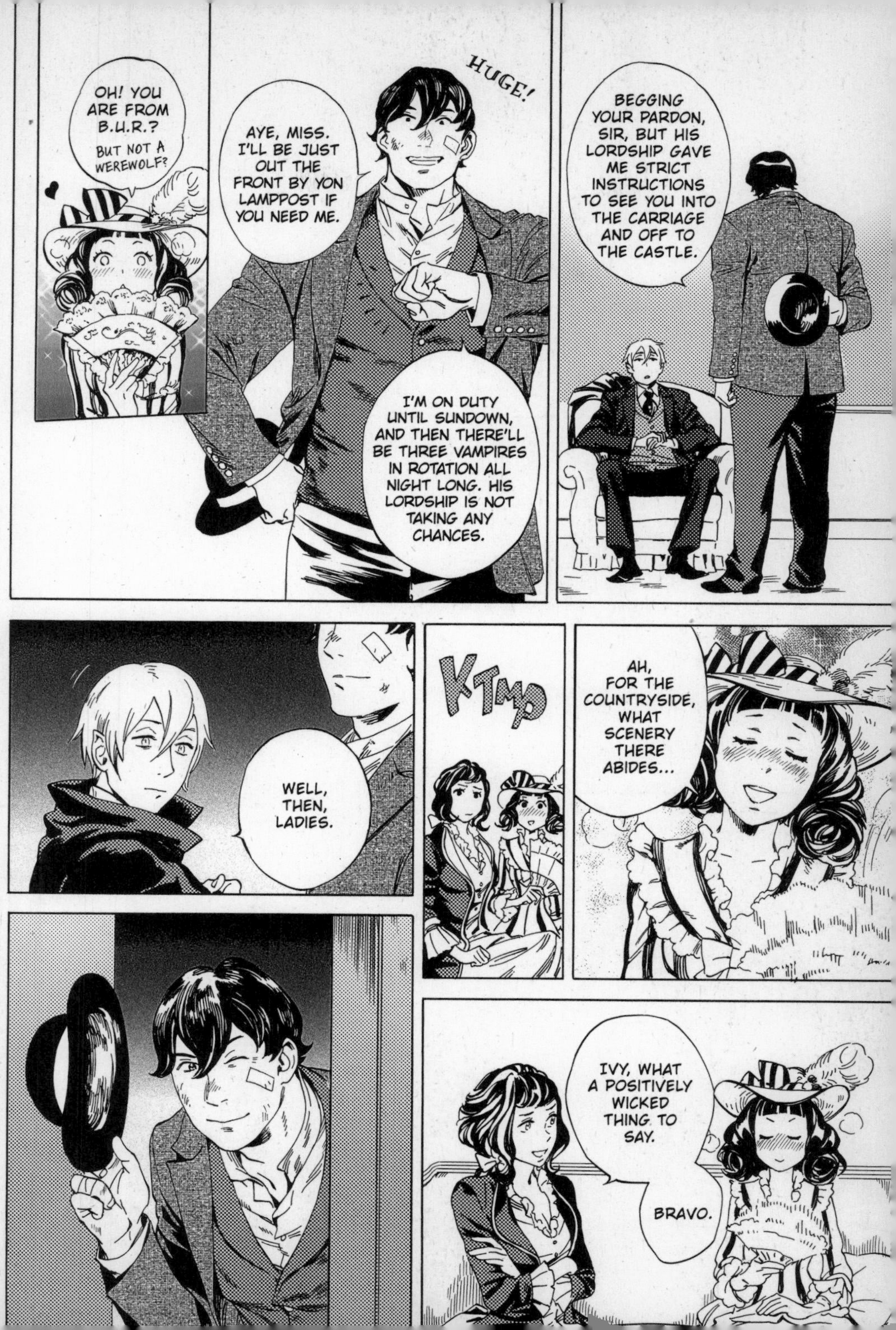
OH! YOU ARE FROM B.U.R.?
BUT NOT A WEREWOLF?
HUGE!
AYE, MISS. I'LL BE JUST OUT THE FRONT BY YON LAMPPOST IF YOU NEED ME.
I'M ON DUTY UNTIL SUNDOWN, AND THEN THERE'LL BE THREE VAMPIRES IN ROTATION ALL NIGHT LONG. HIS LORDSHIP IS NOT TAKING ANY CHANCES.
BEGGING YOUR PARDON, SIR, BUT HIS LORDSHIP GAVE ME STRICT INSTRUCTIONS TO SEE YOU INTO THE CARRIAGE AND OFF TO THE CASTLE.
WELL, THEN, LADIES.
KTMP
AH, FOR THE COUNTRYSIDE, WHAT SCENERY THERE ABIDES...
IVY, WHAT A POSITIVELY WICKED THING TO SAY.
BRAVO.

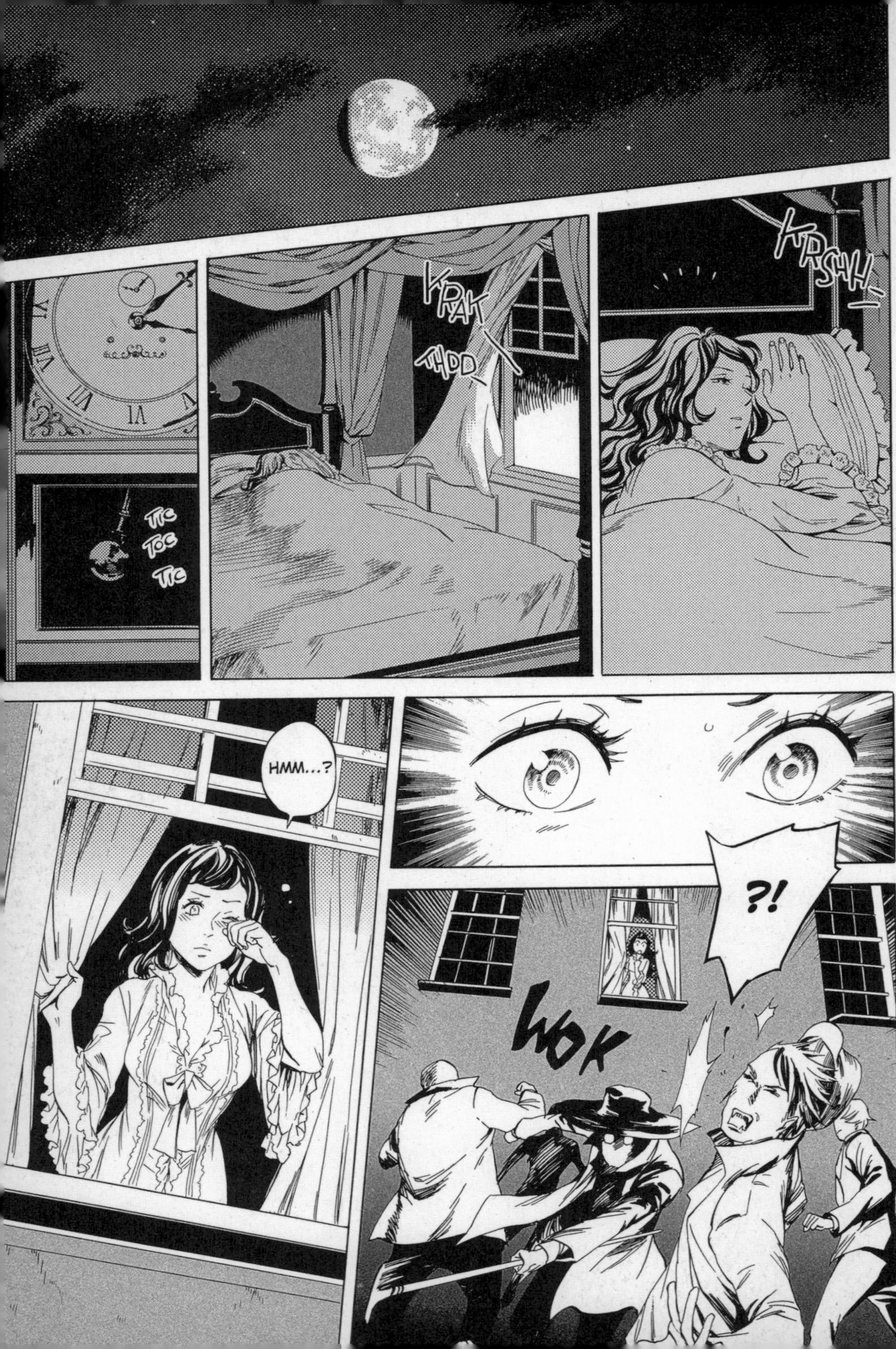
TIC
TOC
TIC
KRAK
THDD
KRSHH
HMM...?
?!
WOK

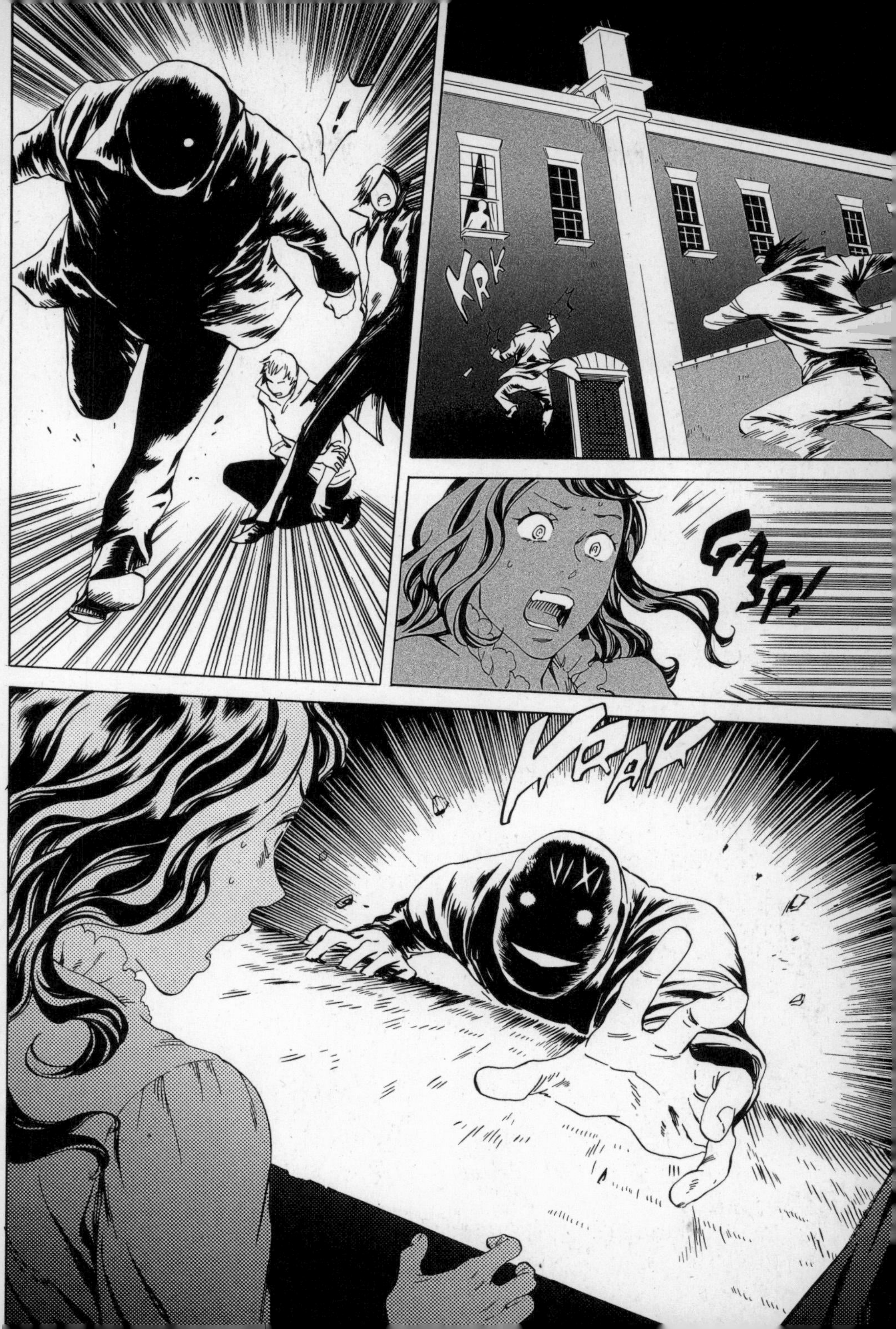
!
KRK
GASP!
KRAK

SOULLESS

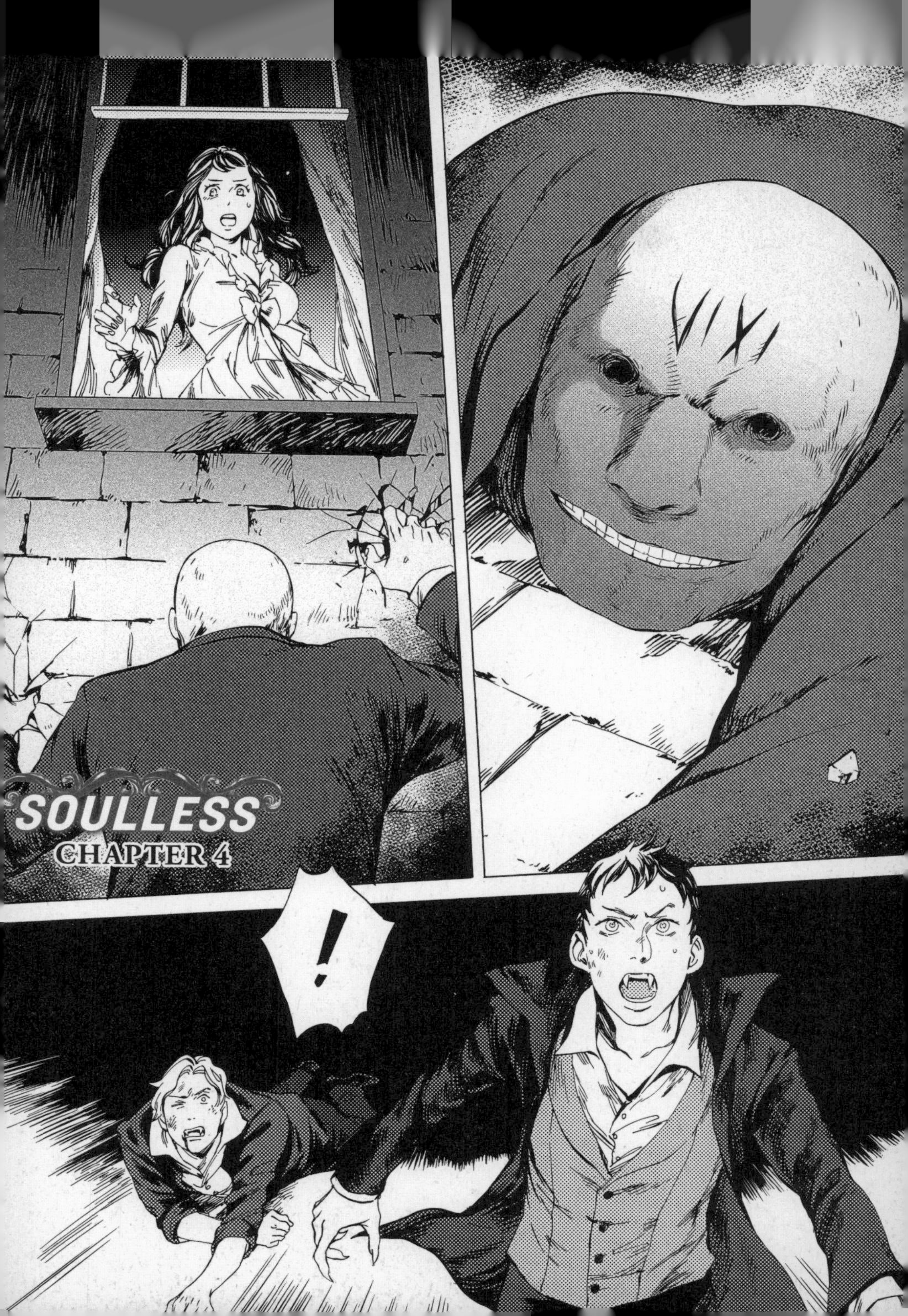
SOULLESS
CHAPTER 4
!

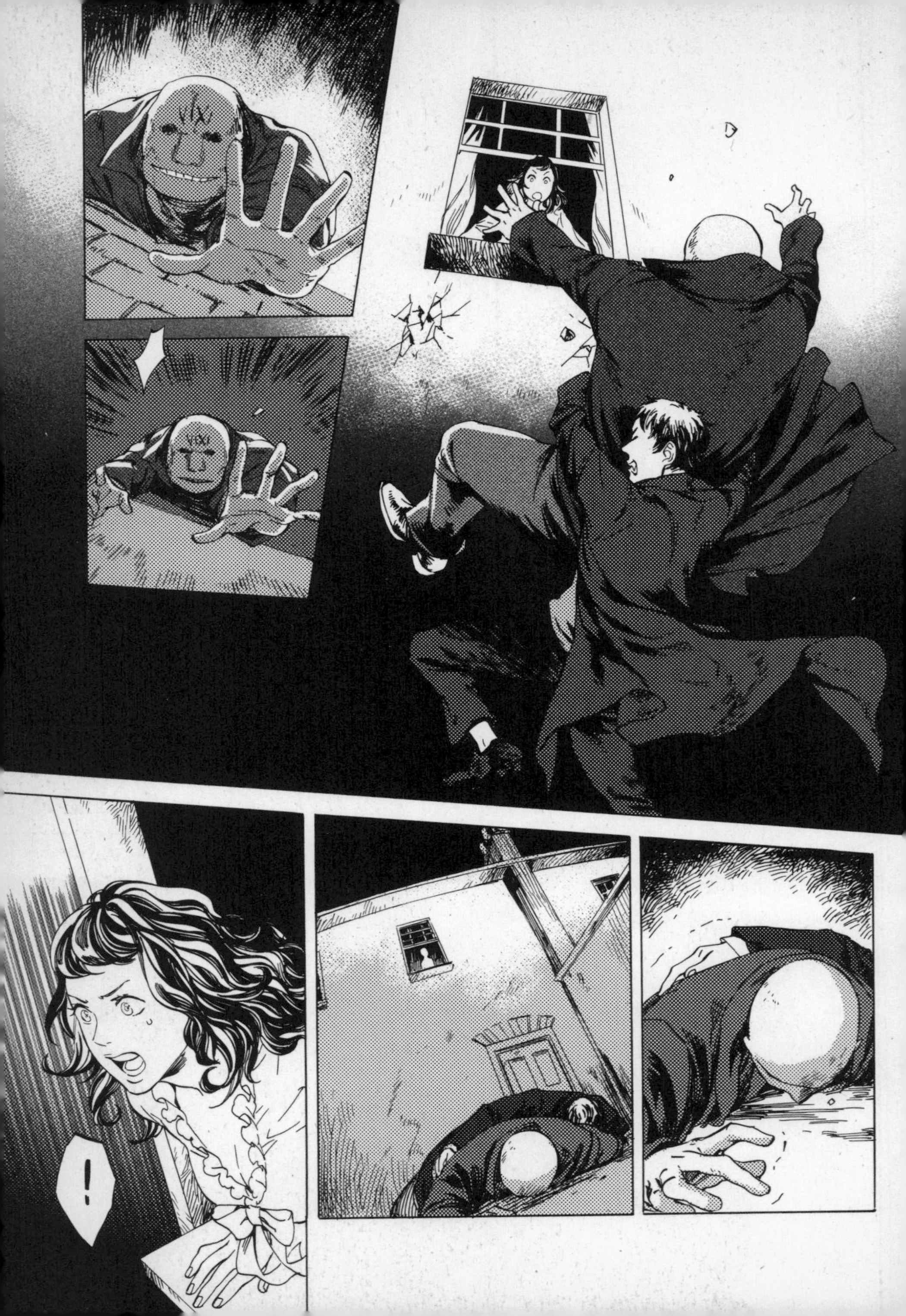
!

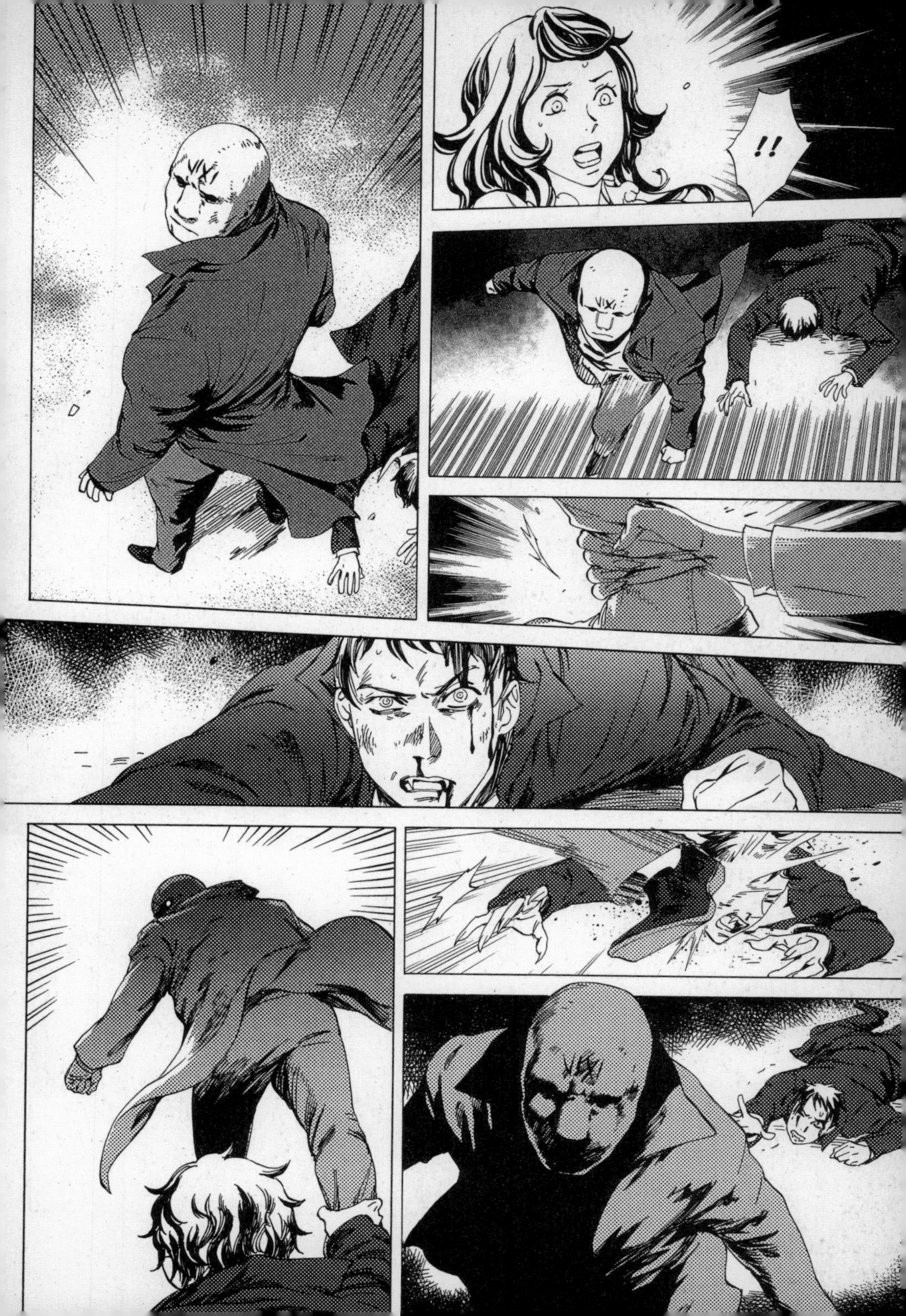
!!

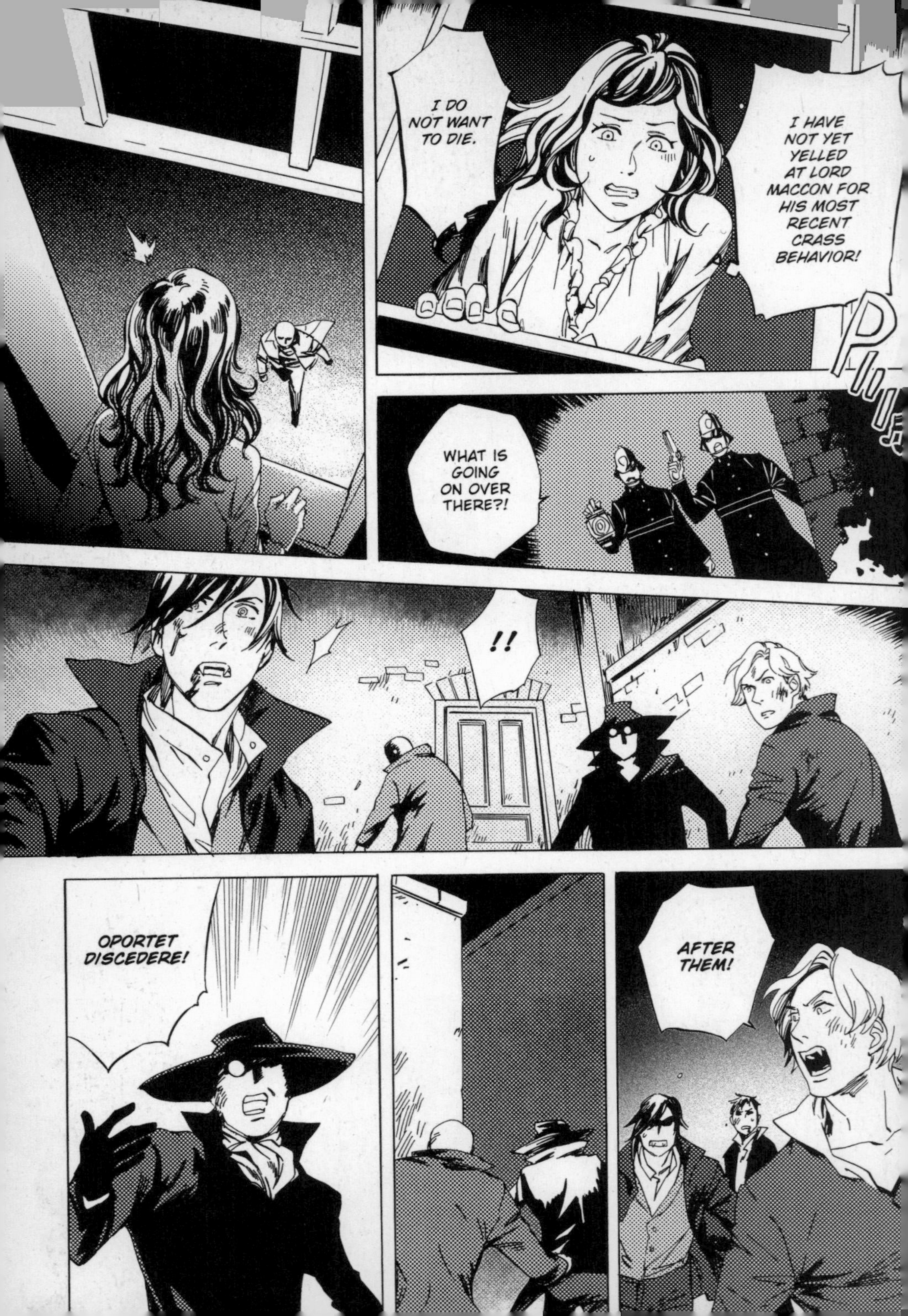
I DO NOT WANT TO DIE.
I HAVE NOT YET YELLED AT LORD MACCON FOR HIS MOST RECENT CRASS BEHAVIOR!
PLUU...
WHAT IS GOING ON OVER THERE?!
!!
OPORTET DISCEDERE!
AFTER THEM!

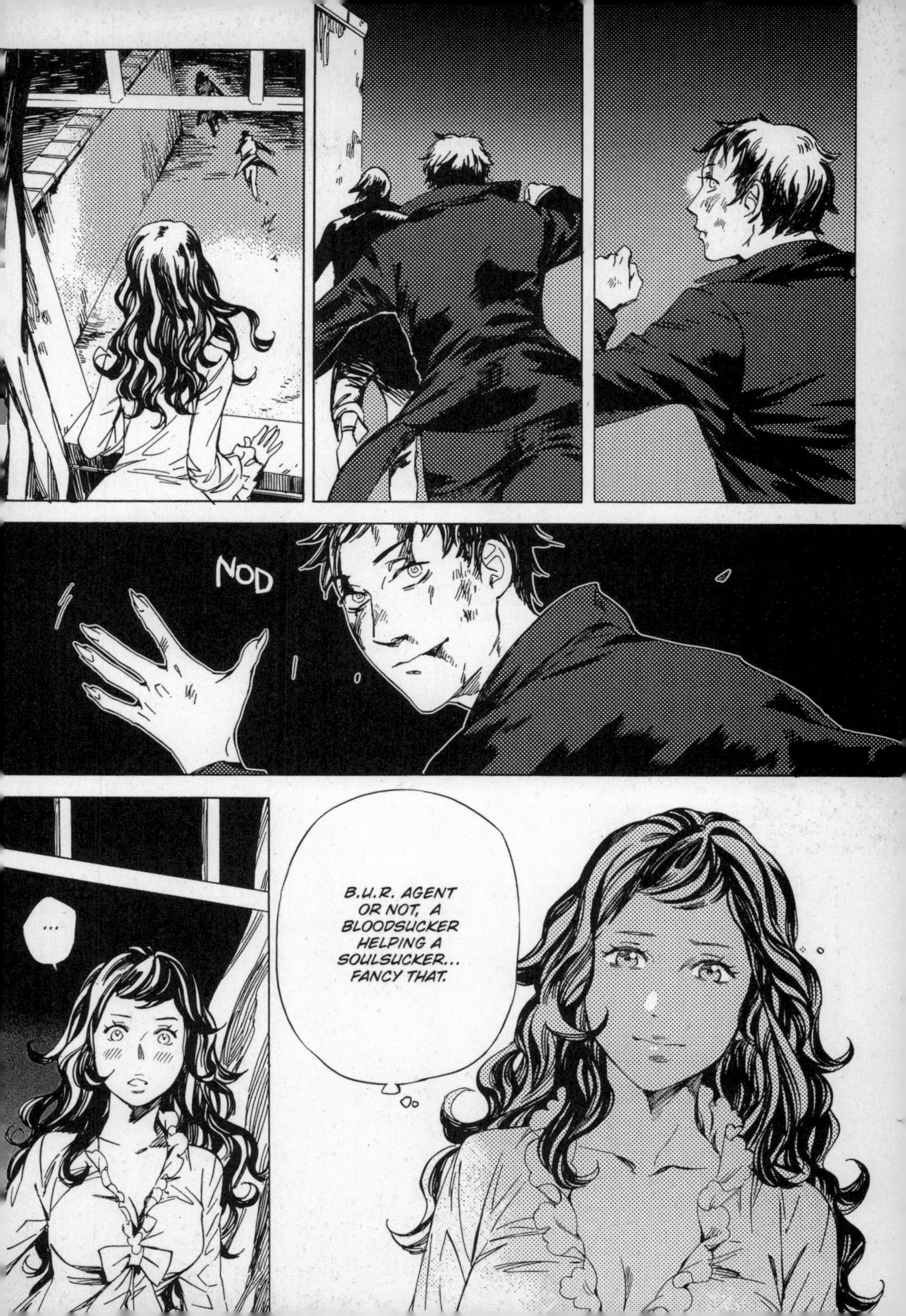
NOD
...
B.U.R. AGENT OR NOT, A BLOODSUCKER HELPING A SOULSUCKER... FANCY THAT.

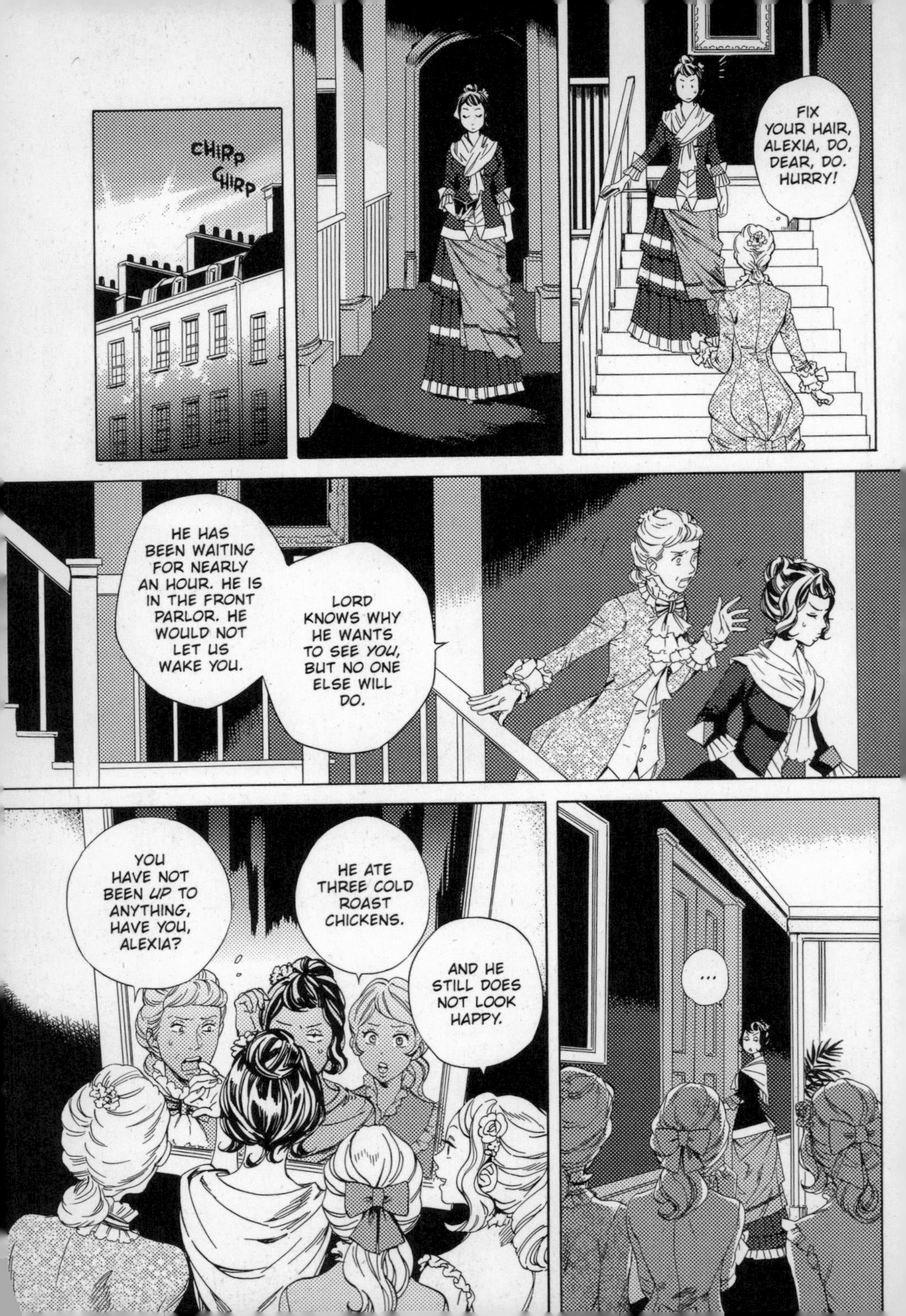
CHIRP CHIRP
FIX YOUR HAIR, ALEXIA, DO, DEAR, DO. HURRY!
HE HAS BEEN WAITING FOR NEARLY AN HOUR. HE IS IN THE FRONT PARLOR. HE WOULD NOT LET US WAKE YOU.
LORD KNOWS WHY HE WANTS TO SEE *YOU*, BUT NO ONE ELSE WILL DO.
YOU HAVE NOT BEEN *UP* TO ANYTHING, HAVE YOU, ALEXIA?
HE ATE THREE COLD ROAST CHICKENS.
AND HE STILL DOES NOT LOOK HAPPY.
...

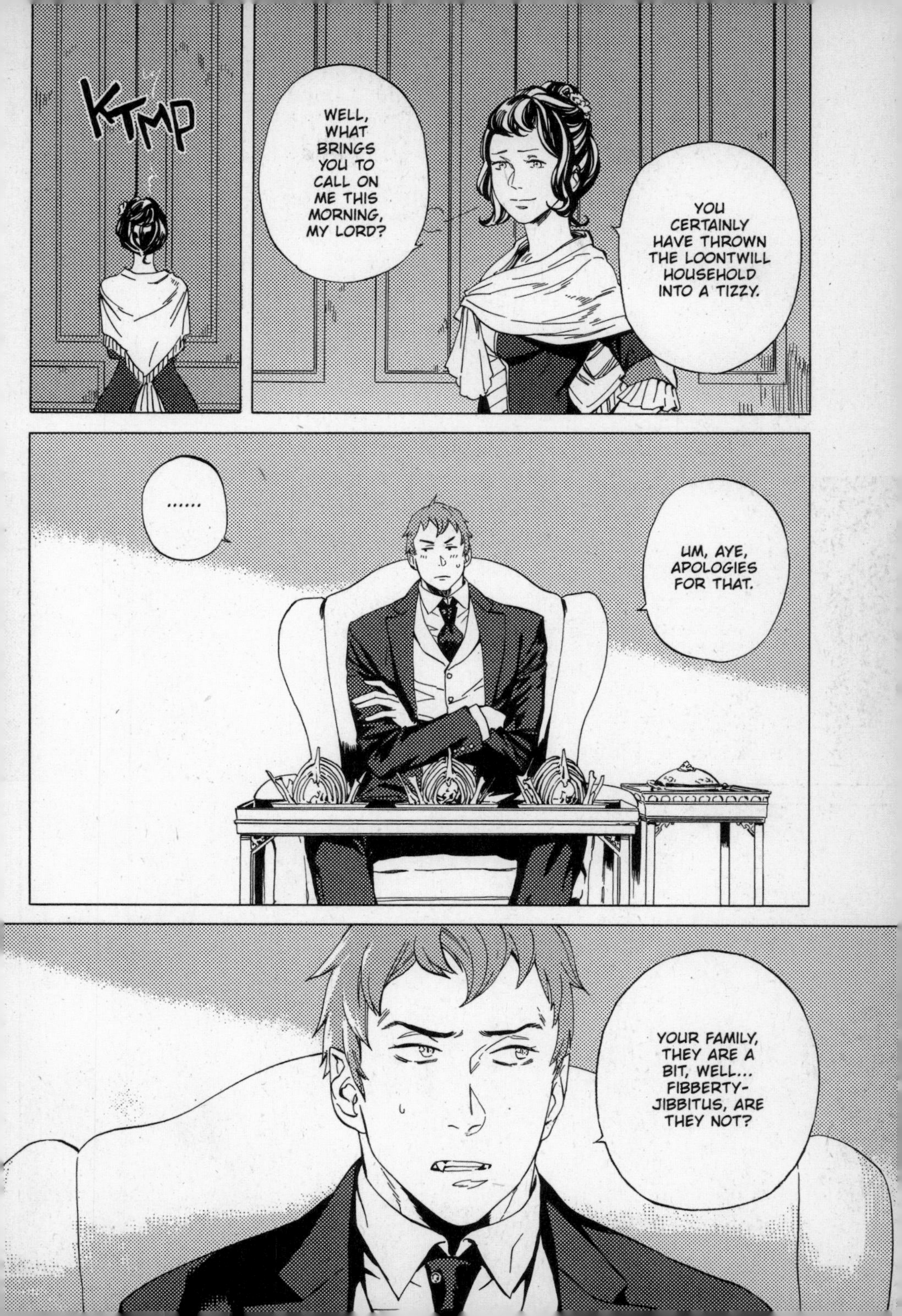
KTMP
WELL, WHAT BRINGS YOU TO CALL ON ME THIS MORNING, MY LORD?
YOU CERTAINLY HAVE THROWN THE LOONTWILL HOUSEHOLD INTO A TIZZY.
......
UM, AYE, APOLOGIES FOR THAT.
YOUR FAMILY, THEY ARE A BIT, WELL... FIBBERTY-JIBBITUS, ARE THEY NOT?

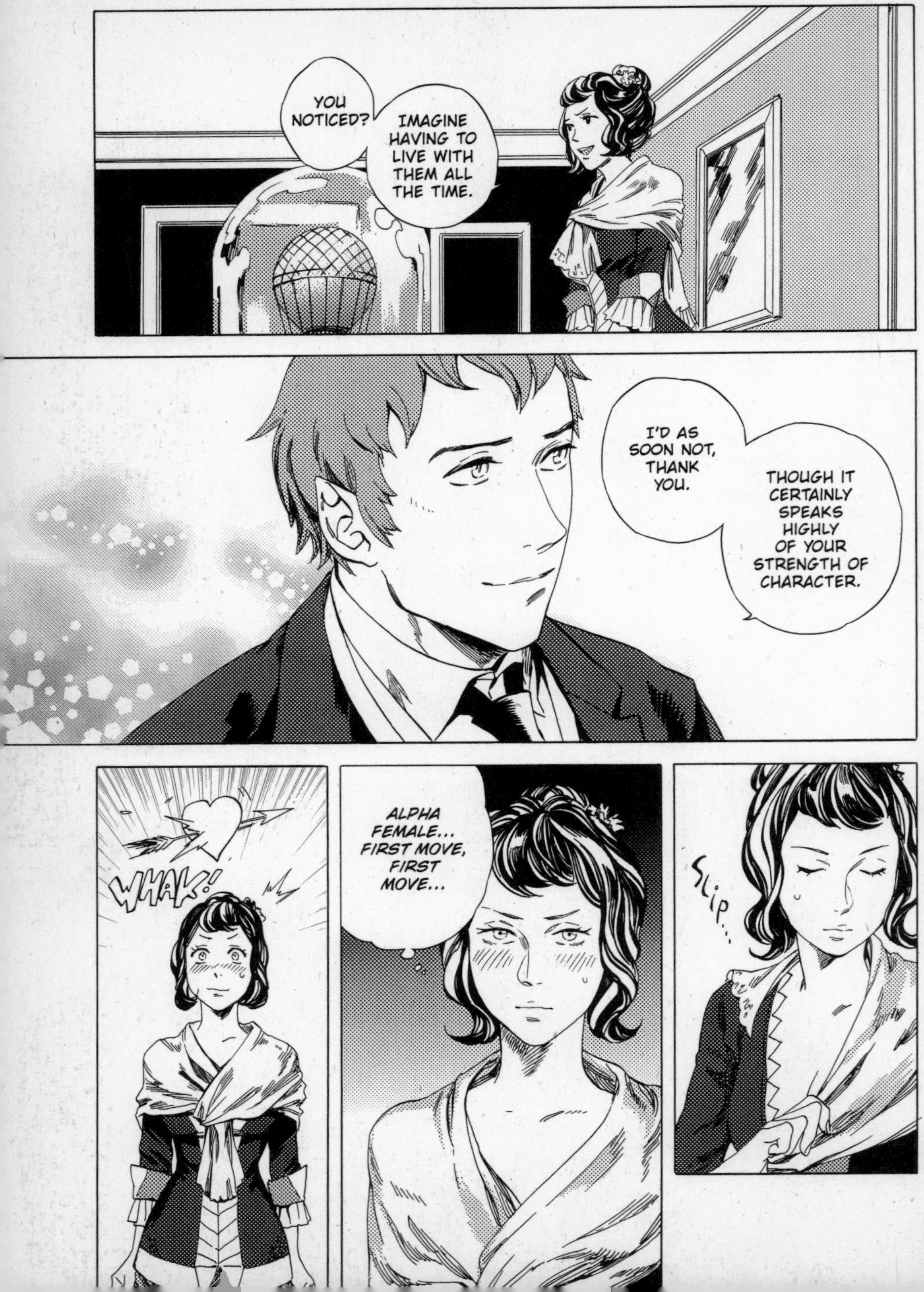
YOU NOTICED?
IMAGINE HAVING TO LIVE WITH THEM ALL THE TIME.
I'D AS SOON NOT, THANK YOU.
THOUGH IT CERTAINLY SPEAKS HIGHLY OF YOUR STRENGTH OF CHARACTER.
WHAK!
ALPHA FEMALE... FIRST MOVE, FIRST MOVE...
SLIP...

IT IS UNSEASONABLY WARM THIS MORNING, WOULDN'T YOU SAY?

AH...

YESTERDAY AFTERNOON, WHILE YOU AND I WERE...

...OTHERWISE ENGAGED, SOMEONE BROKE INTO B.U.R. HEADQUARTERS.

THIS CANNOT POSSIBLY BE GOOD. WAS ANYONE GRIEVOUSLY INJURED? HAVE YOU CAUGHT THE CULPRITS? WAS ANYTHING OF VALUE STOLEN?

NOT SERIOUSLY. NO.

AND MOSTLY ROVE VAMPIRE AND LONER WOLF FILES. SOME OF THE MORE DETAILED RESEARCH DOCUMENTATION ALSO VANISHED, AND...

AND?

YOUR FILES.

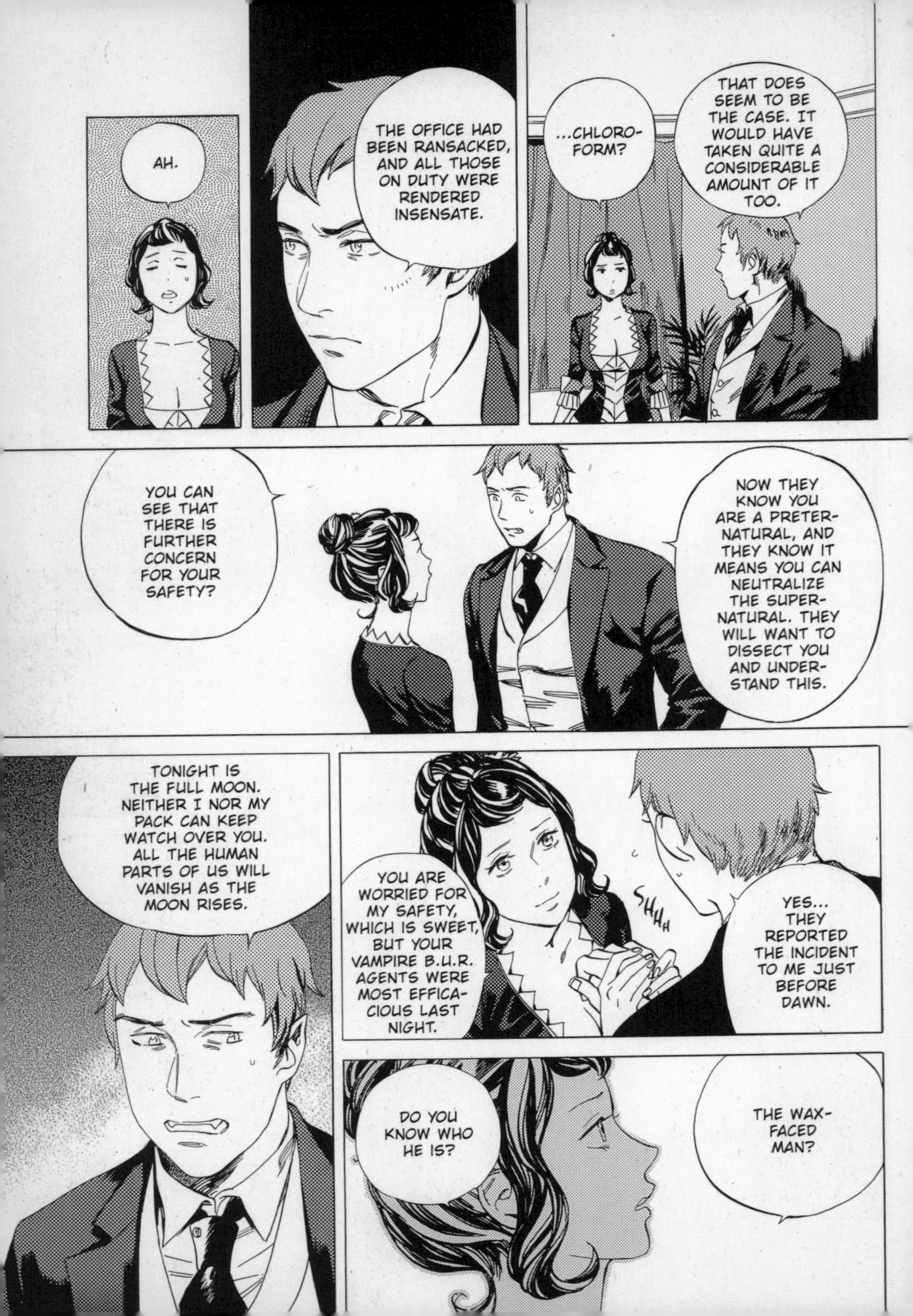
AH.
THE OFFICE HAD BEEN RANSACKED, AND ALL THOSE ON DUTY WERE RENDERED INSENSATE.
...CHLORO-FORM?
THAT DOES SEEM TO BE THE CASE. IT WOULD HAVE TAKEN QUITE A CONSIDERABLE AMOUNT OF IT TOO.
YOU CAN SEE THAT THERE IS FURTHER CONCERN FOR YOUR SAFETY?
NOW THEY KNOW YOU ARE A PRETER-NATURAL, AND THEY KNOW IT MEANS YOU CAN NEUTRALIZE THE SUPER-NATURAL. THEY WILL WANT TO DISSECT YOU AND UNDER-STAND THIS.
TONIGHT IS THE FULL MOON. NEITHER I NOR MY PACK CAN KEEP WATCH OVER YOU. ALL THE HUMAN PARTS OF US WILL VANISH AS THE MOON RISES.
YOU ARE WORRIED FOR MY SAFETY, WHICH IS SWEET, BUT YOUR VAMPIRE B.U.R. AGENTS WERE MOST EFFICA-CIOUS LAST NIGHT.
SHHH
YES... THEY REPORTED THE INCIDENT TO ME JUST BEFORE DAWN.
DO YOU KNOW WHO HE IS?
THE WAX-FACED MAN?

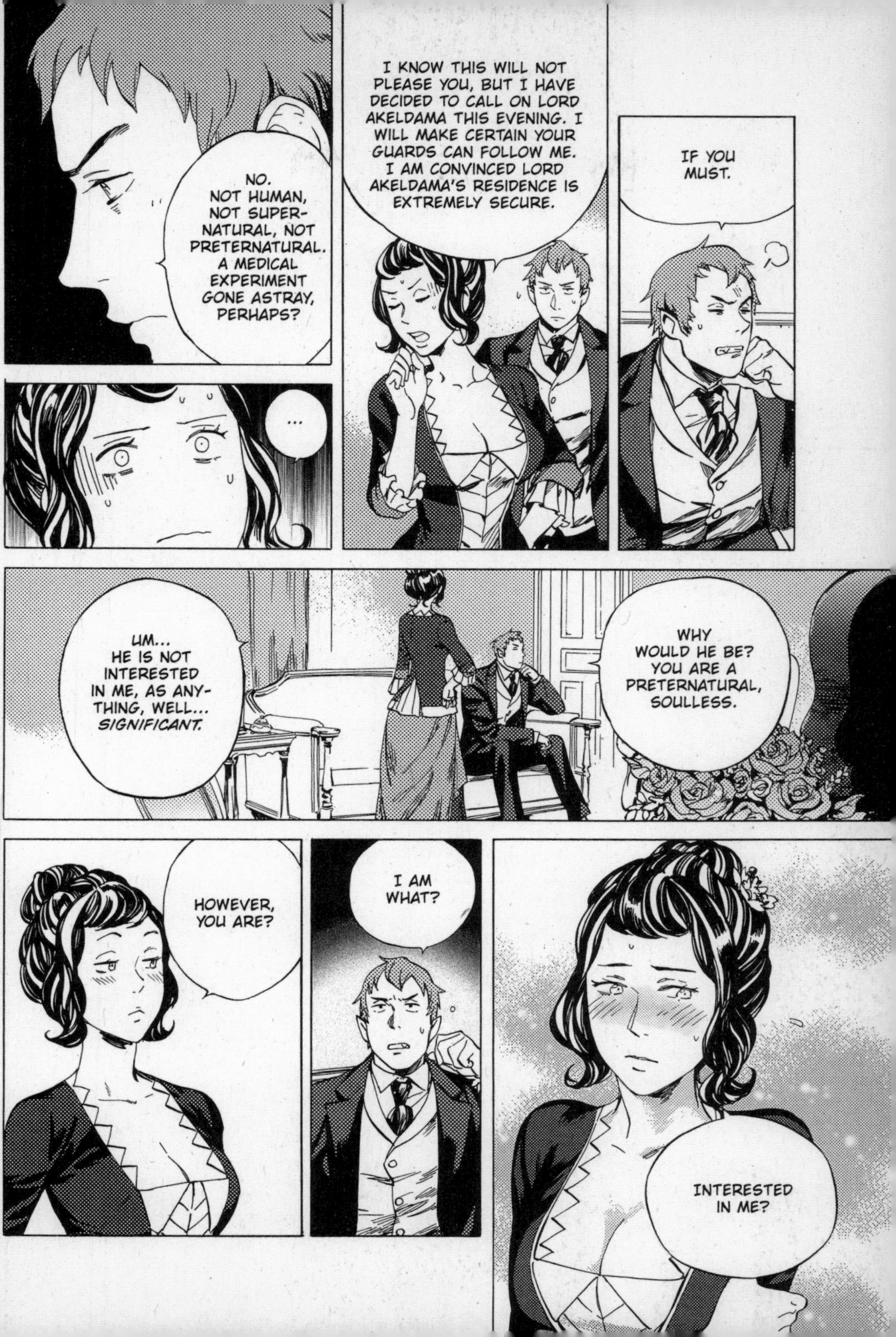
NO. NOT HUMAN, NOT SUPER-NATURAL, NOT PRETERNATURAL. A MEDICAL EXPERIMENT GONE ASTRAY, PERHAPS?
I KNOW THIS WILL NOT PLEASE YOU, BUT I HAVE DECIDED TO CALL ON LORD AKELDAMA THIS EVENING. I WILL MAKE CERTAIN YOUR GUARDS CAN FOLLOW ME. I AM CONVINCED LORD AKELDAMA'S RESIDENCE IS EXTREMELY SECURE.
IF YOU MUST.
...
UM... HE IS NOT INTERESTED IN ME, AS ANY-THING, WELL... *SIGNIFICANT.*
WHY WOULD HE BE? YOU ARE A PRETERNATURAL, SOULLESS.
HOWEVER, YOU ARE?
I AM WHAT?
INTERESTED IN ME?

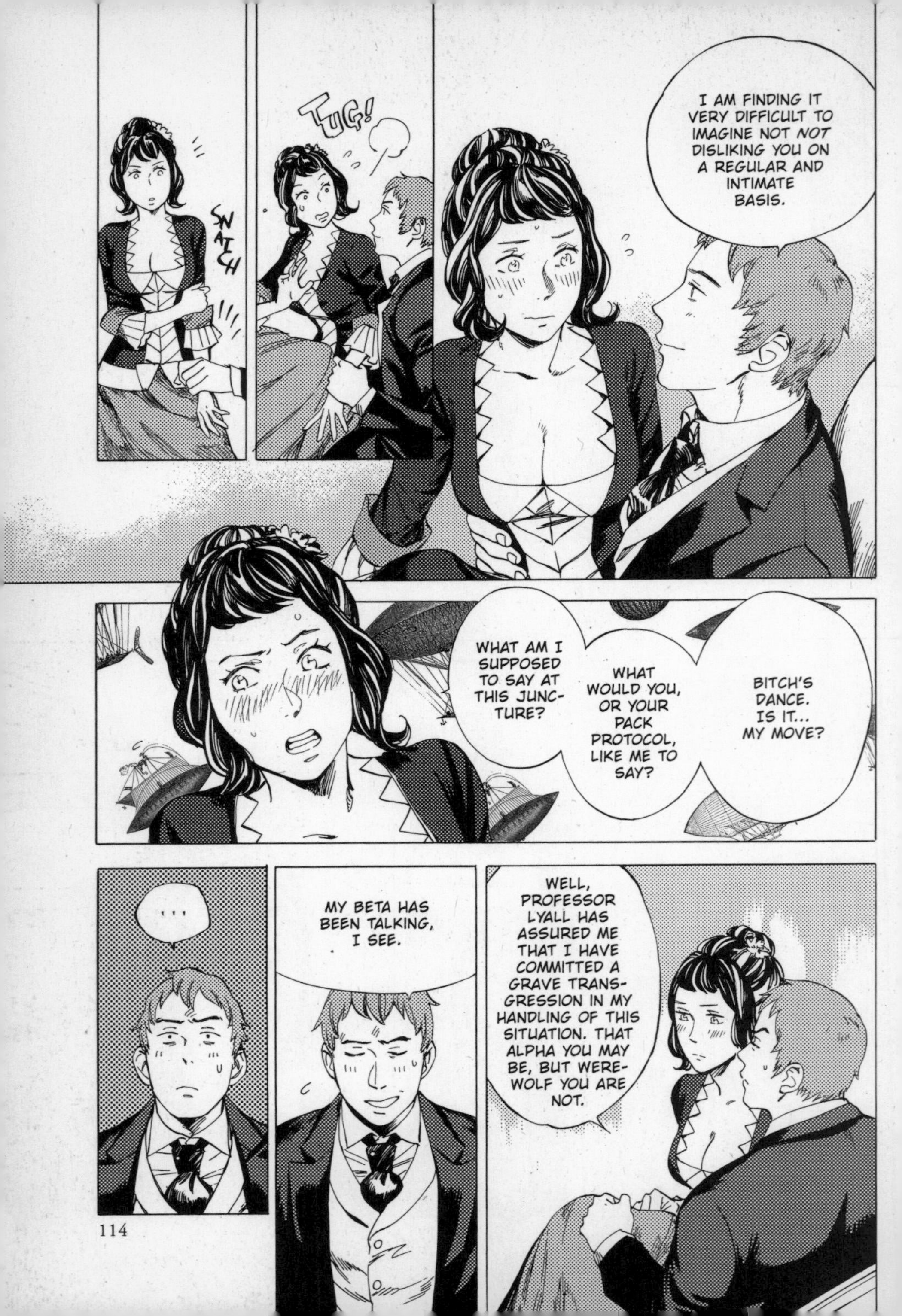
SNATCH
TUG!
I AM FINDING IT VERY DIFFICULT TO IMAGINE NOT *NOT* DISLIKING YOU ON A REGULAR AND INTIMATE BASIS.
WHAT AM I SUPPOSED TO SAY AT THIS JUNCTURE?
WHAT WOULD YOU, OR YOUR PACK PROTOCOL, LIKE ME TO SAY?
BITCH'S DANCE. IS IT... MY MOVE?
...
MY BETA HAS BEEN TALKING, I SEE.
WELL, PROFESSOR LYALL HAS ASSURED ME THAT I HAVE COMMITTED A GRAVE TRANSGRESSION IN MY HANDLING OF THIS SITUATION. THAT ALPHA YOU MAY BE, BUT WEREWOLF YOU ARE NOT.

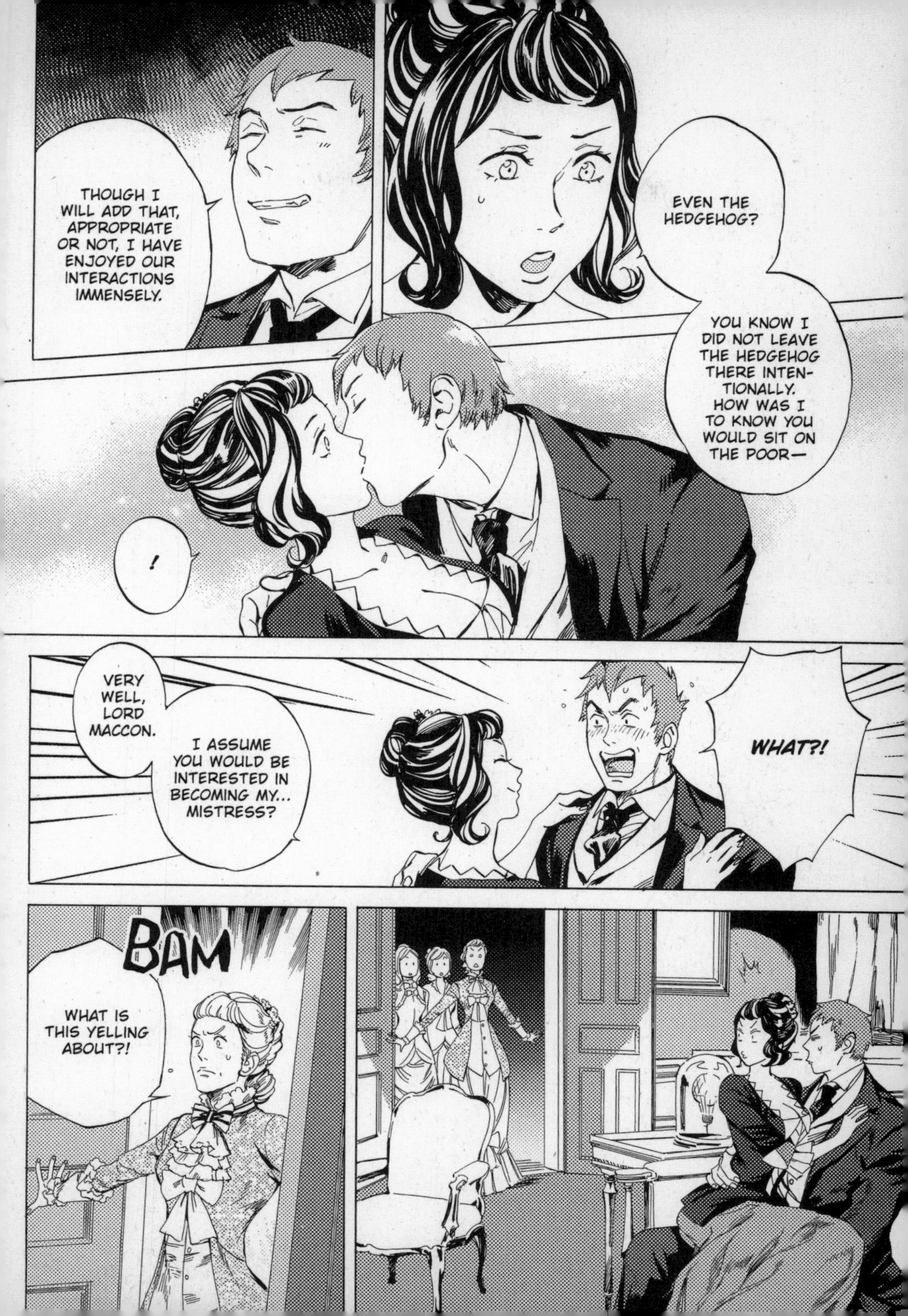
THOUGH I WILL ADD THAT, APPROPRIATE OR NOT, I HAVE ENJOYED OUR INTERACTIONS IMMENSELY.
EVEN THE HEDGEHOG?
YOU KNOW I DID NOT LEAVE THE HEDGEHOG THERE INTEN-TIONALLY. HOW WAS I TO KNOW YOU WOULD SIT ON THE POOR—
!
VERY WELL, LORD MACCON.
I ASSUME YOU WOULD BE INTERESTED IN BECOMING MY... MISTRESS?
WHAT?!
BAM
WHAT IS THIS YELLING ABOUT?!

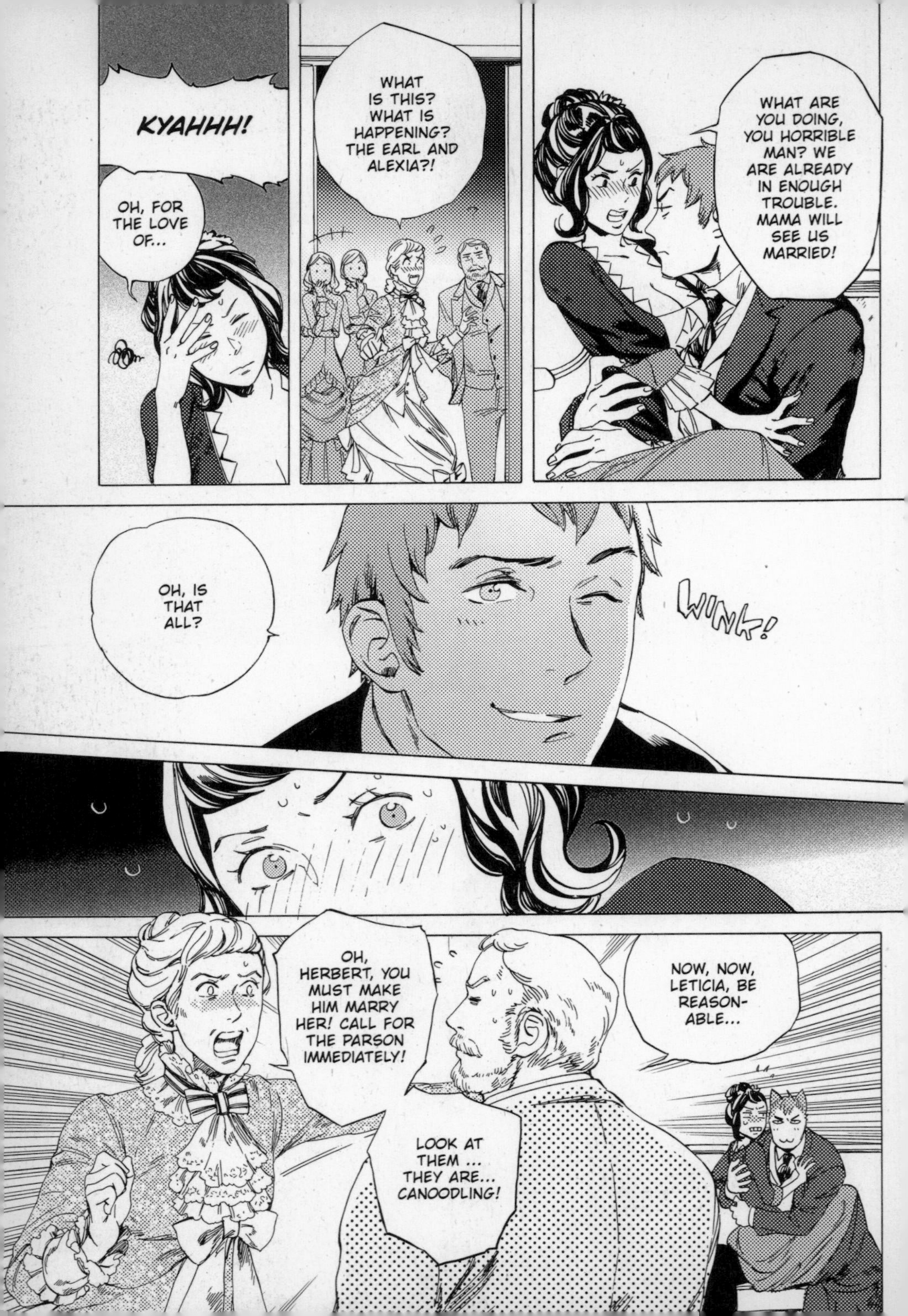
KYAHHH!
OH, FOR THE LOVE OF...
WHAT IS THIS? WHAT IS HAPPENING? THE EARL AND ALEXIA?!
WHAT ARE YOU DOING, YOU HORRIBLE MAN? WE ARE ALREADY IN ENOUGH TROUBLE. MAMA WILL SEE US MARRIED!
OH, IS THAT ALL?
WINK!
OH, HERBERT, YOU MUST MAKE HIM MARRY HER! CALL FOR THE PARSON IMMEDIATELY!
LOOK AT THEM ... THEY ARE... CANOODLING!
NOW, NOW, LETICIA, BE REASON-ABLE...

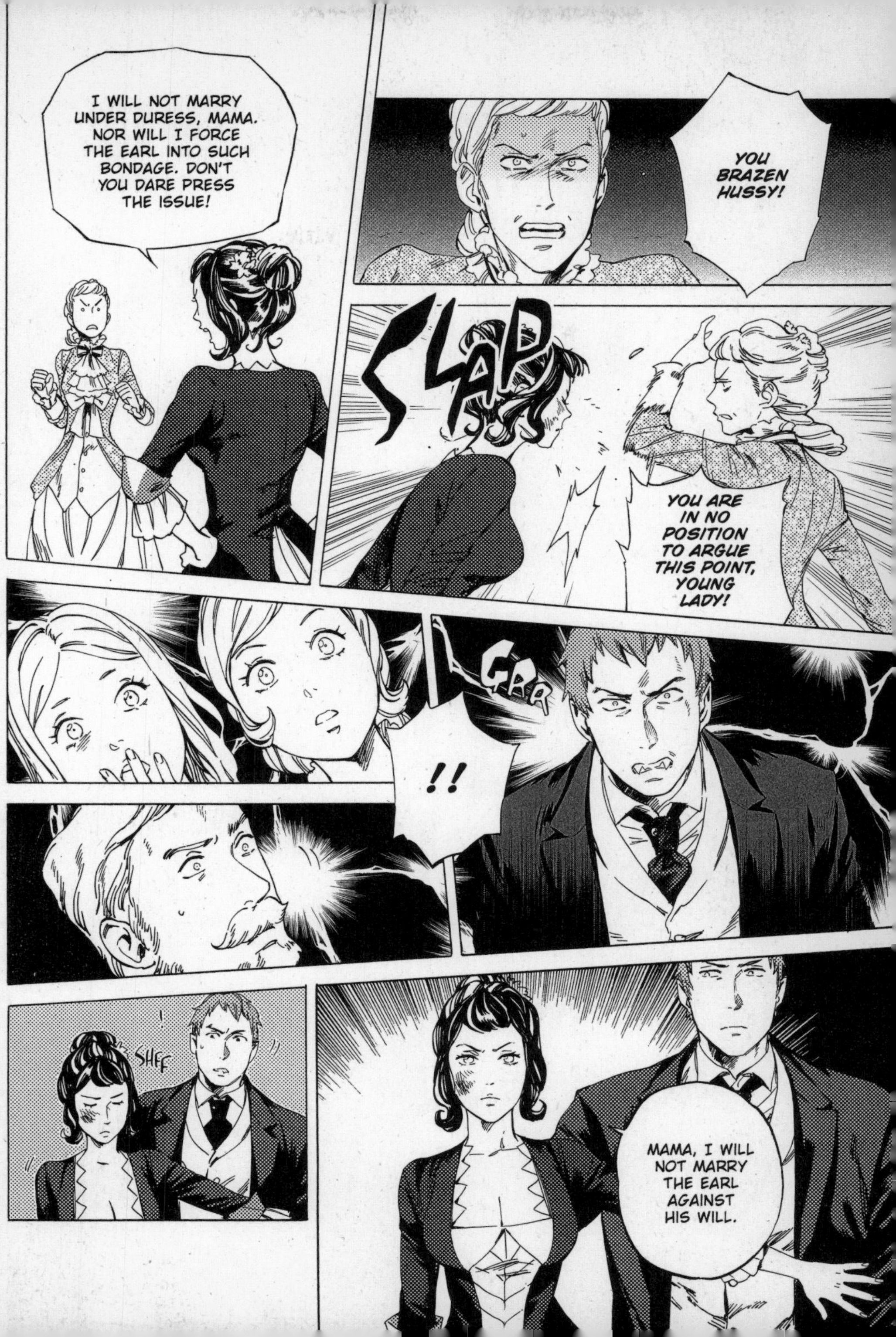
I WILL NOT MARRY UNDER DURESS, MAMA. NOR WILL I FORCE THE EARL INTO SUCH BONDAGE. DON'T YOU DARE PRESS THE ISSUE!
YOU BRAZEN HUSSY!
SLAP
YOU ARE IN NO POSITION TO ARGUE THIS POINT, YOUNG LADY!
GRR
!!
SHFF
MAMA, I WILL NOT MARRY THE EARL AGAINST HIS WILL.

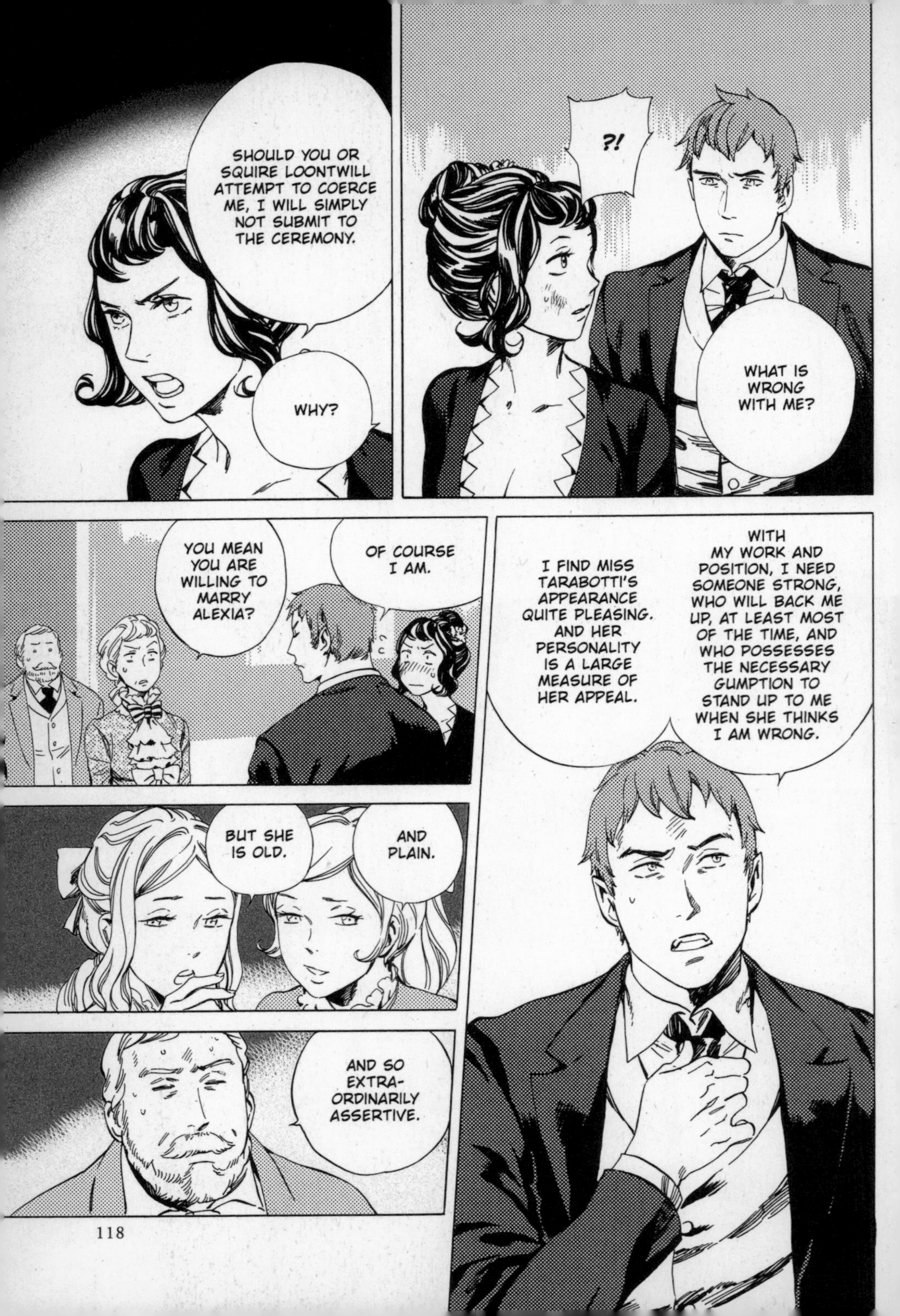

SHOULD YOU OR SQUIRE LOONTWILL ATTEMPT TO COERCE ME, I WILL SIMPLY NOT SUBMIT TO THE CEREMONY.
WHY?
?!
WHAT IS WRONG WITH ME?
YOU MEAN YOU ARE WILLING TO MARRY ALEXIA?
OF COURSE I AM.
BUT SHE IS OLD.
AND PLAIN.
AND SO EXTRA-ORDINARILY ASSERTIVE.
I FIND MISS TARABOTTI'S APPEARANCE QUITE PLEASING. AND HER PERSONALITY IS A LARGE MEASURE OF HER APPEAL.
WITH MY WORK AND POSITION, I NEED SOMEONE STRONG, WHO WILL BACK ME UP, AT LEAST MOST OF THE TIME, AND WHO POSSESSES THE NECESSARY GUMPTION TO STAND UP TO ME WHEN SHE THINKS I AM WRONG.

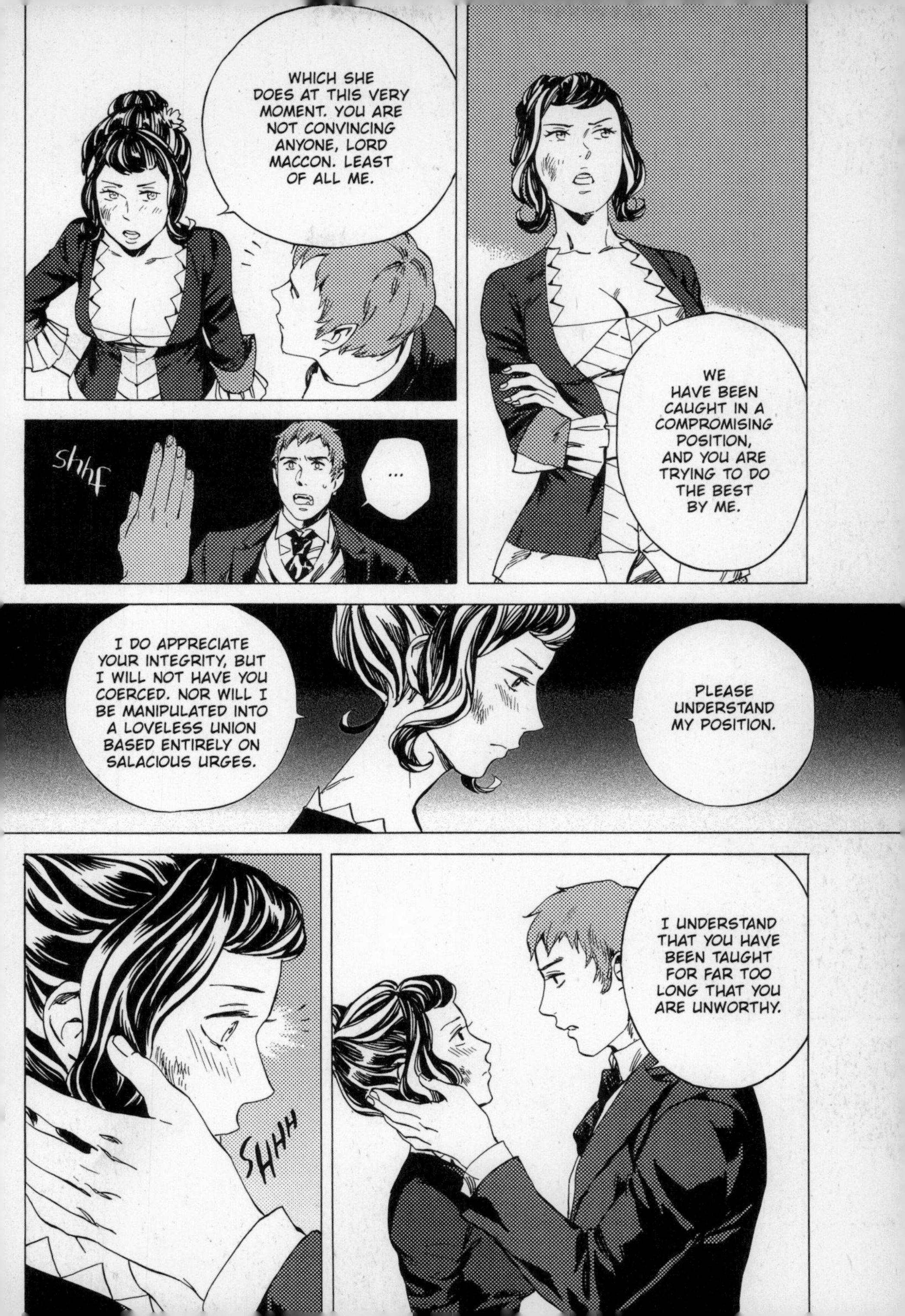
WHICH SHE DOES AT THIS VERY MOMENT. YOU ARE NOT CONVINCING ANYONE, LORD MACCON. LEAST OF ALL ME.
WE HAVE BEEN CAUGHT IN A COMPROMISING POSITION, AND YOU ARE TRYING TO DO THE BEST BY ME.
shhf
...
I DO APPRECIATE YOUR INTEGRITY, BUT I WILL NOT HAVE YOU COERCED. NOR WILL I BE MANIPULATED INTO A LOVELESS UNION BASED ENTIRELY ON SALACIOUS URGES.
PLEASE UNDERSTAND MY POSITION.
SHHH
I UNDERSTAND THAT YOU HAVE BEEN TAUGHT FOR FAR TOO LONG THAT YOU ARE UNWORTHY.

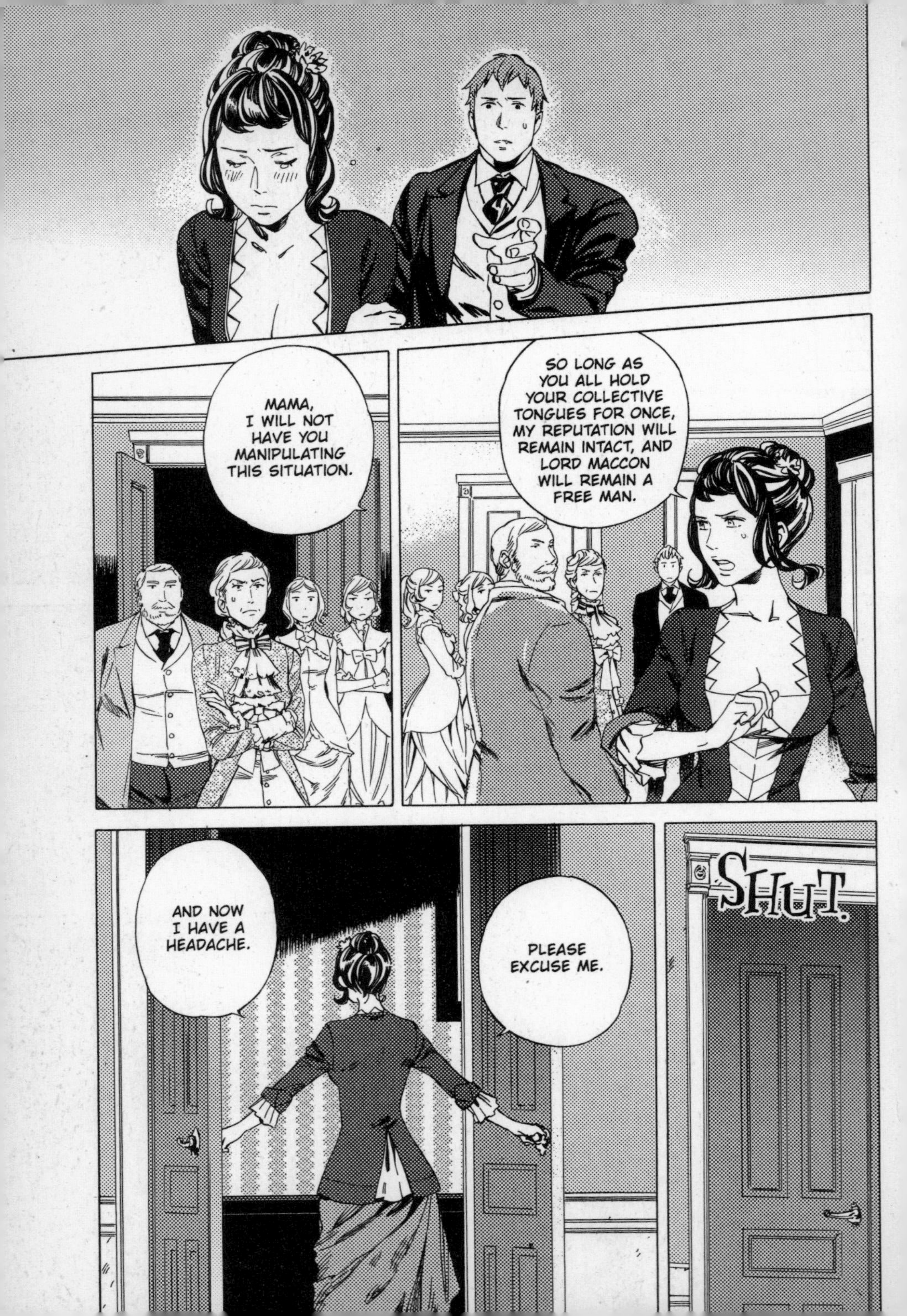
MAMA, I WILL NOT HAVE YOU MANIPULATING THIS SITUATION.
SO LONG AS YOU ALL HOLD YOUR COLLECTIVE TONGUES FOR ONCE, MY REPUTATION WILL REMAIN INTACT, AND LORD MACCON WILL REMAIN A FREE MAN.
AND NOW I HAVE A HEADACHE.
PLEASE EXCUSE ME.
SHUT.

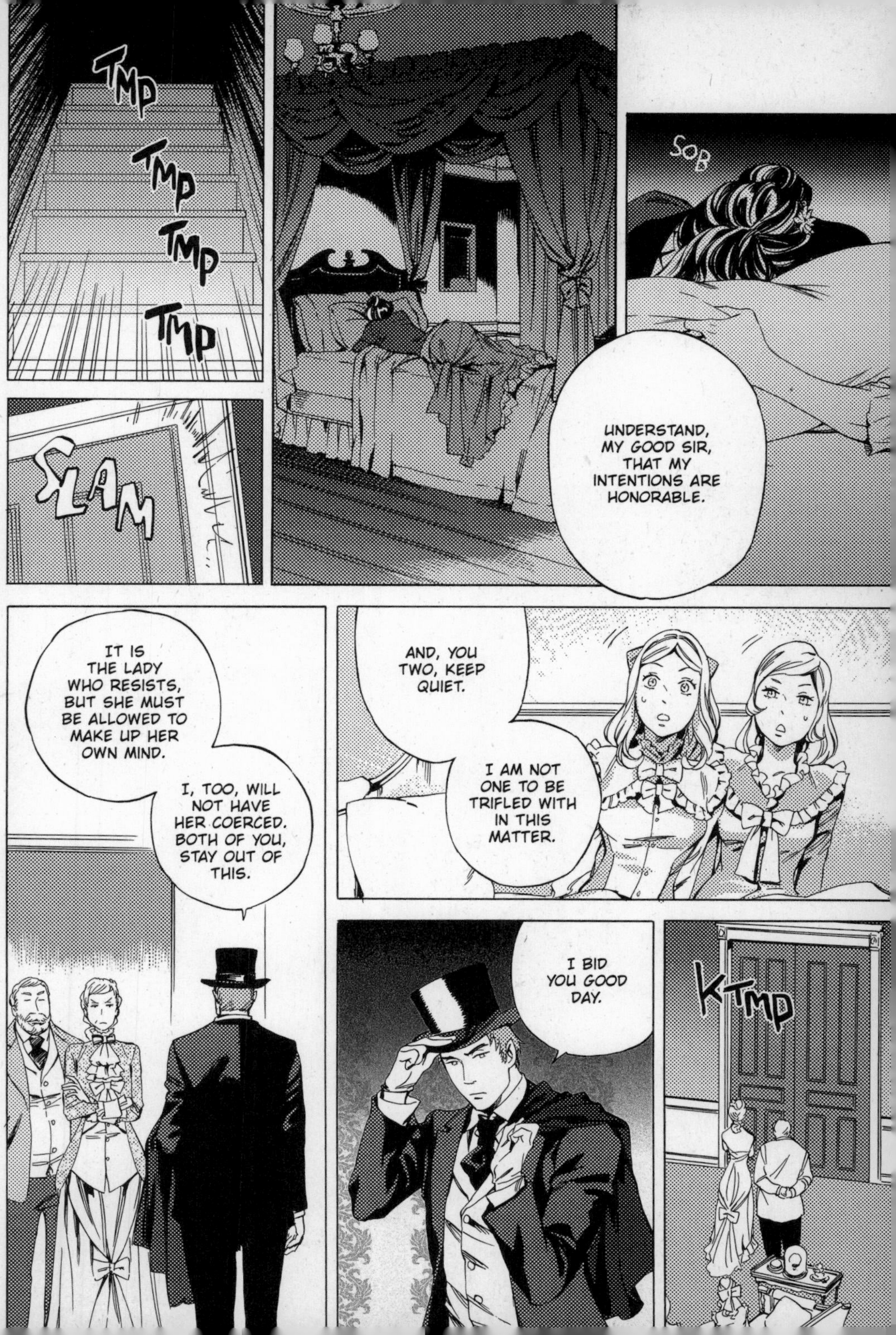
TMP
TMP
TMP
TMP
SLAM
SOB
UNDERSTAND, MY GOOD SIR, THAT MY INTENTIONS ARE HONORABLE.
IT IS THE LADY WHO RESISTS, BUT SHE MUST BE ALLOWED TO MAKE UP HER OWN MIND.
I, TOO, WILL NOT HAVE HER COERCED. BOTH OF YOU, STAY OUT OF THIS.
AND, YOU TWO, KEEP QUIET.
I AM NOT ONE TO BE TRIFLED WITH IN THIS MATTER.
I BID YOU GOOD DAY.
KTMP

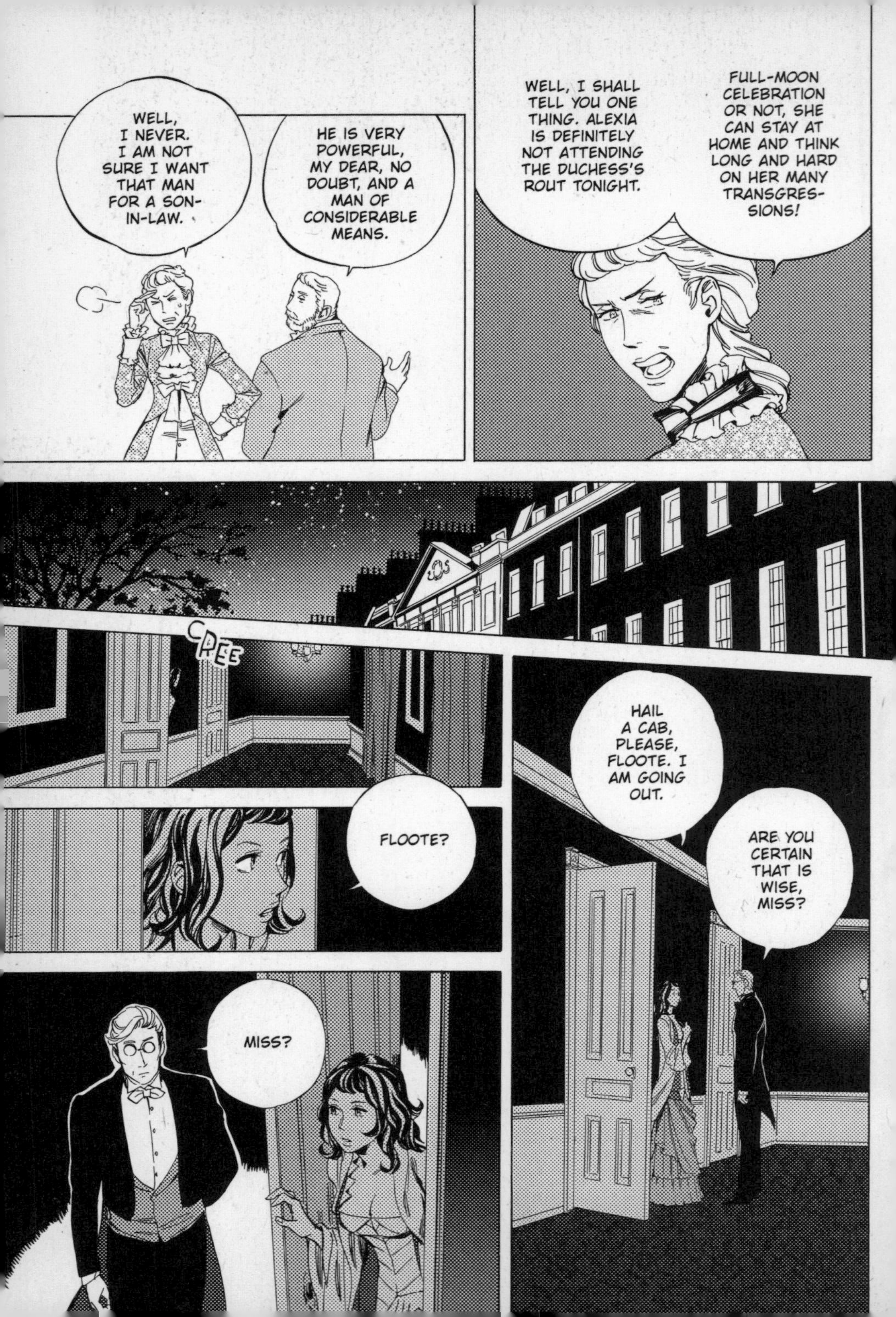
WELL, I NEVER. I AM NOT SURE I WANT THAT MAN FOR A SON-IN-LAW.
HE IS VERY POWERFUL, MY DEAR, NO DOUBT, AND A MAN OF CONSIDERABLE MEANS.
WELL, I SHALL TELL YOU ONE THING. ALEXIA IS DEFINITELY NOT ATTENDING THE DUCHESS'S ROUT TONIGHT.
FULL-MOON CELEBRATION OR NOT, SHE CAN STAY AT HOME AND THINK LONG AND HARD ON HER MANY TRANSGRES-SIONS!
CREE
FLOOTE?
MISS?
HAIL A CAB, PLEASE, FLOOTE. I AM GOING OUT.
ARE YOU CERTAIN THAT IS WISE, MISS?

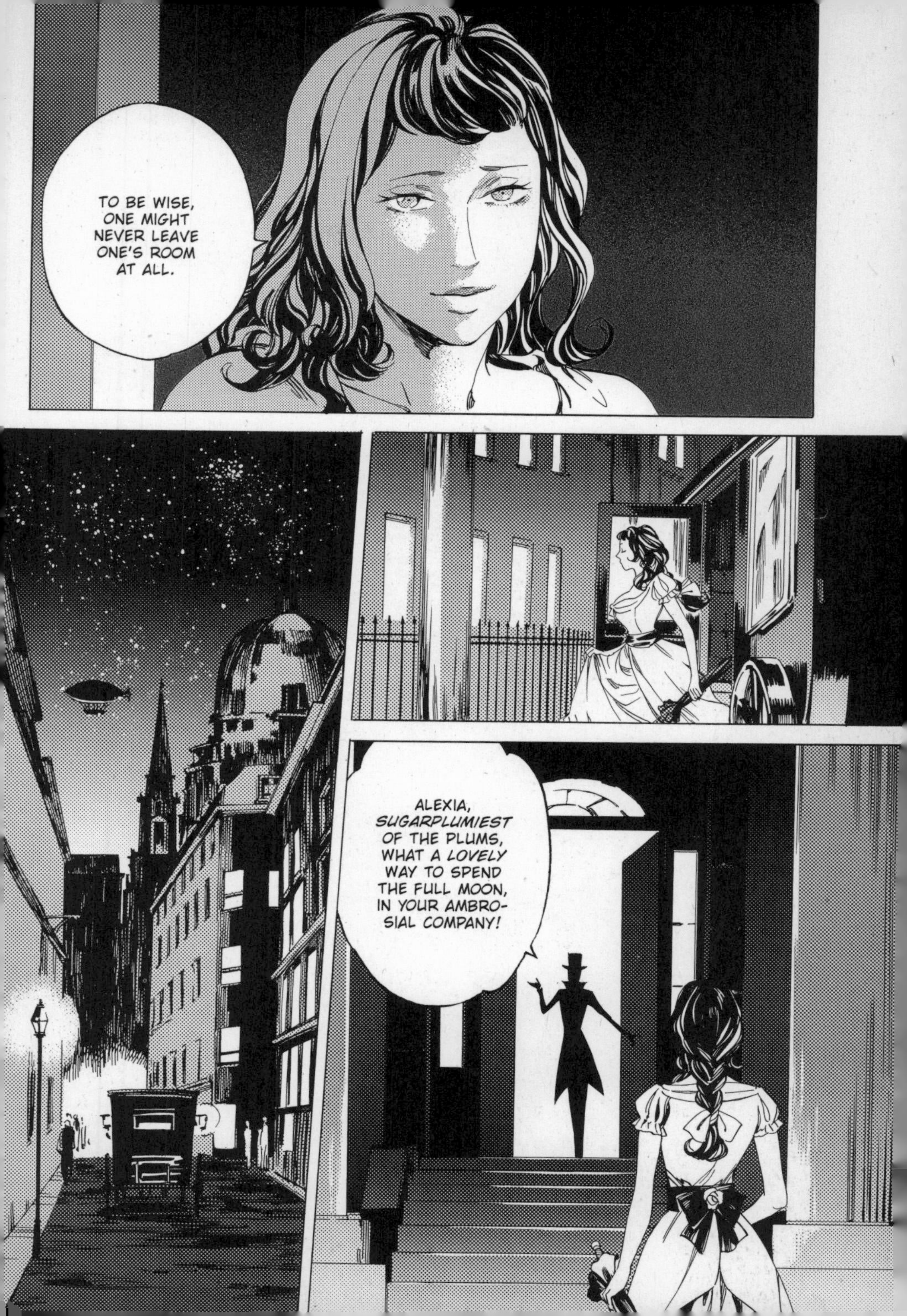
TO BE WISE, ONE MIGHT NEVER LEAVE ONE'S ROOM AT ALL.
ALEXIA, *SUGARPLUMIEST* OF THE PLUMS, WHAT A *LOVELY* WAY TO SPEND THE FULL MOON, IN YOUR AMBROSIAL COMPANY!

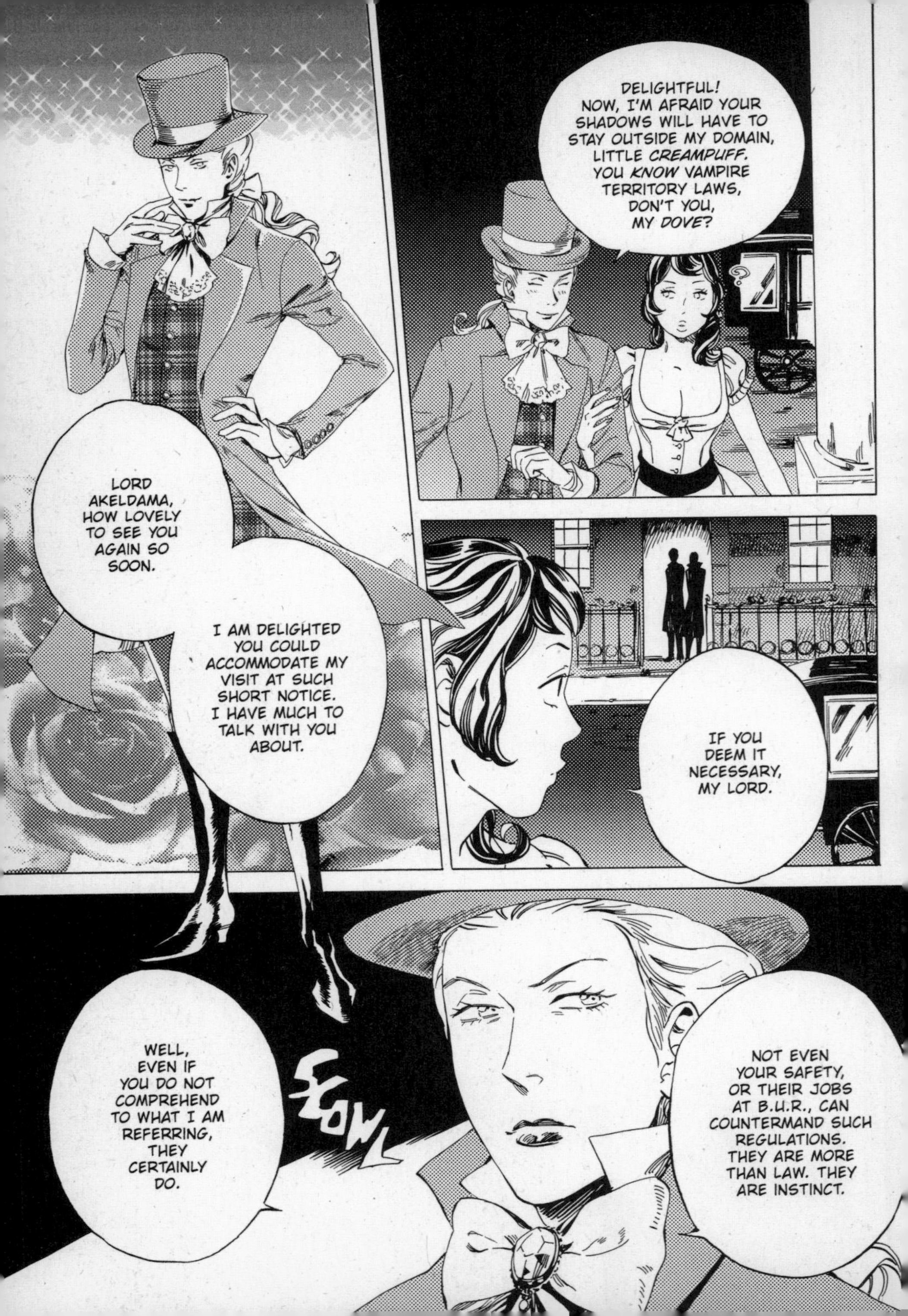
LORD AKELDAMA, HOW LOVELY TO SEE YOU AGAIN SO SOON.
I AM DELIGHTED YOU COULD ACCOMMODATE MY VISIT AT SUCH SHORT NOTICE. I HAVE MUCH TO TALK WITH YOU ABOUT.
DELIGHTFUL! NOW, I'M AFRAID YOUR SHADOWS WILL HAVE TO STAY OUTSIDE MY DOMAIN, LITTLE *CREAMPUFF.* YOU *KNOW* VAMPIRE TERRITORY LAWS, DON'T YOU, MY *DOVE?*
?
IF YOU DEEM IT NECESSARY, MY LORD.
WELL, EVEN IF YOU DO NOT COMPREHEND TO WHAT I AM REFERRING, THEY CERTAINLY DO.
SCOWL
NOT EVEN YOUR SAFETY, OR THEIR JOBS AT B.U.R., CAN COUNTERMAND SUCH REGULATIONS. THEY ARE MORE THAN LAW. THEY ARE INSTINCT.

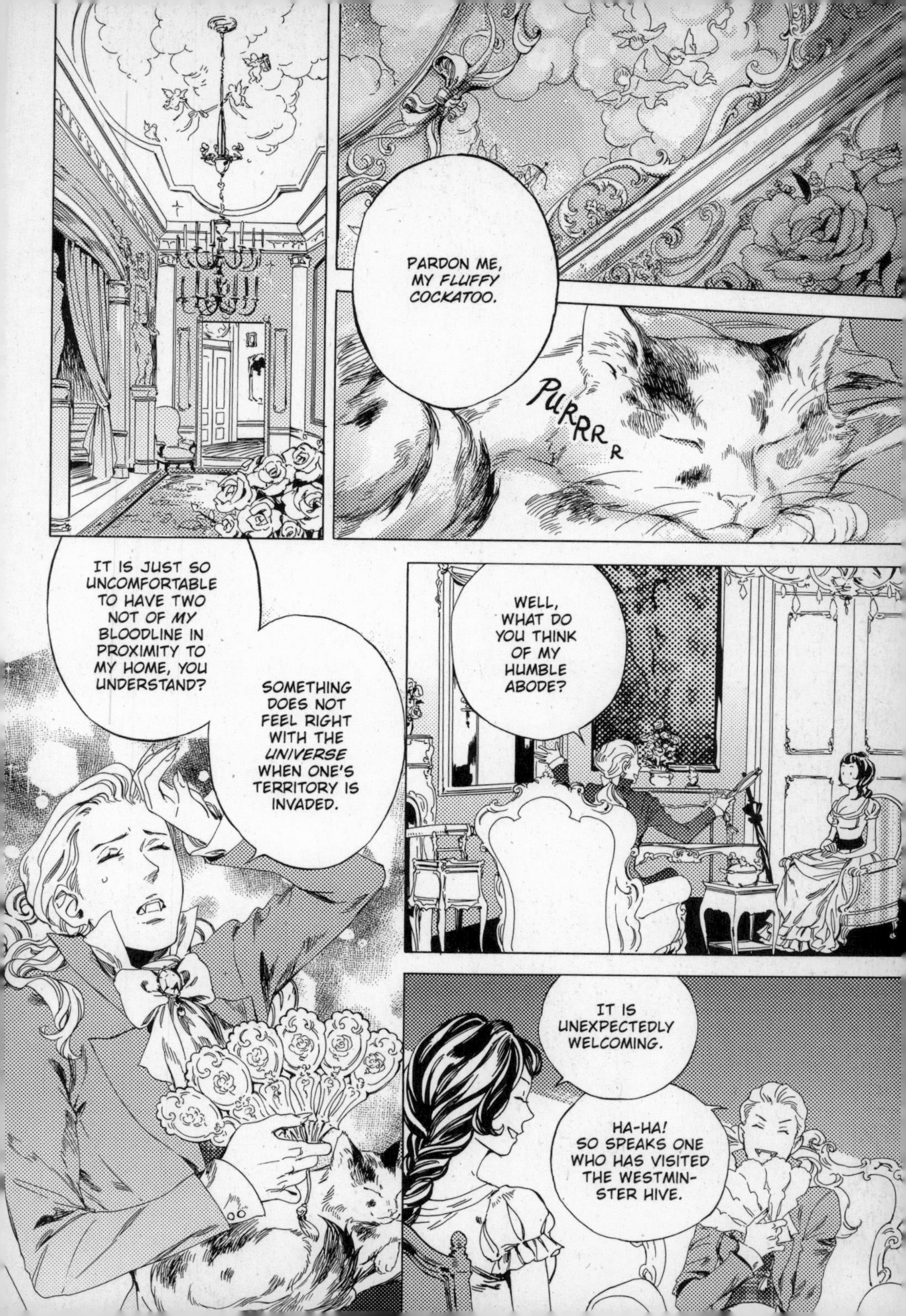
PARDON ME, MY *FLUFFY* COCKATOO.
PURRRRR
IT IS JUST SO UNCOMFORTABLE TO HAVE TWO NOT OF *MY* BLOODLINE IN PROXIMITY TO MY HOME, YOU UNDERSTAND?
SOMETHING DOES NOT FEEL RIGHT WITH THE *UNIVERSE* WHEN ONE'S TERRITORY IS INVADED.
WELL, WHAT DO YOU THINK OF MY HUMBLE ABODE?
IT IS UNEXPECTEDLY WELCOMING.
HA-HA! SO SPEAKS ONE WHO HAS VISITED THE WESTMIN-STER HIVE.

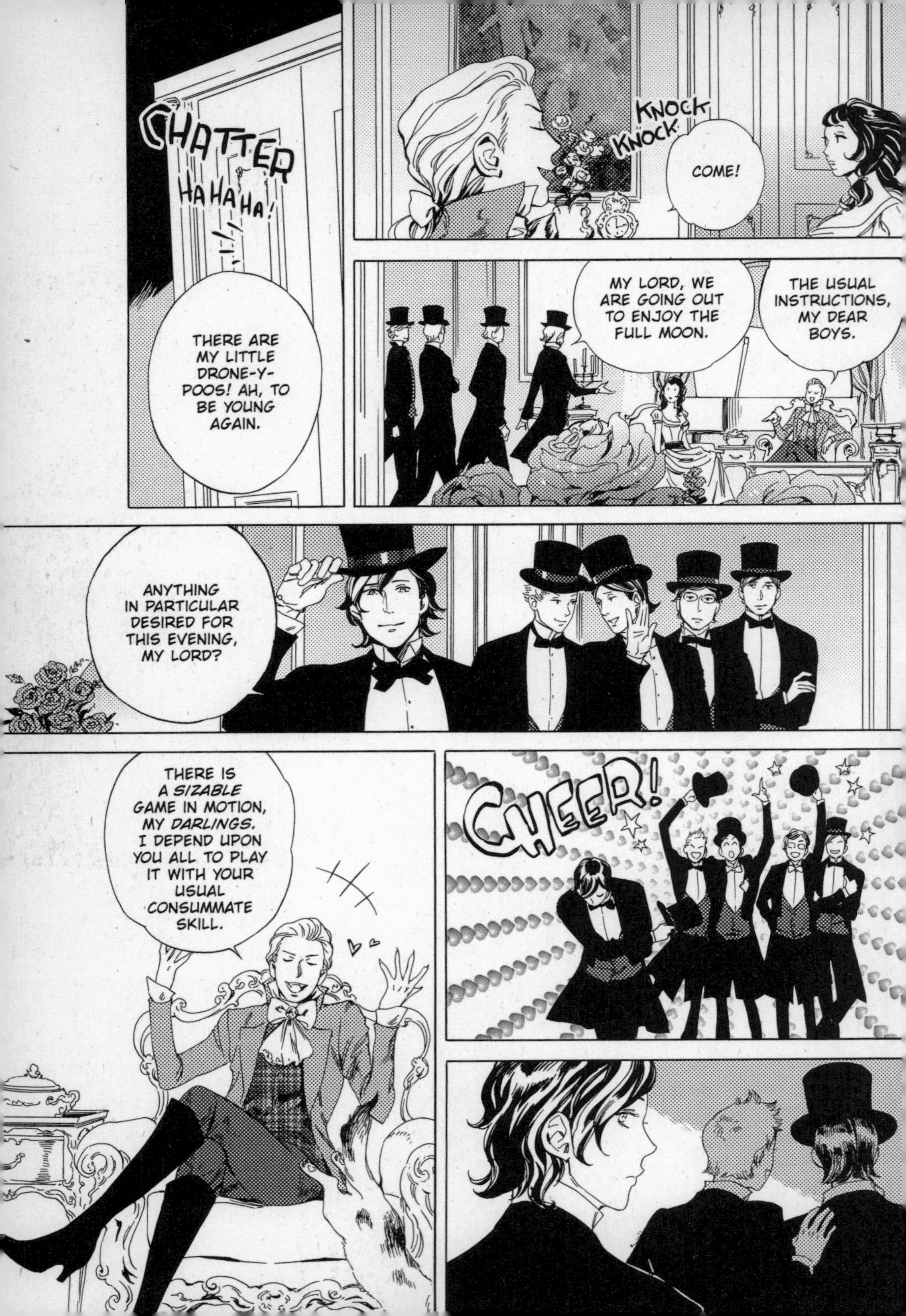
CHATTER
HA HA HA!
THERE ARE MY LITTLE DRONE-Y-POOS! AH, TO BE YOUNG AGAIN.
KNOCK KNOCK
COME!
MY LORD, WE ARE GOING OUT TO ENJOY THE FULL MOON.
THE USUAL INSTRUCTIONS, MY DEAR BOYS.
ANYTHING IN PARTICULAR DESIRED FOR THIS EVENING, MY LORD?
THERE IS A *SIZABLE* GAME IN MOTION, MY *DARLINGS*. I DEPEND UPON YOU ALL TO PLAY IT WITH YOUR USUAL CONSUMMATE SKILL.
CHEER!

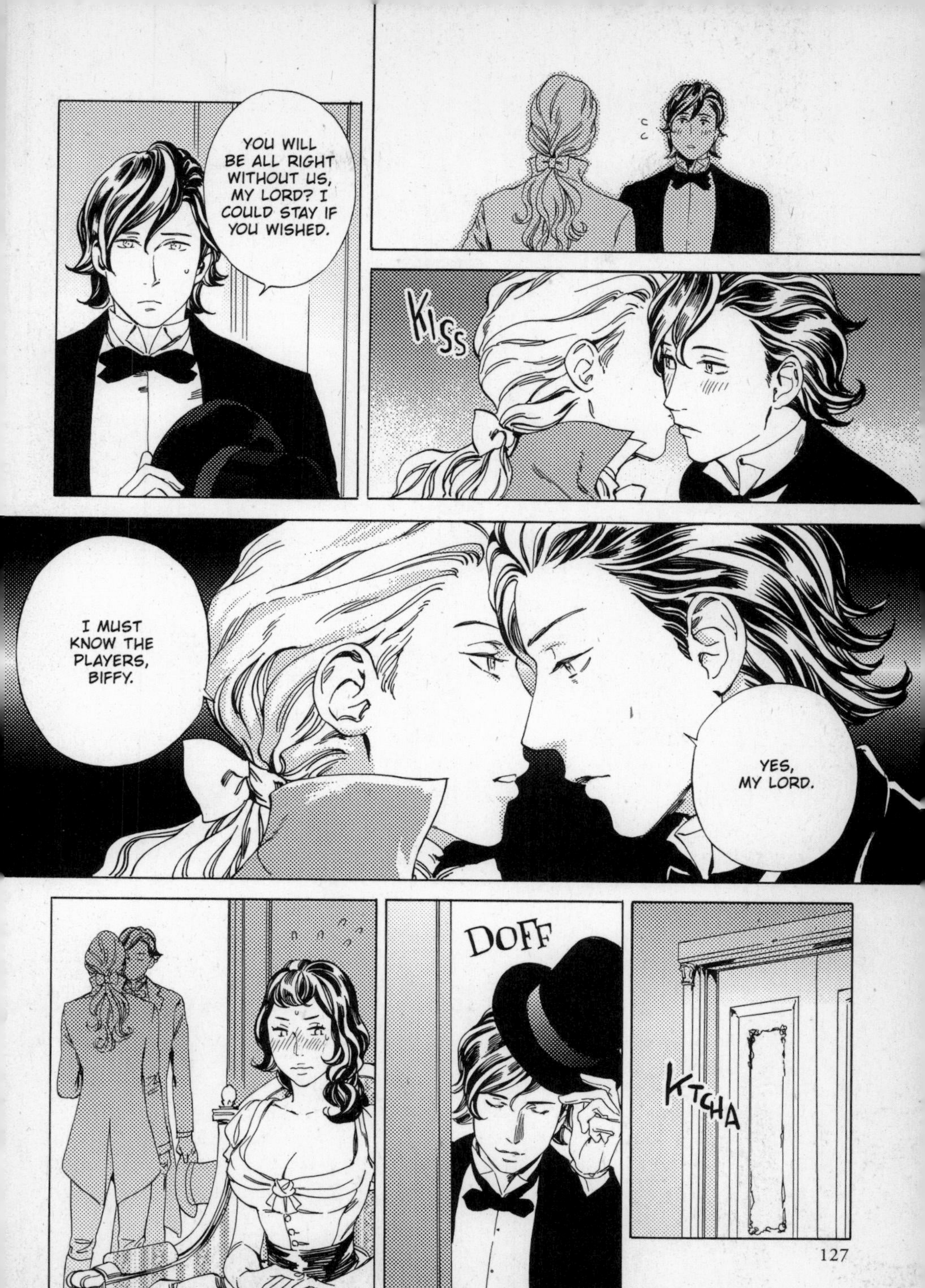
YOU WILL BE ALL RIGHT WITHOUT US, MY LORD? I COULD STAY IF YOU WISHED.
KISS
I MUST KNOW THE PLAYERS, BIFFY.
YES, MY LORD.
DOFF
KTCHA

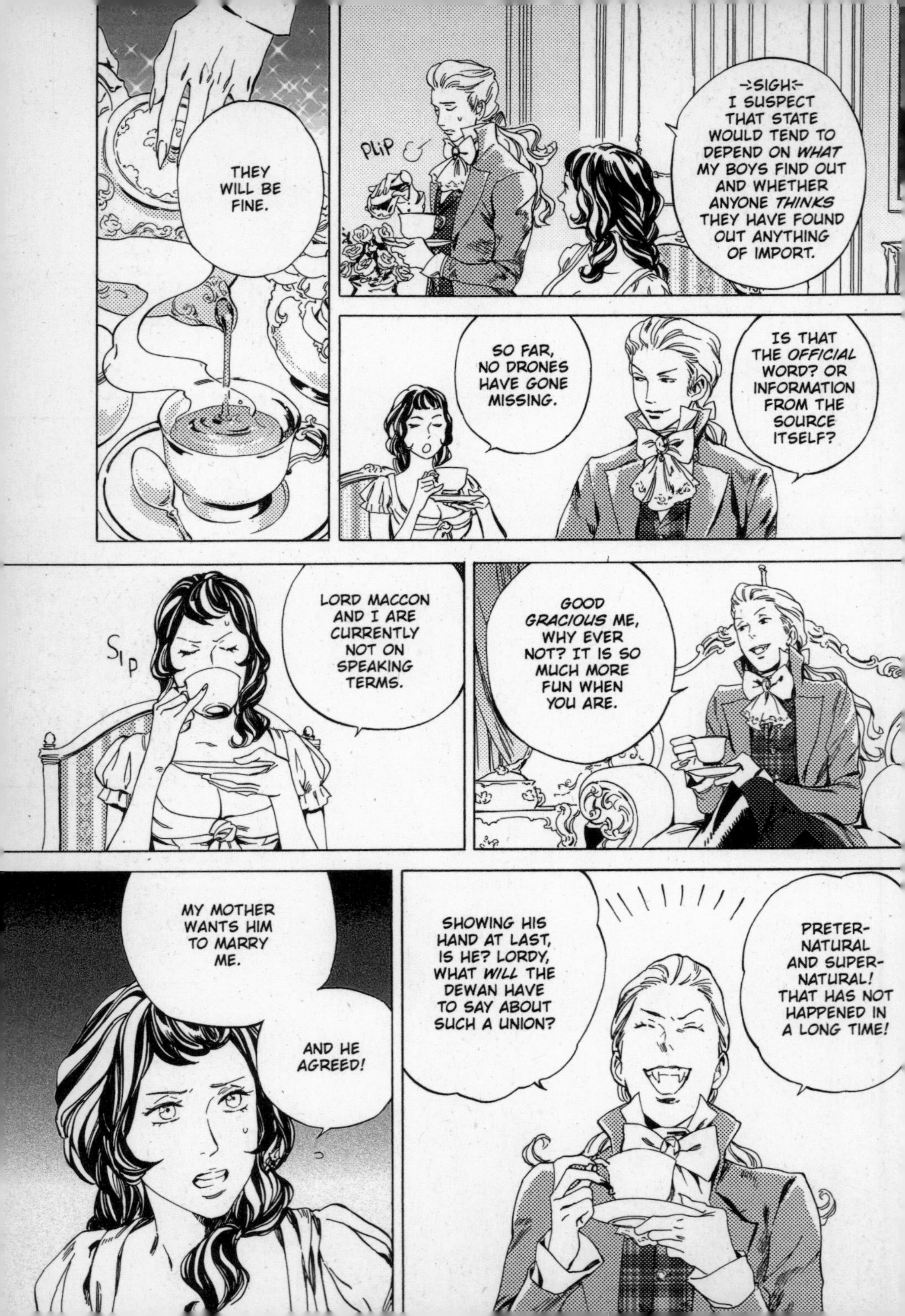
THEY WILL BE FINE.
PLIP
SIGH
I SUSPECT THAT STATE WOULD TEND TO DEPEND ON *WHAT* MY BOYS FIND OUT AND WHETHER ANYONE *THINKS* THEY HAVE FOUND OUT ANYTHING OF IMPORT.
SO FAR, NO DRONES HAVE GONE MISSING.
IS THAT THE *OFFICIAL* WORD? OR INFORMATION FROM THE SOURCE ITSELF?
SIP
LORD MACCON AND I ARE CURRENTLY NOT ON SPEAKING TERMS.
GOOD *GRACIOUS* ME, WHY EVER NOT? IT IS SO MUCH MORE FUN WHEN YOU ARE.
MY MOTHER WANTS HIM TO MARRY ME.
AND HE AGREED!
SHOWING HIS HAND AT LAST, IS HE? LORDY, WHAT *WILL* THE DEWAN HAVE TO SAY ABOUT SUCH A UNION?
PRETER-NATURAL AND SUPER-NATURAL! THAT HAS NOT HAPPENED IN A LONG TIME!

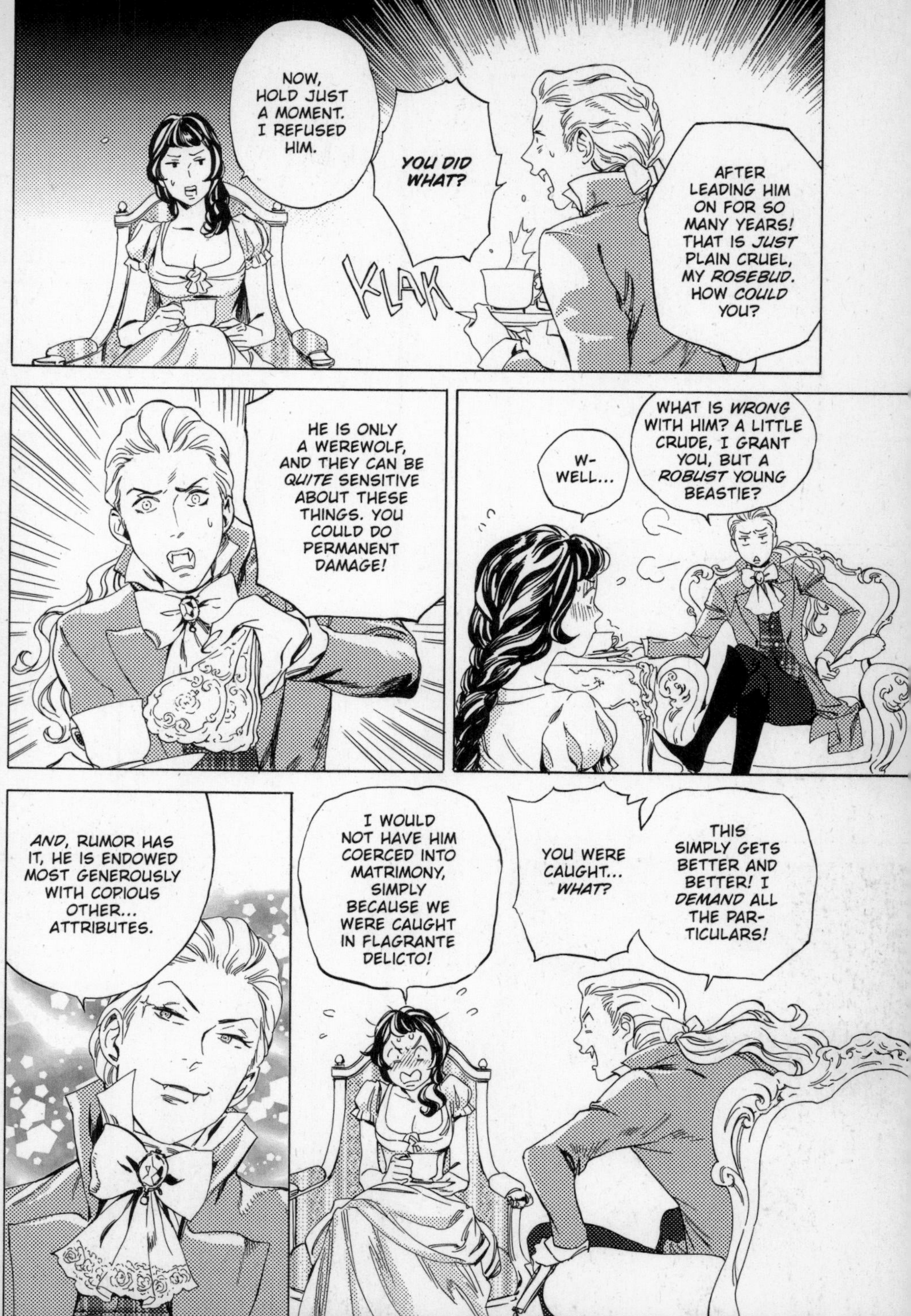
NOW, HOLD JUST A MOMENT. I REFUSED HIM.
YOU DID WHAT?
KLAK
AFTER LEADING HIM ON FOR SO MANY YEARS! THAT IS JUST PLAIN CRUEL, MY ROSEBUD. HOW COULD YOU?
HE IS ONLY A WEREWOLF, AND THEY CAN BE QUITE SENSITIVE ABOUT THESE THINGS. YOU COULD DO PERMANENT DAMAGE!
WHAT IS WRONG WITH HIM? A LITTLE CRUDE, I GRANT YOU, BUT A ROBUST YOUNG BEASTIE?
W-WELL...
AND, RUMOR HAS IT, HE IS ENDOWED MOST GENEROUSLY WITH COPIOUS OTHER... ATTRIBUTES.
I WOULD NOT HAVE HIM COERCED INTO MATRIMONY, SIMPLY BECAUSE WE WERE CAUGHT IN FLAGRANTE DELICTO!
YOU WERE CAUGHT... WHAT?
THIS SIMPLY GETS BETTER AND BETTER! I DEMAND ALL THE PARTICULARS!

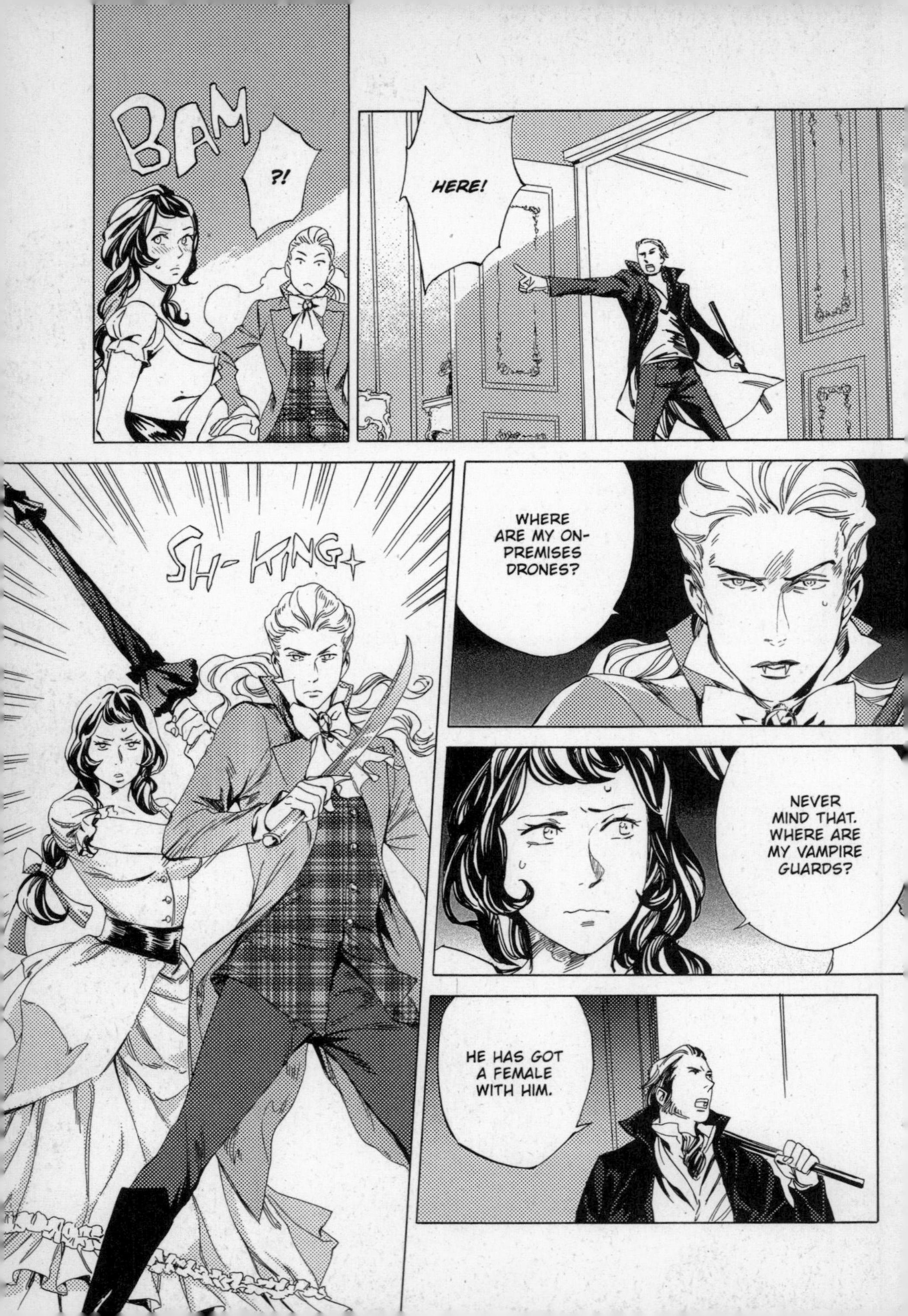
BAM
?!
HERE!
SH-KING
WHERE ARE MY ON-PREMISES DRONES?
NEVER MIND THAT. WHERE ARE MY VAMPIRE GUARDS?
HE HAS GOT A FEMALE WITH HIM.

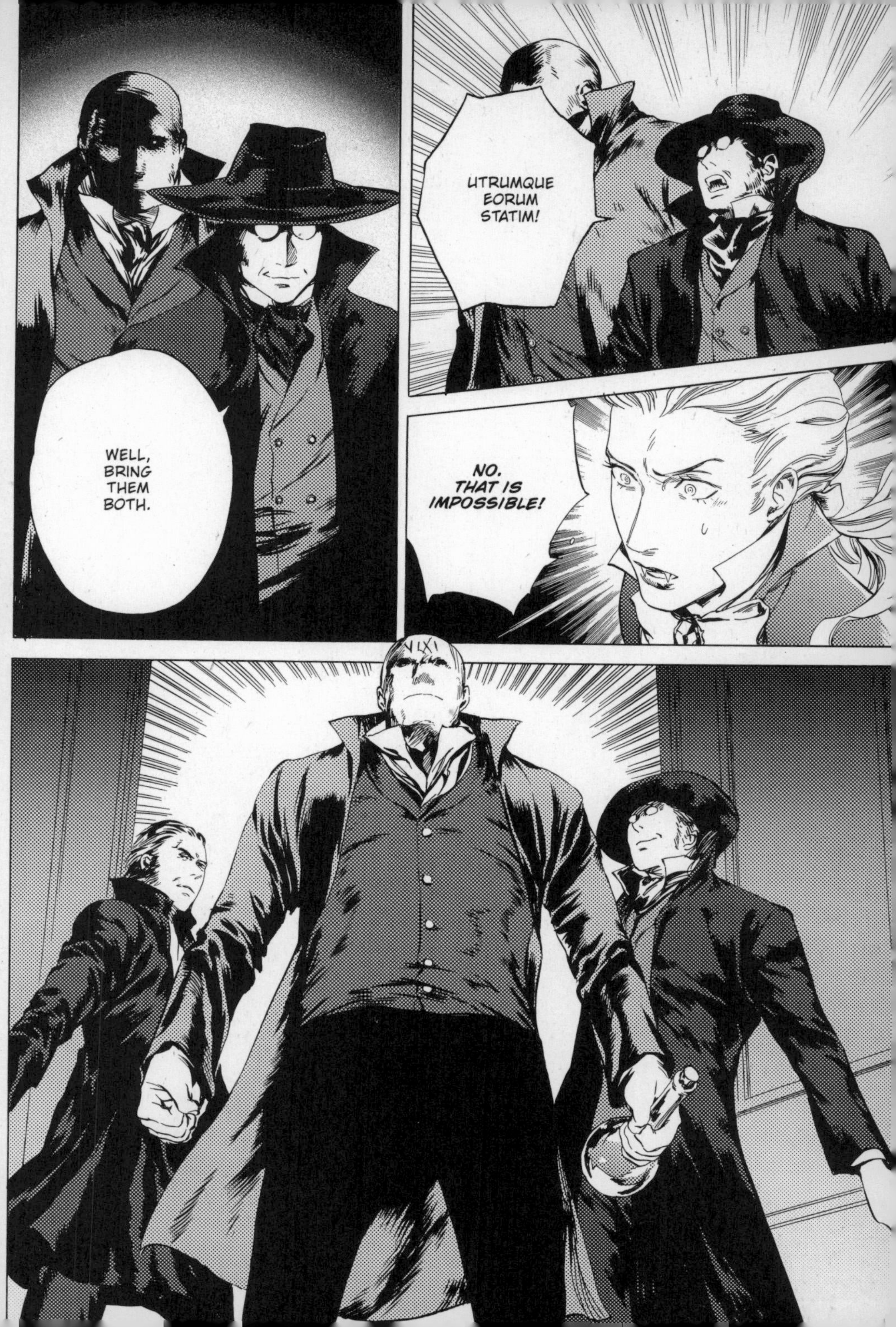
WELL, BRING THEM BOTH.
UTRUMQUE EORUM STATIM!
NO. THAT IS IMPOSSIBLE!

SOULLESS

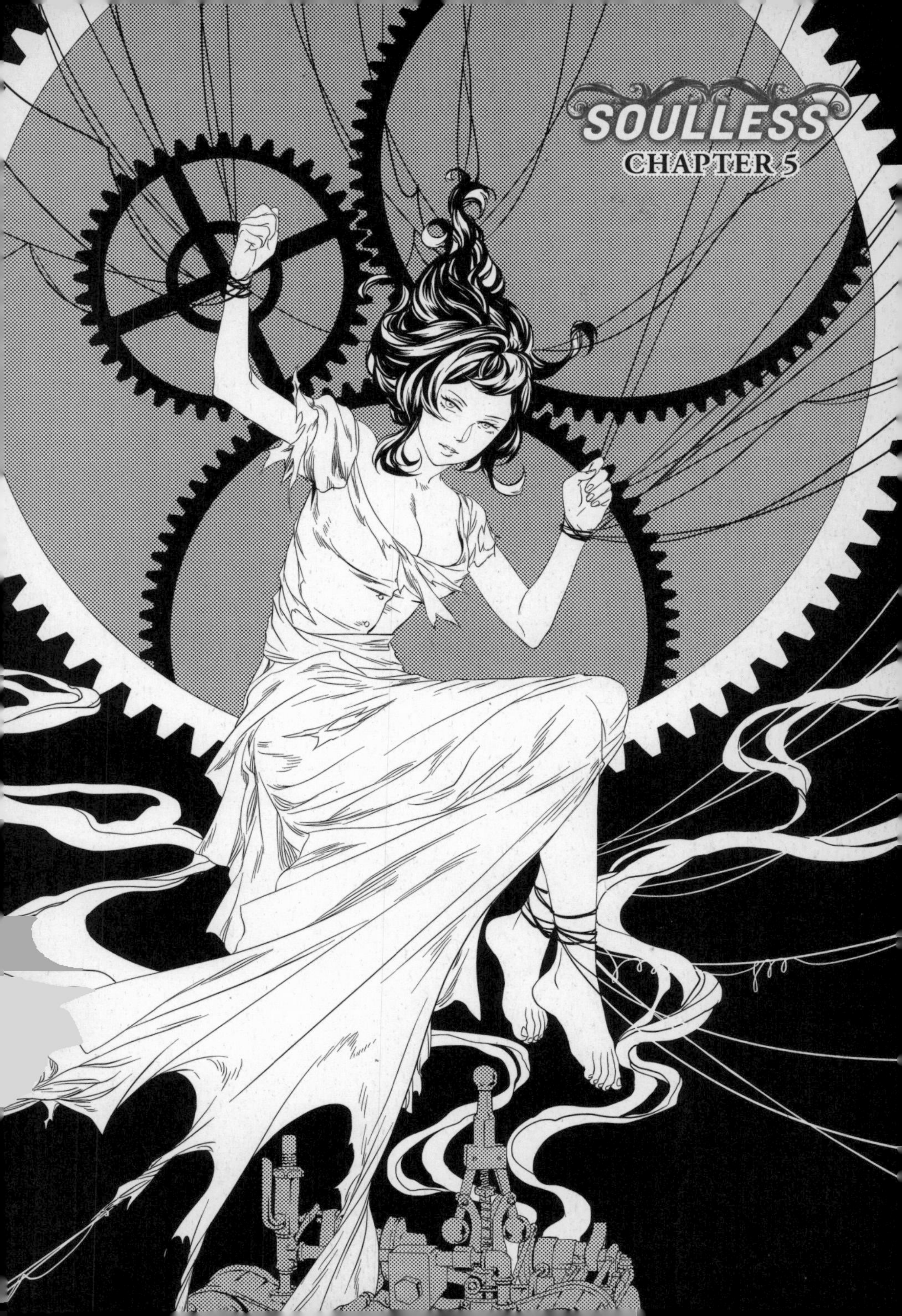
SOULLESS
CHAPTER 5

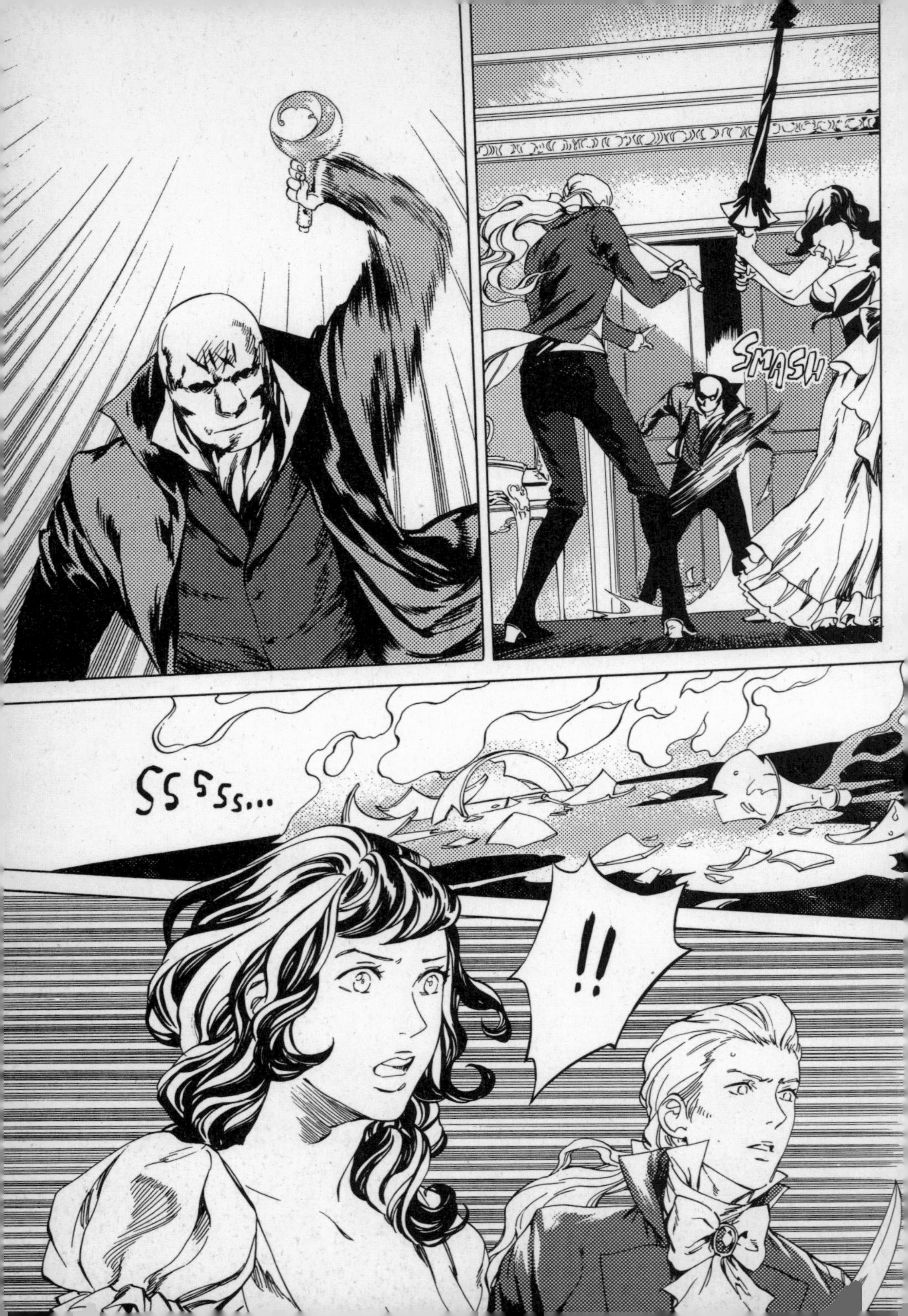
SMASH
SSSSS...
!!

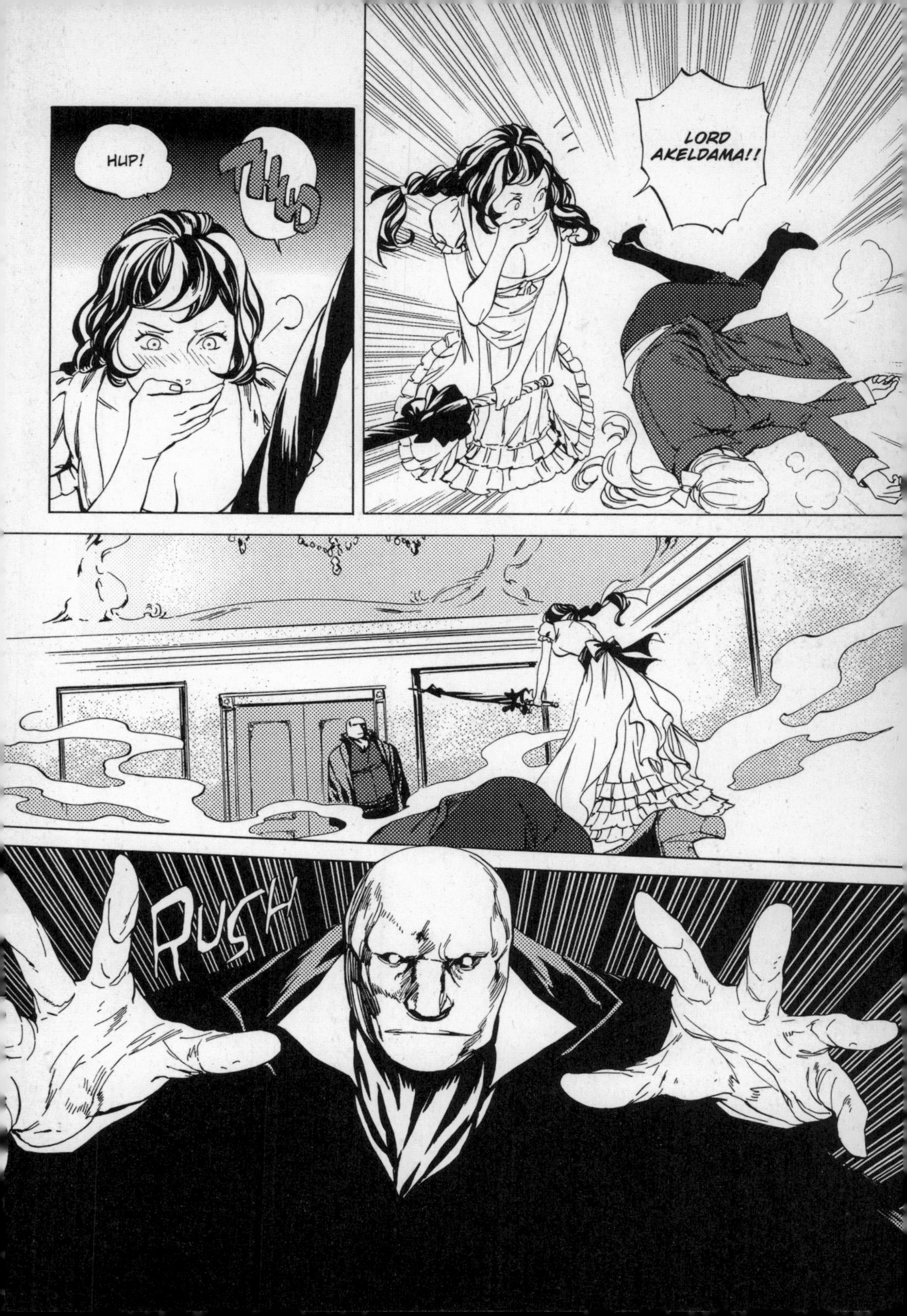
HUP!
THUD
LORD AKELDAMA!!
RUSH

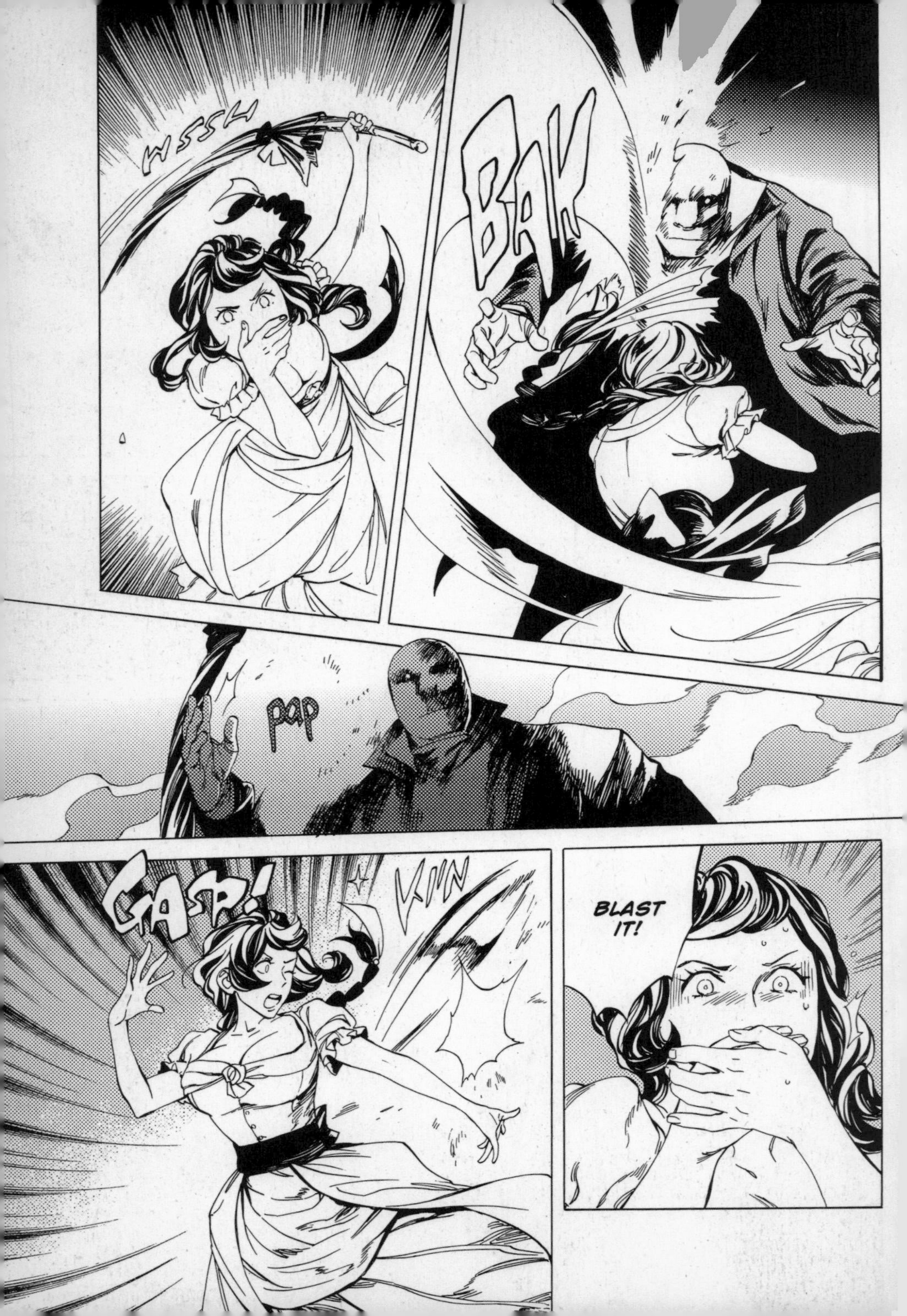
WSSH
BAK
PAP
GASP!
VIIN
BLAST IT!

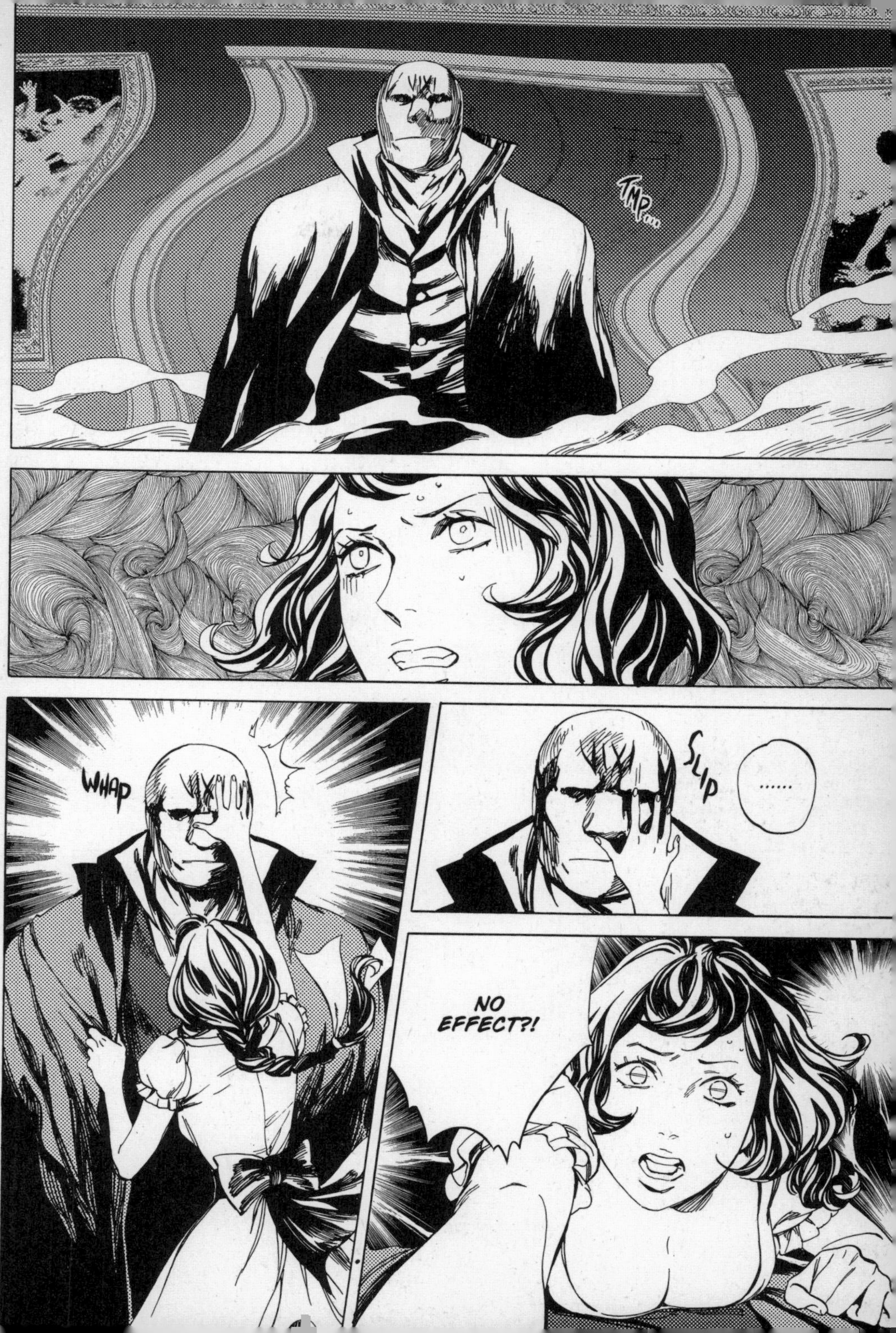
TMP...
WHAP
SLIP
......
NO EFFECT?!

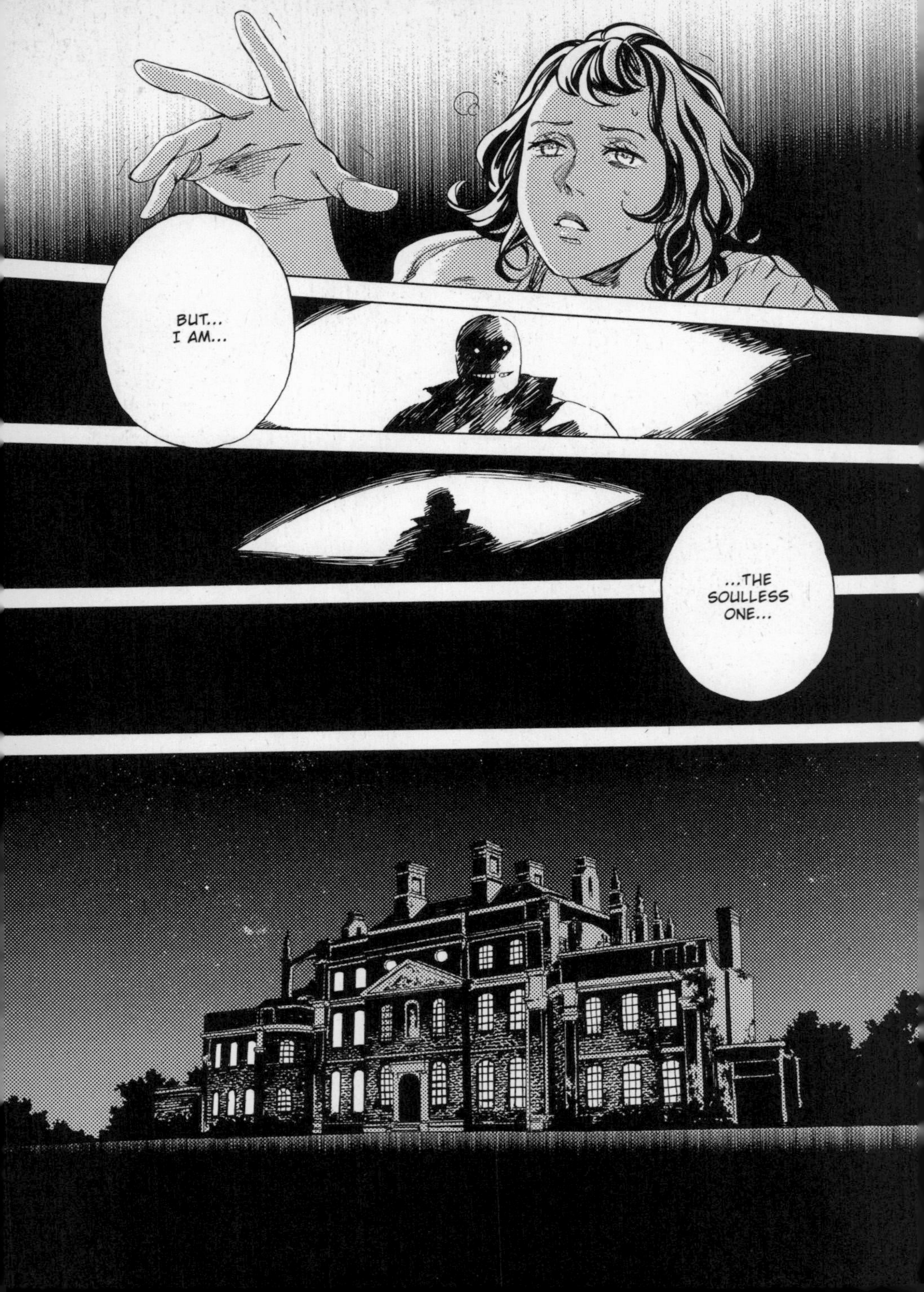
BUT... I AM...
...THE SOULLESS ONE...

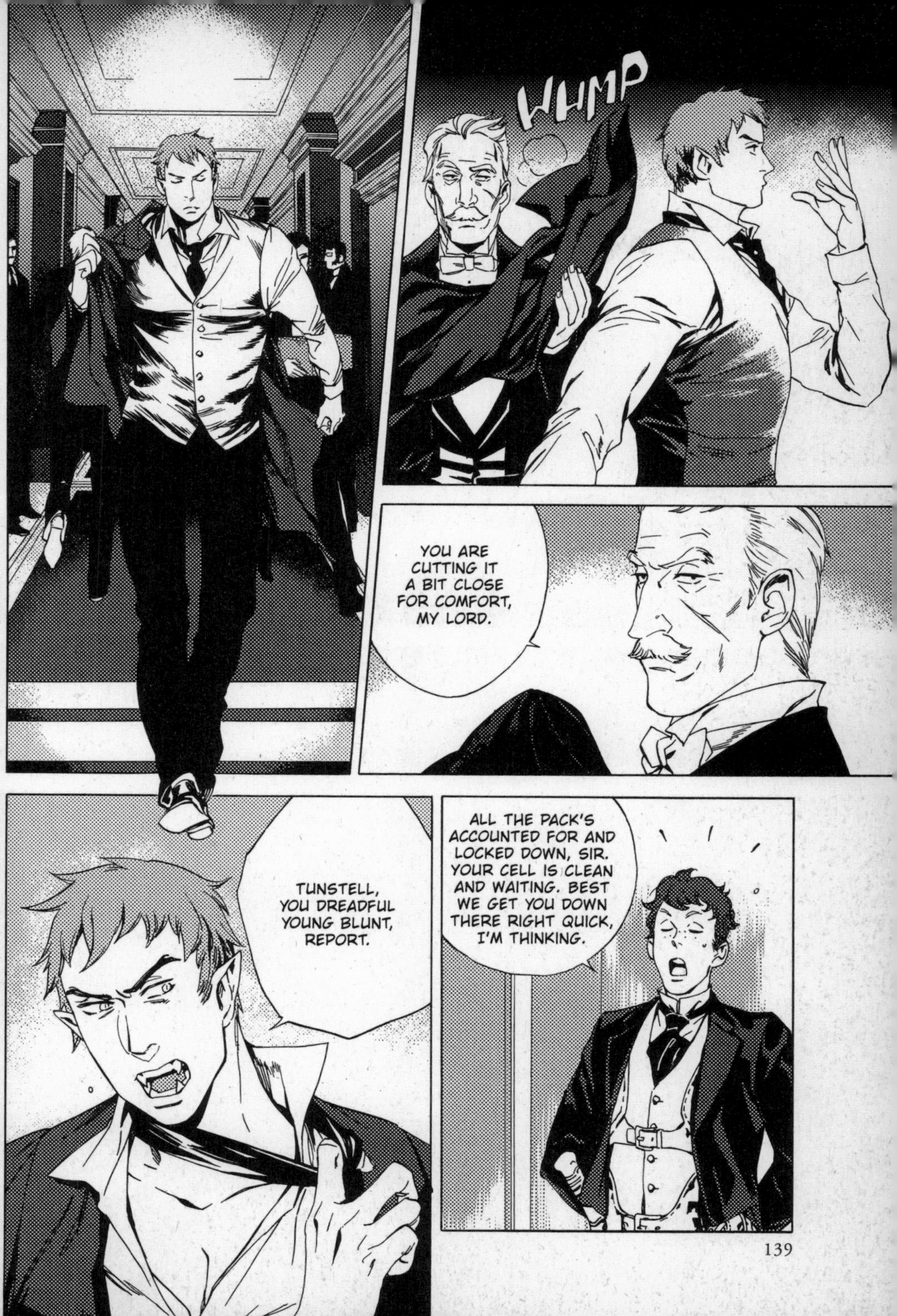
WHMP
YOU ARE CUTTING IT A BIT CLOSE FOR COMFORT, MY LORD.
TUNSTELL, YOU DREADFUL YOUNG BLUNT, REPORT.
ALL THE PACK'S ACCOUNTED FOR AND LOCKED DOWN, SIR. YOUR CELL IS CLEAN AND WAITING. BEST WE GET YOU DOWN THERE RIGHT QUICK, I'M THINKING.

BOFF

THERE YOU GO WITH THE THINKING. WHAT HAVE I TOLD YOU?

PRECAUTIONARY MEASURES, TUNSTELL.

ARE YOU CERTAIN THAT IS NECESSARY, SIR?

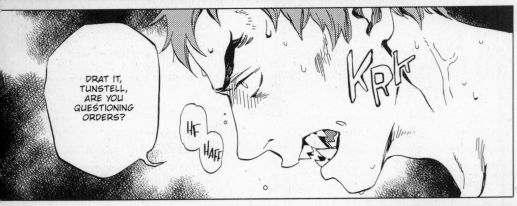

DRAT IT, TUNSTELL, ARE YOU QUESTIONING ORDERS?

HF HAFF

KRIT

MR. TUNSTELL, IF YOU WOULD BE SO KIND.

QUICKLY!!

KLAK

BARK

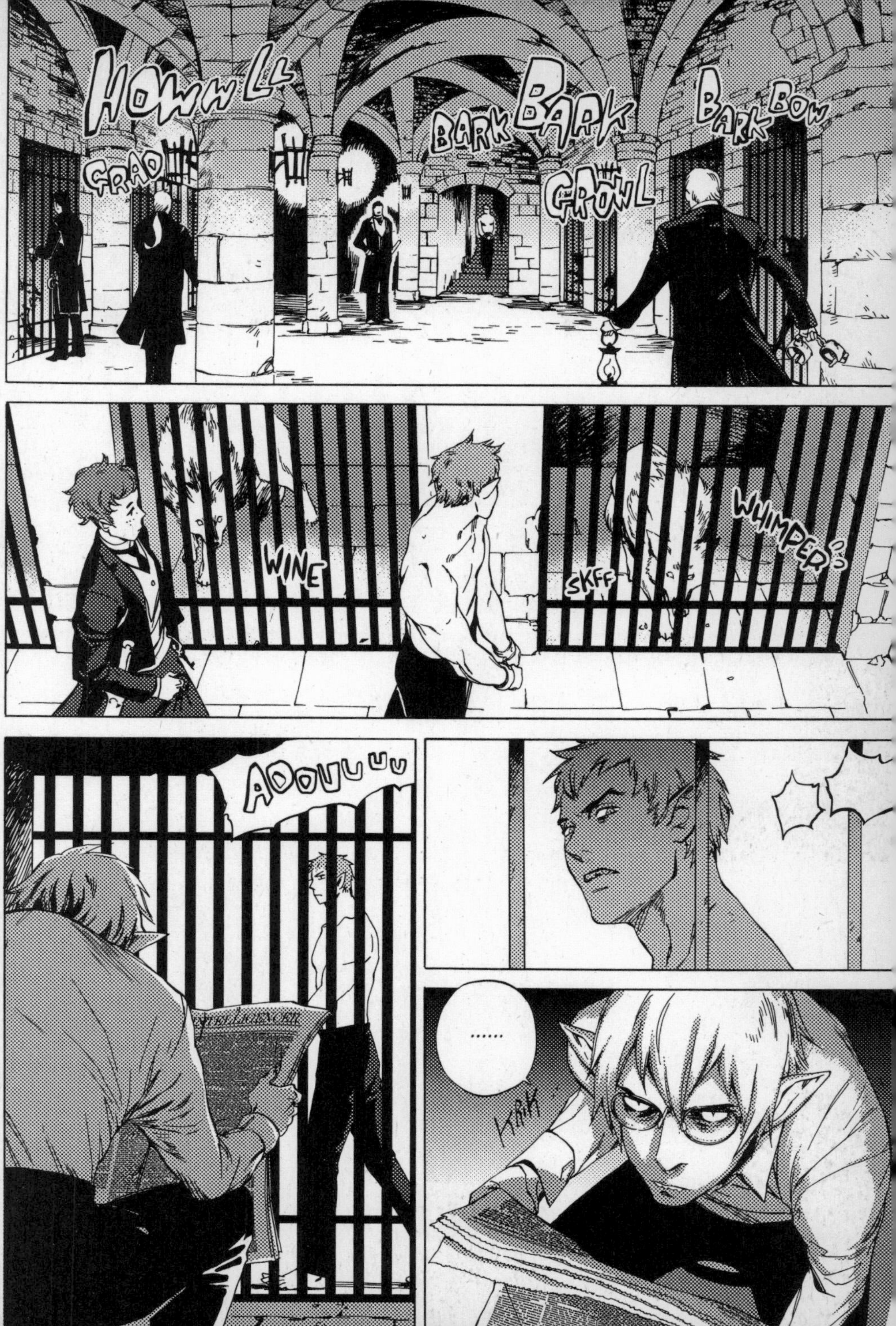
HOWWLL
GRAO
BARK BARK
GROWL
BARK BOW
WINE
SKFF
WHIMPER
ADOULUUU
......
KRIK

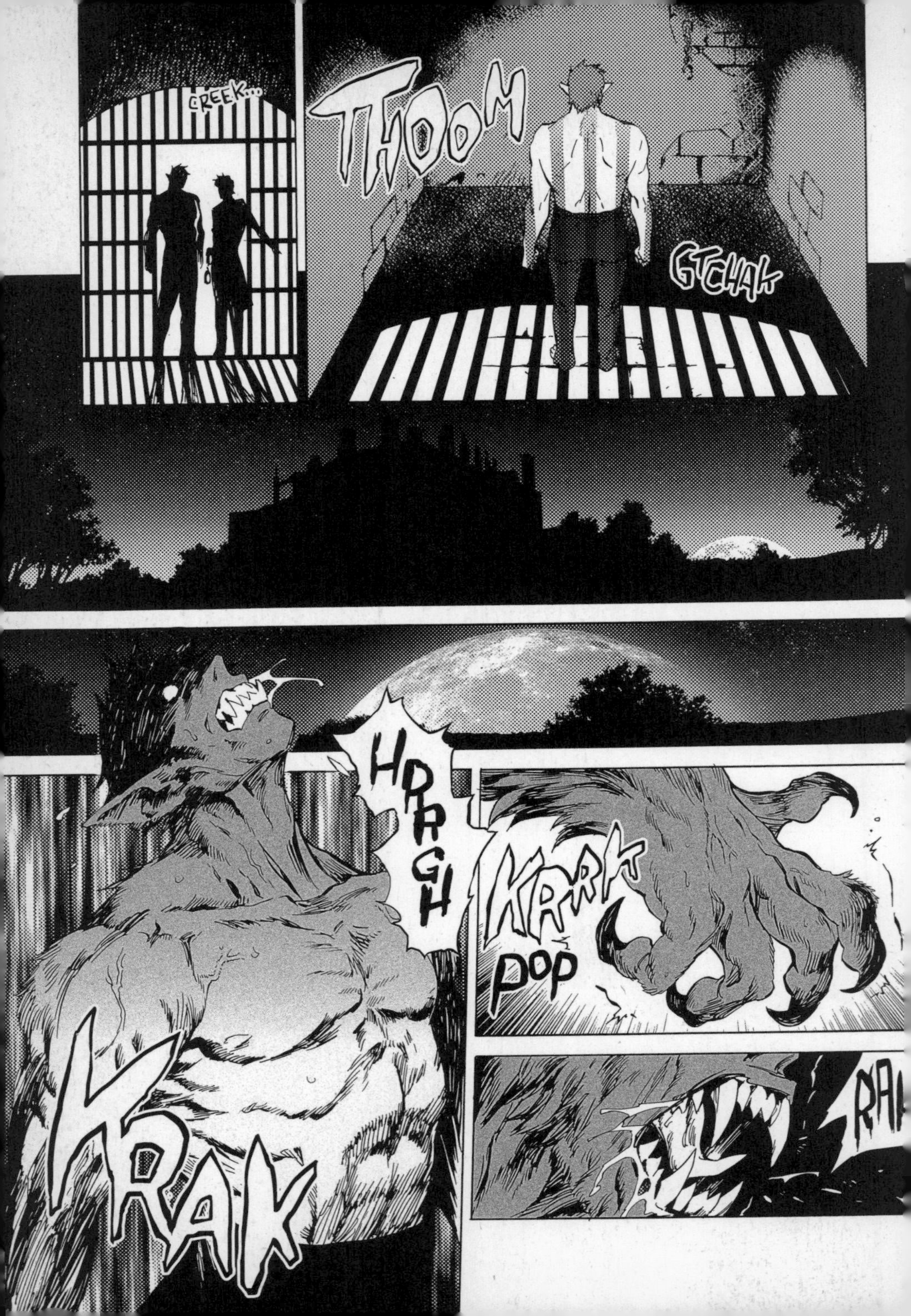
CREEK...
THOOM
GTCHAK
HRRRGH
KRRK
POP
KRAK
RAH

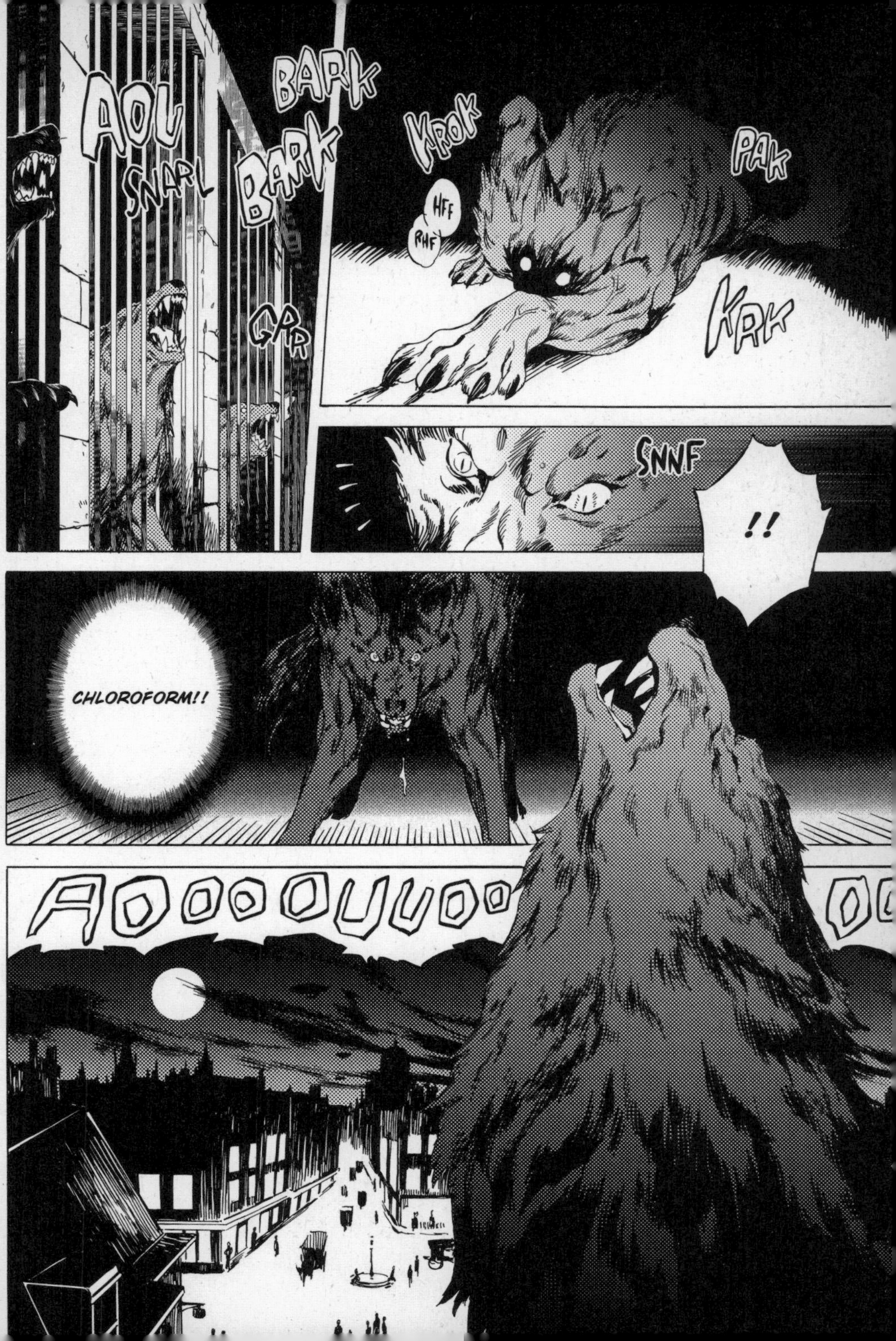
AOU
SNARL
BARK
BARK
GRR
KROK
HFF
RHF
PAK
KRK
SNNF
!!
CHLOROFORM!!
AOOOUUOO OO

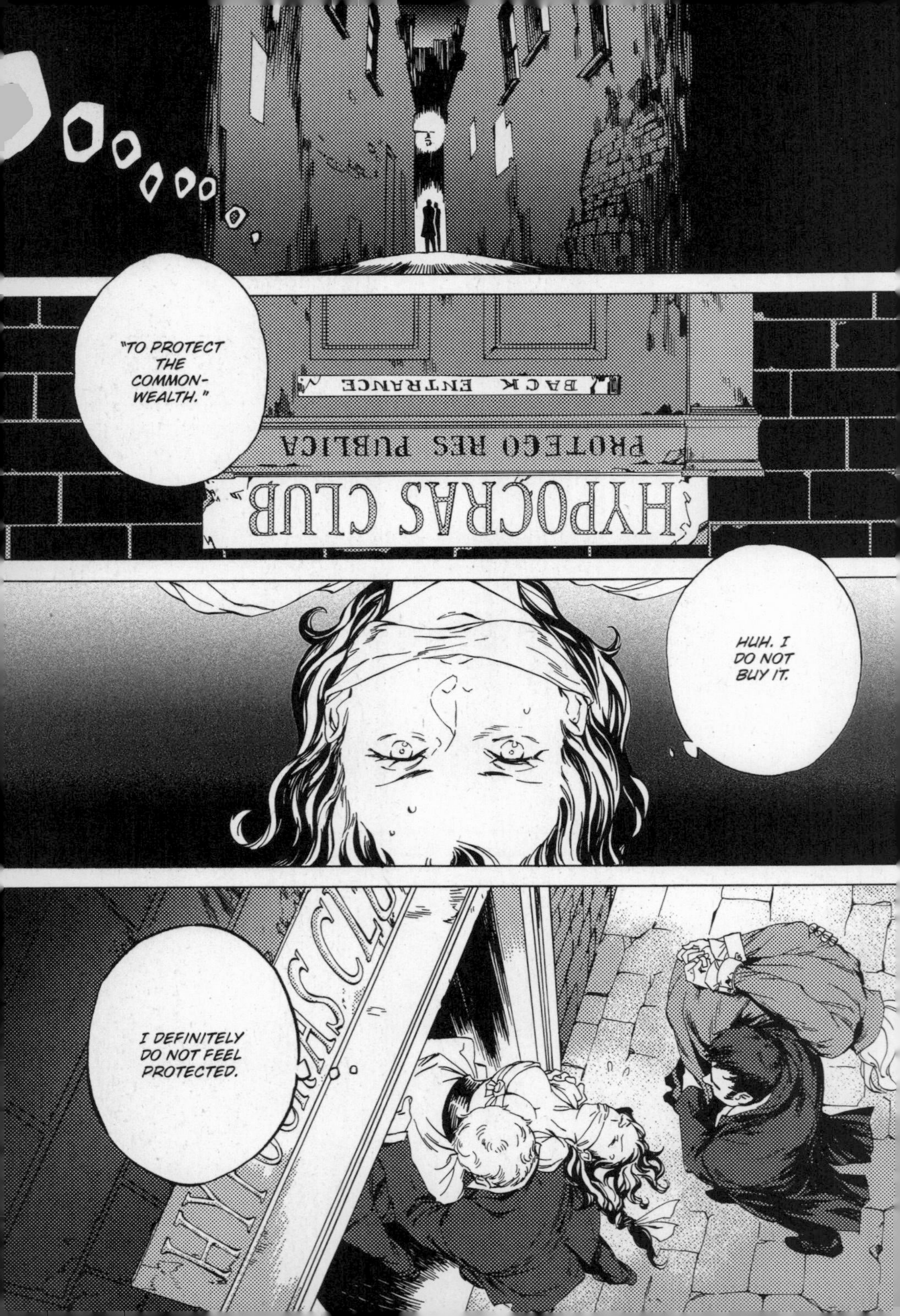
"TO PROTECT THE COMMON-WEALTH."
BACK ENTRANCE
PROTEGO RES PUBLICA
HYPOCRAS CLUB
HUH. I DO NOT BUY IT.
I DEFINITELY DO NOT FEEL PROTECTED.

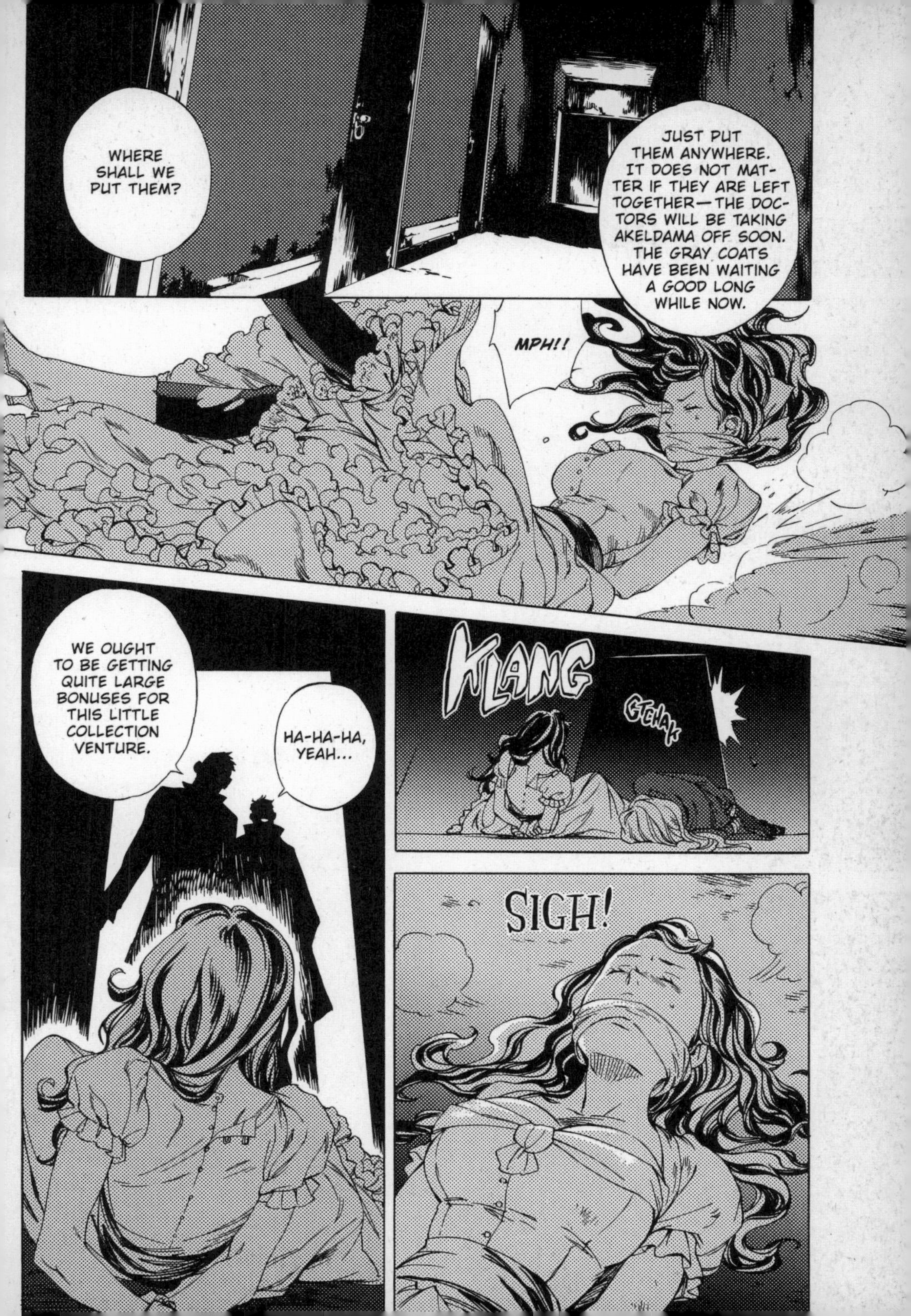
WHERE SHALL WE PUT THEM?
JUST PUT THEM ANYWHERE. IT DOES NOT MATTER IF THEY ARE LEFT TOGETHER—THE DOCTORS WILL BE TAKING AKELDAMA OFF SOON. THE GRAY COATS HAVE BEEN WAITING A GOOD LONG WHILE NOW.
MPH!!
WE OUGHT TO BE GETTING QUITE LARGE BONUSES FOR THIS LITTLE COLLECTION VENTURE.
HA-HA-HA, YEAH...
KLANG
GTCHAK
SIGH!

turn...

!!

WELL, THIS IS *A PRETTY* KETTLE OF FISH.

I AM SORRY TO HAVE DRAGGED YOU INTO THIS, MY DEAR, ALMOST AS MUCH AS HAVING DRAGGED ONE OF MY BEST EVENING JACKETS INTO IT.

FWIP

OH, DON'T BE SO RIDICULOUS. MY HEAD IS STILL SPINNING FROM THAT BLASTED CHLOROFORM, AND THERE IS NO NEED FOR YOU TO BE TIRESOME ON TOP OF IT. THIS SITUATION COULD NOT POSSIBLY BE MIS-CONSTRUED AS YOUR FAULT.

BUT THEY WERE AFTER ME.

THEY WOULD HAVE BEEN AFTER ME AS WELL, IF THEY ONLY KNEW MY NAME, SO LET US HEAR NOTHING MORE ABOUT IT.

SCOOCH

WELL, MY *BUTTERCUP*, I SUGGEST WE *KEEP* THAT NAME OF YOURS QUIET AS LONG AS POSSIBLE.

nom

WE MAY NOT NEED TO BOTHER.

THE WAX-FACED MAN KNOWS, AND HE WILL TELL THEM WHO I AM.

PBBTH

CANNOT BE DONE, *DEWDROP*.

HOW COULD YOU POSSIBLY KNOW THAT?

THE *HOMUNCULUS SIMULACRUM*, OR THE WAX-FACED MAN, AS YOU CALL IT, CANNOT TELL ANYONE ANYTHING.

IT HAS NO VOICE, *LITTLE TULIP*, NONE AT ALL.

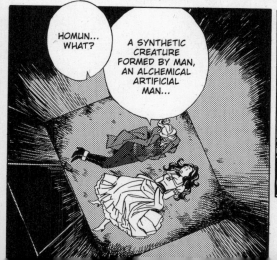

HOMUN... WHAT?

A SYNTHETIC CREATURE FORMED BY MAN, AN ALCHEMICAL ARTIFICIAL MAN...

AN AUTO-MATON?

EXACTLY! THEY HAVE EXISTED BEFORE.

147

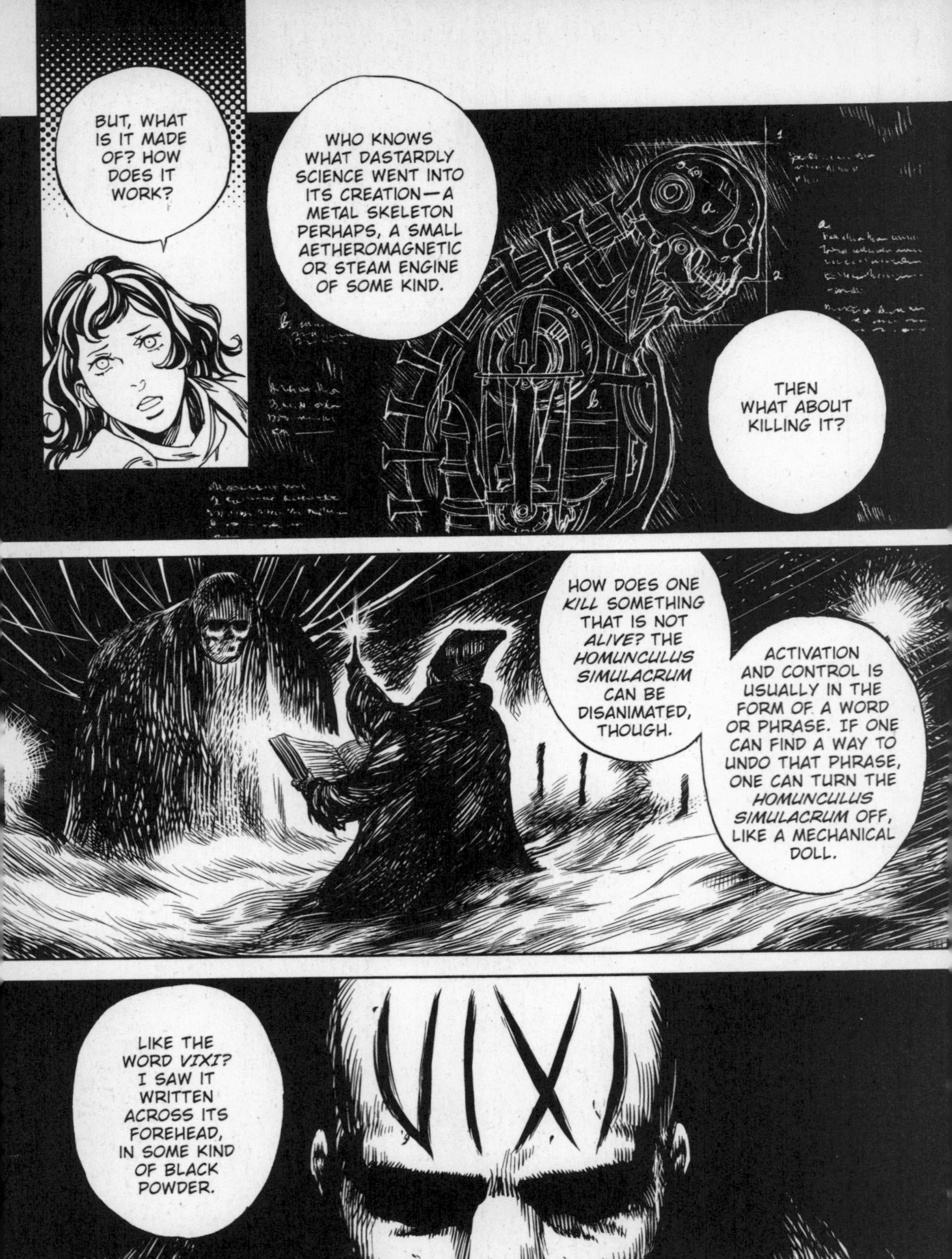
BUT, WHAT IS IT MADE OF? HOW DOES IT WORK?
WHO KNOWS WHAT DASTARDLY SCIENCE WENT INTO ITS CREATION—A METAL SKELETON PERHAPS, A SMALL AETHEROMAGNETIC OR STEAM ENGINE OF SOME KIND.
THEN WHAT ABOUT KILLING IT?
HOW DOES ONE *KILL* SOMETHING THAT IS NOT *ALIVE*? THE *HOMUNCULUS SIMULACRUM* CAN BE DISANIMATED, THOUGH.
ACTIVATION AND CONTROL IS USUALLY IN THE FORM OF A WORD OR PHRASE. IF ONE CAN FIND A WAY TO UNDO THAT PHRASE, ONE CAN TURN THE *HOMUNCULUS SIMULACRUM* OFF, LIKE A MECHANICAL DOLL.
LIKE THE WORD *VIXI*? I SAW IT WRITTEN ACROSS ITS FOREHEAD, IN SOME KIND OF BLACK POWDER.
VIXI

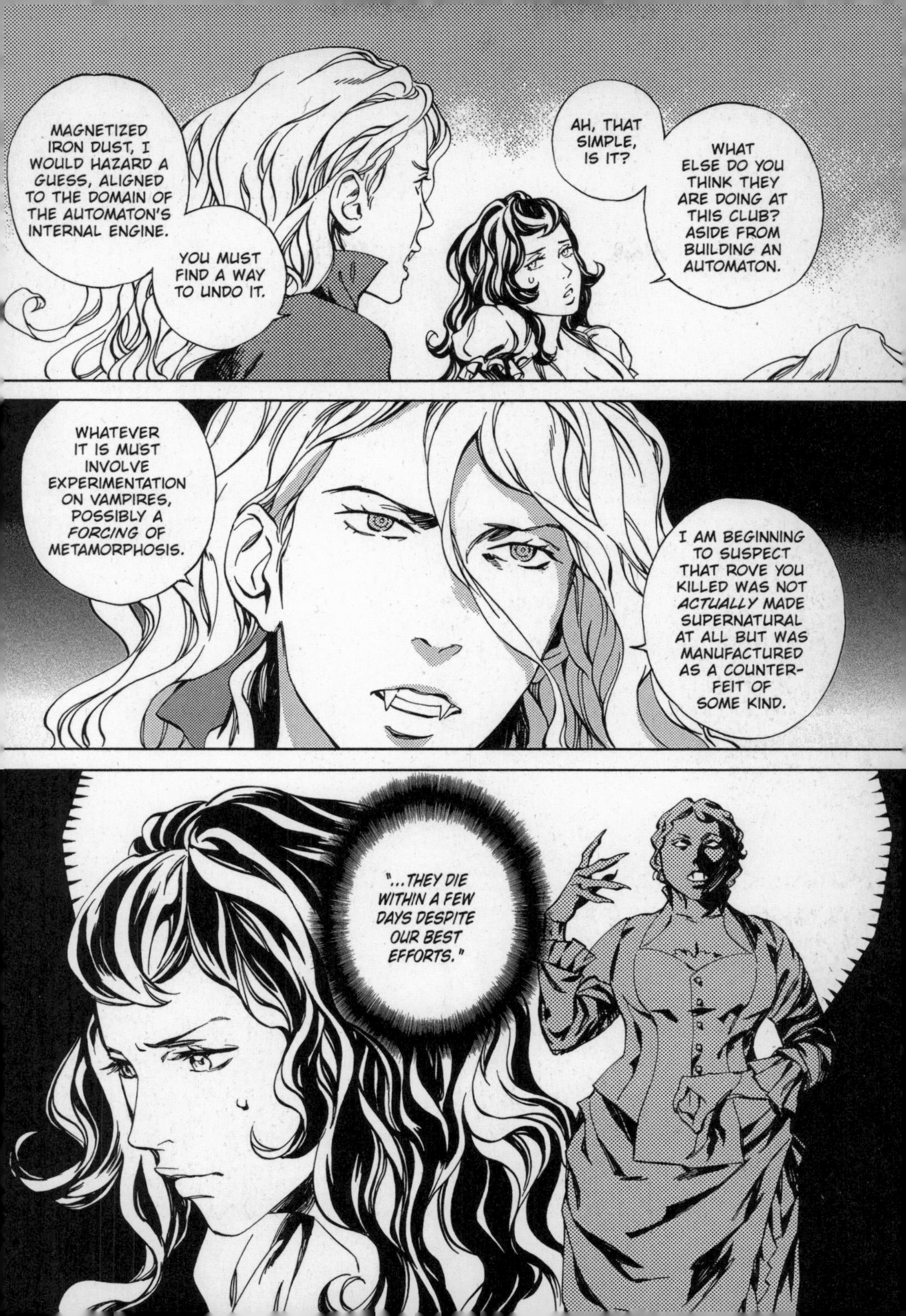
MAGNETIZED IRON DUST, I WOULD HAZARD A GUESS, ALIGNED TO THE DOMAIN OF THE AUTOMATON'S INTERNAL ENGINE.
YOU MUST FIND A WAY TO UNDO IT.
AH, THAT SIMPLE, IS IT?
WHAT ELSE DO YOU THINK THEY ARE DOING AT THIS CLUB? ASIDE FROM BUILDING AN AUTOMATON.
WHATEVER IT IS MUST INVOLVE EXPERIMENTATION ON VAMPIRES, POSSIBLY A *FORCING* OF METAMORPHOSIS.
I AM BEGINNING TO SUSPECT THAT ROVE YOU KILLED WAS NOT *ACTUALLY* MADE SUPERNATURAL AT ALL BUT WAS MANUFACTURED AS A COUNTER-FEIT OF SOME KIND.
"...THEY DIE WITHIN A FEW DAYS DESPITE OUR BEST EFFORTS."

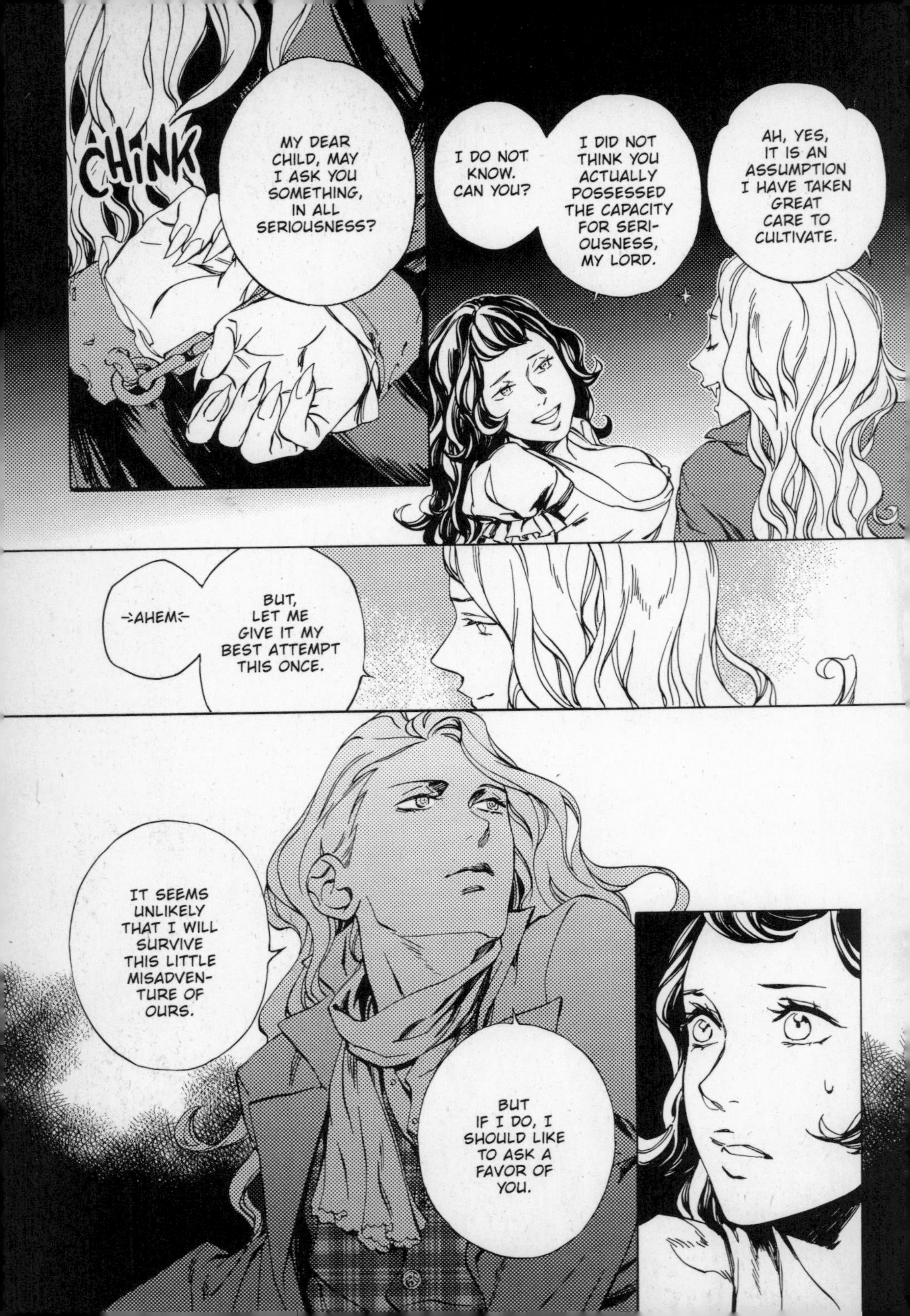
CHINK
MY DEAR CHILD, MAY I ASK YOU SOMETHING, IN ALL SERIOUSNESS?
I DO NOT KNOW. CAN YOU?
I DID NOT THINK YOU ACTUALLY POSSESSED THE CAPACITY FOR SERI-OUSNESS, MY LORD.
AH, YES, IT IS AN ASSUMPTION I HAVE TAKEN GREAT CARE TO CULTIVATE.
-AHEM-
BUT, LET ME GIVE IT MY BEST ATTEMPT THIS ONCE.
IT SEEMS UNLIKELY THAT I WILL SURVIVE THIS LITTLE MISADVEN-TURE OF OURS.
BUT IF I DO, I SHOULD LIKE TO ASK A FAVOR OF YOU.

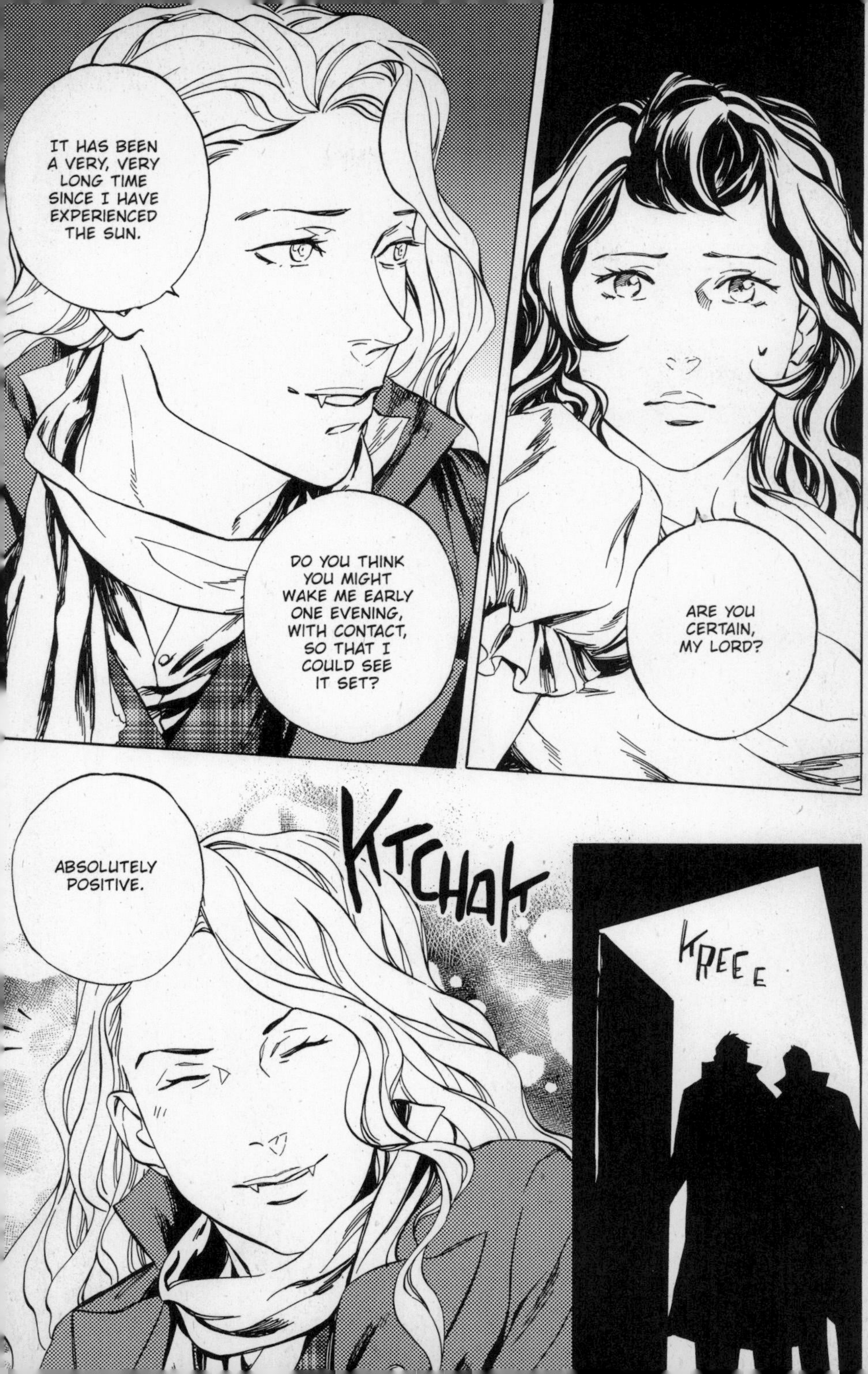
IT HAS BEEN A VERY, VERY LONG TIME SINCE I HAVE EXPERIENCED THE SUN.
DO YOU THINK YOU MIGHT WAKE ME EARLY ONE EVENING, WITH CONTACT, SO THAT I COULD SEE IT SET?
ARE YOU CERTAIN, MY LORD?
ABSOLUTELY POSITIVE.
KTCHAK
KREEE

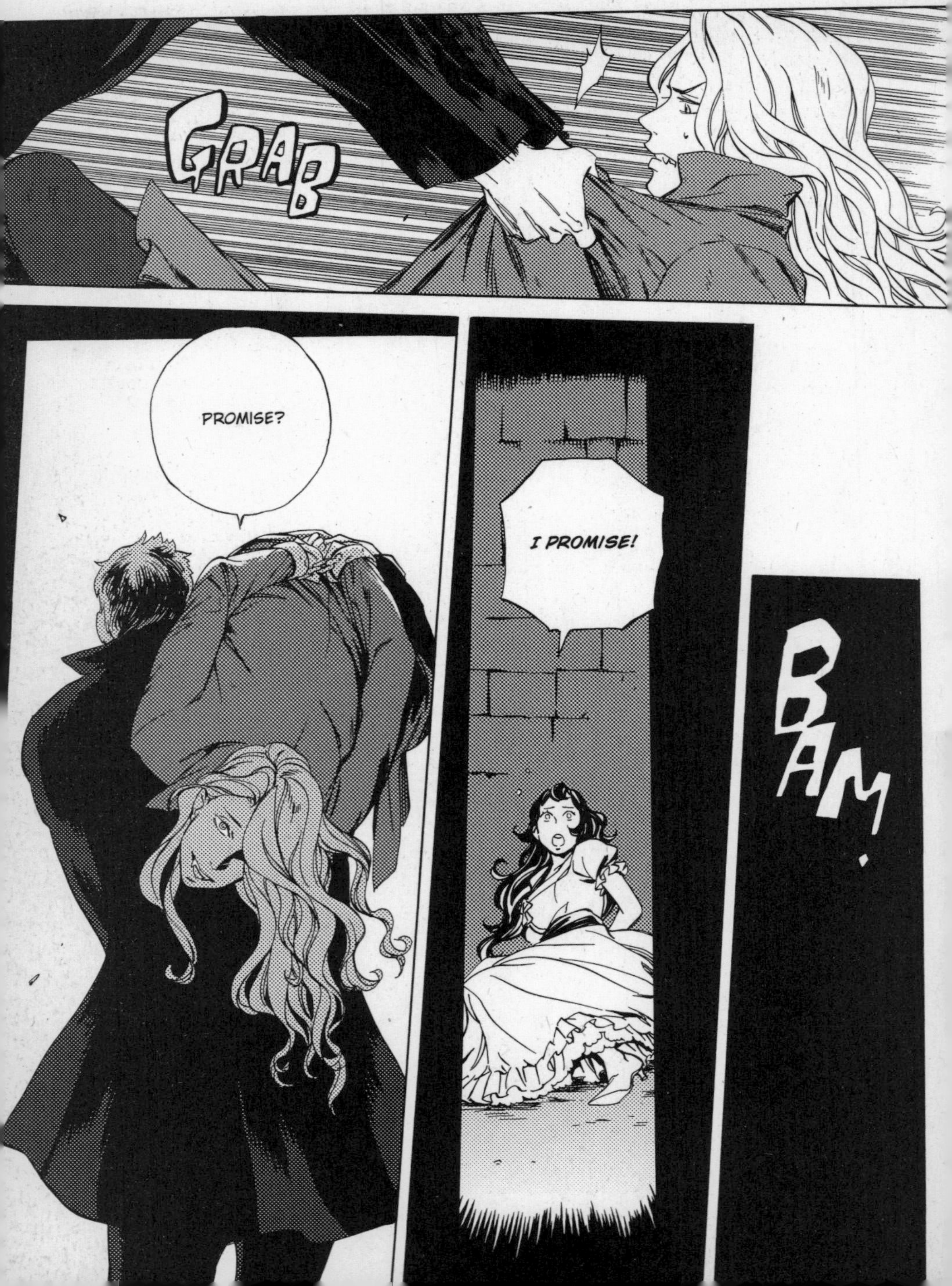
GRAB
PROMISE?
I PROMISE!
BAM!

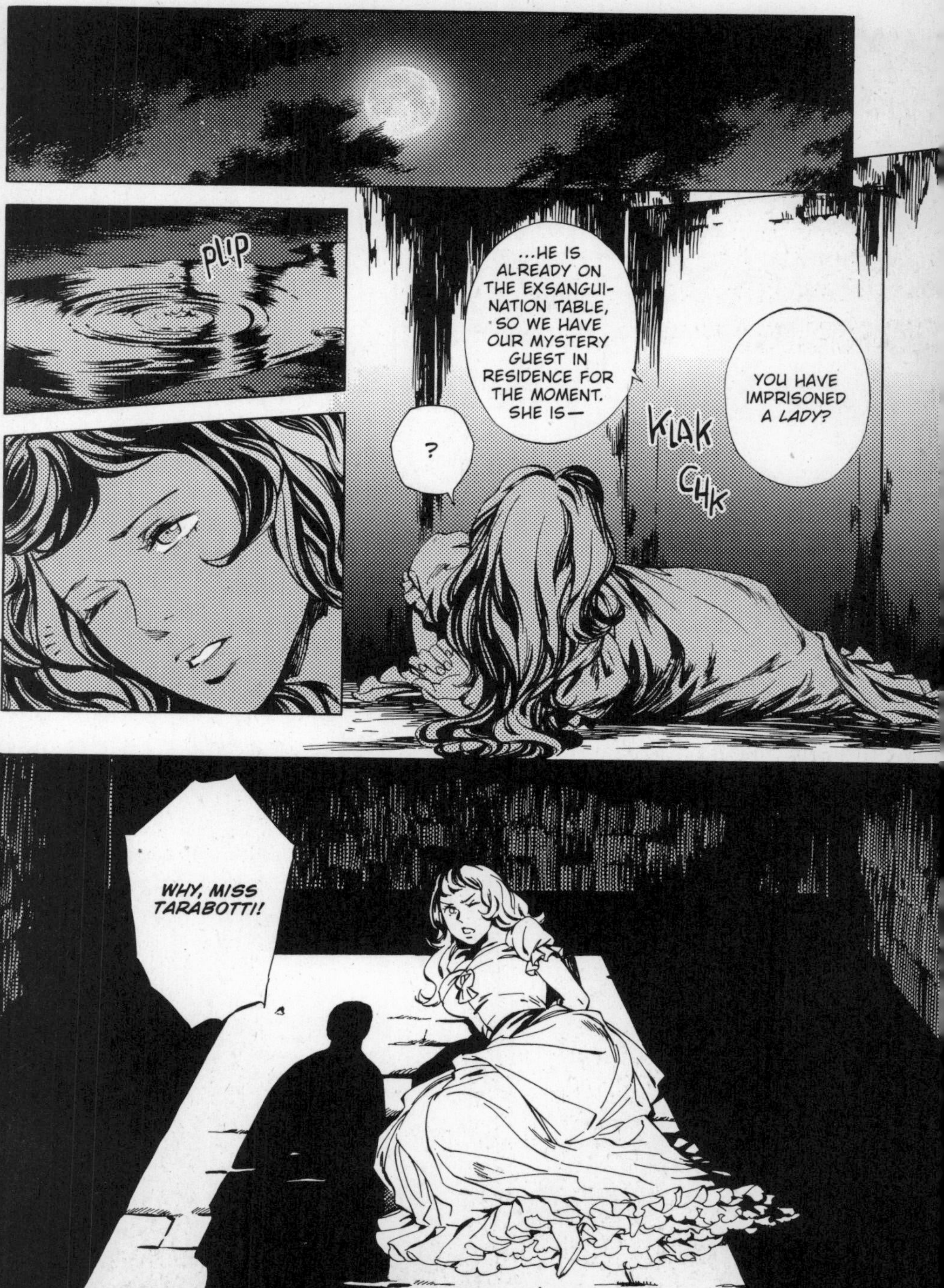
PLIP
...HE IS ALREADY ON THE EXSANGUINATION TABLE, SO WE HAVE OUR MYSTERY GUEST IN RESIDENCE FOR THE MOMENT. SHE IS—
?
KLAK
CHK
YOU HAVE IMPRISONED A *LADY*?
WHY, MISS TARABOTTI!

GOOD EVENING, MR. MAC-DOUGALL.

HOW NICE TO SEE YOU AGAIN.

YOU KNOW THE YOUNG LADY?

I CERTAINLY DO. THIS IS MISS ALEXIA TARABOTTI.

TO TREAT A YOUNG LADY OF SUCH STANDING AS SHABBILY AS THIS!

OH DEAR, THE CAT IS WELL AND TRULY OUT OF THE BAG.

IT IS A GRAVE BLOW, NOT ONLY TO THE HONOR OF THE CLUB, BUT ALSO TO THAT OF THE SCIENTIFIC PROFESSION AS A WHOLE. WE SHOULD REMOVE HER RESTRAINTS THIS MOMENT!

SHAME ON YOU!

WHY DOES THAT NAME SOUND FAMILIAR?

OF COURSE— THE B.U.R. RECORDS!

SNAP!

ARE YOU TELLING ME THIS IS *THE* ALEXIA TARABOTTI?

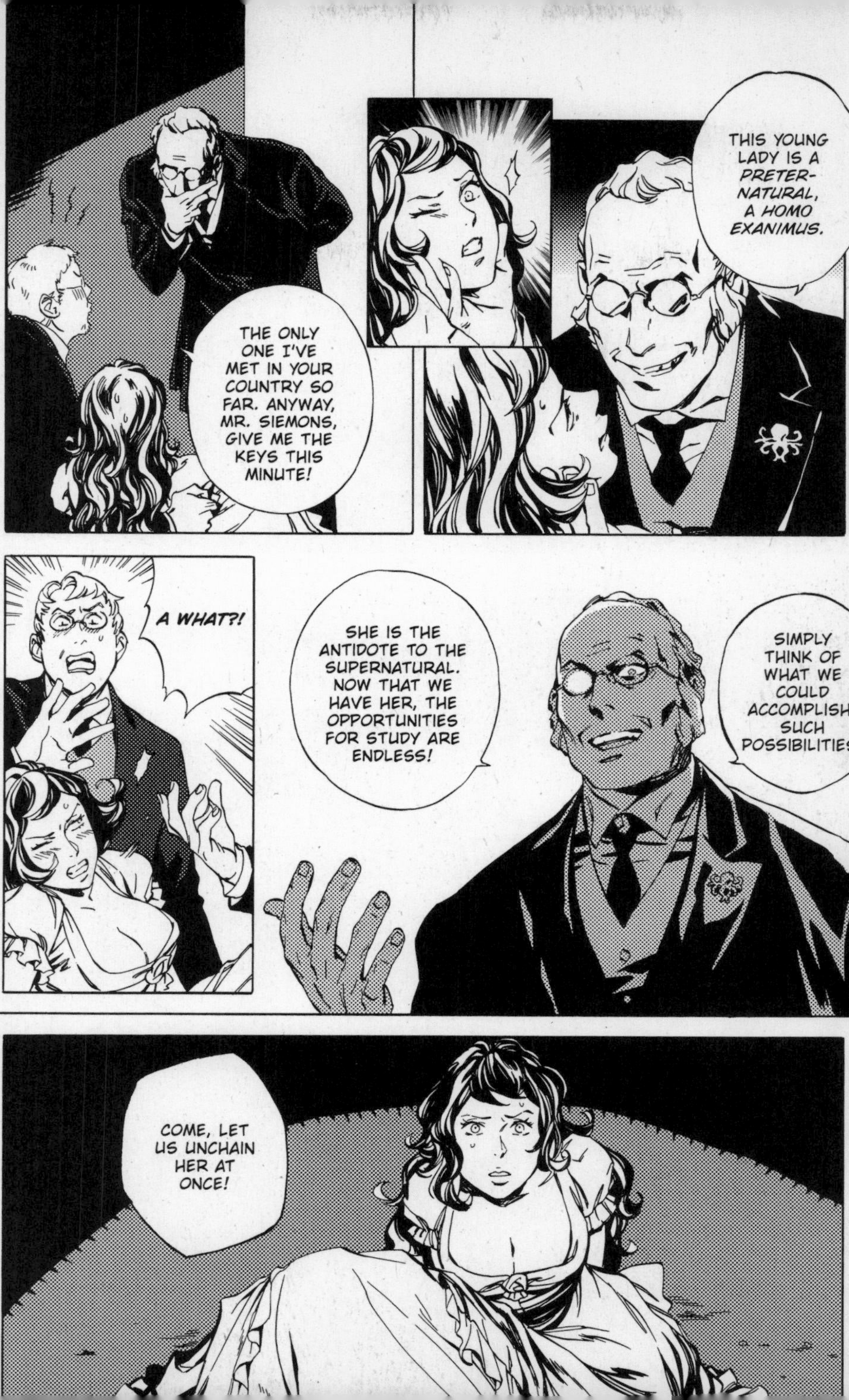
THE ONLY ONE I'VE MET IN YOUR COUNTRY SO FAR. ANYWAY, MR. SIEMONS, GIVE ME THE KEYS THIS MINUTE!
THIS YOUNG LADY IS A PRETER-NATURAL, A HOMO EXANIMUS.
A WHAT?!
SHE IS THE ANTIDOTE TO THE SUPERNATURAL. NOW THAT WE HAVE HER, THE OPPORTUNITIES FOR STUDY ARE ENDLESS!
SIMPLY THINK OF WHAT WE COULD ACCOMPLISH. SUCH POSSIBILITIES.
COME, LET US UNCHAIN HER AT ONCE!

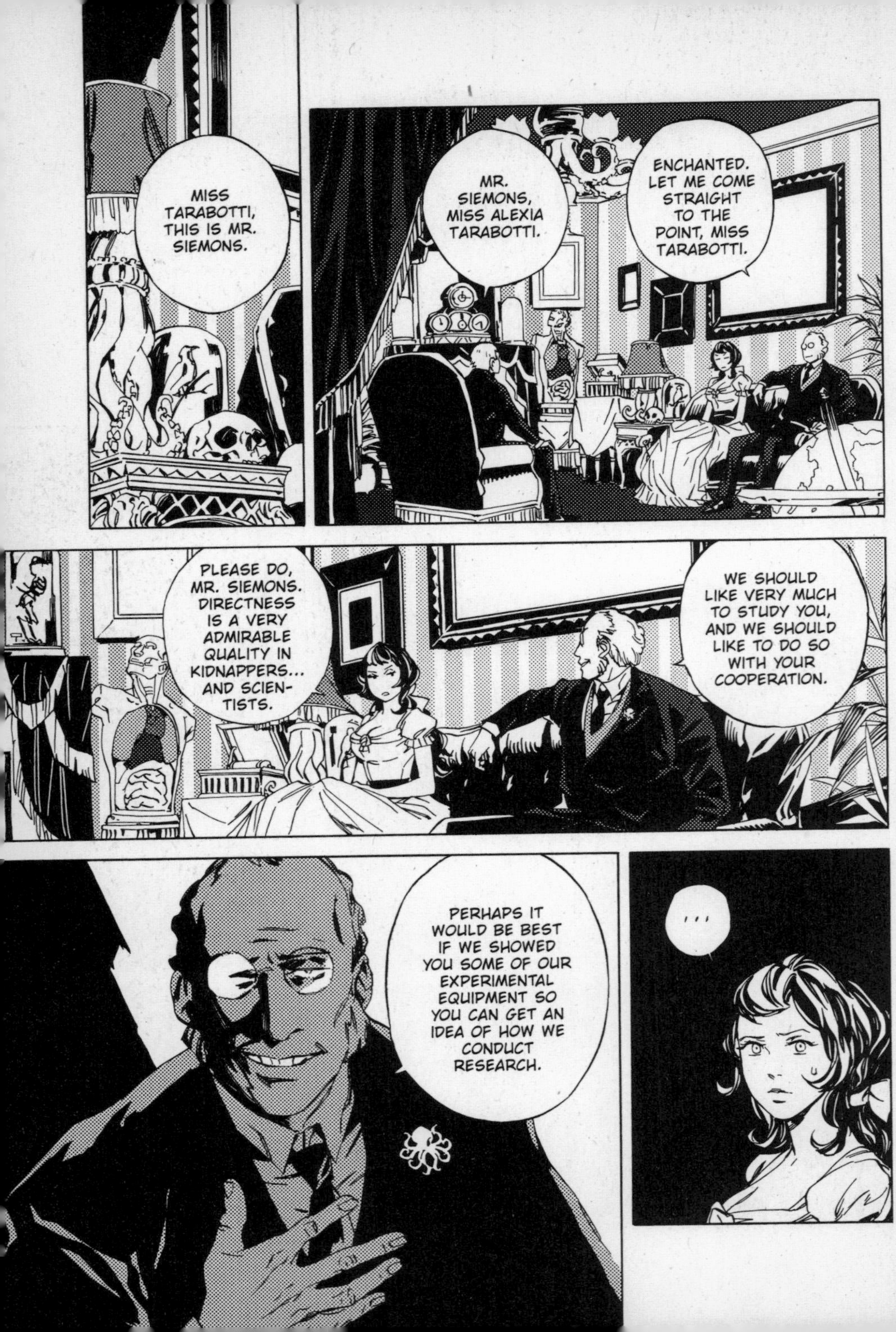
MISS TARABOTTI, THIS IS MR. SIEMONS.
MR. SIEMONS, MISS ALEXIA TARABOTTI.
ENCHANTED. LET ME COME STRAIGHT TO THE POINT, MISS TARABOTTI.
PLEASE DO, MR. SIEMONS. DIRECTNESS IS A VERY ADMIRABLE QUALITY IN KIDNAPPERS... AND SCIEN-TISTS.
WE SHOULD LIKE VERY MUCH TO STUDY YOU, AND WE SHOULD LIKE TO DO SO WITH YOUR COOPERATION.
PERHAPS IT WOULD BE BEST IF WE SHOWED YOU SOME OF OUR EXPERIMENTAL EQUIPMENT SO YOU CAN GET AN IDEA OF HOW WE CONDUCT RESEARCH.
...

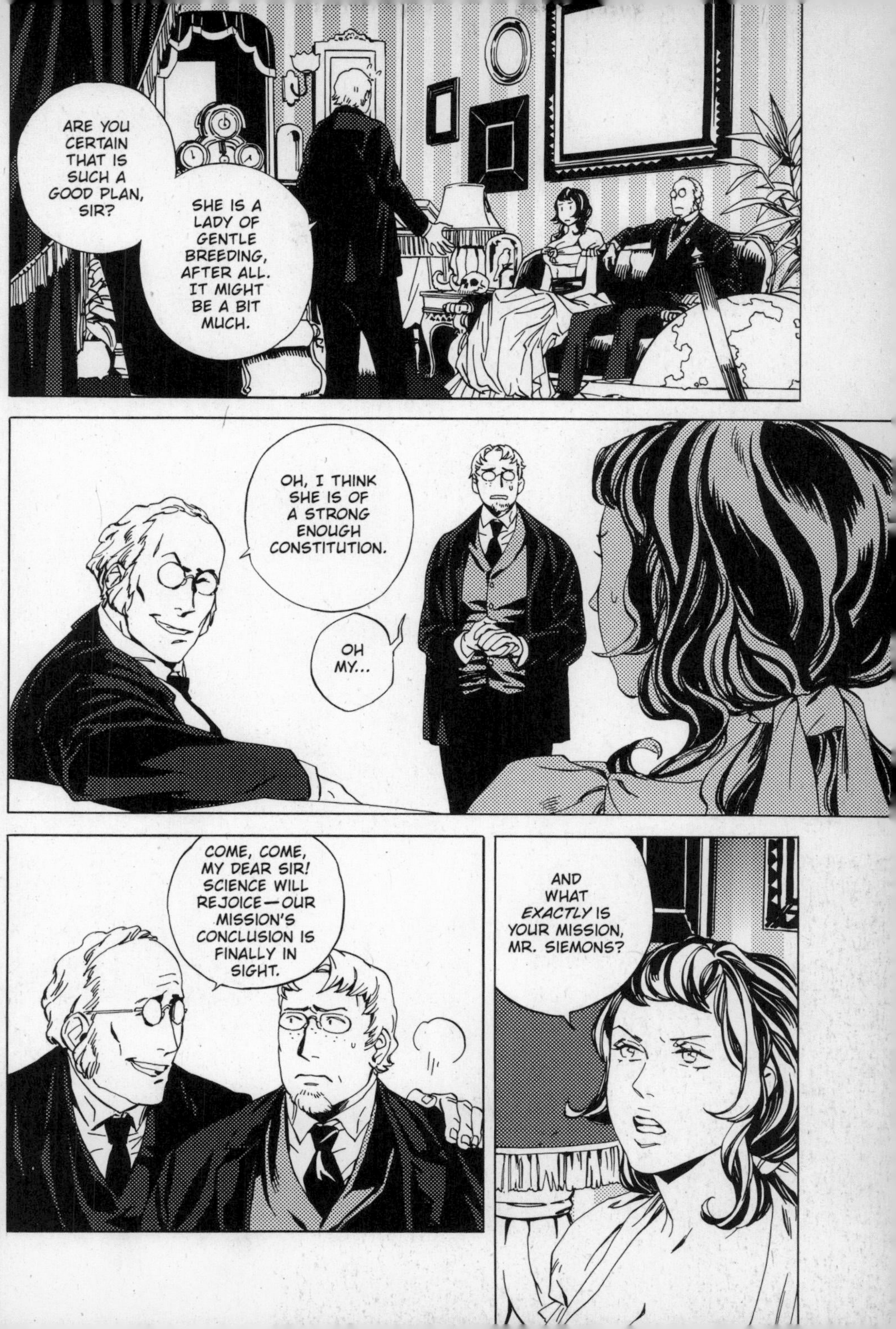
ARE YOU CERTAIN THAT IS SUCH A GOOD PLAN, SIR?
SHE IS A LADY OF GENTLE BREEDING, AFTER ALL. IT MIGHT BE A BIT MUCH.
OH, I THINK SHE IS OF A STRONG ENOUGH CONSTITUTION.
OH MY...
COME, COME, MY DEAR SIR! SCIENCE WILL REJOICE—OUR MISSION'S CONCLUSION IS FINALLY IN SIGHT.
AND WHAT *EXACTLY* IS YOUR MISSION, MR. SIEMONS?

WHY, TO PROTECT THE COMMON-WEALTH, OF COURSE.

FROM WHOM?

FROM THE SUPER-NATURAL THREAT, WHAT ELSE?

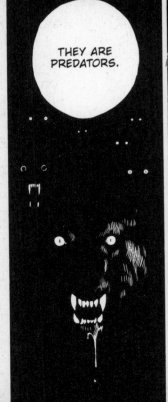

THEY ARE PREDATORS.

FOR THOUSANDS OF YEARS, THEY FED UPON US AND ATTACKED US.

WHAT THEY HAVE GIVEN US IN MILITARY KNOWLEDGE HAS ALLOWED US TO BUILD AN EMPIRE, TRUE, BUT AT WHAT COST?

THEY PERMEATE OUR GOVERNMENT AND OUR DEFENSES, BUT THEY ARE NOT MOTIVATED TO PROTECT THE BEST INTEREST OF THE FULLY HUMAN SPECIES.

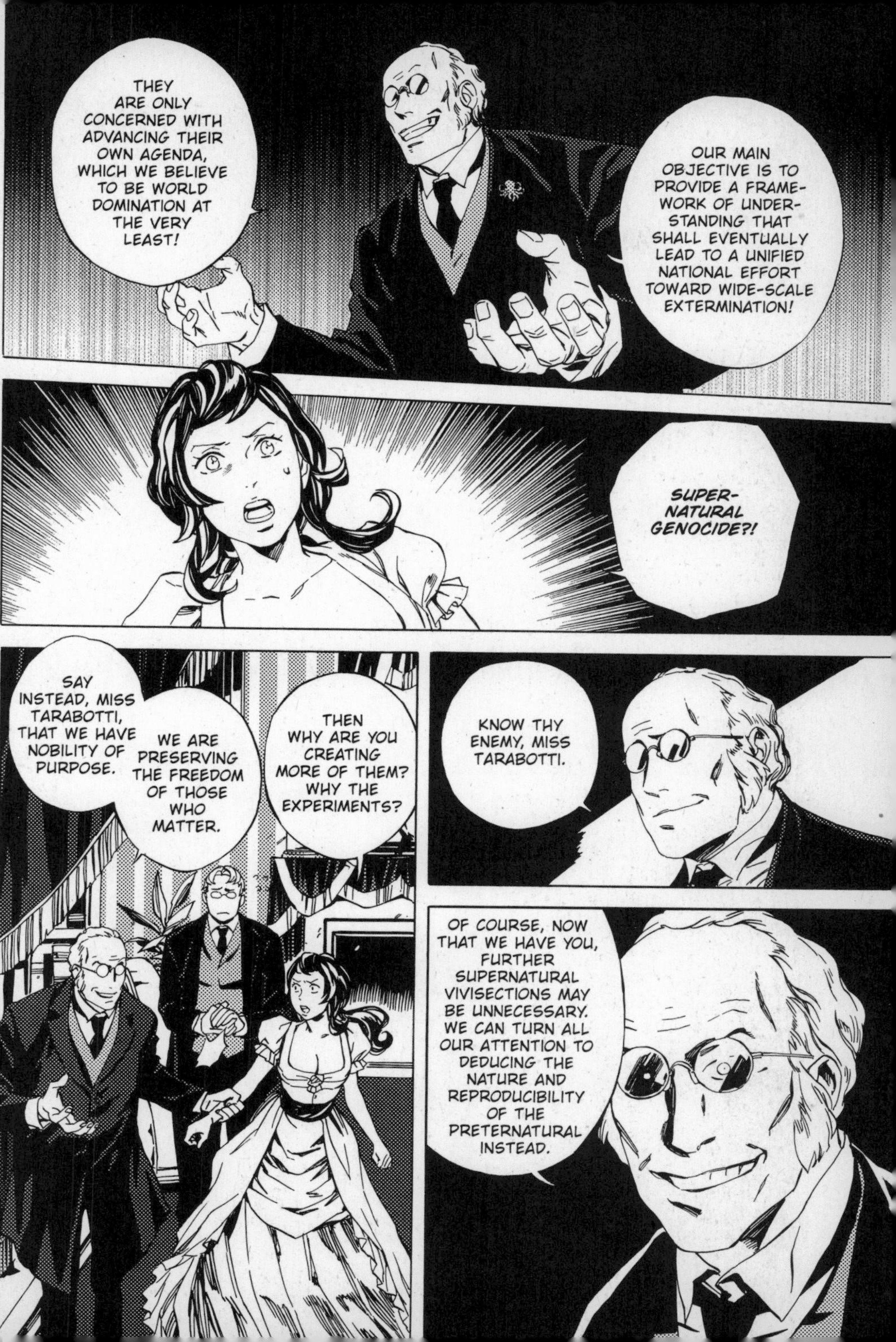

THEY ARE ONLY CONCERNED WITH ADVANCING THEIR OWN AGENDA, WHICH WE BELIEVE TO BE WORLD DOMINATION AT THE VERY LEAST!
OUR MAIN OBJECTIVE IS TO PROVIDE A FRAME-WORK OF UNDER-STANDING THAT SHALL EVENTUALLY LEAD TO A UNIFIED NATIONAL EFFORT TOWARD WIDE-SCALE EXTERMINATION!
SUPER-NATURAL GENOCIDE?!
SAY INSTEAD, MISS TARABOTTI, THAT WE HAVE NOBILITY OF PURPOSE.
WE ARE PRESERVING THE FREEDOM OF THOSE WHO MATTER.
THEN WHY ARE YOU CREATING MORE OF THEM? WHY THE EXPERIMENTS?
KNOW THY ENEMY, MISS TARABOTTI.
OF COURSE, NOW THAT WE HAVE YOU, FURTHER SUPERNATURAL VIVISECTIONS MAY BE UNNECESSARY. WE CAN TURN ALL OUR ATTENTION TO DEDUCING THE NATURE AND REPRODUCIBILITY OF THE PRETERNATURAL INSTEAD.

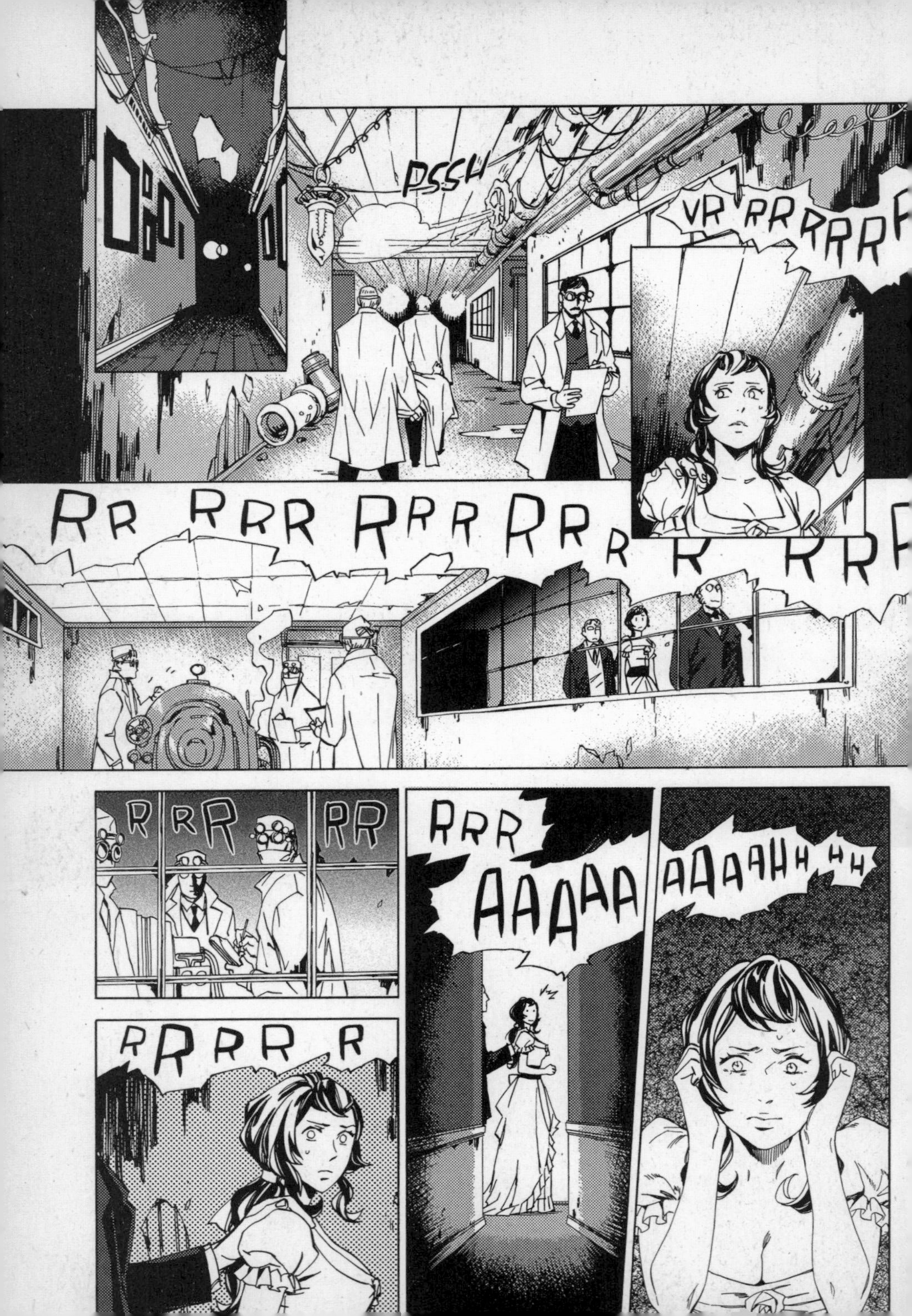
PSSH
VR RRRRRRRR
RR RRR RRR RRR R R RRR
RRR RR
RRRRR R
RRR
AAAAA AAAAHH HH

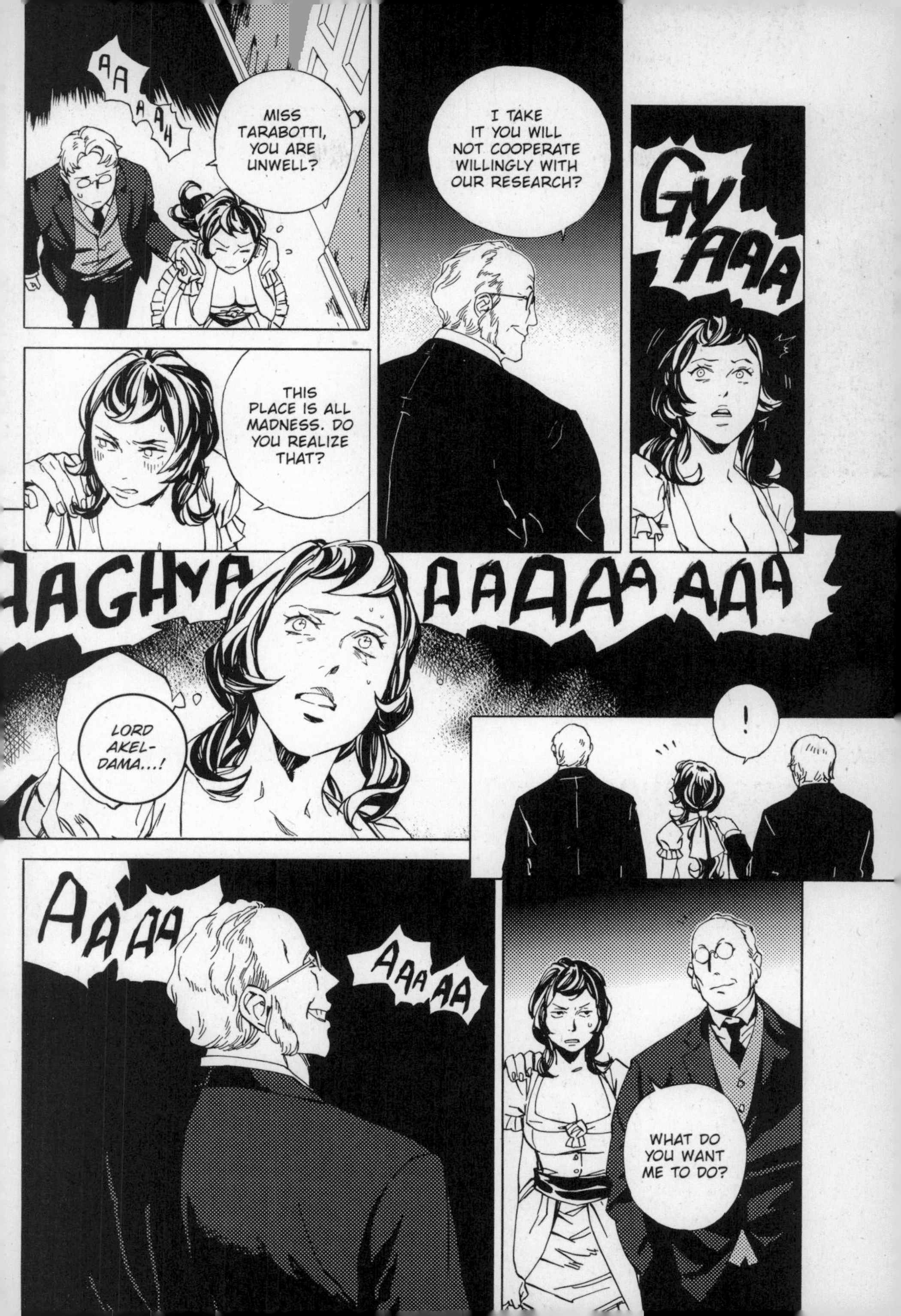
AAAAH
MISS TARABOTTI, YOU ARE UNWELL?
I TAKE IT YOU WILL NOT COOPERATE WILLINGLY WITH OUR RESEARCH?
THIS PLACE IS ALL MADNESS. DO YOU REALIZE THAT?
GYAAA
AAGHYAAAAAAAAAAA
LORD AKEL-DAMA...!
!
AAAA
AAAAA
WHAT DO YOU WANT ME TO DO?

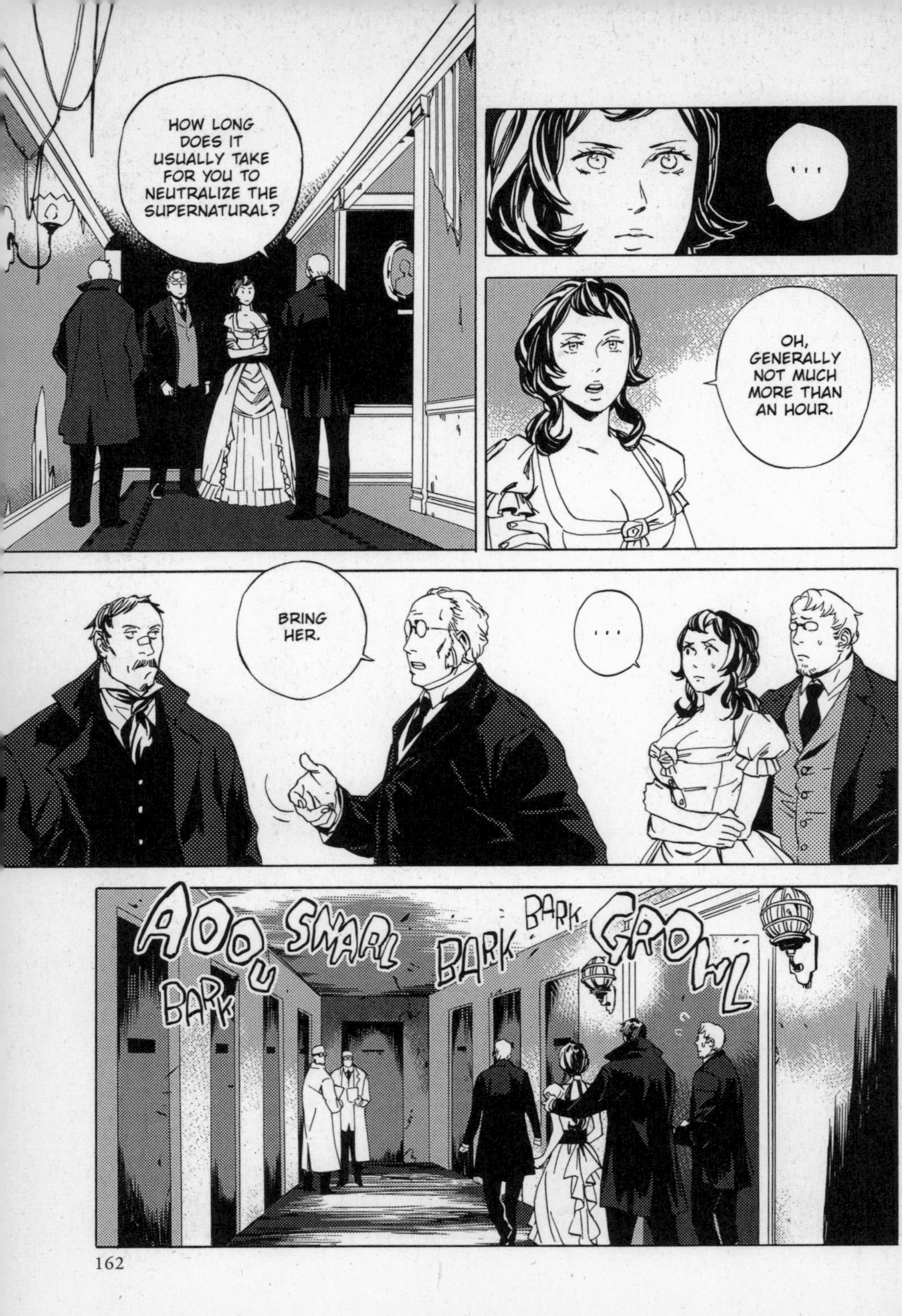
HOW LONG DOES IT USUALLY TAKE FOR YOU TO NEUTRALIZE THE SUPERNATURAL?
...
OH, GENERALLY NOT MUCH MORE THAN AN HOUR.
BRING HER.
...
AOOU
SNARL
BARK
BARK
GROWL
BARK

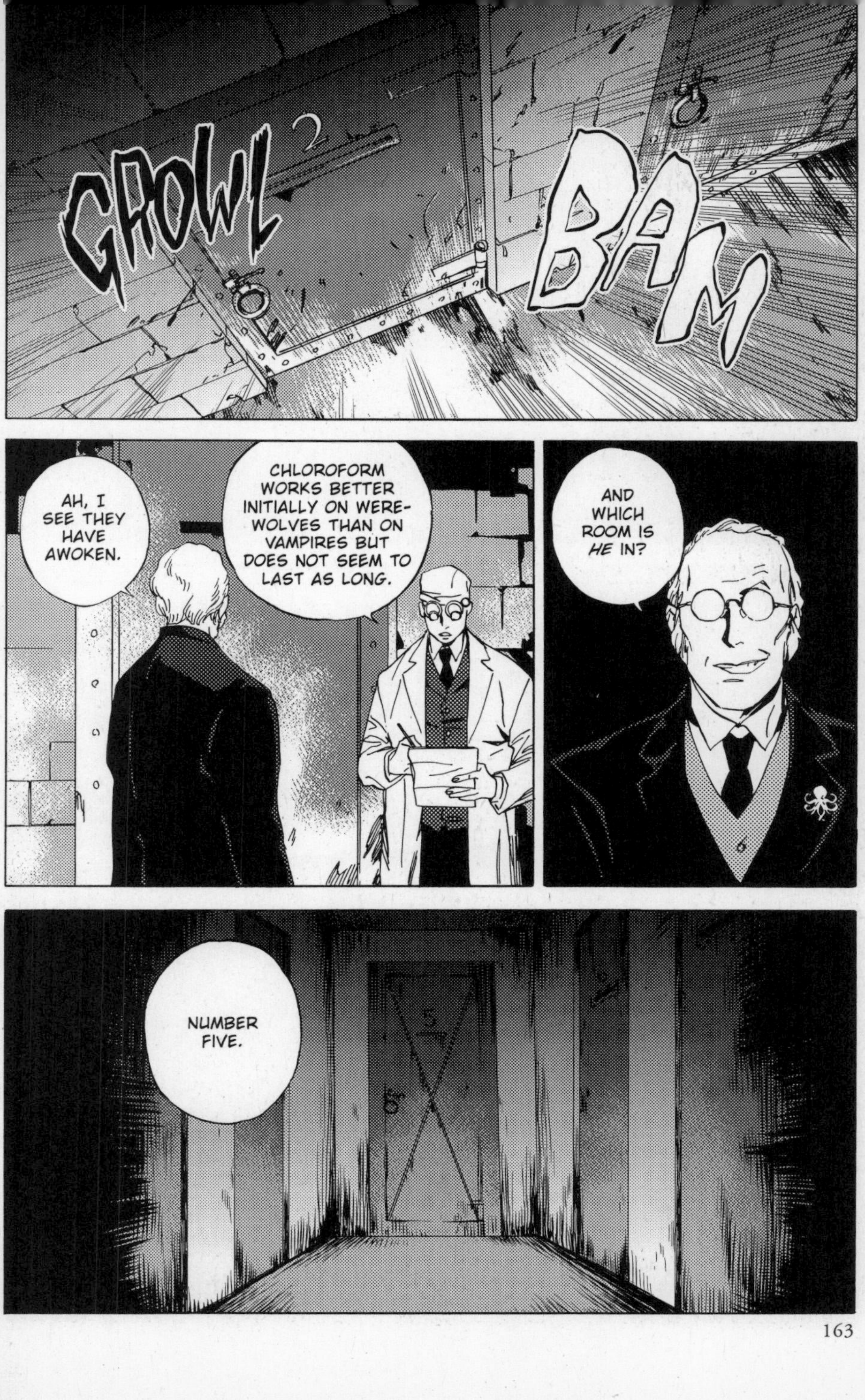
GROWL
BAM
AH, I SEE THEY HAVE AWOKEN.
CHLOROFORM WORKS BETTER INITIALLY ON WERE-WOLVES THAN ON VAMPIRES BUT DOES NOT SEEM TO LAST AS LONG.
AND WHICH ROOM IS *HE* IN?
NUMBER FIVE.

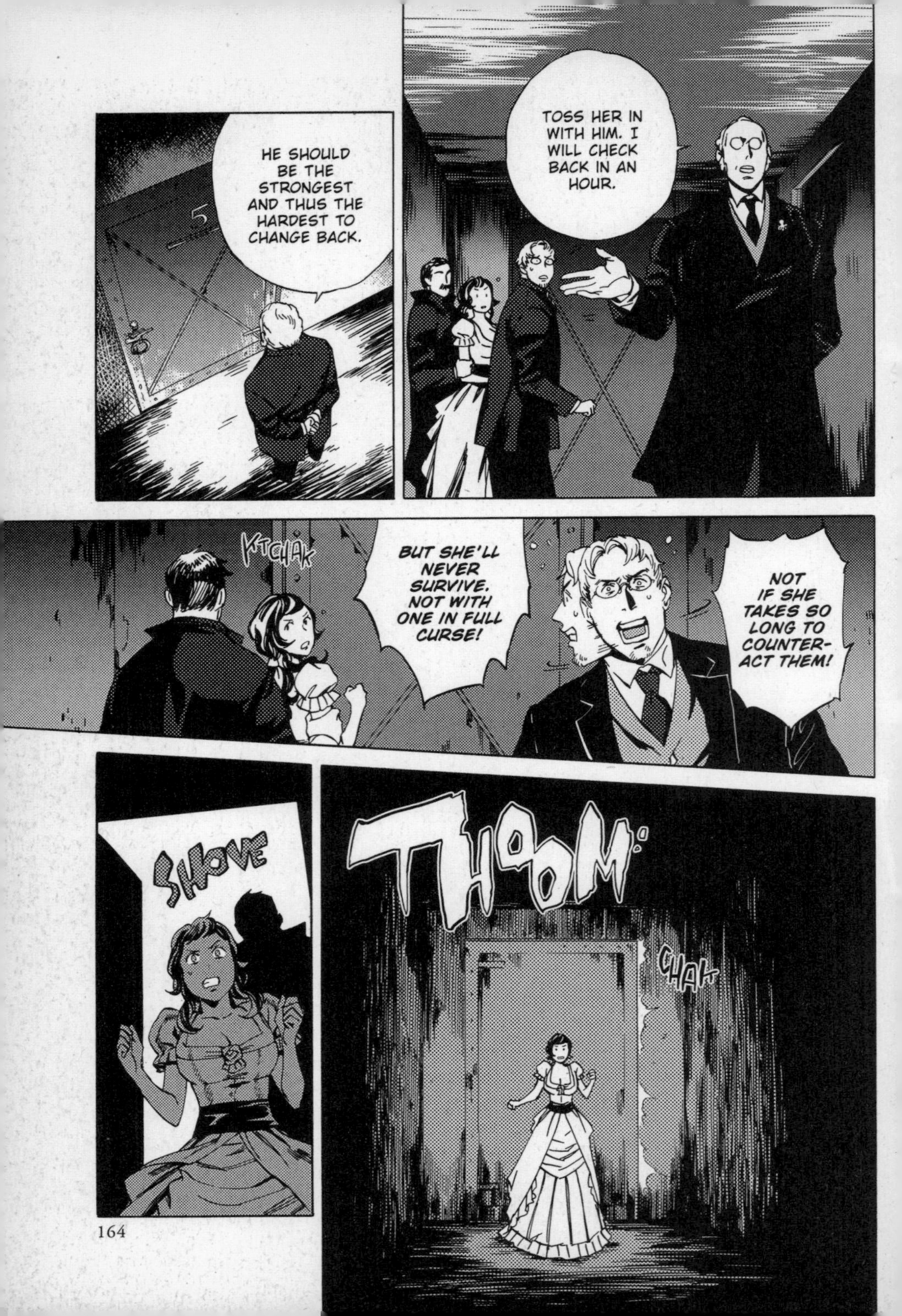
HE SHOULD BE THE STRONGEST AND THUS THE HARDEST TO CHANGE BACK.
TOSS HER IN WITH HIM. I WILL CHECK BACK IN AN HOUR.
KTCHAK
BUT SHE'LL NEVER SURVIVE. NOT WITH ONE IN FULL CURSE!
NOT IF SHE TAKES SO LONG TO COUNTER-ACT THEM!
SHOVE
THOOM
CHAK

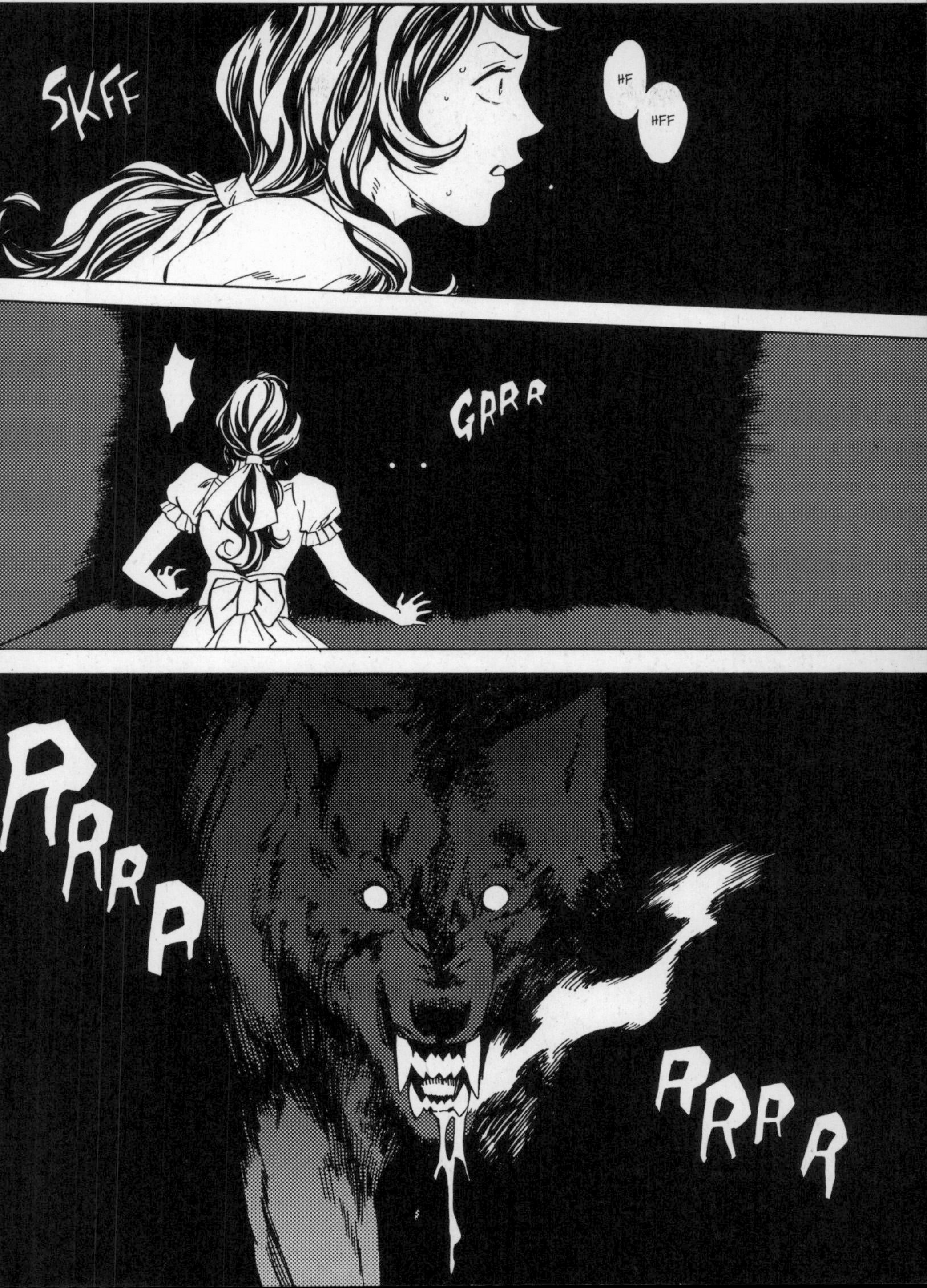
SKFF
HF
HFF
GRRR
RRRRA
RRRR

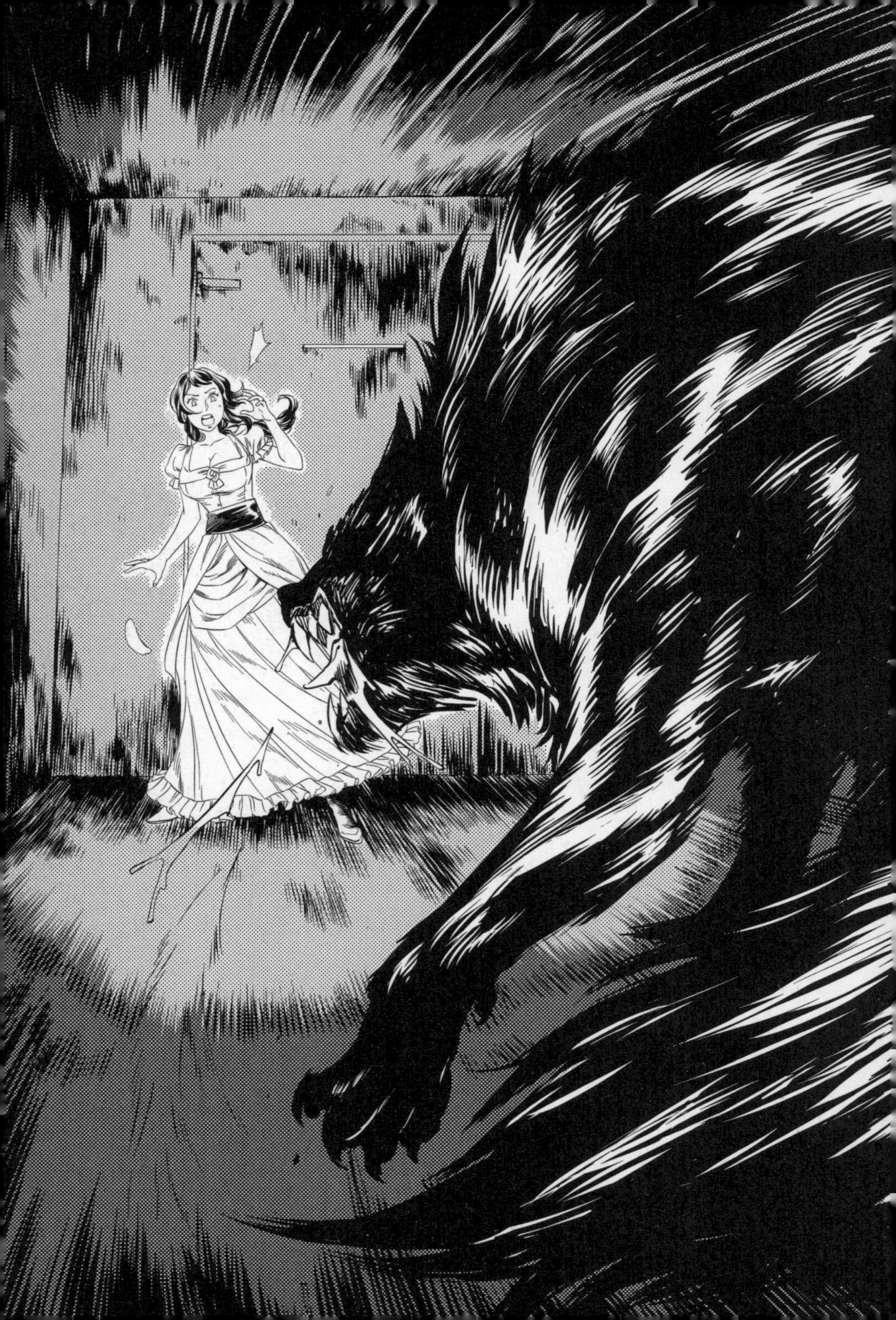

SOULLESS

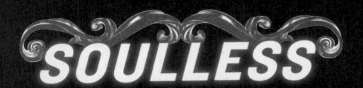

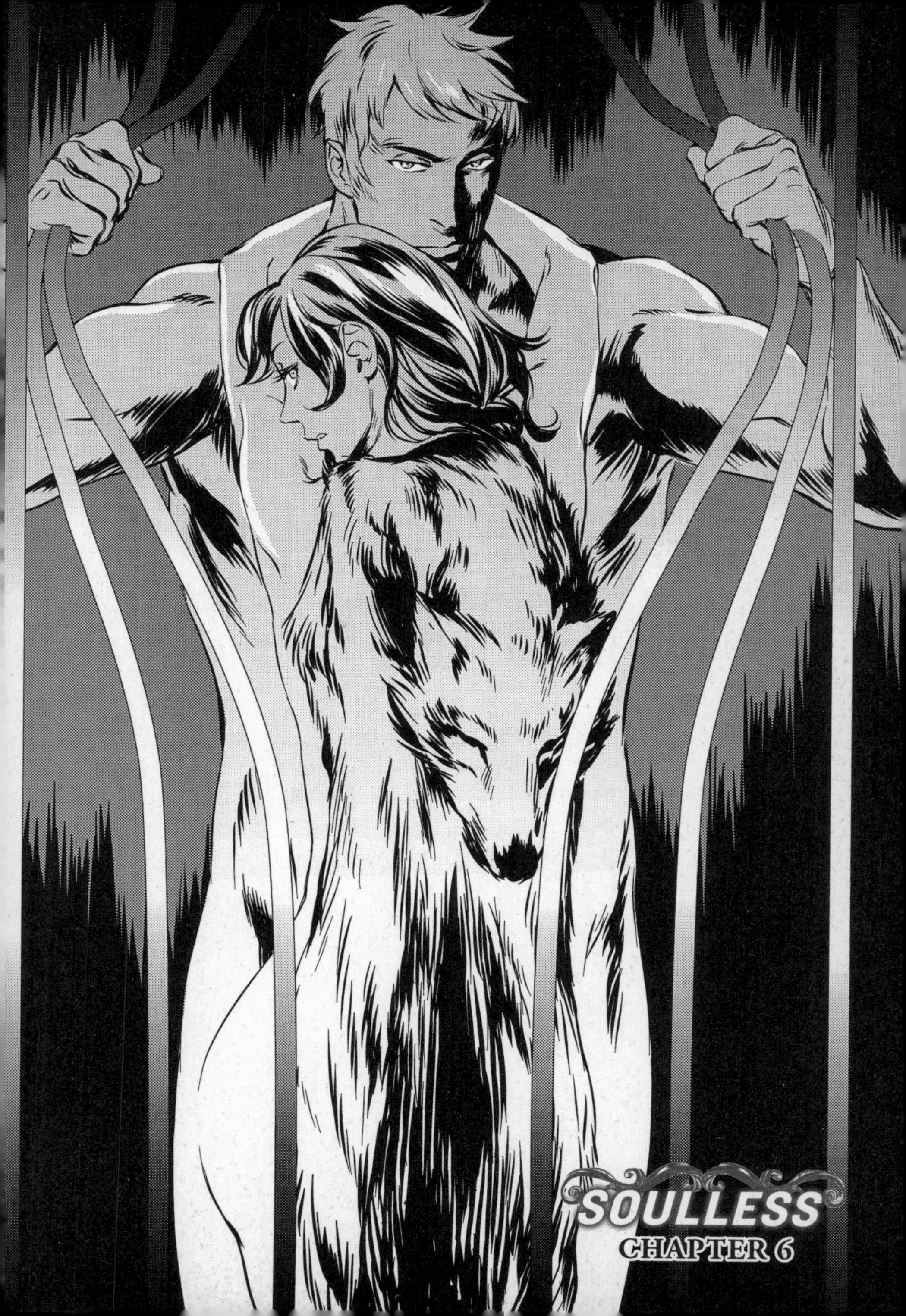
SOULLESS
CHAPTER 6

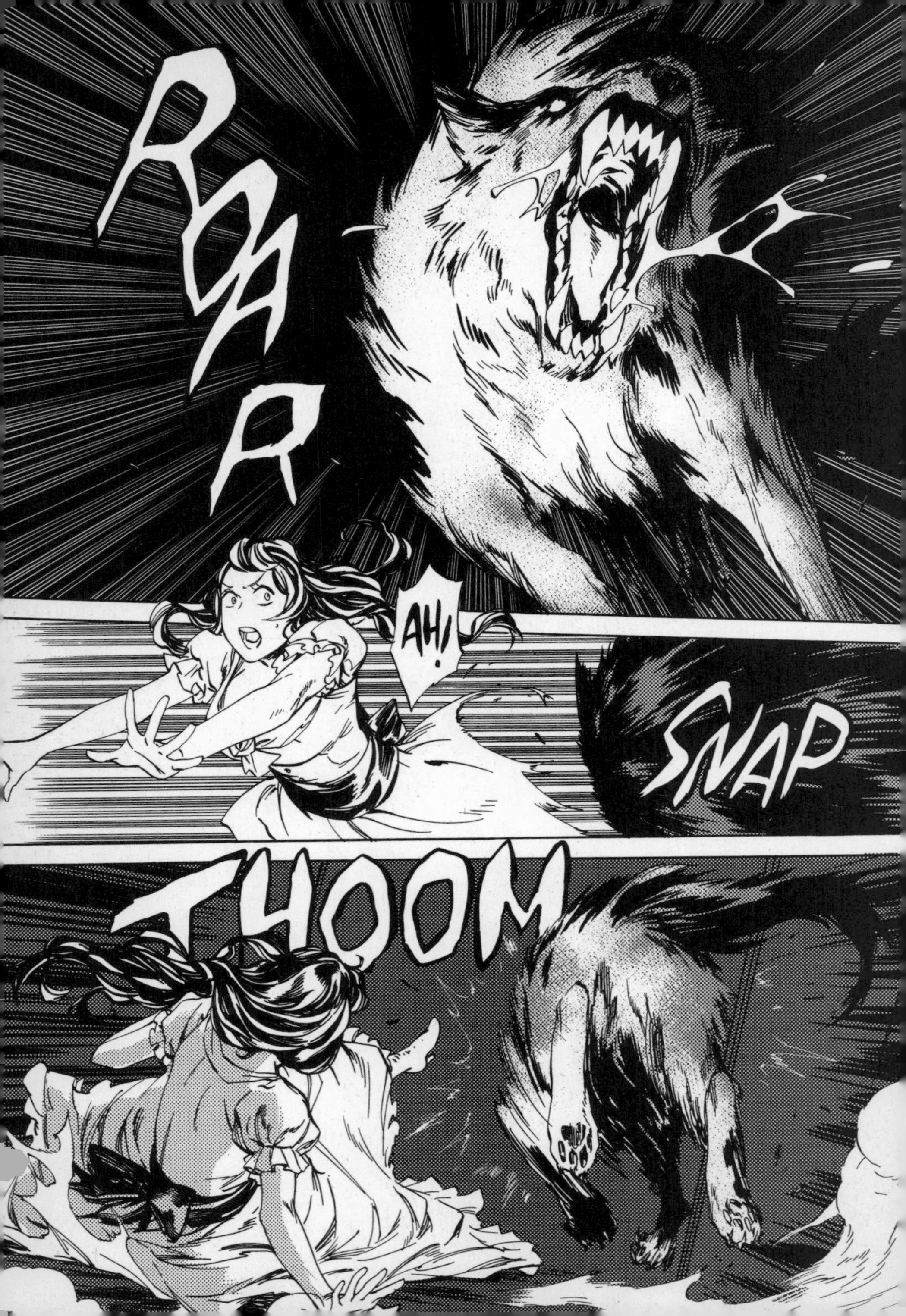
ROAAR
AH!
SNAP
THOOM

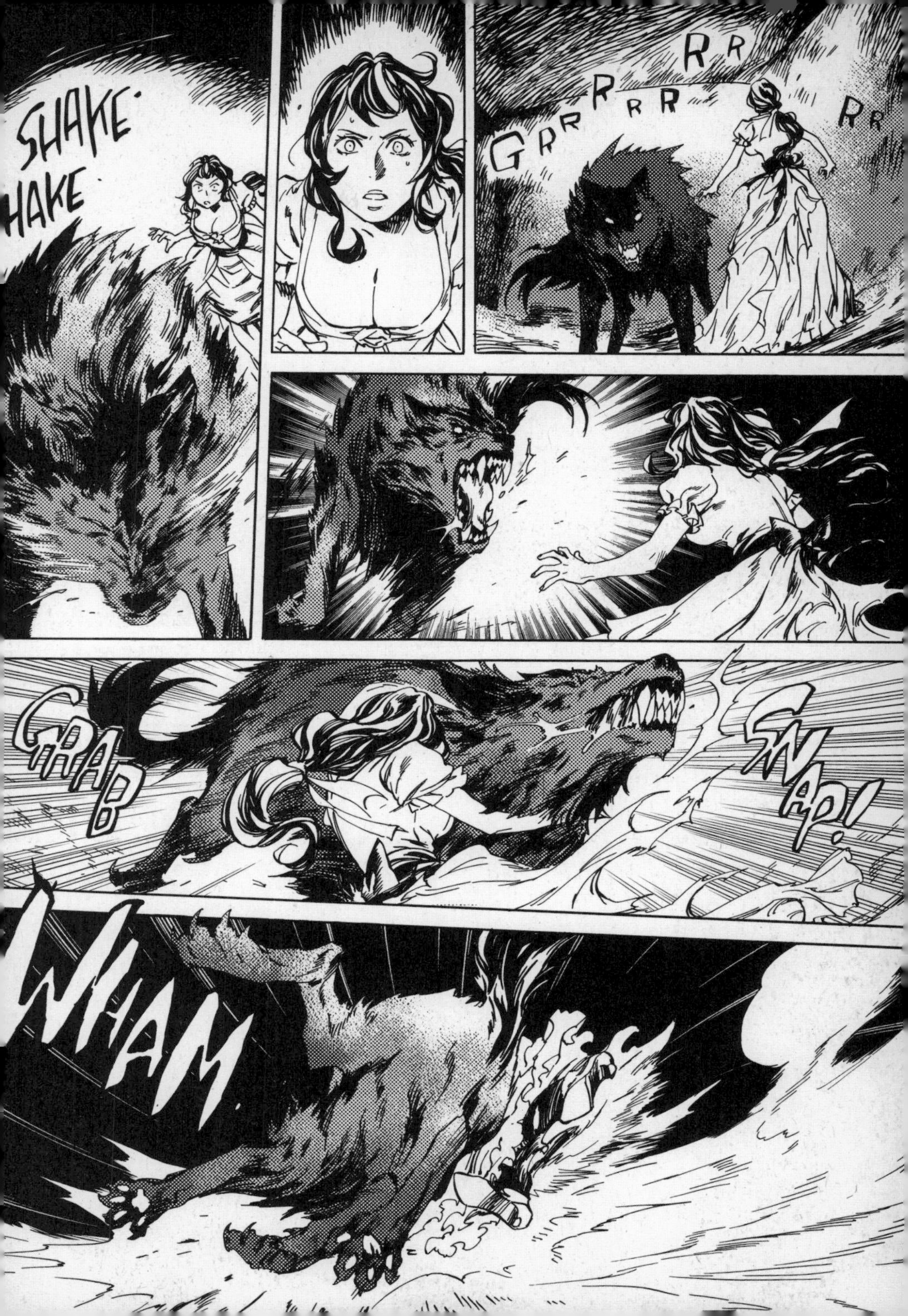
SHAKE
SHAKE
GRRRRRRRRRR
GRAB
SNAP!
WHAM

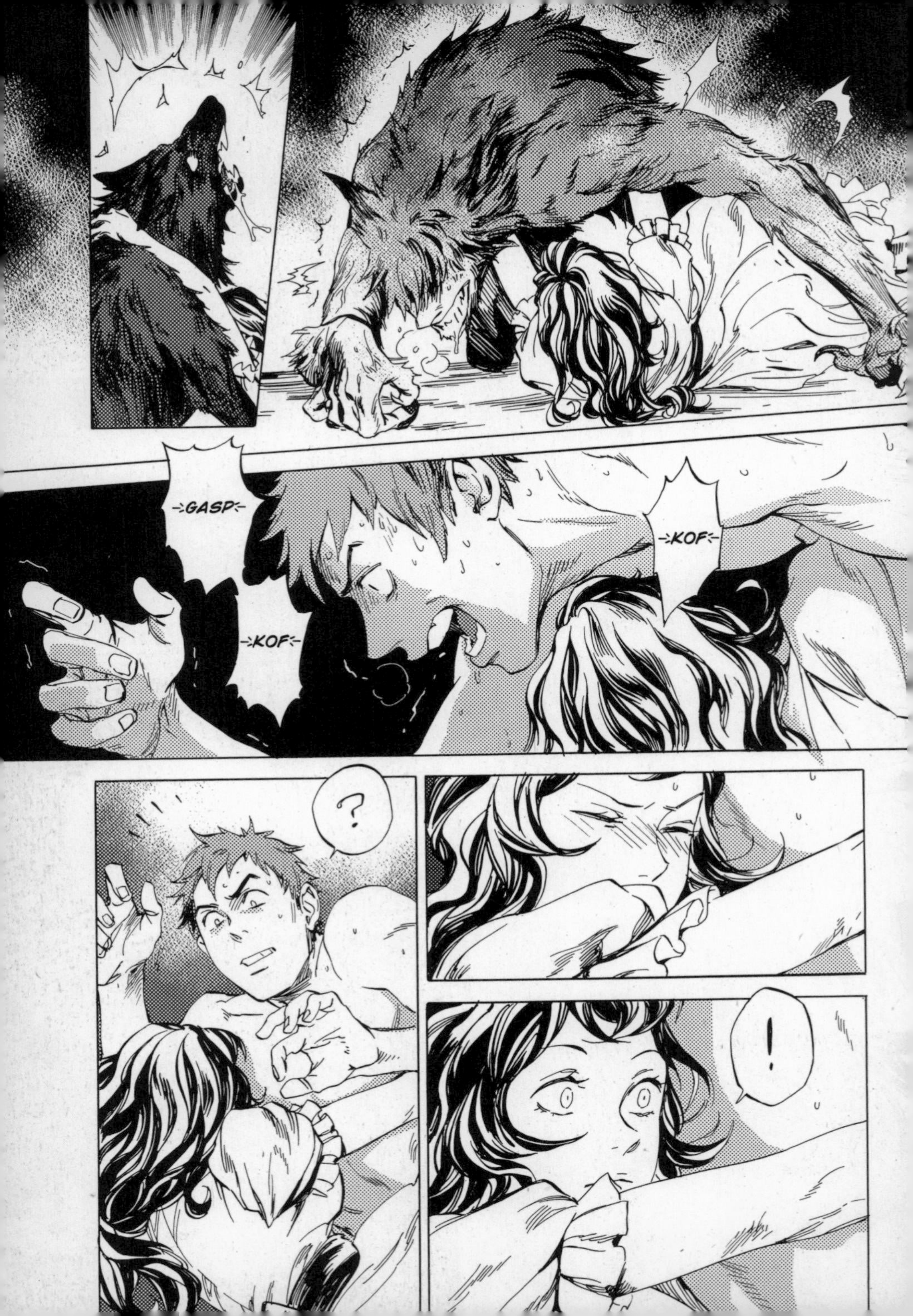
GASP
KOF
KOF
?
!

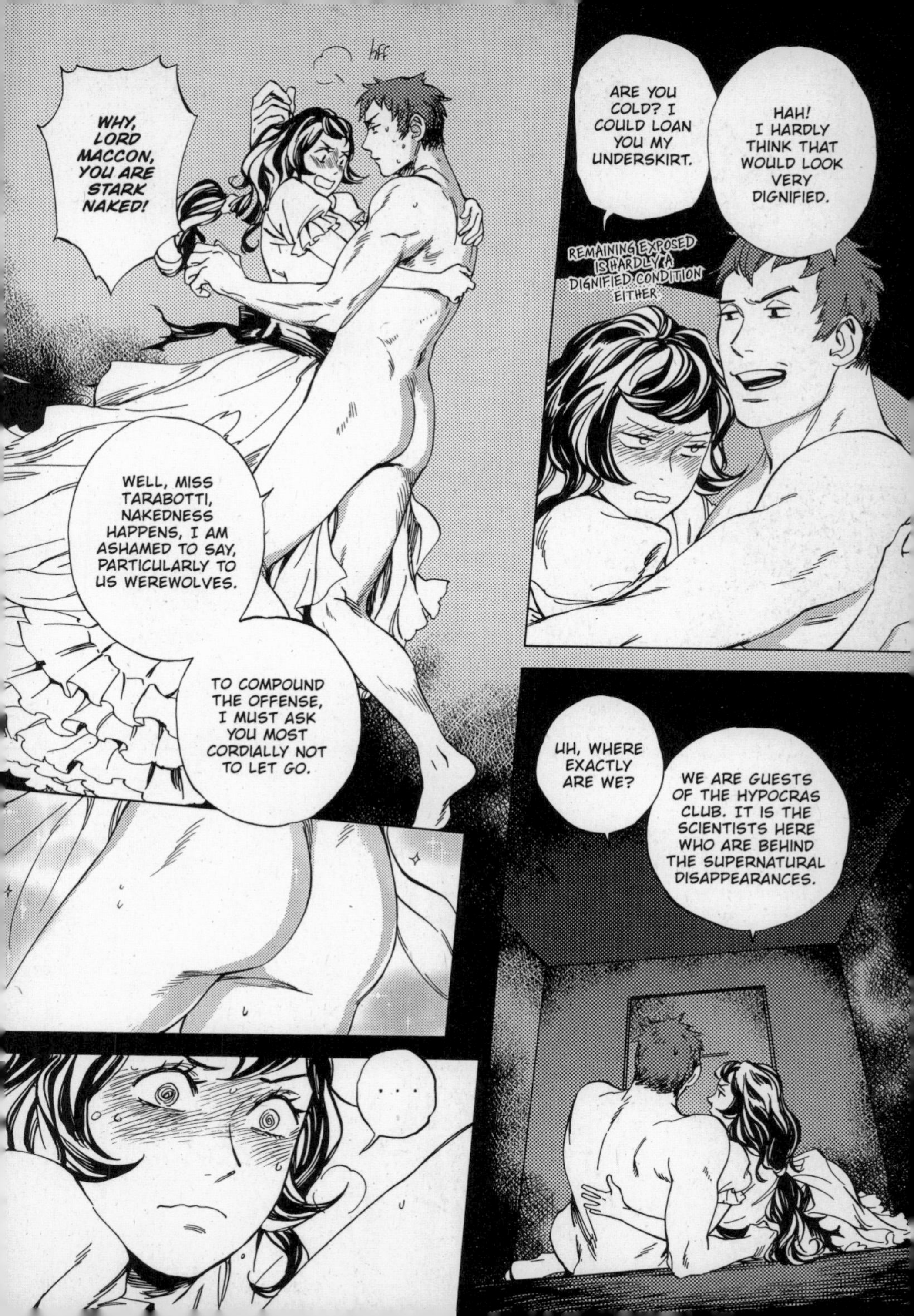

hff
WHY, LORD MACCON, YOU ARE STARK NAKED!
WELL, MISS TARABOTTI, NAKEDNESS HAPPENS, I AM ASHAMED TO SAY, PARTICULARLY TO US WEREWOLVES.
TO COMPOUND THE OFFENSE, I MUST ASK YOU MOST CORDIALLY NOT TO LET GO.
...
ARE YOU COLD? I COULD LOAN YOU MY UNDERSKIRT.
HAH! I HARDLY THINK THAT WOULD LOOK VERY DIGNIFIED.
REMAINING EXPOSED IS HARDLY A DIGNIFIED CONDITION EITHER.
UH, WHERE EXACTLY ARE WE?
WE ARE GUESTS OF THE HYPOCRAS CLUB. IT IS THE SCIENTISTS HERE WHO ARE BEHIND THE SUPERNATURAL DISAPPEARANCES.

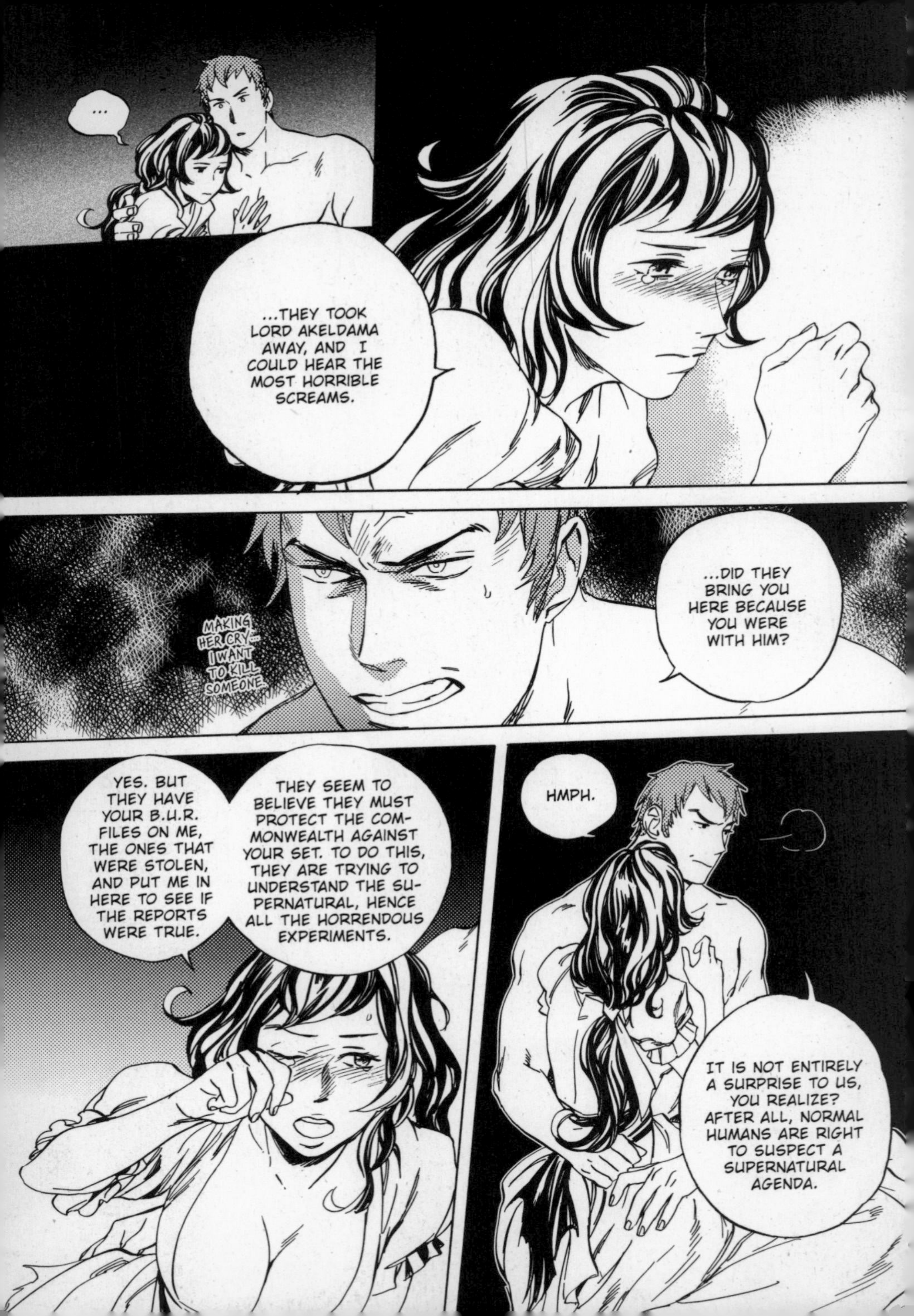
...
...THEY TOOK LORD AKELDAMA AWAY, AND I COULD HEAR THE MOST HORRIBLE SCREAMS.
MAKING HER CRY... I WANT TO KILL SOMEONE.
...DID THEY BRING YOU HERE BECAUSE YOU WERE WITH HIM?
YES. BUT THEY HAVE YOUR B.U.R. FILES ON ME, THE ONES THAT WERE STOLEN, AND PUT ME IN HERE TO SEE IF THE REPORTS WERE TRUE.
THEY SEEM TO BELIEVE THEY MUST PROTECT THE COM-MONWEALTH AGAINST YOUR SET. TO DO THIS, THEY ARE TRYING TO UNDERSTAND THE SU-PERNATURAL, HENCE ALL THE HORRENDOUS EXPERIMENTS.
HMPH.
IT IS NOT ENTIRELY A SURPRISE TO US, YOU REALIZE? AFTER ALL, NORMAL HUMANS ARE RIGHT TO SUSPECT A SUPERNATURAL AGENDA.

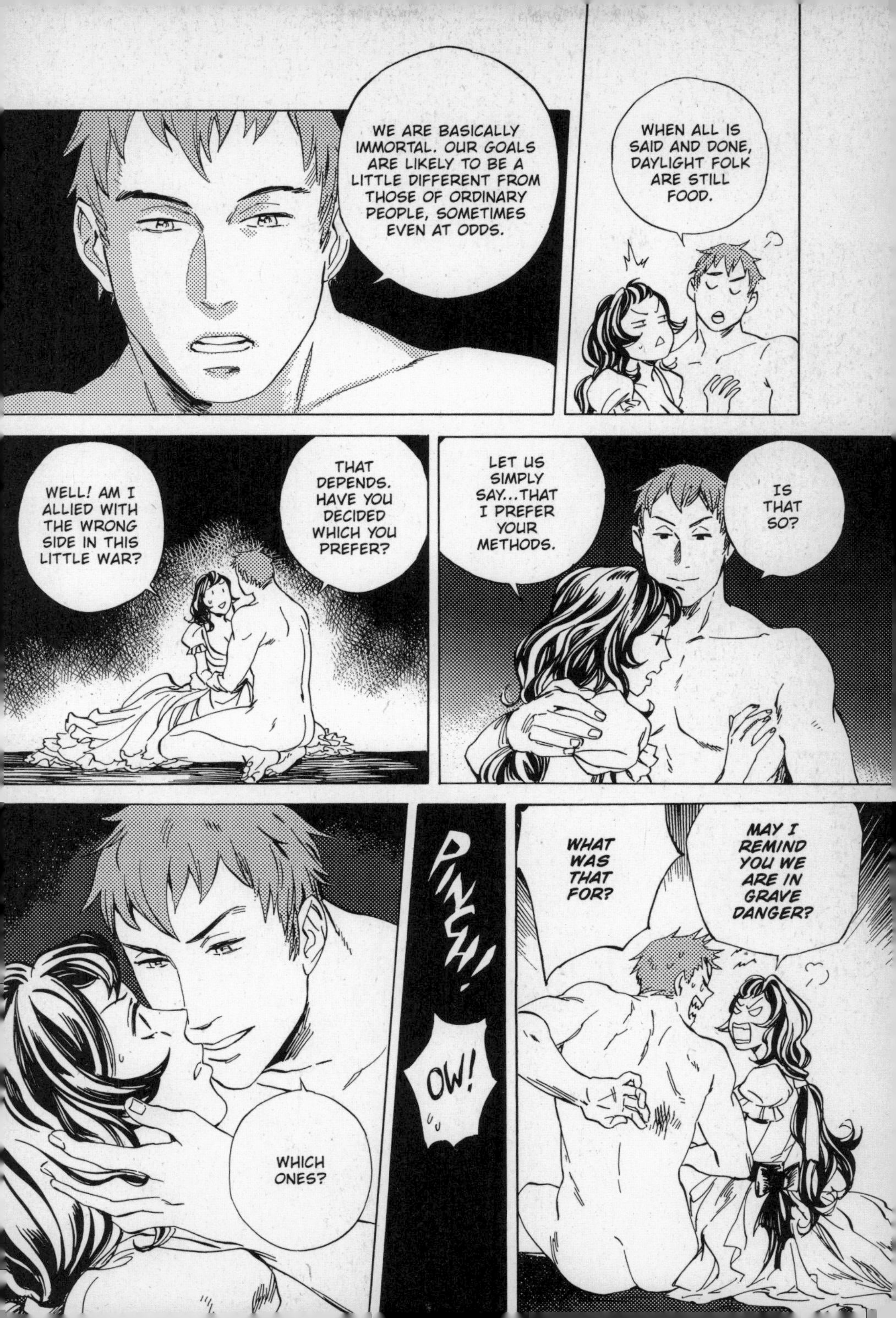
WE ARE BASICALLY IMMORTAL. OUR GOALS ARE LIKELY TO BE A LITTLE DIFFERENT FROM THOSE OF ORDINARY PEOPLE, SOMETIMES EVEN AT ODDS.
WHEN ALL IS SAID AND DONE, DAYLIGHT FOLK ARE STILL FOOD.
WELL! AM I ALLIED WITH THE WRONG SIDE IN THIS LITTLE WAR?
THAT DEPENDS. HAVE YOU DECIDED WHICH YOU PREFER?
LET US SIMPLY SAY...THAT I PREFER YOUR METHODS.
IS THAT SO?
WHICH ONES?
PINCH!
OW!
WHAT WAS THAT FOR?
MAY I REMIND YOU WE ARE IN GRAVE DANGER?

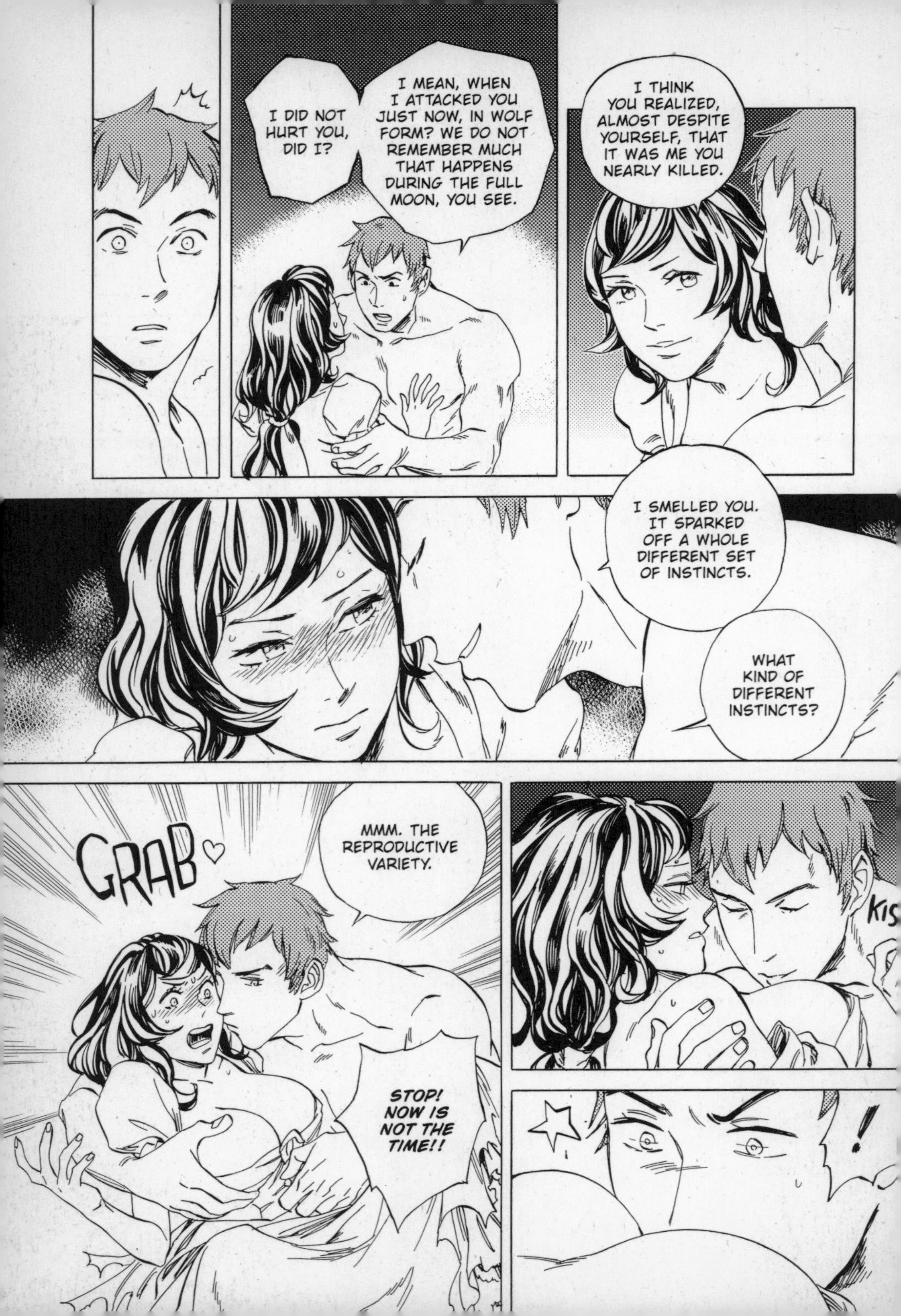

I DID NOT HURT YOU, DID I?
I MEAN, WHEN I ATTACKED YOU JUST NOW, IN WOLF FORM? WE DO NOT REMEMBER MUCH THAT HAPPENS DURING THE FULL MOON, YOU SEE.
I THINK YOU REALIZED, ALMOST DESPITE YOURSELF, THAT IT WAS ME YOU NEARLY KILLED.
I SMELLED YOU. IT SPARKED OFF A WHOLE DIFFERENT SET OF INSTINCTS.
WHAT KIND OF DIFFERENT INSTINCTS?
GRAB ♡
MMM. THE REPRODUCTIVE VARIETY.
STOP! NOW IS NOT THE TIME!!
KIS
!

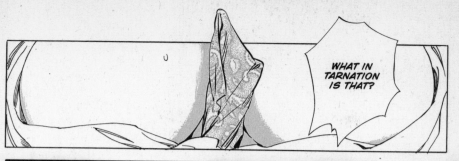

WHAT IN TARNATION IS THAT?

OH, I FORGOT ABOUT THAT.

I PINCHED IT FROM THE DRESSING ROOM WHEN THE SCIENTISTS LEFT ME ALONE FOR A MOMENT. THOUGHT IT MIGHT COME IN HANDY.

VERY RESOURCEFUL, MY DEAR. IT IS AT TIMES LIKE THIS WHEN I REALLY WISH YOU COULD BE ON THE B.U.R. ROSTER.

S-SO, WHAT IS THE PLAN?

ANY MOMENT NOW, EVIL SCIENTISTS MAY COME CHARGING IN.

ALL THE MORE REASON TO GRASP THE OPPORTUNITY. JUST THINK OF THIS AS A SORT OF WEDDING-NIGHT PRELUDE.

NO CHOICE AT THIS POINT, ALEXIA. YOU SIMPLY MUST CALL ME CONALL.

REALLY, LORD MACCON! WHERE DO YOU KEEP GETTING THIS IDEA THAT WE SHOULD MARRY?

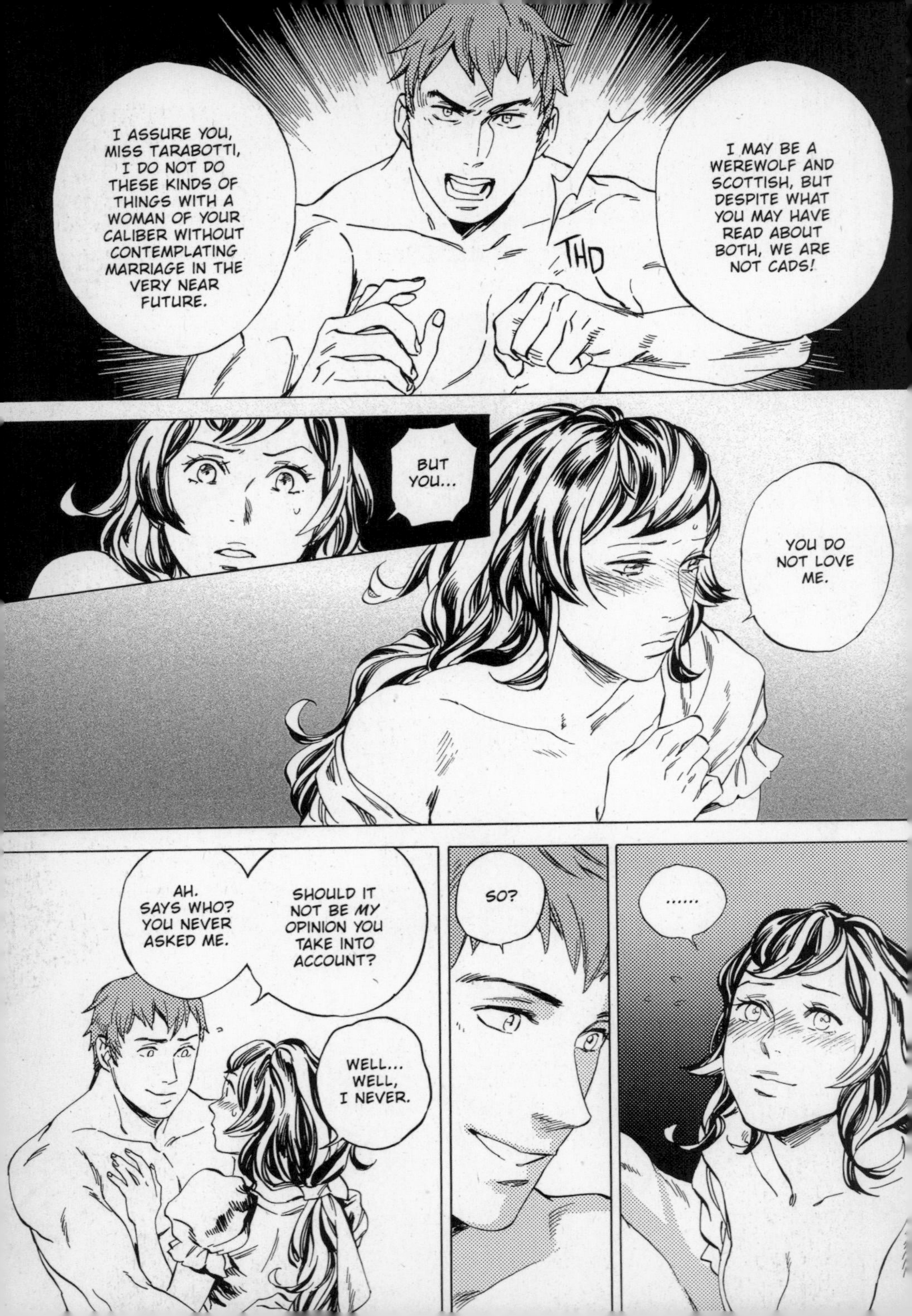
I ASSURE YOU, MISS TARABOTTI, I DO NOT DO THESE KINDS OF THINGS WITH A WOMAN OF YOUR CALIBER WITHOUT CONTEMPLATING MARRIAGE IN THE VERY NEAR FUTURE.
THD
I MAY BE A WEREWOLF AND SCOTTISH, BUT DESPITE WHAT YOU MAY HAVE READ ABOUT BOTH, WE ARE NOT CADS!
BUT YOU...
YOU DO NOT LOVE ME.
AH. SAYS WHO? YOU NEVER ASKED ME.
SHOULD IT NOT BE *MY* OPINION YOU TAKE INTO ACCOUNT?
WELL... WELL, I NEVER.
SO?
......

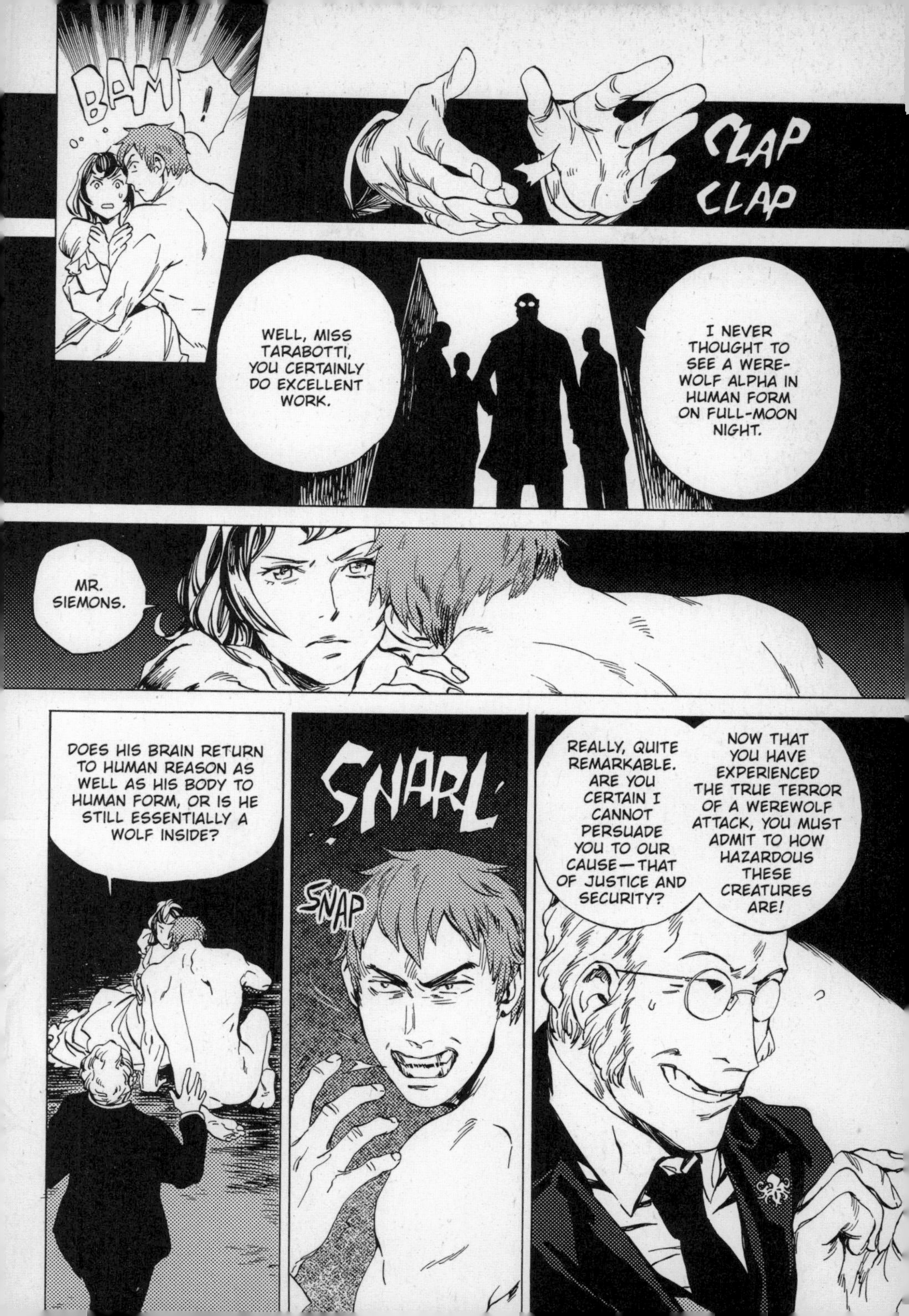
BAM!
CLAP CLAP
WELL, MISS TARABOTTI, YOU CERTAINLY DO EXCELLENT WORK.
I NEVER THOUGHT TO SEE A WERE-WOLF ALPHA IN HUMAN FORM ON FULL-MOON NIGHT.
MR. SIEMONS.
DOES HIS BRAIN RETURN TO HUMAN REASON AS WELL AS HIS BODY TO HUMAN FORM, OR IS HE STILL ESSENTIALLY A WOLF INSIDE?
SNARL
SNAP
REALLY, QUITE REMARKABLE. ARE YOU CERTAIN I CANNOT PERSUADE YOU TO OUR CAUSE—THAT OF JUSTICE AND SECURITY?
NOW THAT YOU HAVE EXPERIENCED THE TRUE TERROR OF A WEREWOLF ATTACK, YOU MUST ADMIT TO HOW HAZARDOUS THESE CREATURES ARE!

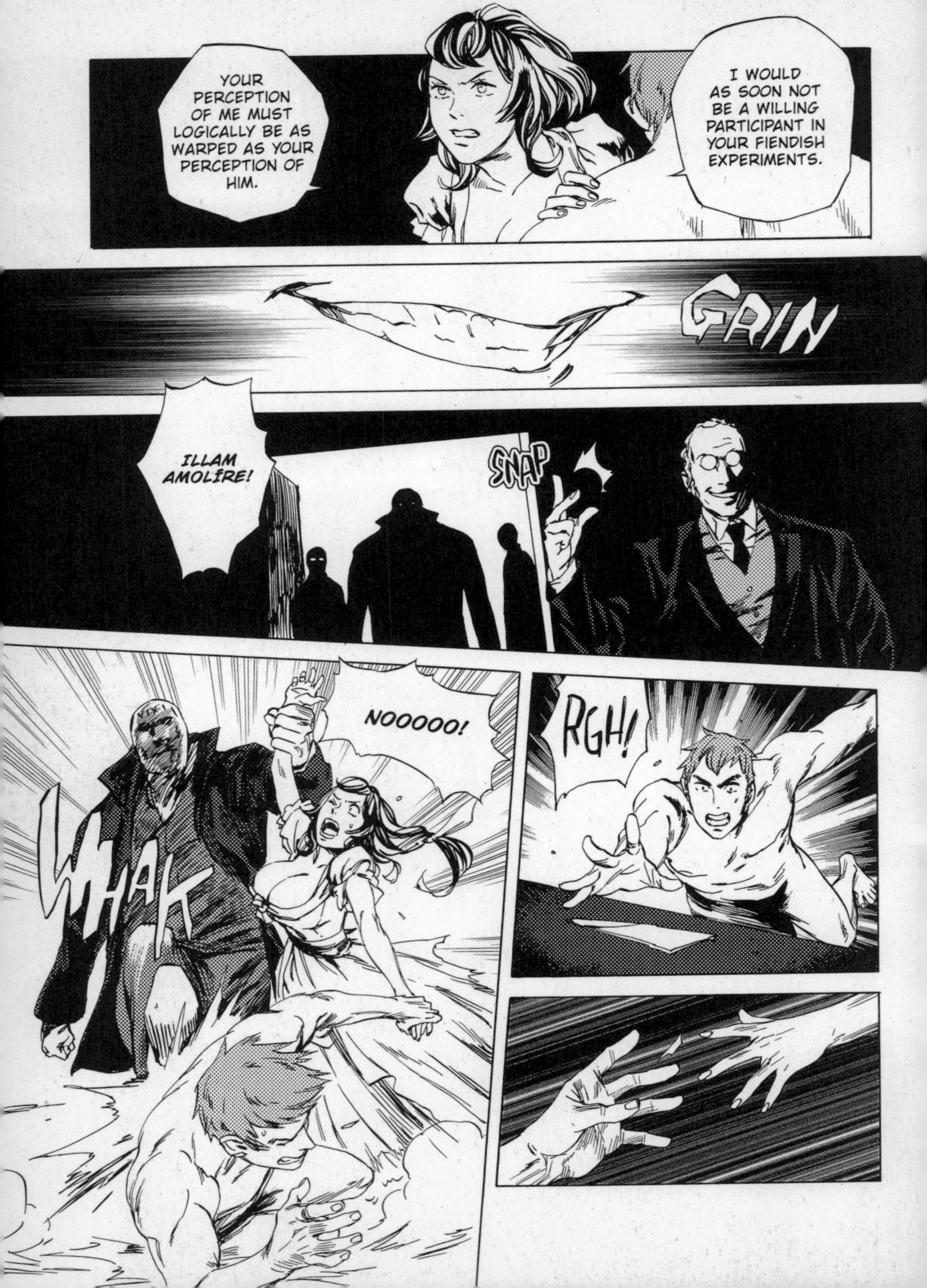
YOUR PERCEPTION OF ME MUST LOGICALLY BE AS WARPED AS YOUR PERCEPTION OF HIM.
I WOULD AS SOON NOT BE A WILLING PARTICIPANT IN YOUR FIENDISH EXPERIMENTS.
GRIN
ILLAM AMOLÎRE!
SNAP
WHAK
NOOOOO!
RGH!

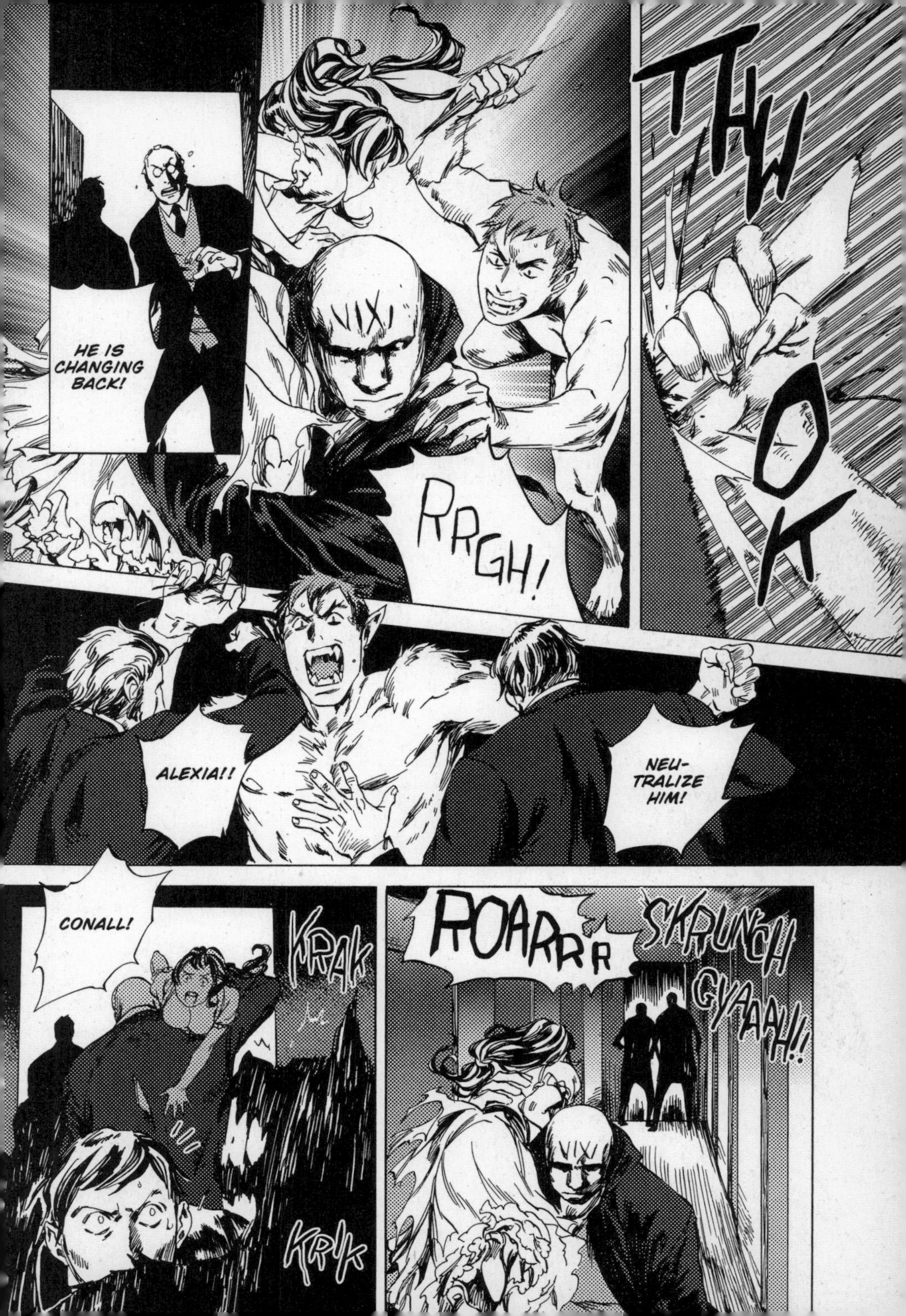

HE IS CHANGING BACK!
RRGH!
THWOK
ALEXIA!!
NEU-TRALIZE HIM!
CONALL!
KRAK
KRIK
ROARRRR
SKRUNCH
GYAAAH!!

UGH!

OOZE...

...WHY HAD LORD MACCON BEEN SO INTENT ON WOUNDING THE AUTOMATON?

...HE NEEDS A TRAIL TO FOLLOW.

THIS WILL NEVER DO. IT'S NOT BLEEDING ENOUGH TO LEAVE DROPS BEHIND.

SLASH!

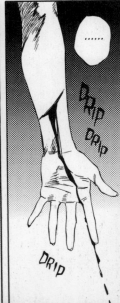

......

DRIP DRIP

DRIP

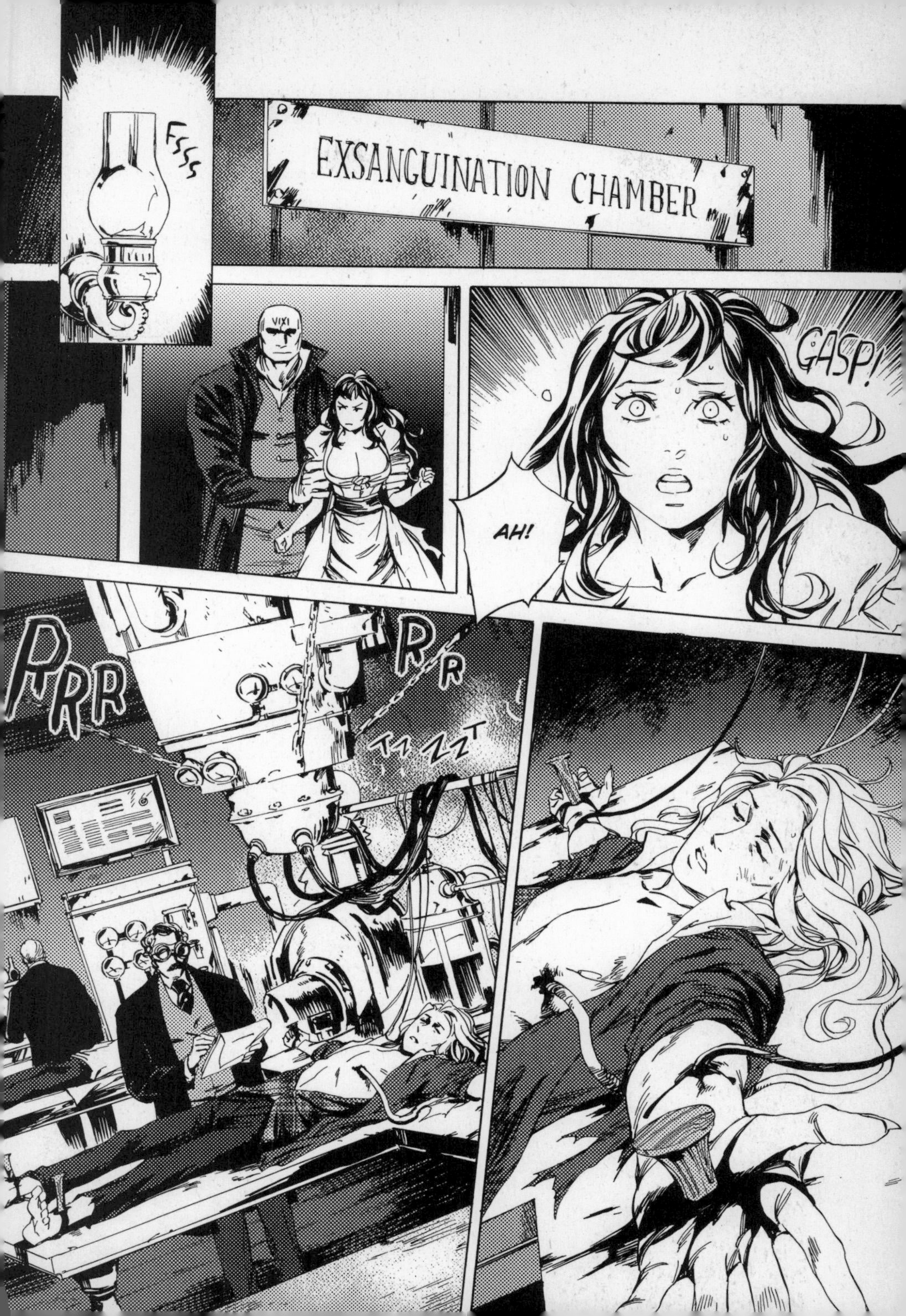
FSSS
EXSANGUINATION CHAMBER
VIXI
GASP!
AH!
RRR
RR
TZZZT

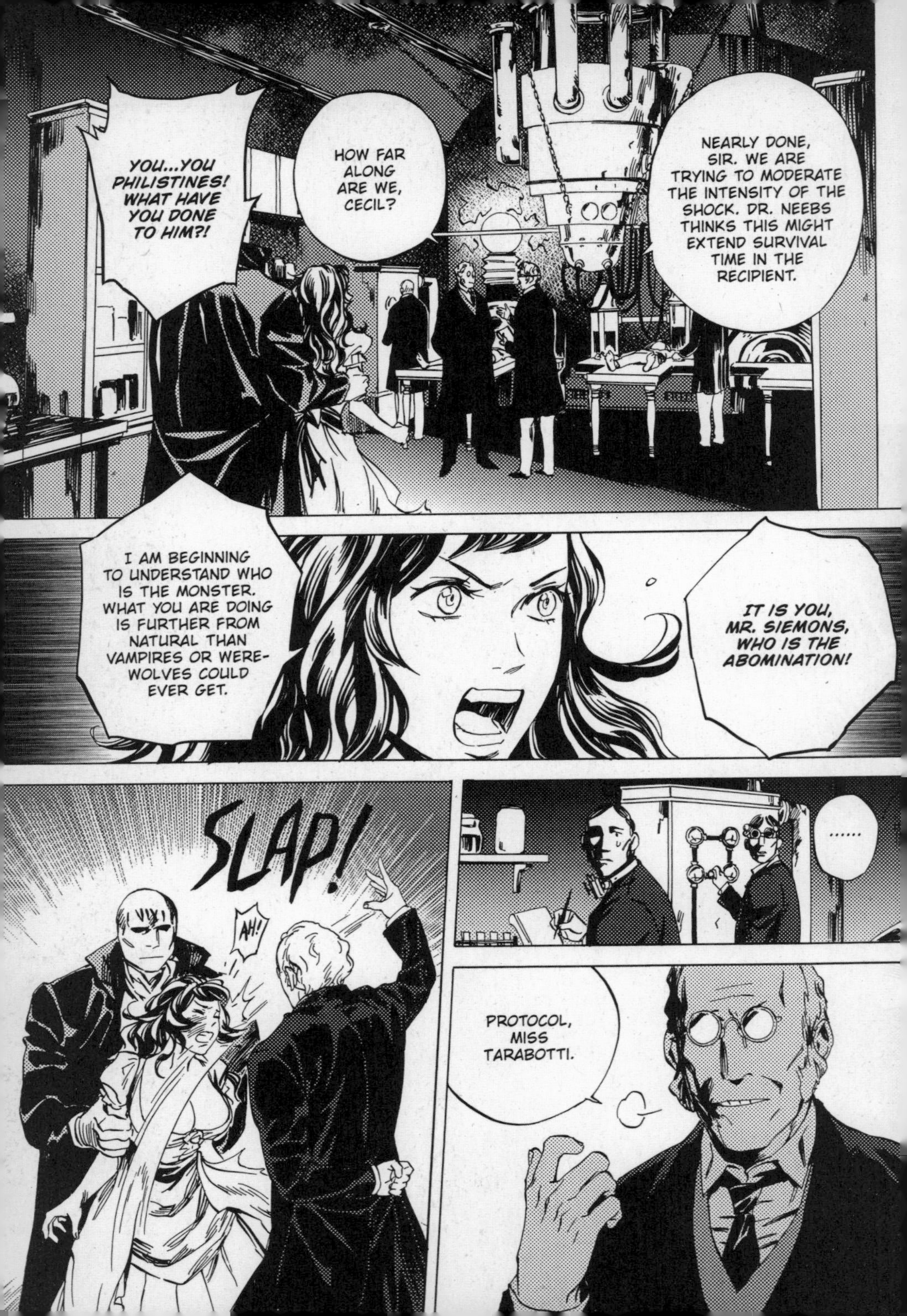
YOU...YOU PHILISTINES! WHAT HAVE YOU DONE TO HIM?!
HOW FAR ALONG ARE WE, CECIL?
NEARLY DONE, SIR. WE ARE TRYING TO MODERATE THE INTENSITY OF THE SHOCK. DR. NEEBS THINKS THIS MIGHT EXTEND SURVIVAL TIME IN THE RECIPIENT.
I AM BEGINNING TO UNDERSTAND WHO IS THE MONSTER. WHAT YOU ARE DOING IS FURTHER FROM NATURAL THAN VAMPIRES OR WEREWOLVES COULD EVER GET.
IT IS YOU, MR. SIEMONS, WHO IS THE ABOMINATION!
SLAP!
AH!
......
PROTOCOL, MISS TARABOTTI.

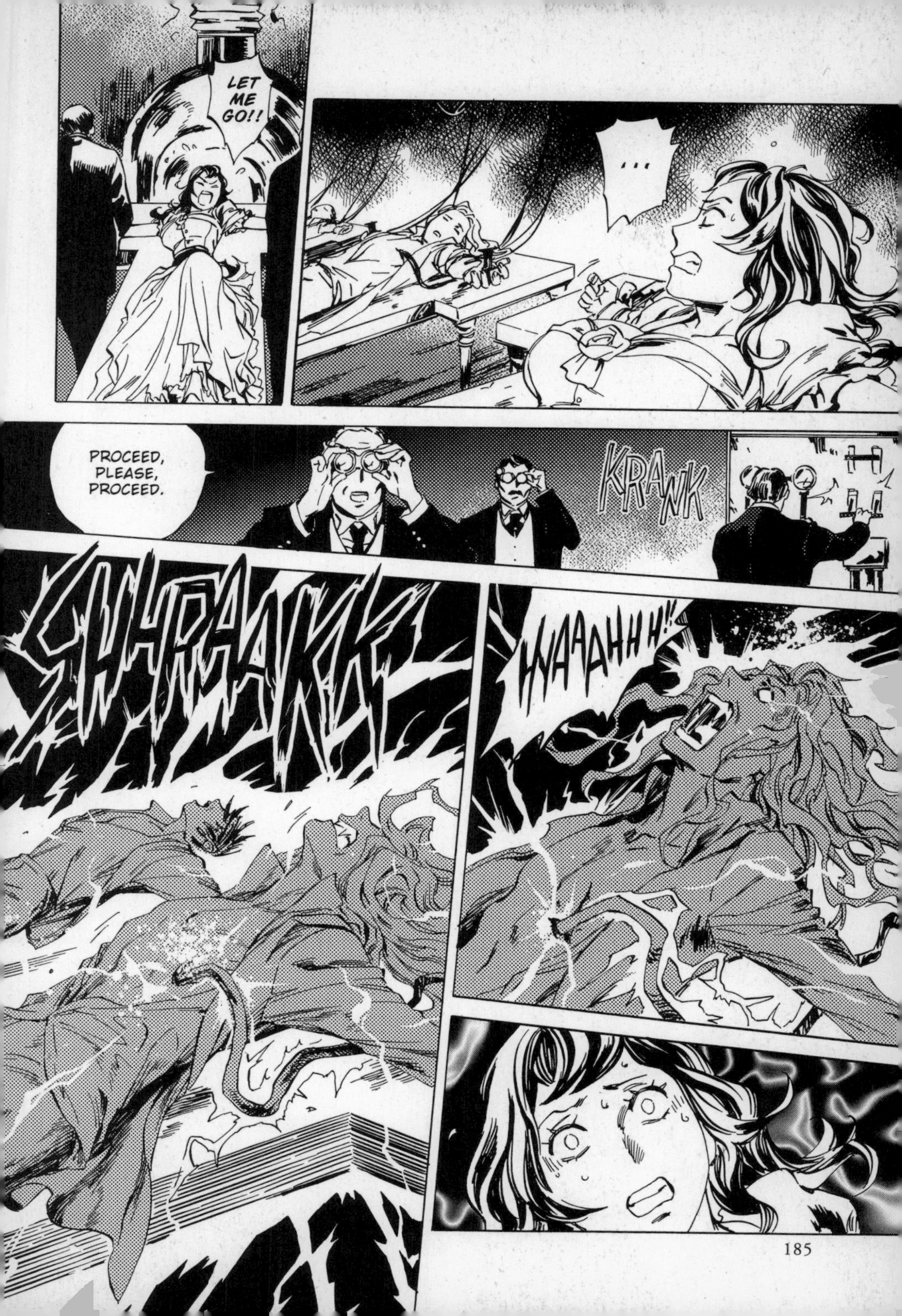
LET ME GO!!
...
PROCEED, PLEASE, PROCEED.
KRANK
SHRAAKK
WAAAHHH!!

FSSSHH

AH...

AH, THERE HE GOES.

YES, YES... PERFECT!

URK

GOOD LORD, MISS TARABOTTI!!!

WHDO

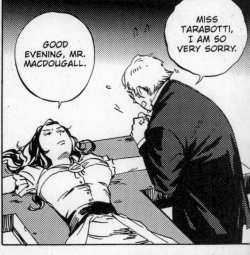

GOOD EVENING, MR. MACDOUGALL.

MISS TARABOTTI, I AM SO VERY SORRY.

IF I HAD ONLY KNOWN WHAT YOU WERE AT THE COMMENCEMENT OF OUR ACQUAINTANCE, I MIGHT HAVE PREVENTED THIS.

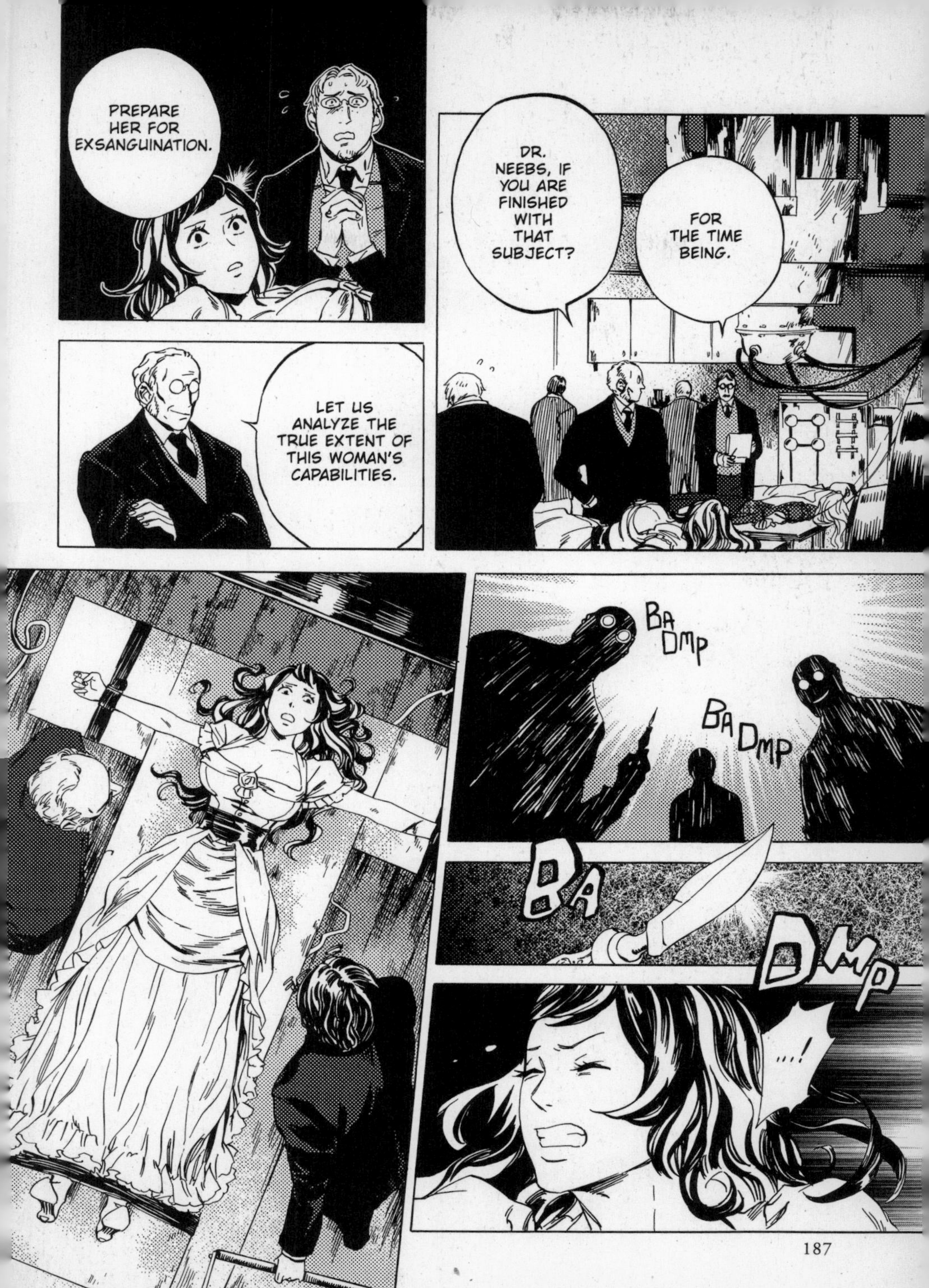
PREPARE HER FOR EXSANGUINATION.
DR. NEEBS, IF YOU ARE FINISHED WITH THAT SUBJECT?
FOR THE TIME BEING.
LET US ANALYZE THE TRUE EXTENT OF THIS WOMAN'S CAPABILITIES.
BADMP
BADMP
BA
DMP
...!

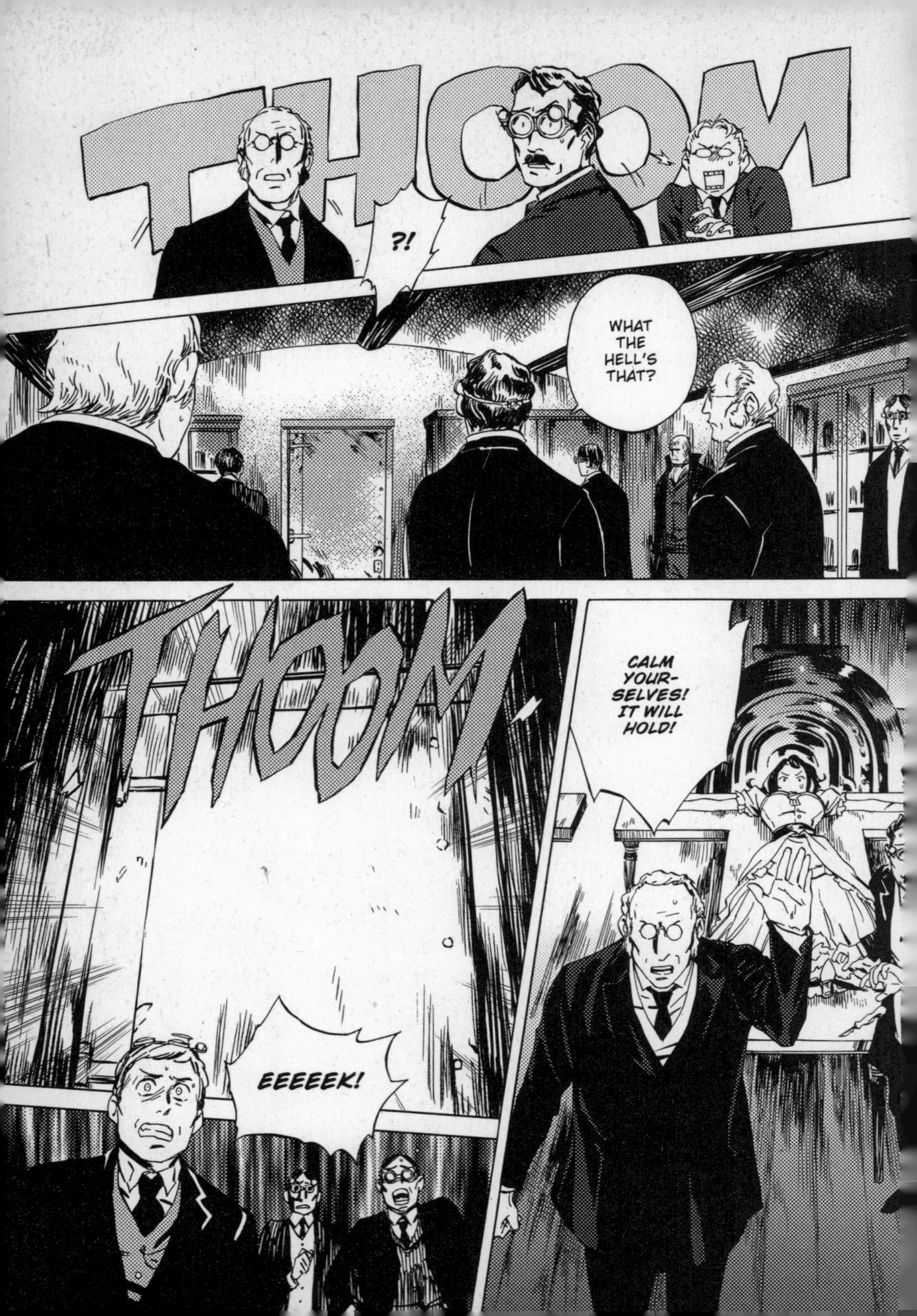
THOOM
?!
WHAT THE HELL'S THAT?
THOOM
EEEEEK!
CALM YOUR-SELVES! IT WILL HOLD!

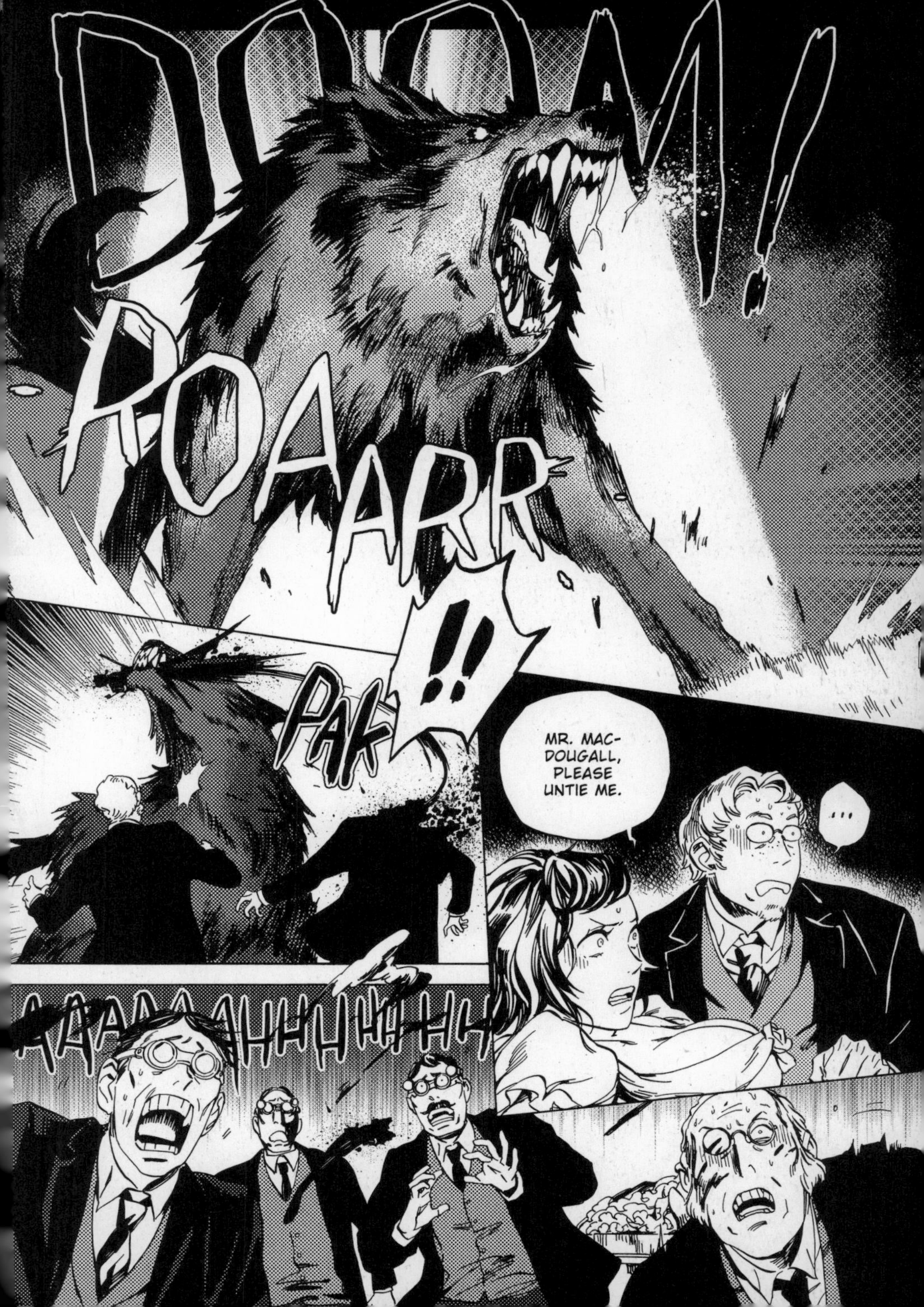
DOOM!!
ROAARR
PAK!!
MR. MAC-DOUGALL, PLEASE UNTIE ME.
...
AAAAAAHHHHHHHH

UNTIE ME THIS INSTANT, YOU RIDICULOUS MAN!!

hff

GRAWL

AAM

ILLUM NECÃ!

RUSH

VIXII

GRK·

SHKR

VIXII

KRR

-ACK.

HURRY!! I CAN STOP HIM!!

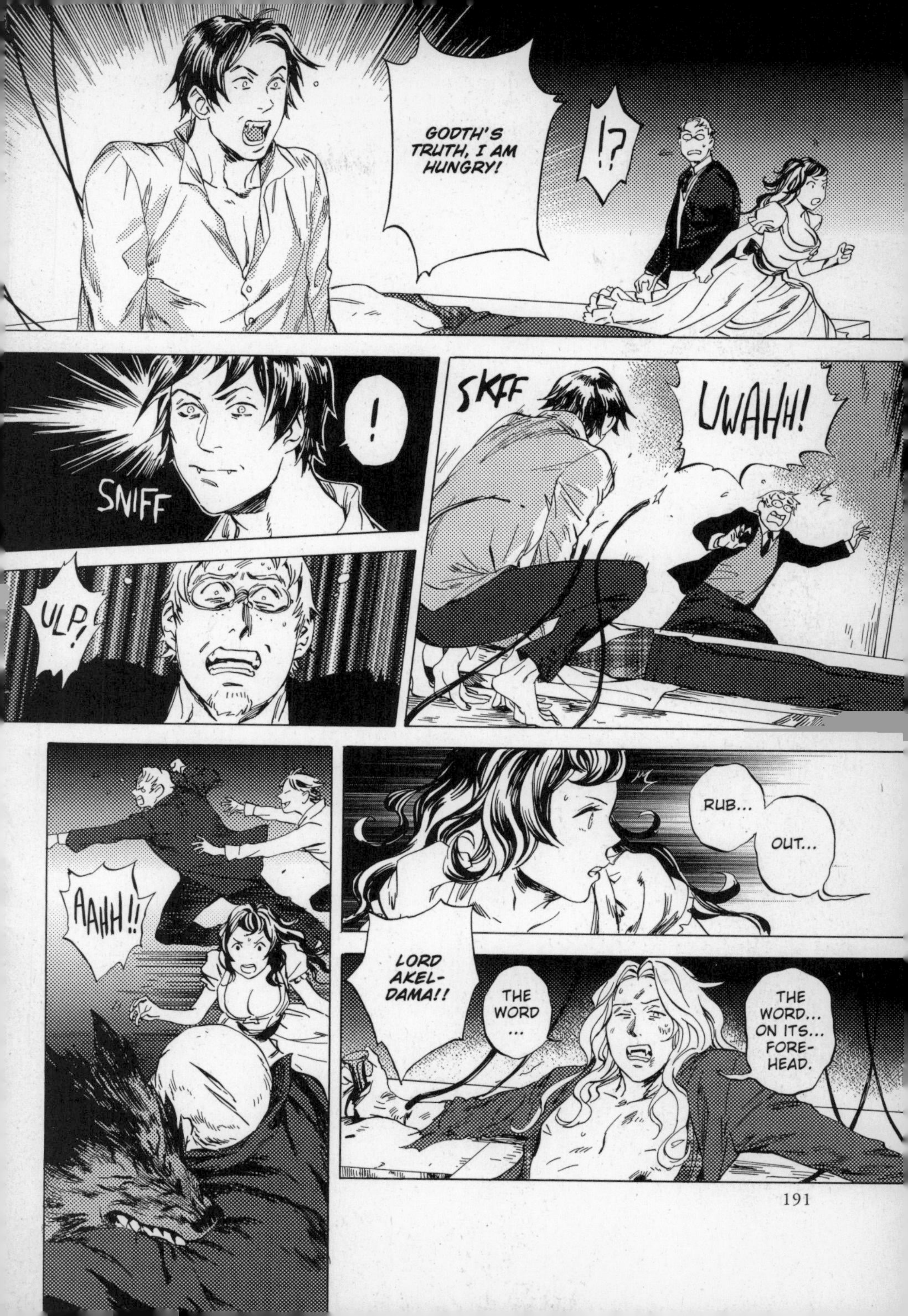
GODTH'S TRUTH, I AM HUNGRY!
!?
!
SNIFF
ULP!
SKFF
UWAHH!
AAHH!!
RUB...
OUT...
LORD AKEL-DAMA!!
THE WORD ...
THE WORD... ON ITS... FORE-HEAD.

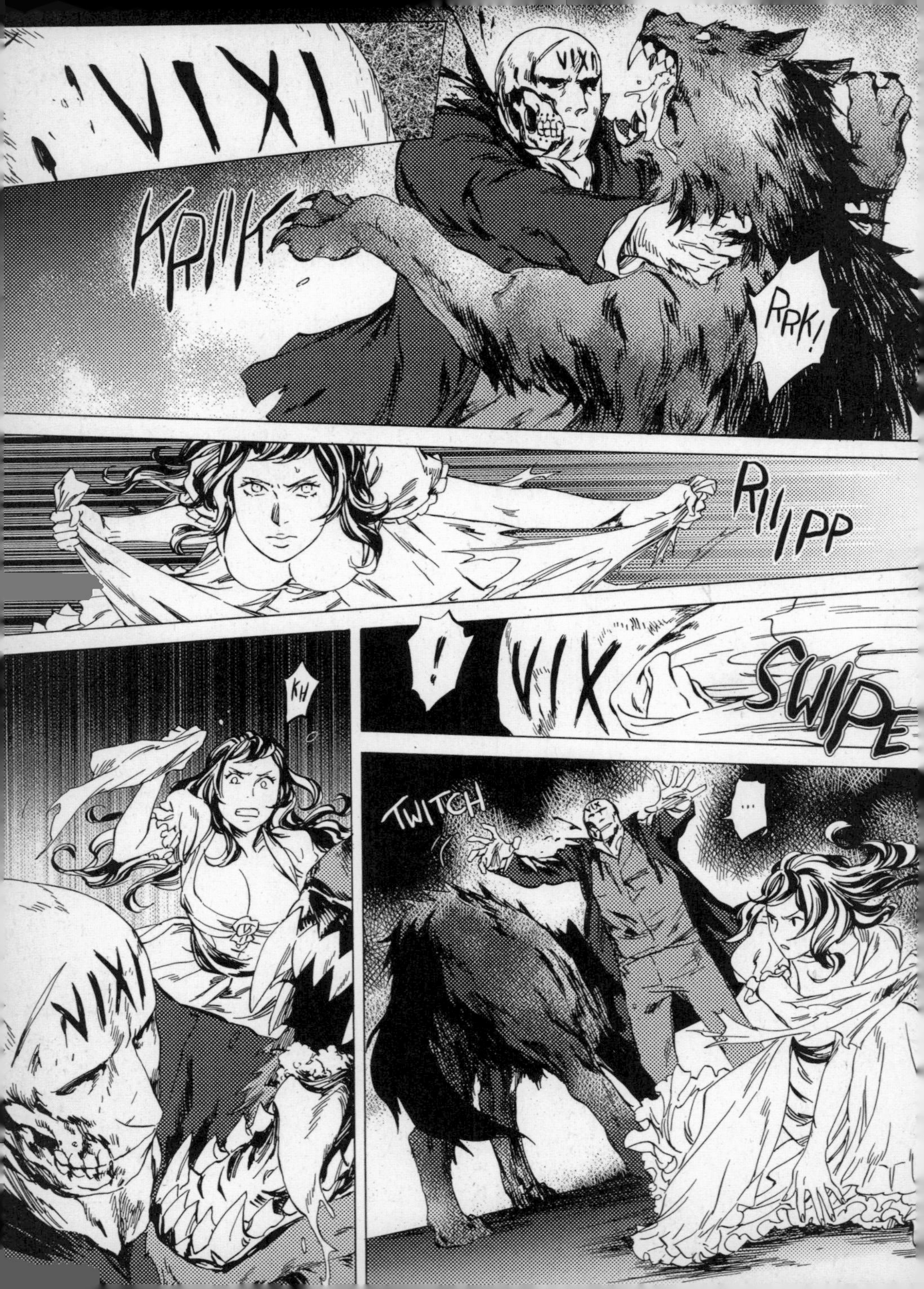
VIXI
KRIIK
VIXI
RRRK!
RIIIPP
KH
VIXI
!
VIX
SWIPE
TWITCH
...

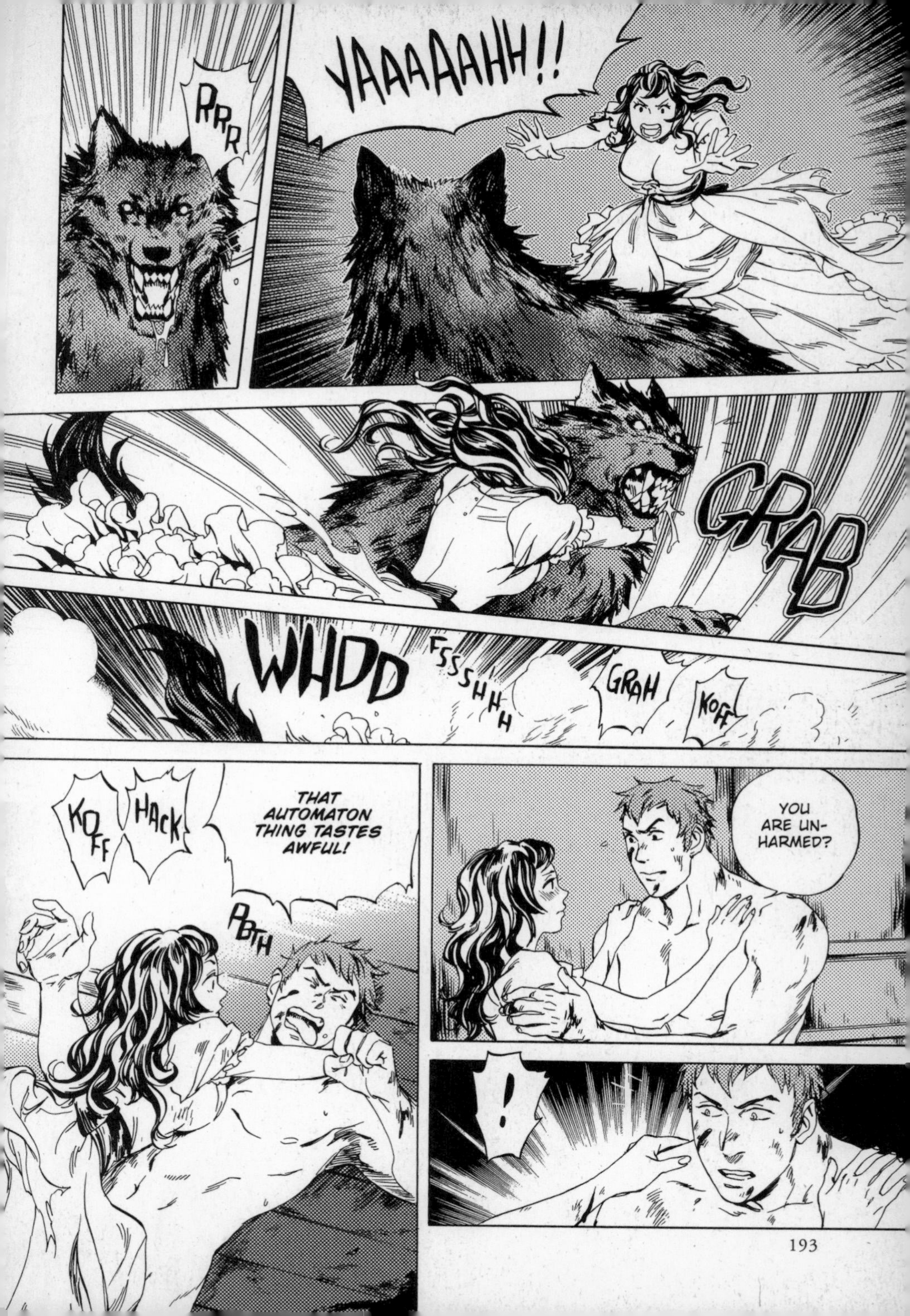
RRR
YAAAAAHH!!
GRAB
WHDD
FSSSHHH
GRAH
KOFF
KOFF
HACK
THAT AUTOMATON THING TASTES AWFUL!
PBTH
YOU ARE UN-HARMED?
!

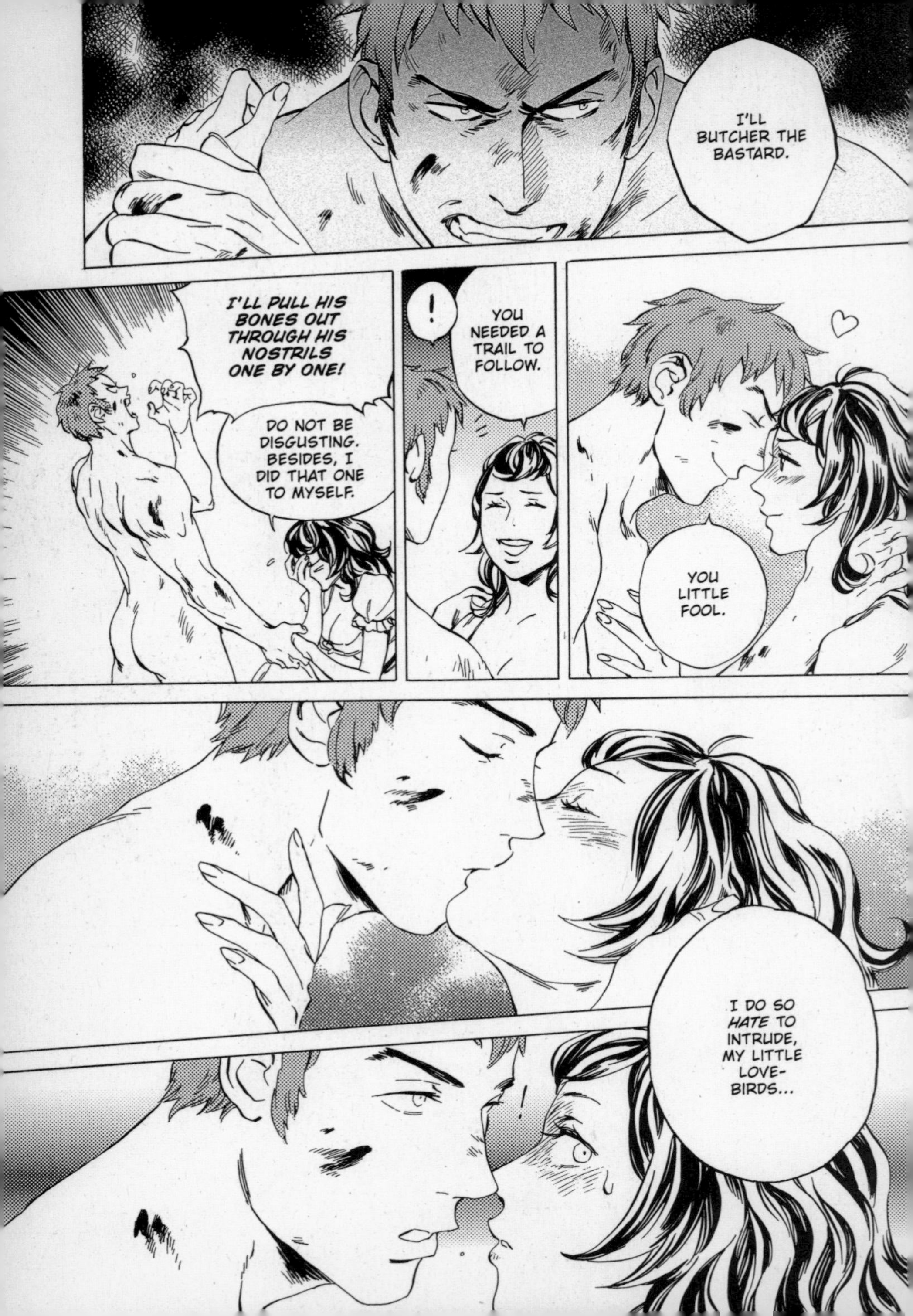

I'LL BUTCHER THE BASTARD.
I'LL PULL HIS BONES OUT THROUGH HIS NOSTRILS ONE BY ONE!
DO NOT BE DISGUSTING. BESIDES, I DID THAT ONE TO MYSELF.
!
YOU NEEDED A TRAIL TO FOLLOW.
♡
YOU LITTLE FOOL.
I DO SO *HATE* TO INTRUDE, MY LITTLE LOVE-BIRDS...

...BUT IF YOU COULD SEE YOUR WAY CLEAR TO MAYBE RELEASING ME?

......

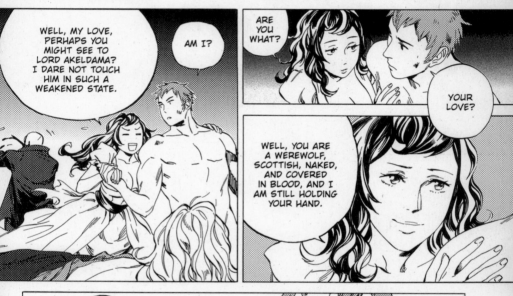

WELL, MY LOVE, PERHAPS YOU MIGHT SEE TO LORD AKELDAMA? I DARE NOT TOUCH HIM IN SUCH A WEAKENED STATE.

AM I?

ARE YOU WHAT?

YOUR LOVE?

WELL, YOU ARE A WEREWOLF, SCOTTISH, NAKED, AND COVERED IN BLOOD, AND I AM STILL HOLDING YOUR HAND.

GOOD.

THAT IS SETTLED, THEN.

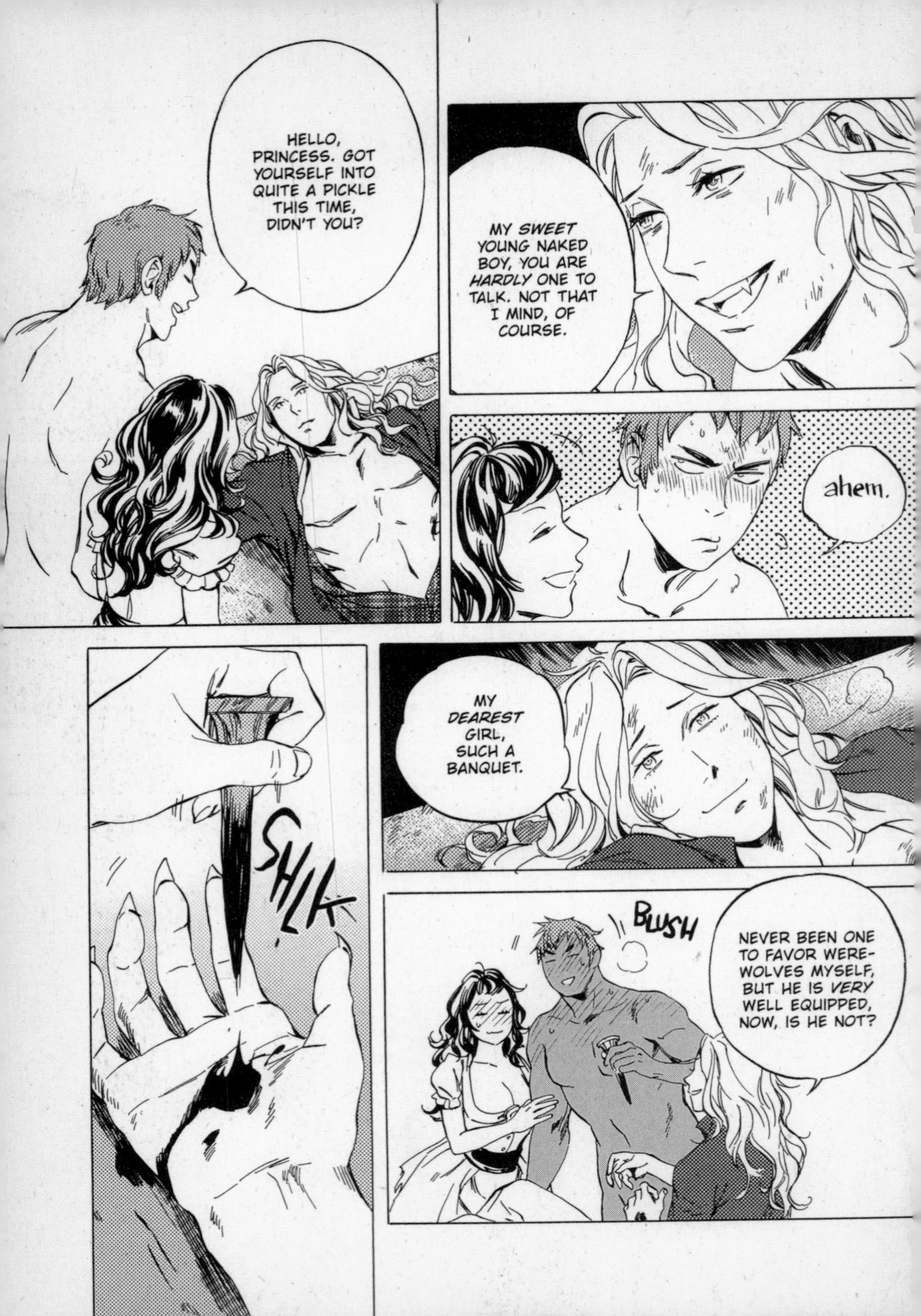
HELLO, PRINCESS. GOT YOURSELF INTO QUITE A PICKLE THIS TIME, DIDN'T YOU?
MY *SWEET* YOUNG NAKED BOY, YOU ARE *HARDLY* ONE TO TALK. NOT THAT I MIND, OF COURSE.
ahem.
SHLK
MY *DEAREST* GIRL, SUCH A BANQUET.
BLUSH
NEVER BEEN ONE TO FAVOR WERE-WOLVES MYSELF, BUT HE IS *VERY* WELL EQUIPPED, NOW, IS HE NOT?

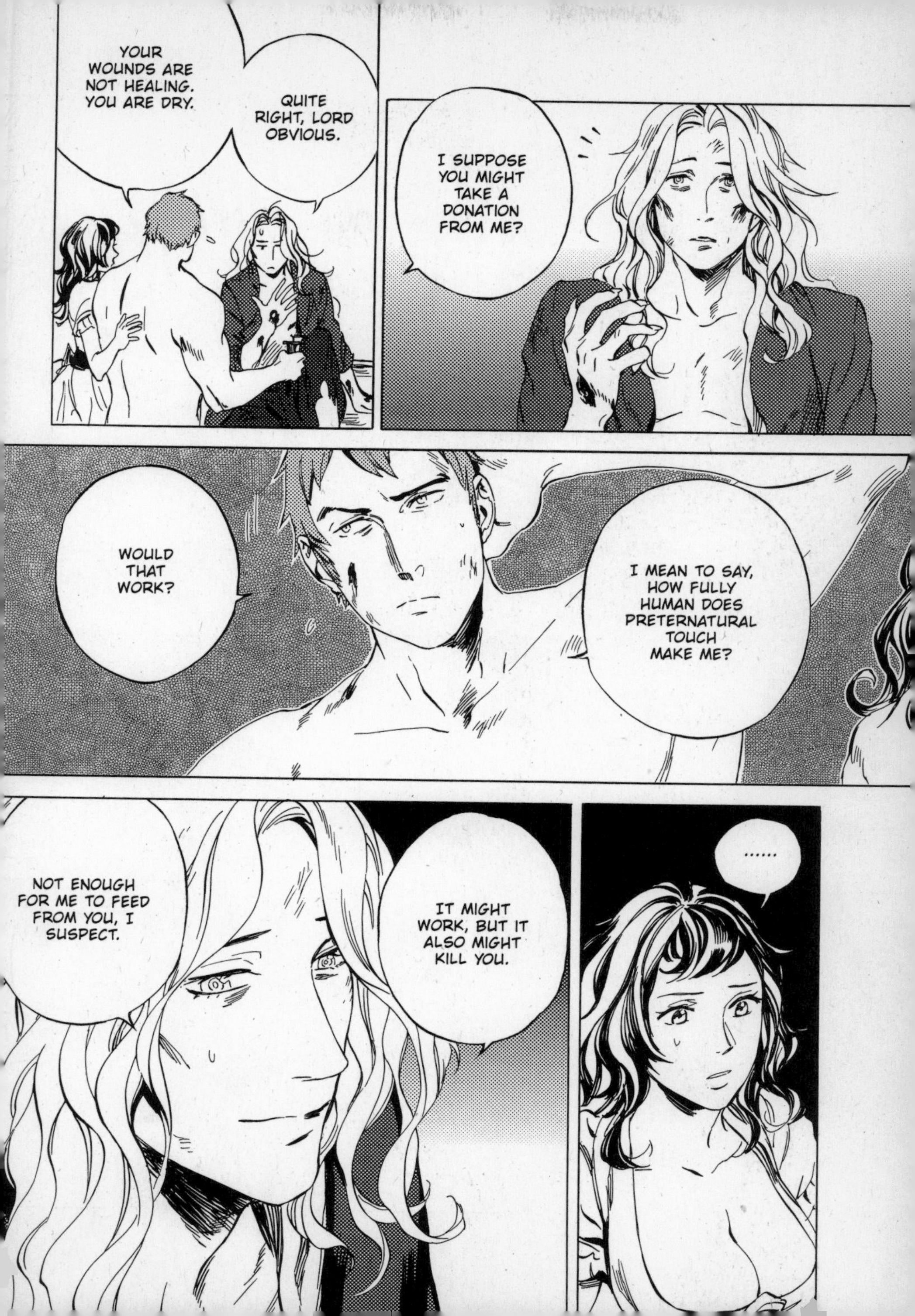
YOUR WOUNDS ARE NOT HEALING. YOU ARE DRY.
QUITE RIGHT, LORD OBVIOUS.
I SUPPOSE YOU MIGHT TAKE A DONATION FROM ME?
WOULD THAT WORK?
I MEAN TO SAY, HOW FULLY HUMAN DOES PRETERNATURAL TOUCH MAKE ME?
NOT ENOUGH FOR ME TO FEED FROM YOU, I SUSPECT.
IT MIGHT WORK, BUT IT ALSO MIGHT KILL YOU.
......

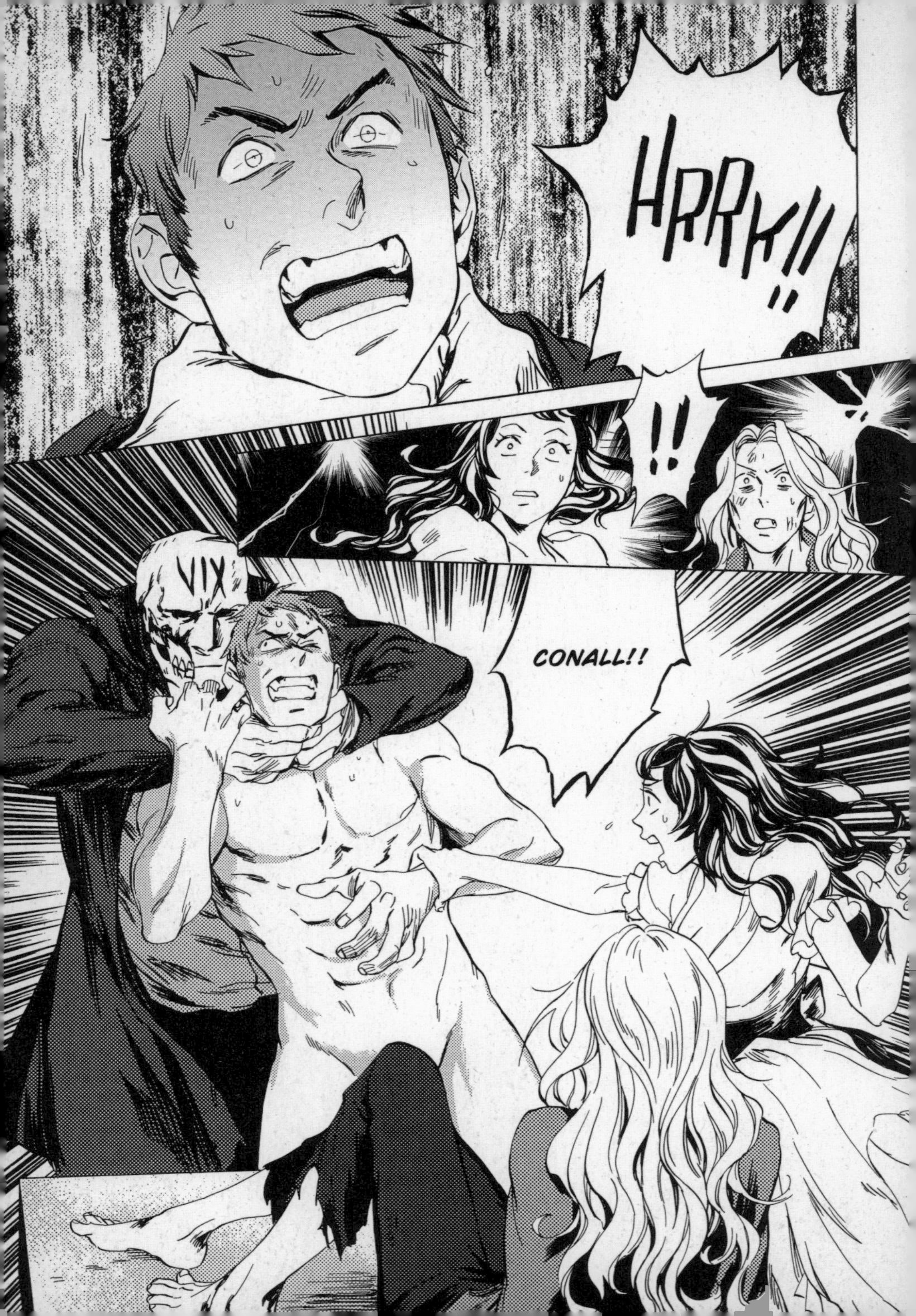
HRRK!!
!!
CONALL!!

SOULLESS

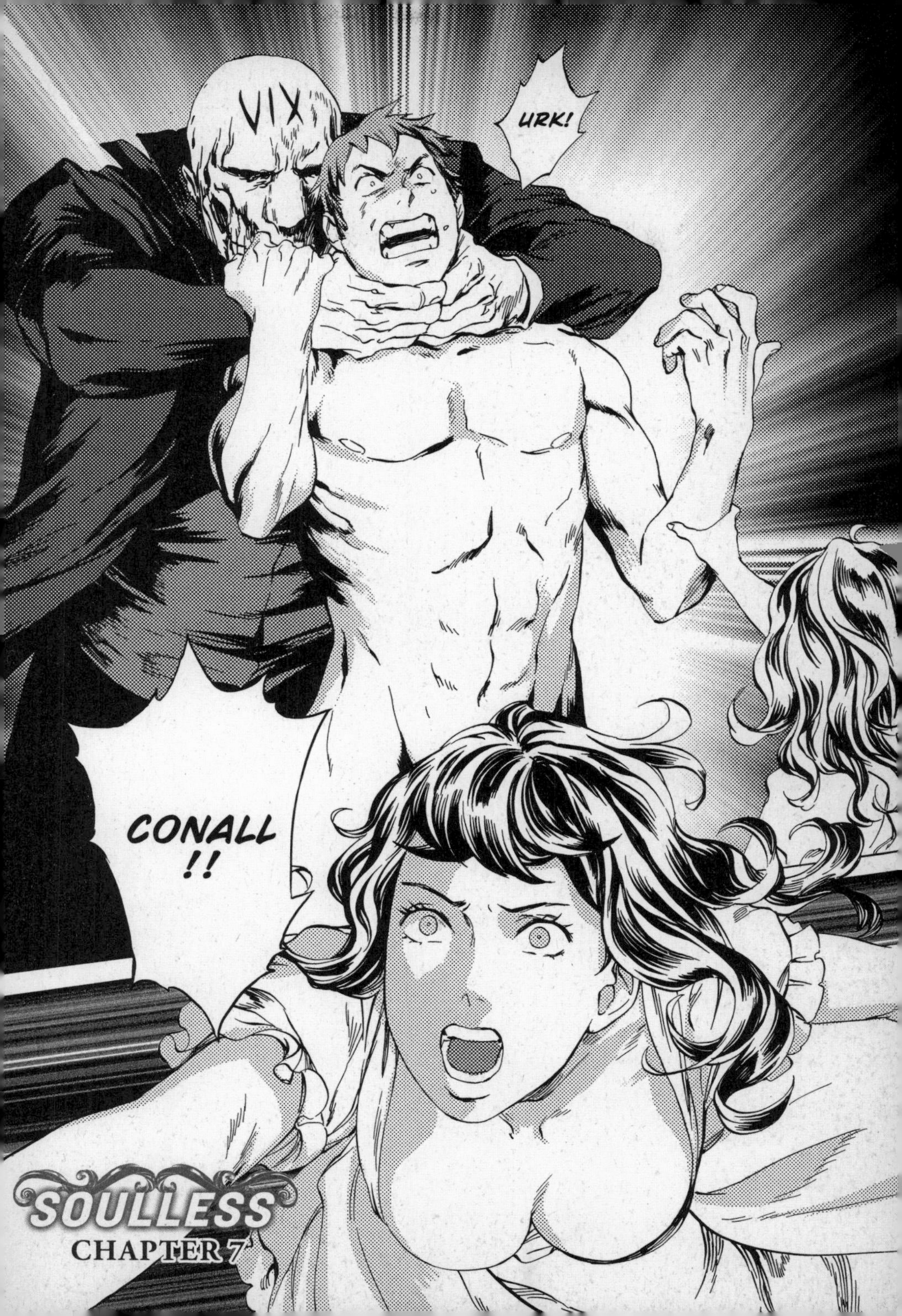
URK!
CONALL !!
SOULLESS
CHAPTER 7

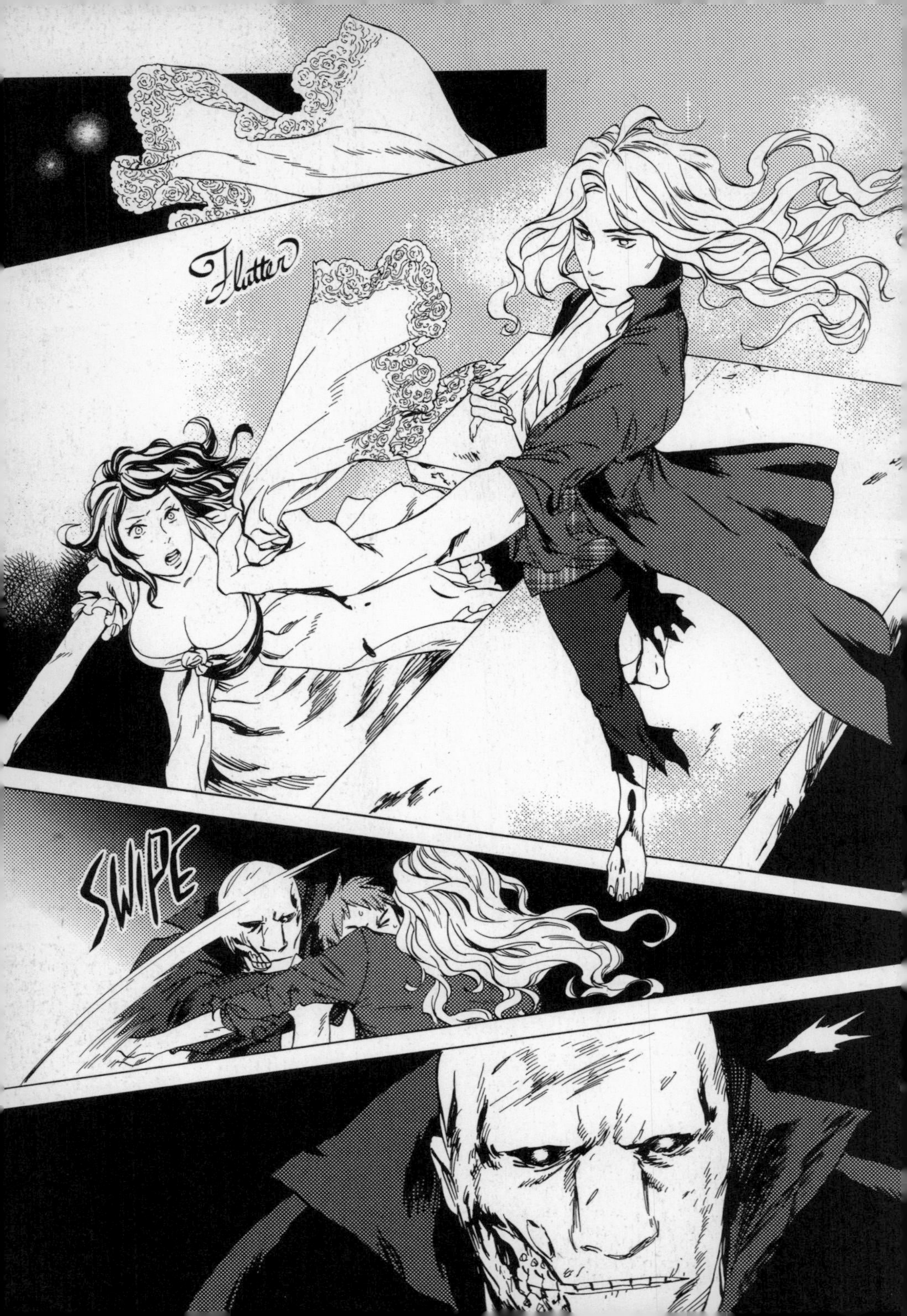
Flutter
SWIPE

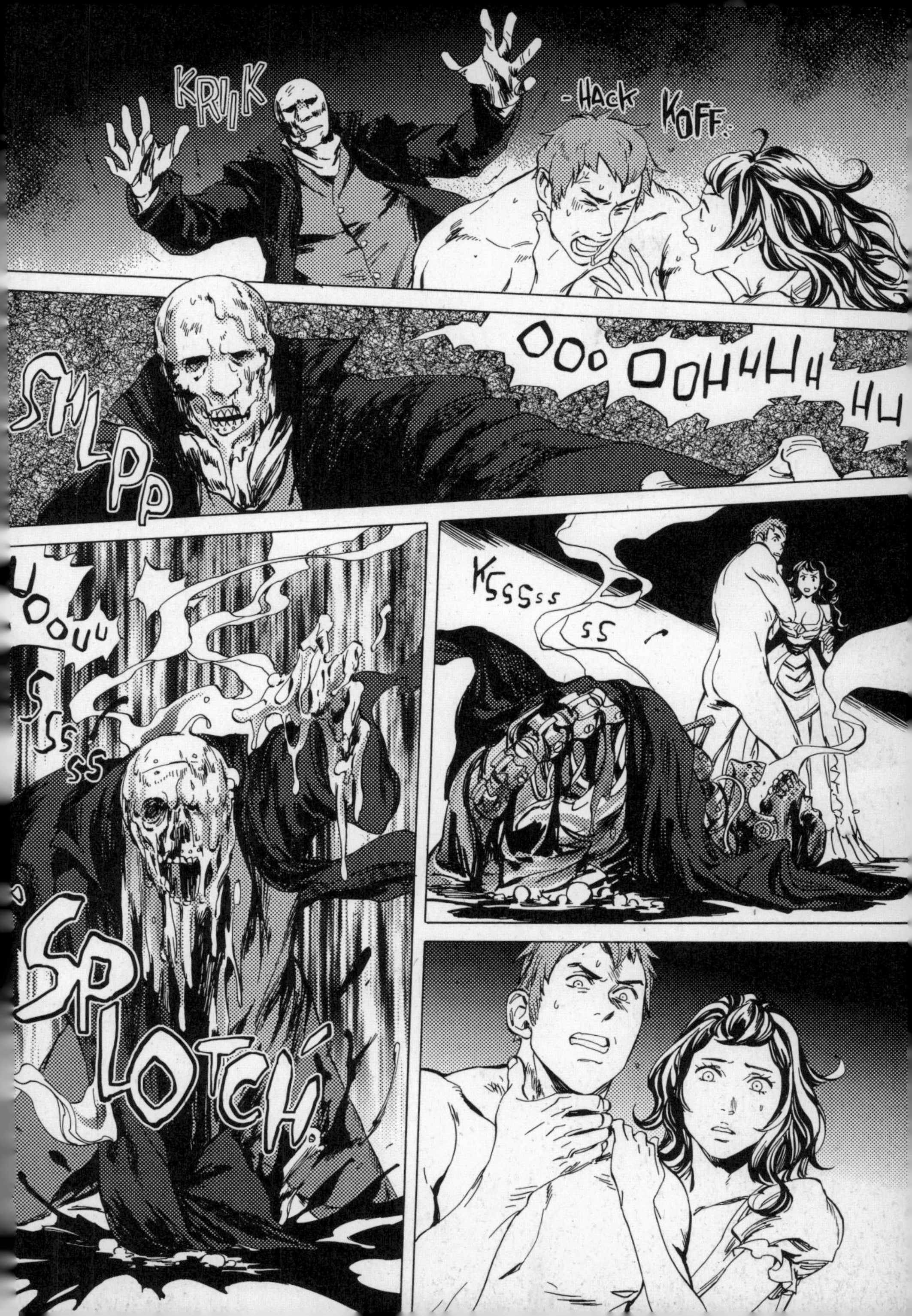
KRIIIK
-HACK
KOFF
OOOOOHHHHHU
SHLPP
UOOOUU
SSSSS
SPLOTCH
KSSSSS
SS

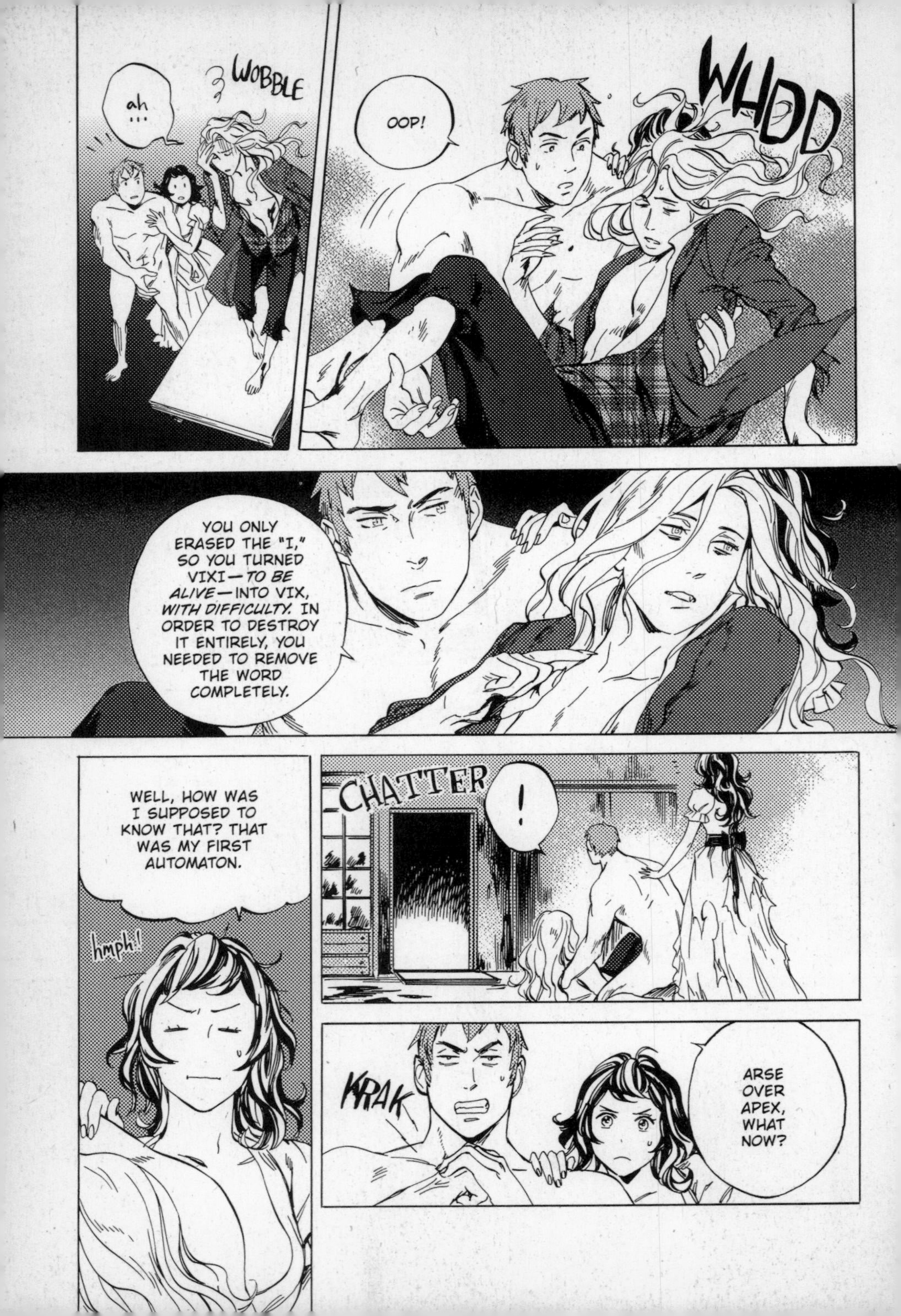
ah ...
WOBBLE
OOP!
WHDD
YOU ONLY ERASED THE "I," SO YOU TURNED VIXI—*TO BE ALIVE*—INTO VIX, *WITH DIFFICULTY.* IN ORDER TO DESTROY IT ENTIRELY, YOU NEEDED TO REMOVE THE WORD COMPLETELY.
WELL, HOW WAS I SUPPOSED TO KNOW THAT? THAT WAS MY FIRST AUTOMATON.
hmph!
CHATTER
!
KRAK
ARSE OVER APEX, WHAT NOW?

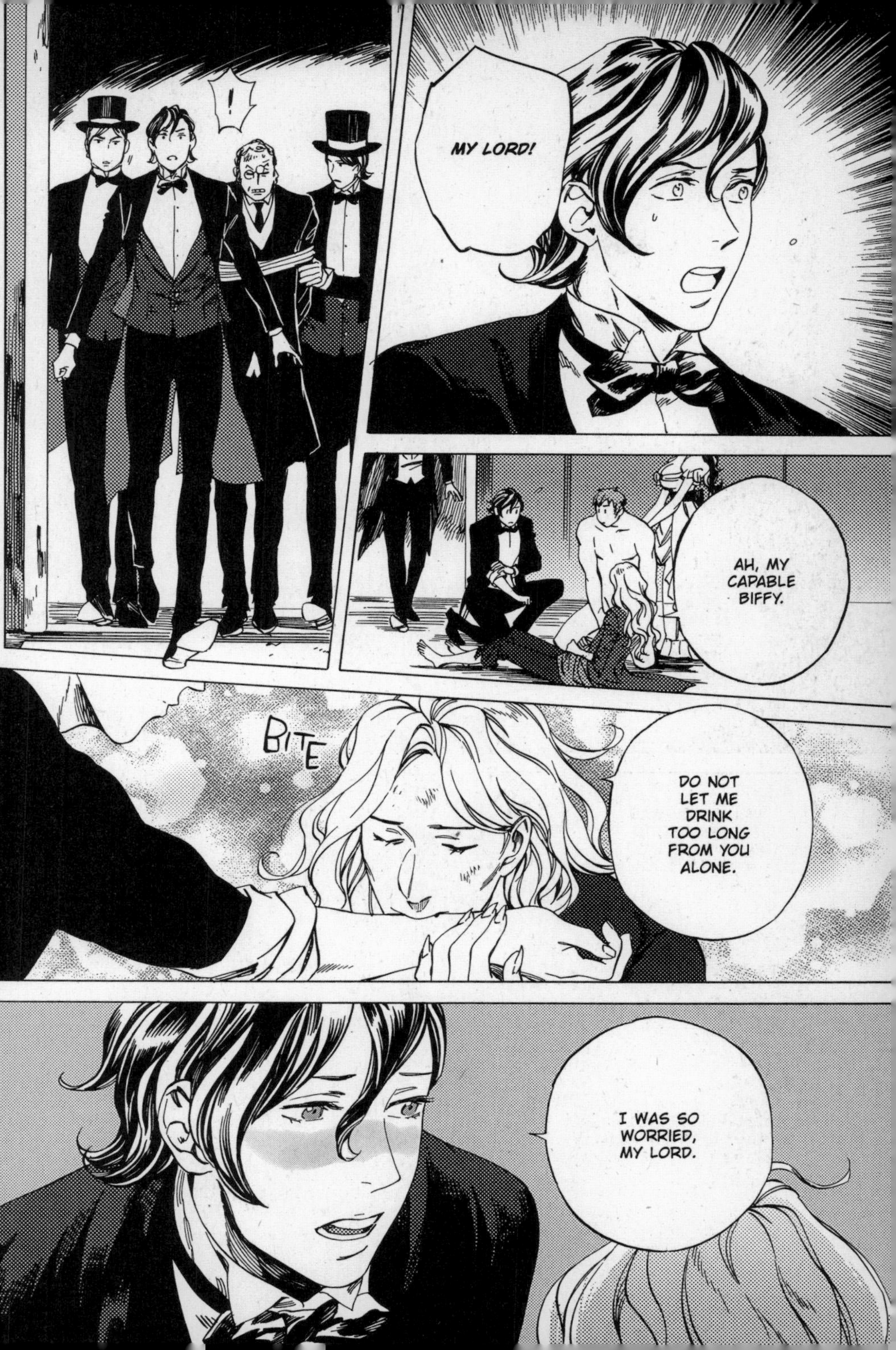
!
MY LORD!
AH, MY CAPABLE BIFFY.
BITE
DO NOT LET ME DRINK TOO LONG FROM YOU ALONE.
I WAS SO WORRIED, MY LORD.

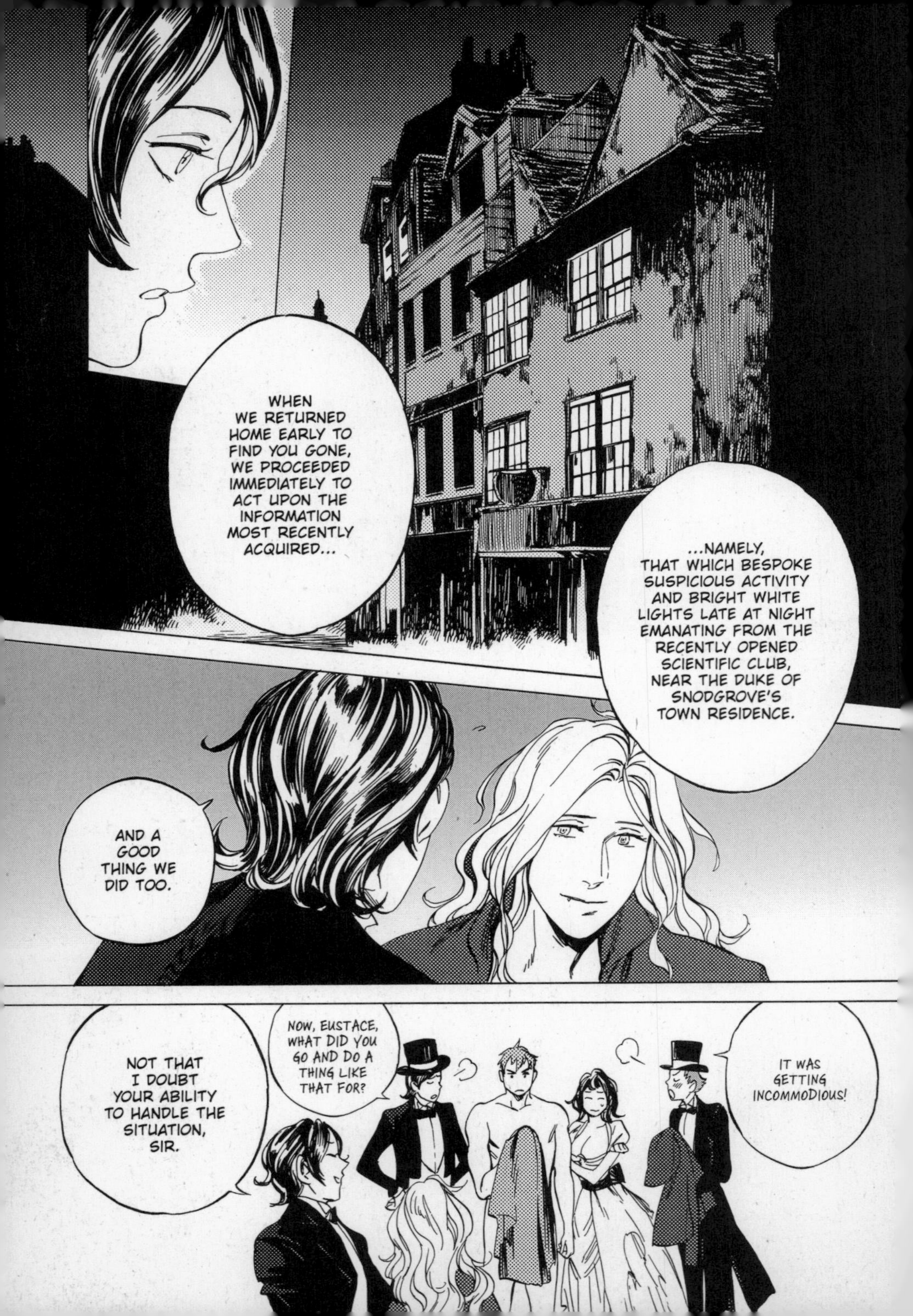
WHEN WE RETURNED HOME EARLY TO FIND YOU GONE, WE PROCEEDED IMMEDIATELY TO ACT UPON THE INFORMATION MOST RECENTLY ACQUIRED...
...NAMELY, THAT WHICH BESPOKE SUSPICIOUS ACTIVITY AND BRIGHT WHITE LIGHTS LATE AT NIGHT EMANATING FROM THE RECENTLY OPENED SCIENTIFIC CLUB, NEAR THE DUKE OF SNODGROVE'S TOWN RESIDENCE.
AND A GOOD THING WE DID TOO.
NOT THAT I DOUBT YOUR ABILITY TO HANDLE THE SITUATION, SIR.
NOW, EUSTACE, WHAT DID YOU GO AND DO A THING LIKE THAT FOR?
IT WAS GETTING INCOMMODIOUS!

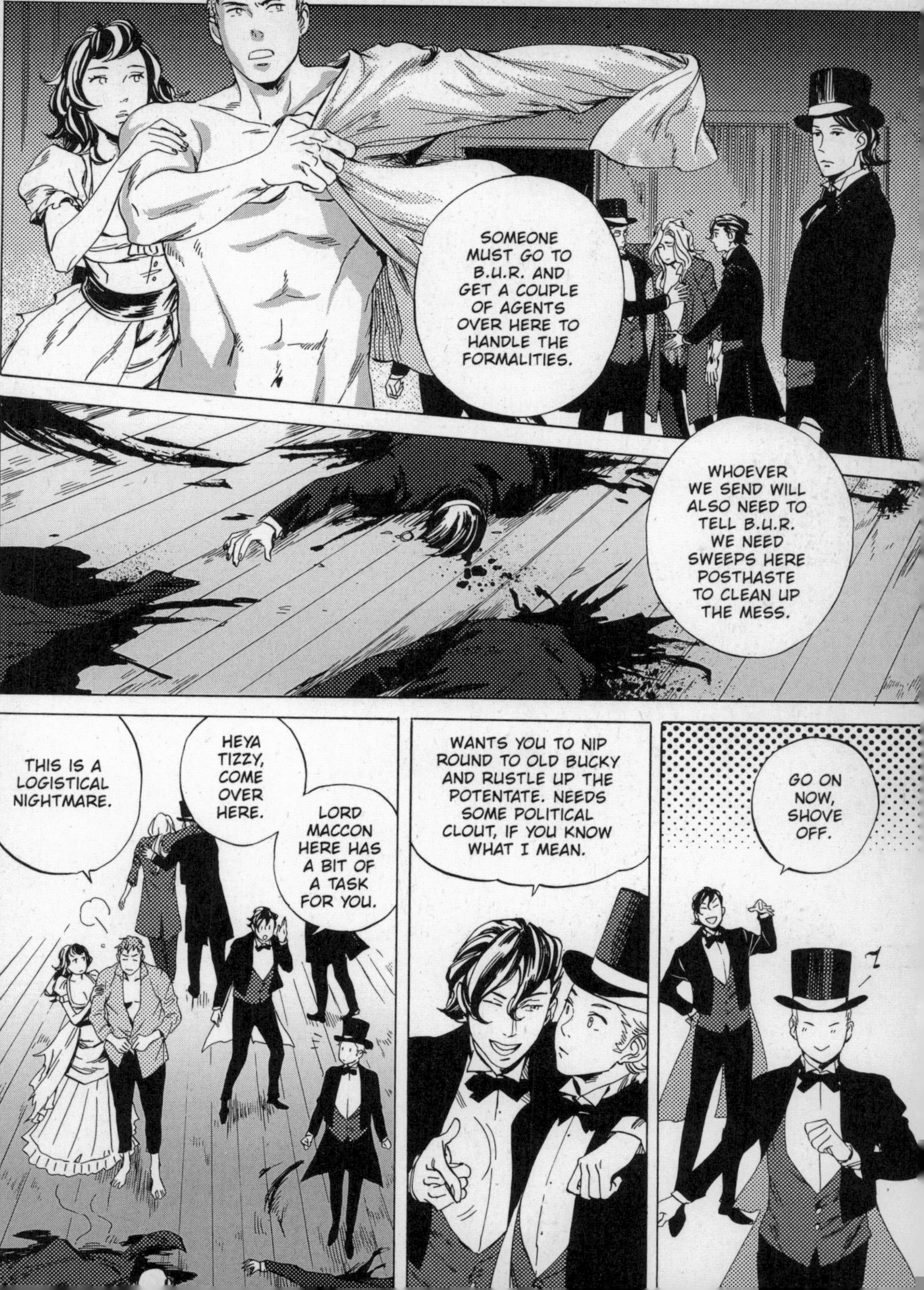
SOMEONE MUST GO TO B.U.R. AND GET A COUPLE OF AGENTS OVER HERE TO HANDLE THE FORMALITIES.
WHOEVER WE SEND WILL ALSO NEED TO TELL B.U.R. WE NEED SWEEPS HERE POSTHASTE TO CLEAN UP THE MESS.
THIS IS A LOGISTICAL NIGHTMARE.
HEYA TIZZY, COME OVER HERE.
LORD MACCON HERE HAS A BIT OF A TASK FOR YOU.
WANTS YOU TO NIP ROUND TO OLD BUCKY AND RUSTLE UP THE POTENTATE. NEEDS SOME POLITICAL CLOUT, IF YOU KNOW WHAT I MEAN.
GO ON NOW, SHOVE OFF.

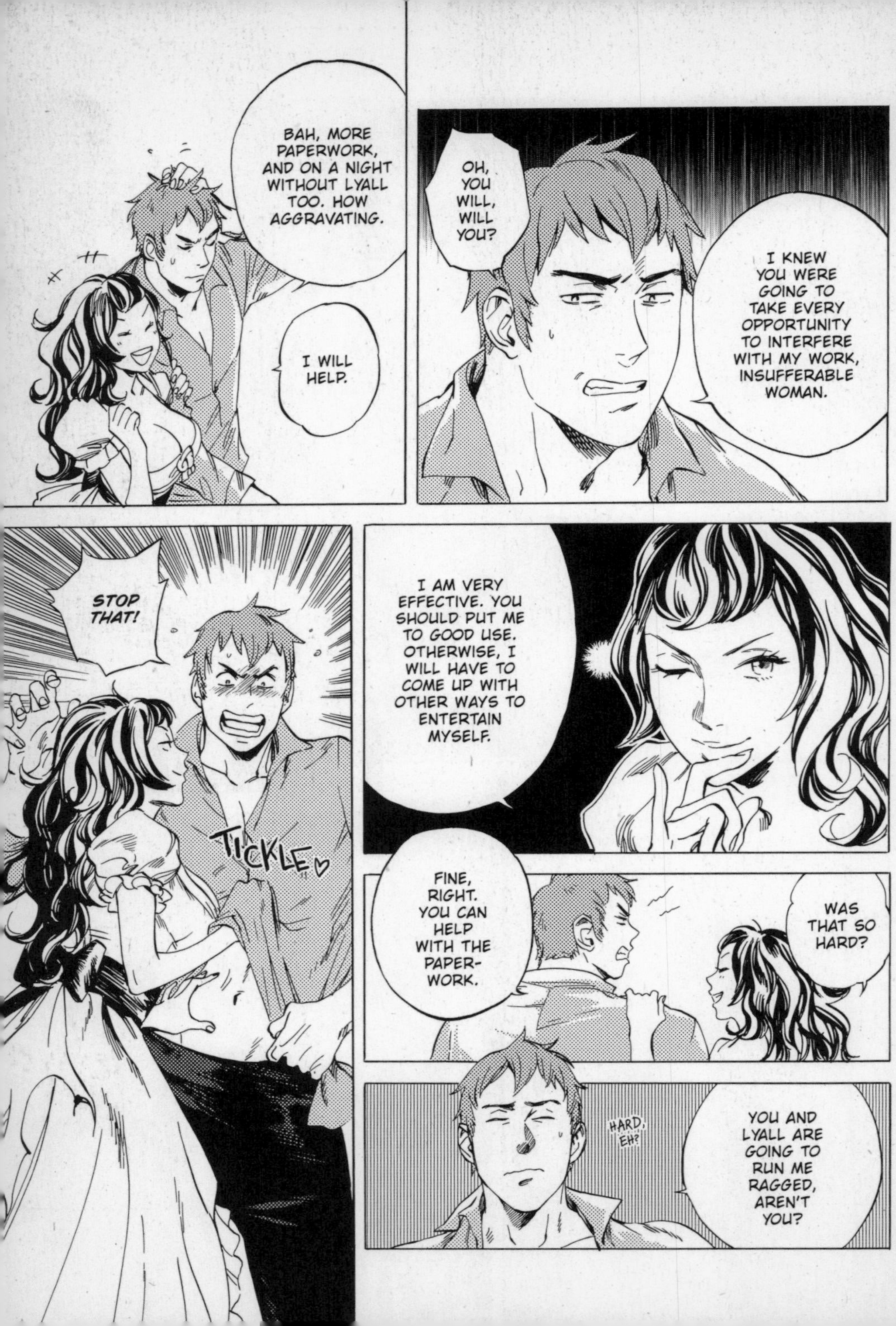
BAH, MORE PAPERWORK, AND ON A NIGHT WITHOUT LYALL TOO. HOW AGGRAVATING.
I WILL HELP.
OH, YOU WILL, WILL YOU?
I KNEW YOU WERE GOING TO TAKE EVERY OPPORTUNITY TO INTERFERE WITH MY WORK, INSUFFERABLE WOMAN.
STOP THAT!
TICKLE
I AM VERY EFFECTIVE. YOU SHOULD PUT ME TO GOOD USE. OTHERWISE, I WILL HAVE TO COME UP WITH OTHER WAYS TO ENTERTAIN MYSELF.
FINE, RIGHT. YOU CAN HELP WITH THE PAPER-WORK.
WAS THAT SO HARD?
HARD, EH?
YOU AND LYALL ARE GOING TO RUN ME RAGGED, AREN'T YOU?

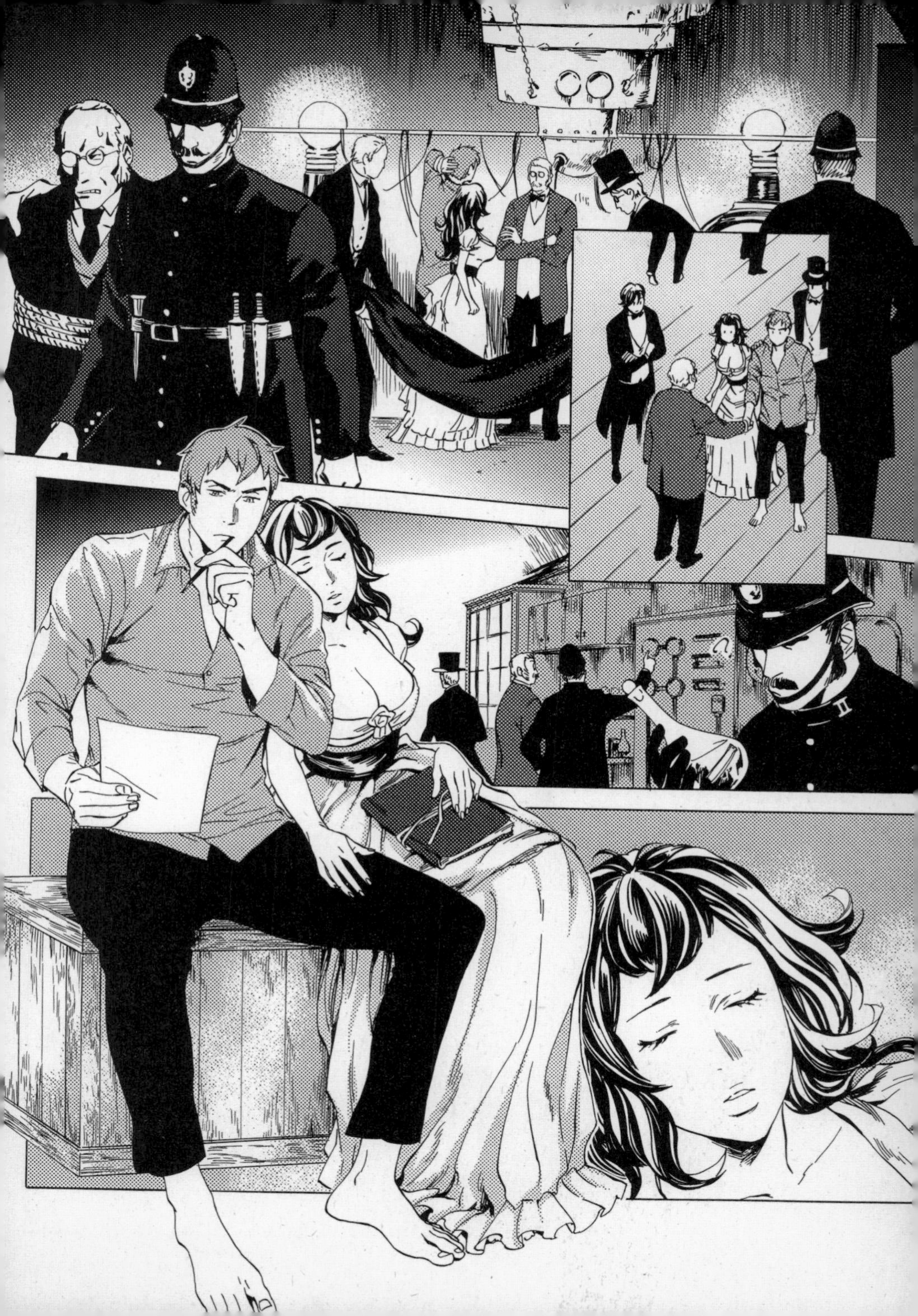

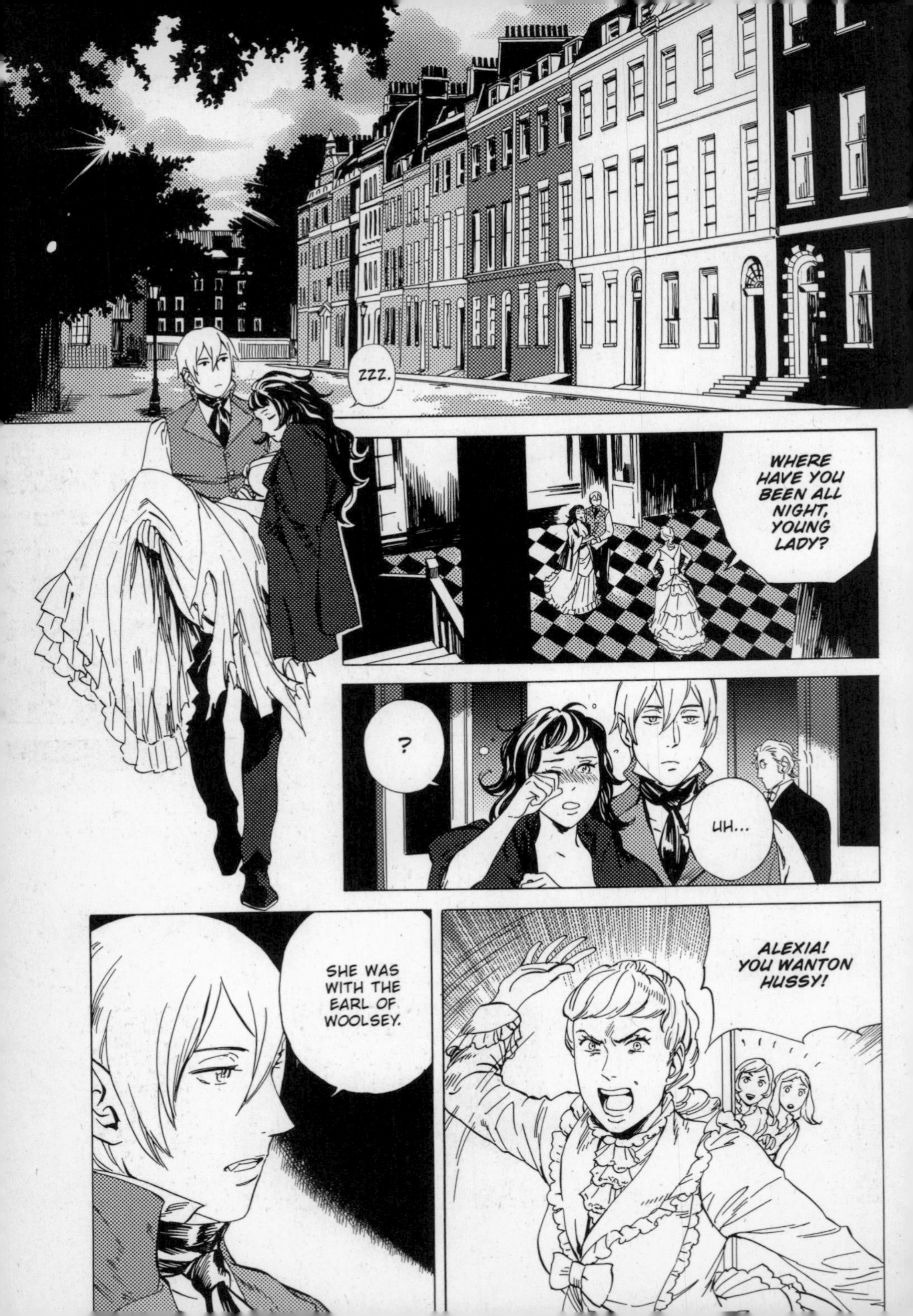
ZZZ.
WHERE HAVE YOU BEEN ALL NIGHT, YOUNG LADY?
?
UH...
SHE WAS WITH THE EARL OF WOOLSEY.
ALEXIA! YOU WANTON HUSSY!

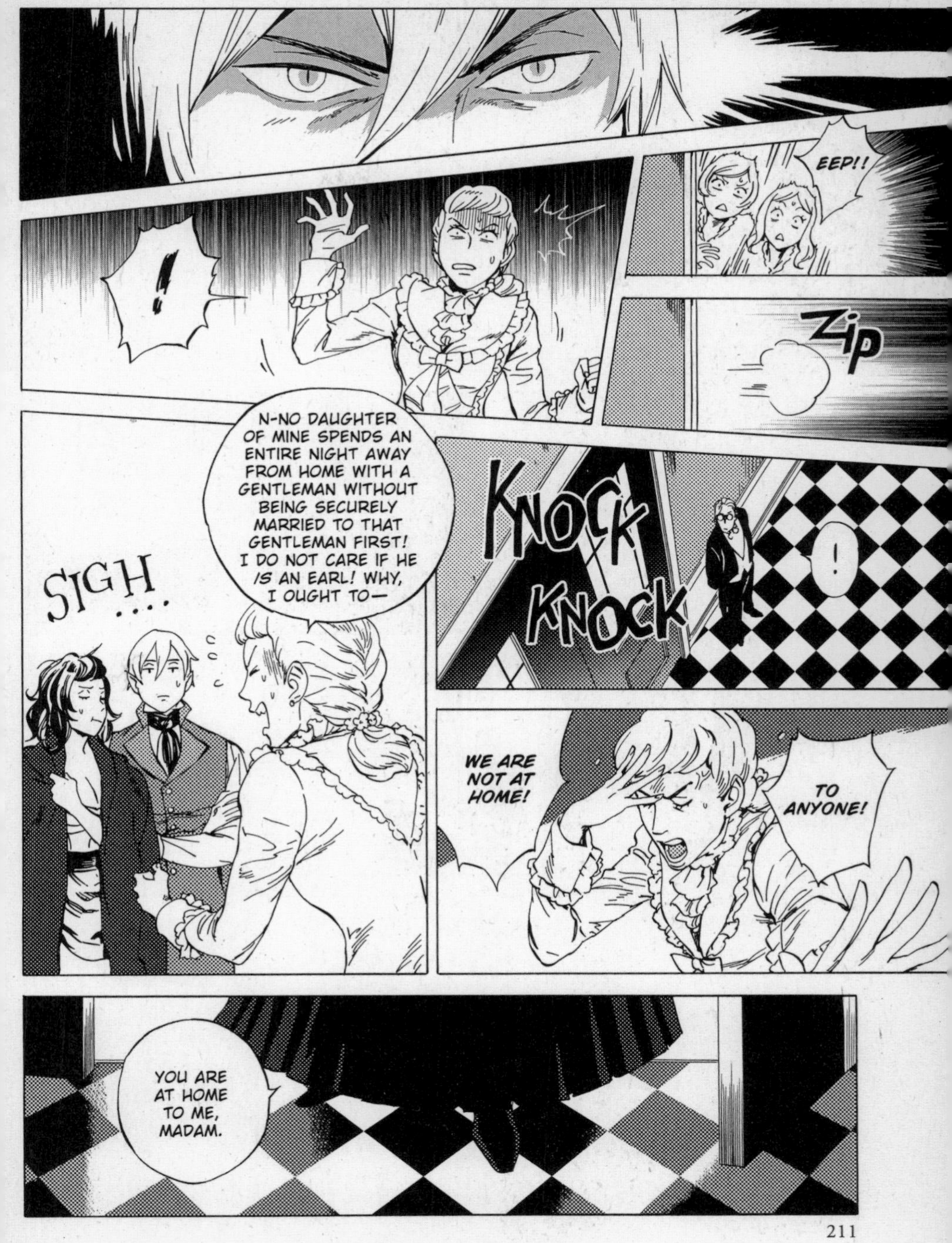

!
EEP!!
ZIP
N-NO DAUGHTER OF MINE SPENDS AN ENTIRE NIGHT AWAY FROM HOME WITH A GENTLEMAN WITHOUT BEING SECURELY MARRIED TO THAT GENTLEMAN FIRST! I DO NOT CARE IF HE IS AN EARL! WHY, I OUGHT TO—
SIGH....
KNOCK KNOCK
!
WE ARE NOT AT HOME!
TO ANYONE!
YOU ARE AT HOME TO ME, MADAM.

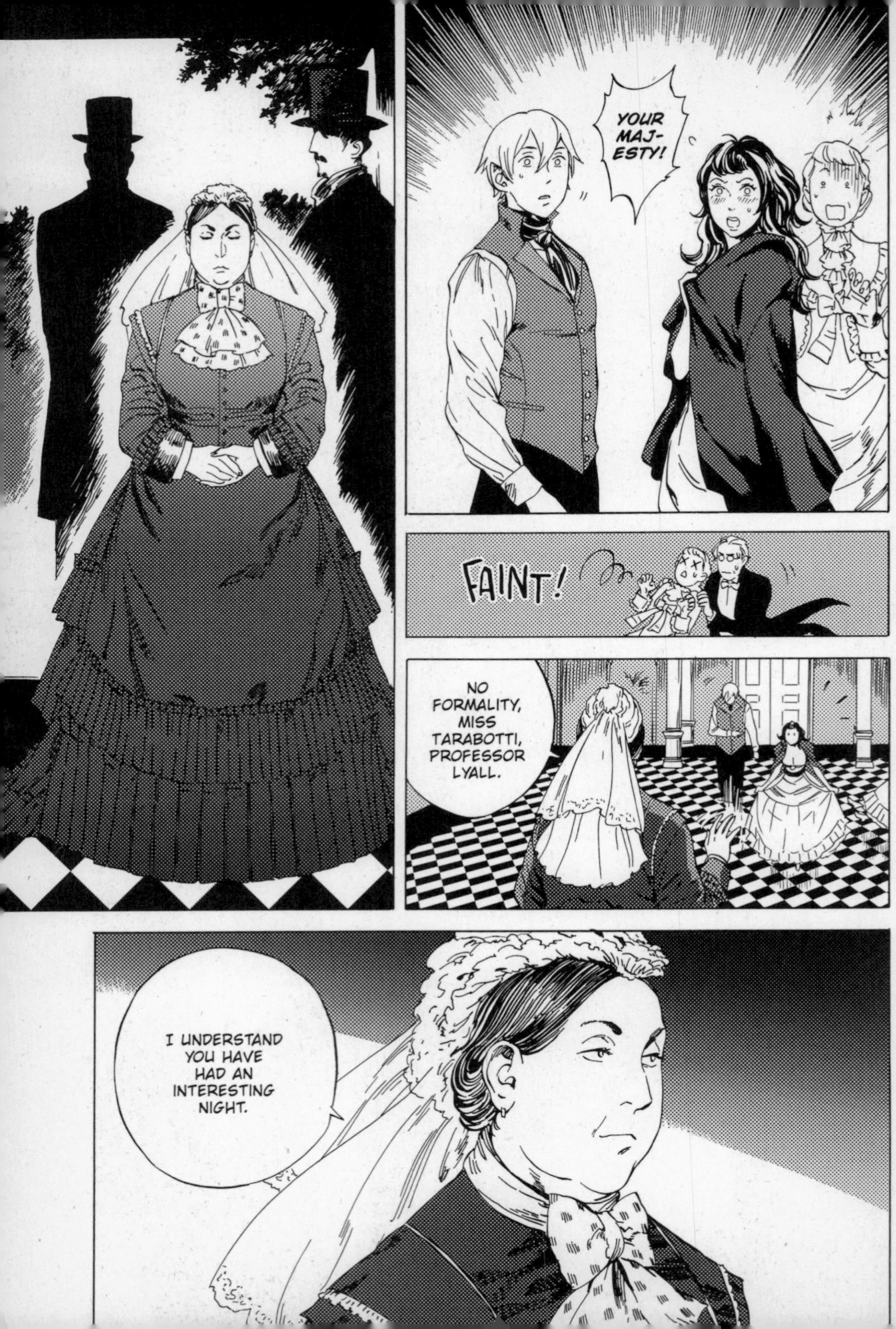
YOUR MAJ-ESTY!
FAINT!
NO FORMALITY, MISS TARABOTTI, PROFESSOR LYALL.
I UNDERSTAND YOU HAVE HAD AN INTERESTING NIGHT.

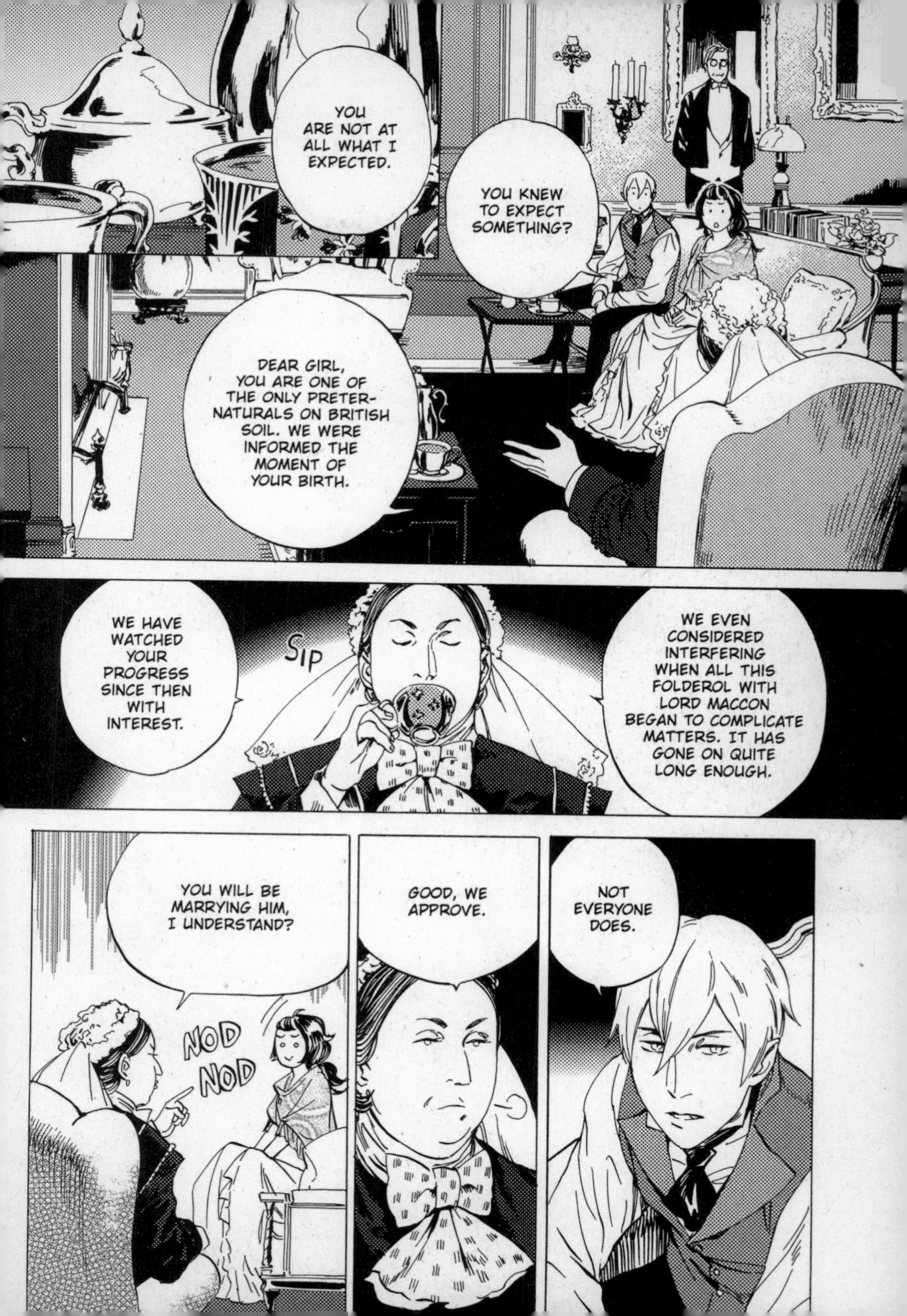
YOU ARE NOT AT ALL WHAT I EXPECTED.
YOU KNEW TO EXPECT SOMETHING?
DEAR GIRL, YOU ARE ONE OF THE ONLY PRETER-NATURALS ON BRITISH SOIL. WE WERE INFORMED THE MOMENT OF YOUR BIRTH.
WE HAVE WATCHED YOUR PROGRESS SINCE THEN WITH INTEREST.
SIP
WE EVEN CONSIDERED INTERFERING WHEN ALL THIS FOLDEROL WITH LORD MACCON BEGAN TO COMPLICATE MATTERS. IT HAS GONE ON QUITE LONG ENOUGH.
YOU WILL BE MARRYING HIM, I UNDERSTAND?
NOD NOD
GOOD, WE APPROVE.
NOT EVERYONE DOES.

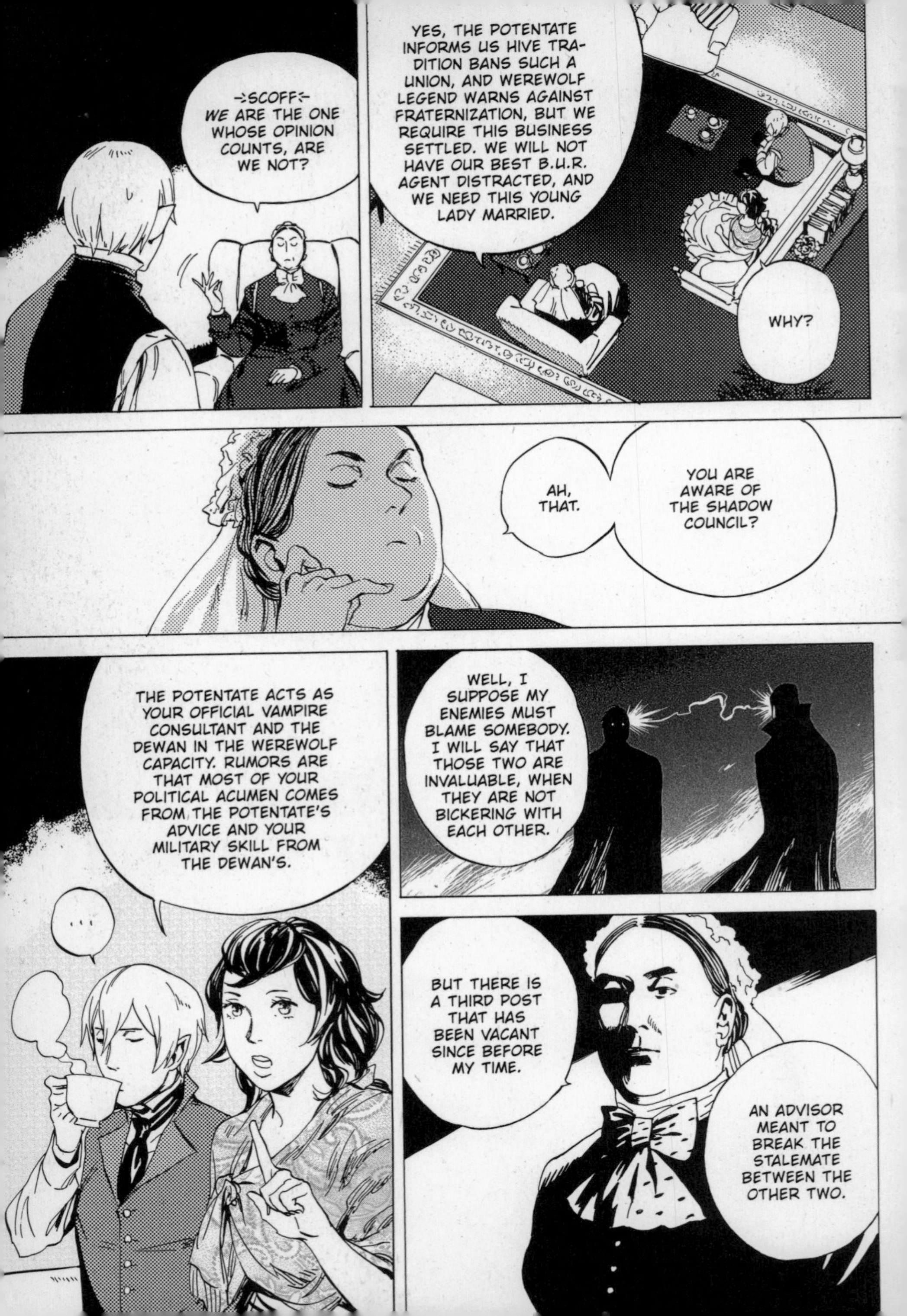

⇉SCOFF⇇ WE ARE THE ONE WHOSE OPINION COUNTS, ARE WE NOT?
YES, THE POTENTATE INFORMS US HIVE TRADITION BANS SUCH A UNION, AND WEREWOLF LEGEND WARNS AGAINST FRATERNIZATION, BUT WE REQUIRE THIS BUSINESS SETTLED. WE WILL NOT HAVE OUR BEST B.U.R. AGENT DISTRACTED, AND WE NEED THIS YOUNG LADY MARRIED.
WHY?
AH, THAT.
YOU ARE AWARE OF THE SHADOW COUNCIL?
THE POTENTATE ACTS AS YOUR OFFICIAL VAMPIRE CONSULTANT AND THE DEWAN IN THE WEREWOLF CAPACITY. RUMORS ARE THAT MOST OF YOUR POLITICAL ACUMEN COMES FROM THE POTENTATE'S ADVICE AND YOUR MILITARY SKILL FROM THE DEWAN'S.
...
WELL, I SUPPOSE MY ENEMIES MUST BLAME SOMEBODY. I WILL SAY THAT THOSE TWO ARE INVALUABLE, WHEN THEY ARE NOT BICKERING WITH EACH OTHER.
BUT THERE IS A THIRD POST THAT HAS BEEN VACANT SINCE BEFORE MY TIME.
AN ADVISOR MEANT TO BREAK THE STALEMATE BETWEEN THE OTHER TWO.

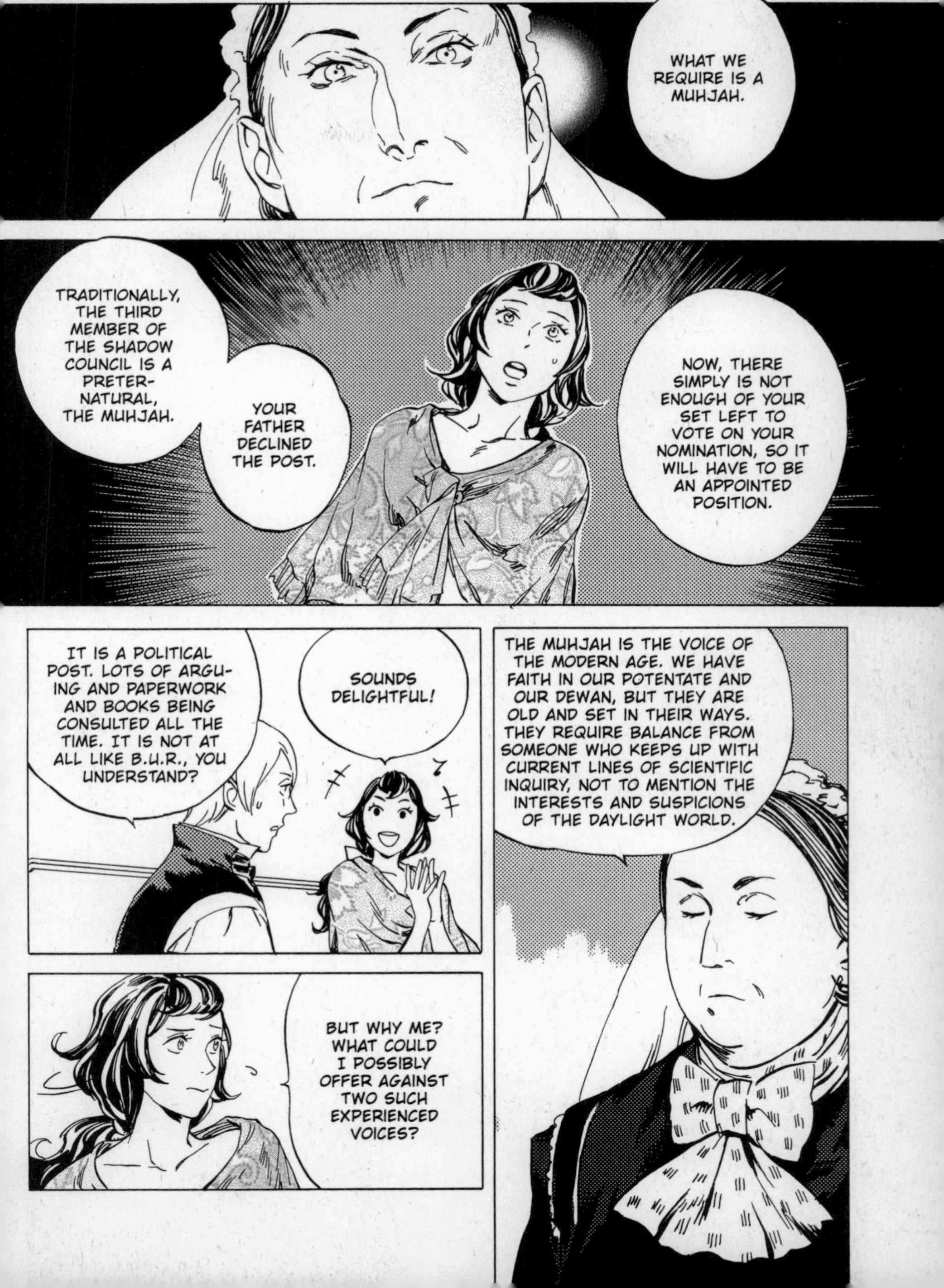
WHAT WE REQUIRE IS A MUHJAH.
TRADITIONALLY, THE THIRD MEMBER OF THE SHADOW COUNCIL IS A PRETER-NATURAL, THE MUHJAH.
YOUR FATHER DECLINED THE POST.
NOW, THERE SIMPLY IS NOT ENOUGH OF YOUR SET LEFT TO VOTE ON YOUR NOMINATION, SO IT WILL HAVE TO BE AN APPOINTED POSITION.
IT IS A POLITICAL POST. LOTS OF ARGUING AND PAPERWORK AND BOOKS BEING CONSULTED ALL THE TIME. IT IS NOT AT ALL LIKE B.U.R., YOU UNDERSTAND?
SOUNDS DELIGHTFUL!
BUT WHY ME? WHAT COULD I POSSIBLY OFFER AGAINST TWO SUCH EXPERIENCED VOICES?
THE MUHJAH IS THE VOICE OF THE MODERN AGE. WE HAVE FAITH IN OUR POTENTATE AND OUR DEWAN, BUT THEY ARE OLD AND SET IN THEIR WAYS. THEY REQUIRE BALANCE FROM SOMEONE WHO KEEPS UP WITH CURRENT LINES OF SCIENTIFIC INQUIRY, NOT TO MENTION THE INTERESTS AND SUSPICIONS OF THE DAYLIGHT WORLD.

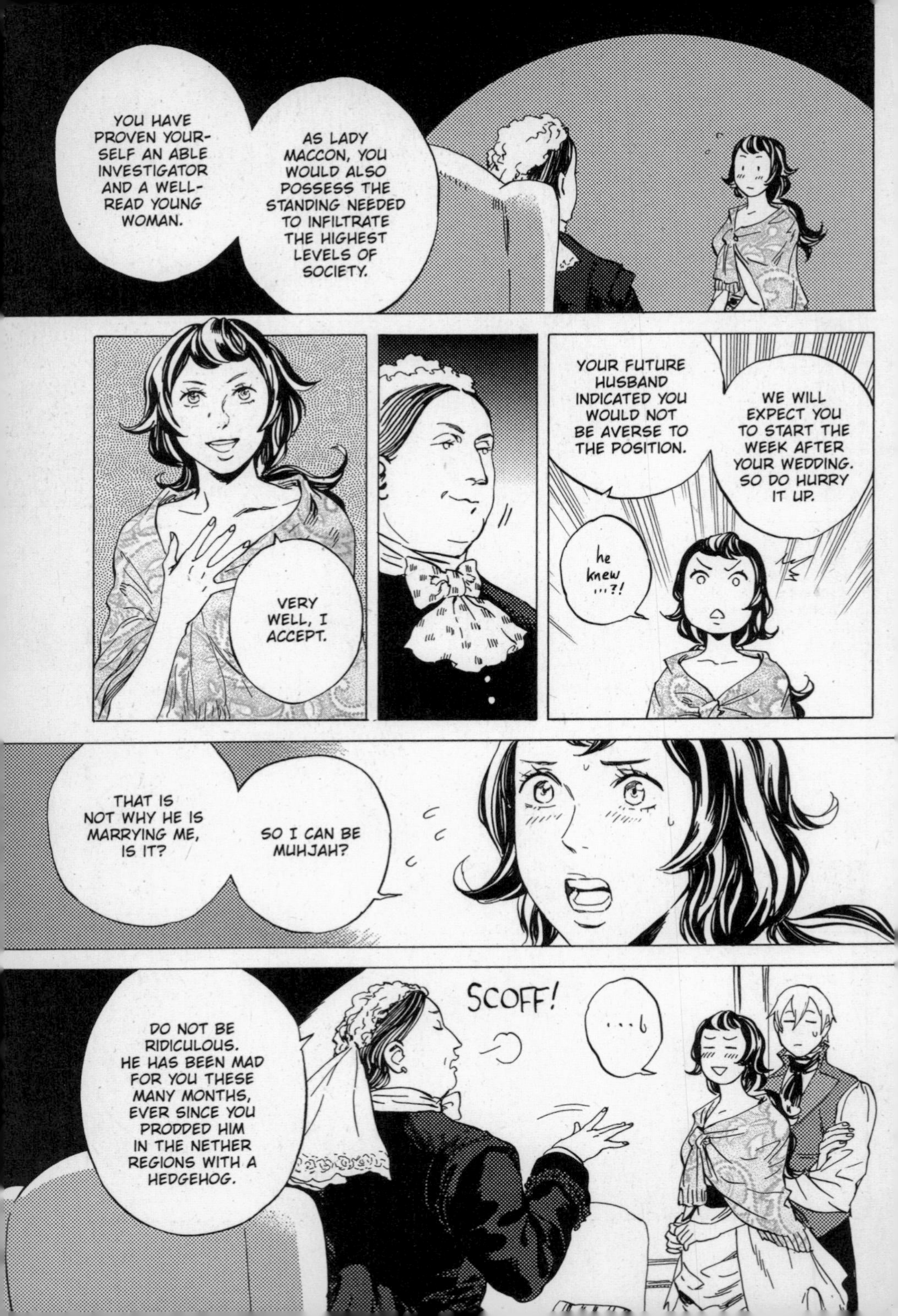

YOU HAVE PROVEN YOURSELF AN ABLE INVESTIGATOR AND A WELL-READ YOUNG WOMAN.
AS LADY MACCON, YOU WOULD ALSO POSSESS THE STANDING NEEDED TO INFILTRATE THE HIGHEST LEVELS OF SOCIETY.
VERY WELL, I ACCEPT.
YOUR FUTURE HUSBAND INDICATED YOU WOULD NOT BE AVERSE TO THE POSITION.
WE WILL EXPECT YOU TO START THE WEEK AFTER YOUR WEDDING. SO DO HURRY IT UP.
he knew ...?!
THAT IS NOT WHY HE IS MARRYING ME, IS IT?
SO I CAN BE MUHJAH?
DO NOT BE RIDICULOUS. HE HAS BEEN MAD FOR YOU THESE MANY MONTHS, EVER SINCE YOU PRODDED HIM IN THE NETHER REGIONS WITH A HEDGEHOG.
SCOFF!
...

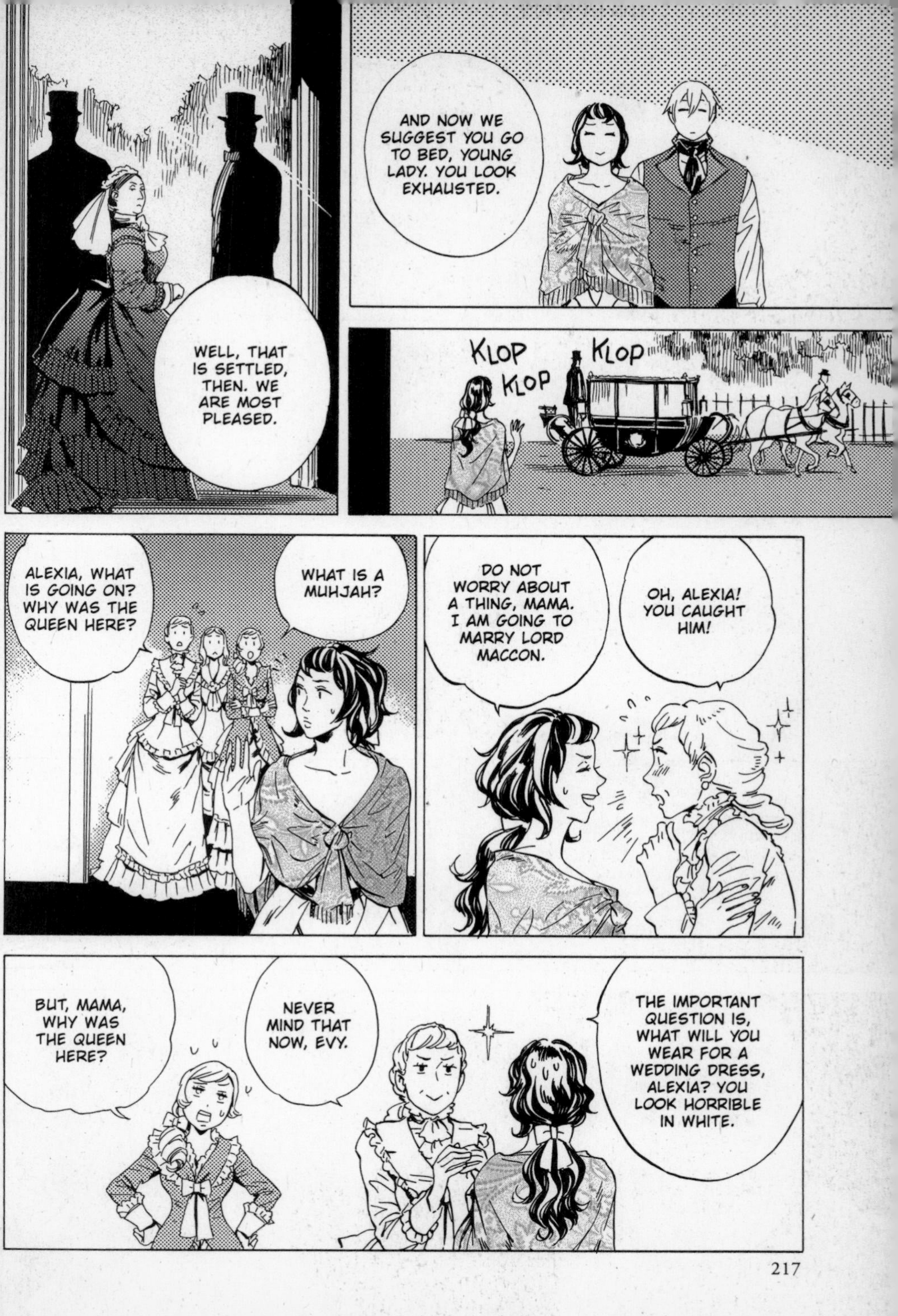
WELL, THAT IS SETTLED, THEN. WE ARE MOST PLEASED.
AND NOW WE SUGGEST YOU GO TO BED, YOUNG LADY. YOU LOOK EXHAUSTED.
KLOP KLOP KLOP
ALEXIA, WHAT IS GOING ON? WHY WAS THE QUEEN HERE?
WHAT IS A MUHJAH?
DO NOT WORRY ABOUT A THING, MAMA. I AM GOING TO MARRY LORD MACCON.
OH, ALEXIA! YOU CAUGHT HIM!
BUT, MAMA, WHY WAS THE QUEEN HERE?
NEVER MIND THAT NOW, EVY.
THE IMPORTANT QUESTION IS, WHAT WILL YOU WEAR FOR A WEDDING DRESS, ALEXIA? YOU LOOK HORRIBLE IN WHITE.

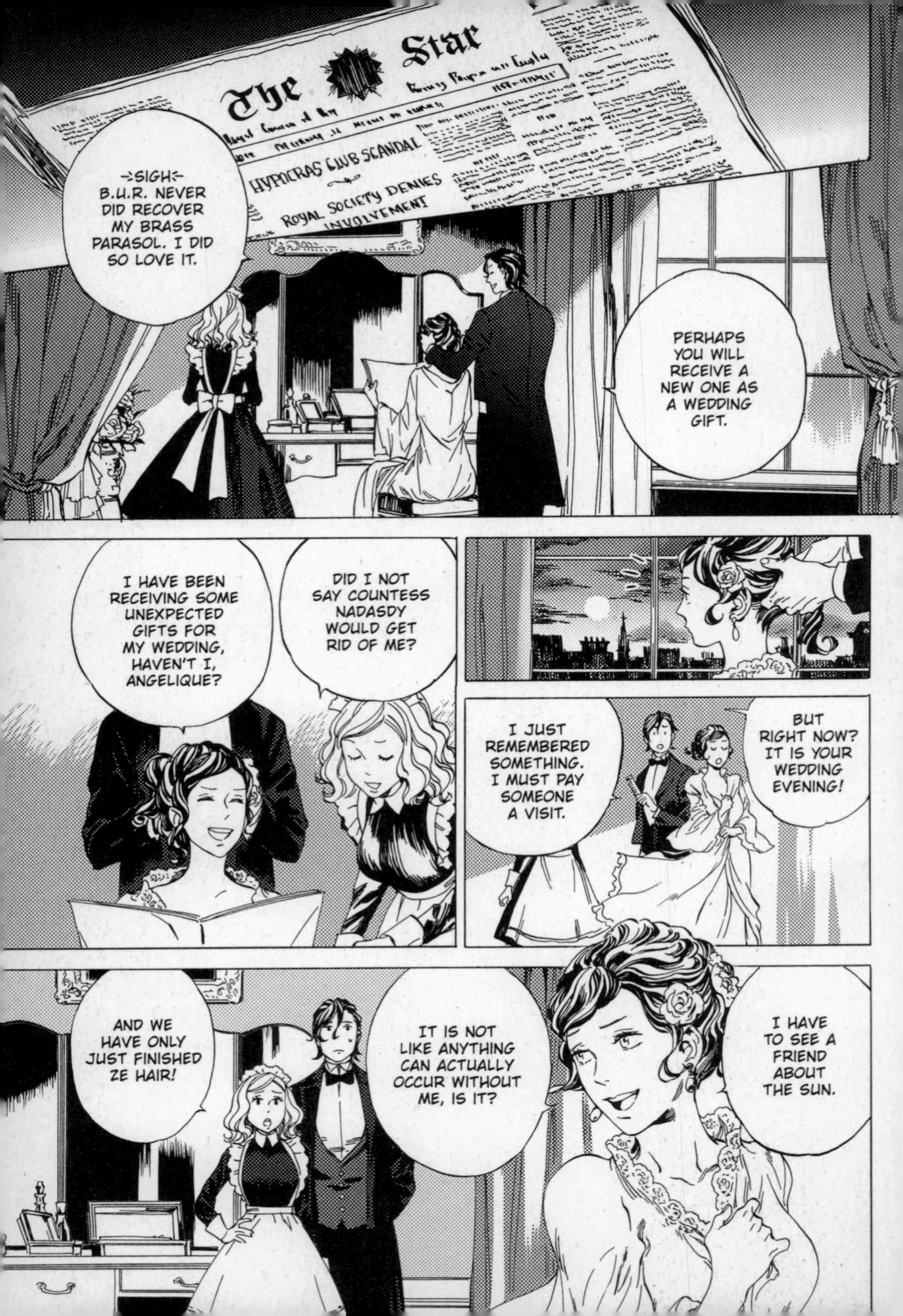
The Star
HYPOCRAS CLUB SCANDAL
ROYAL SOCIETY DENIES INVOLVEMENT
-SIGH- B.U.R. NEVER DID RECOVER MY BRASS PARASOL. I DID SO LOVE IT.
PERHAPS YOU WILL RECEIVE A NEW ONE AS A WEDDING GIFT.
I HAVE BEEN RECEIVING SOME UNEXPECTED GIFTS FOR MY WEDDING, HAVEN'T I, ANGELIQUE?
DID I NOT SAY COUNTESS NADASDY WOULD GET RID OF ME?
I JUST REMEMBERED SOMETHING. I MUST PAY SOMEONE A VISIT.
BUT RIGHT NOW? IT IS YOUR WEDDING EVENING!
AND WE HAVE ONLY JUST FINISHED ZE HAIR!
IT IS NOT LIKE ANYTHING CAN ACTUALLY OCCUR WITHOUT ME, IS IT?
I HAVE TO SEE A FRIEND ABOUT THE SUN.

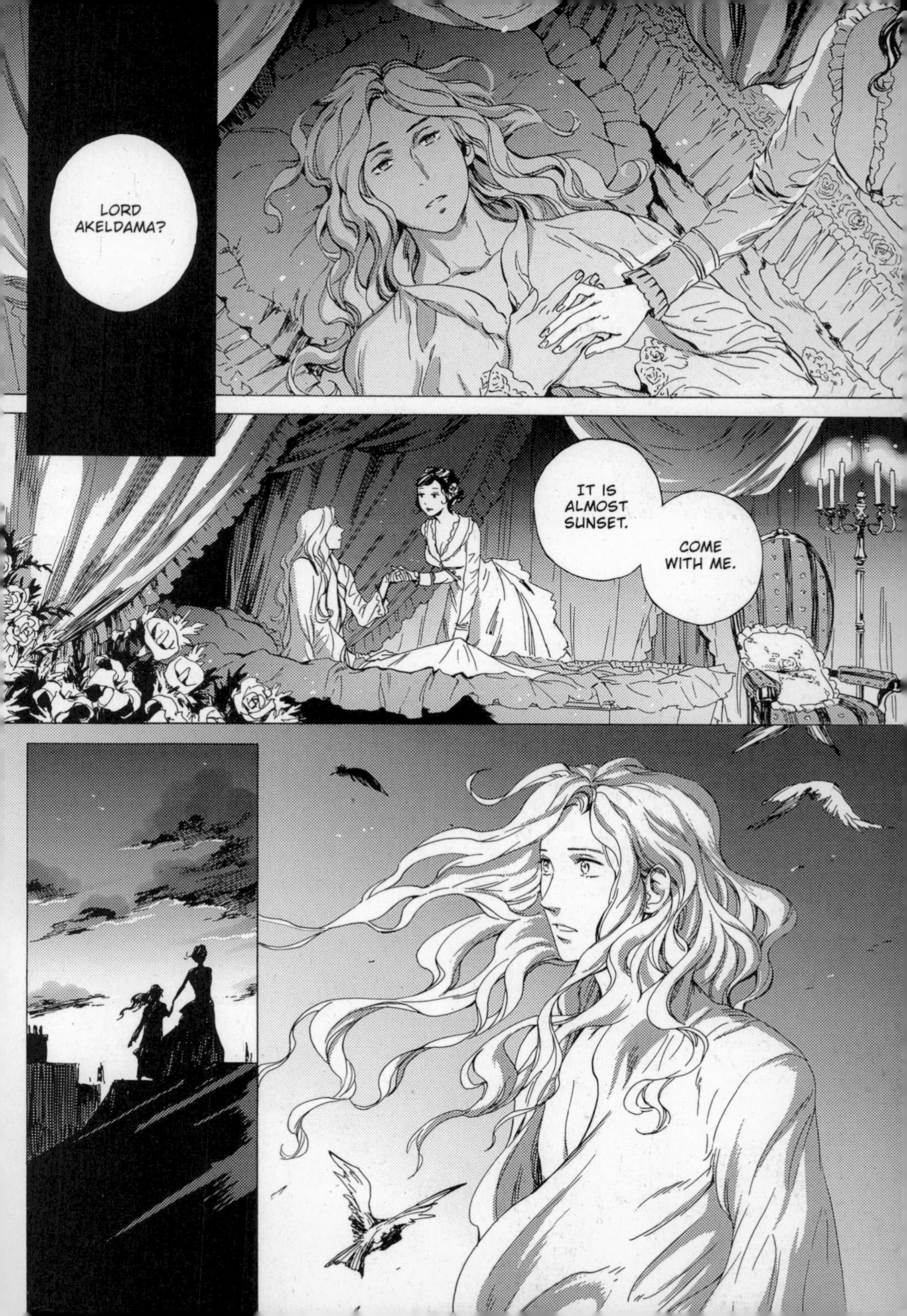
LORD AKELDAMA?
IT IS ALMOST SUNSET.
COME WITH ME.

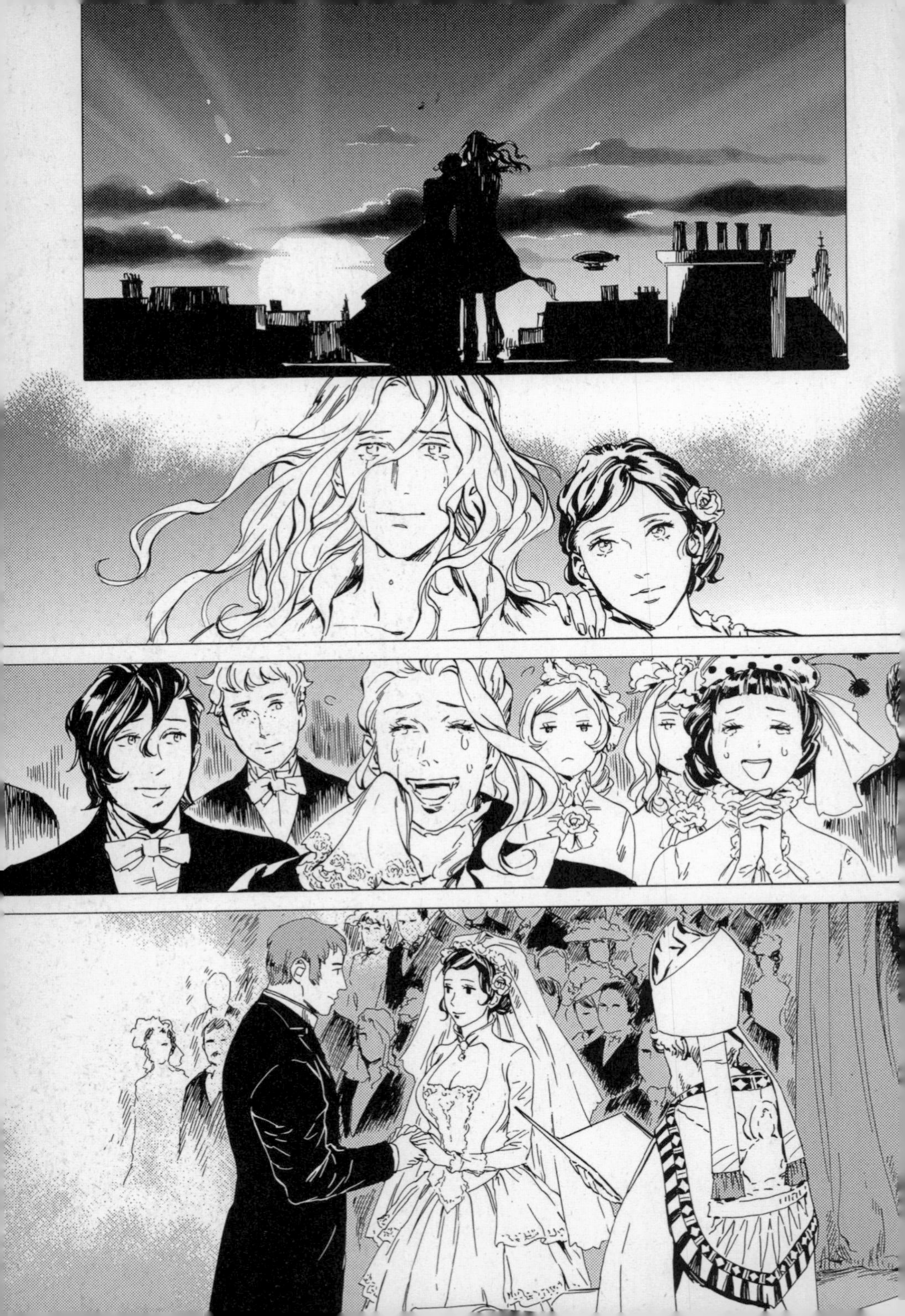

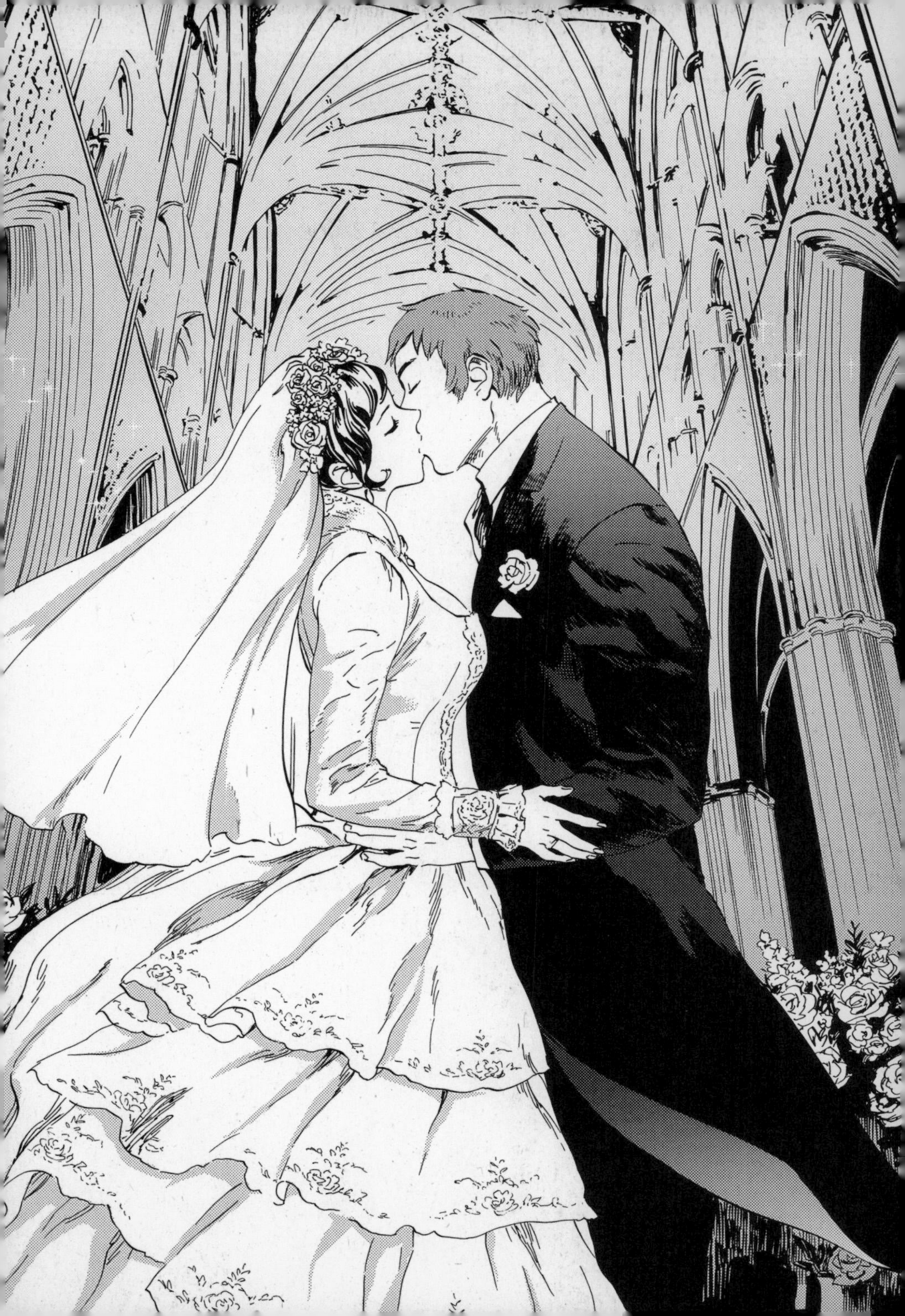

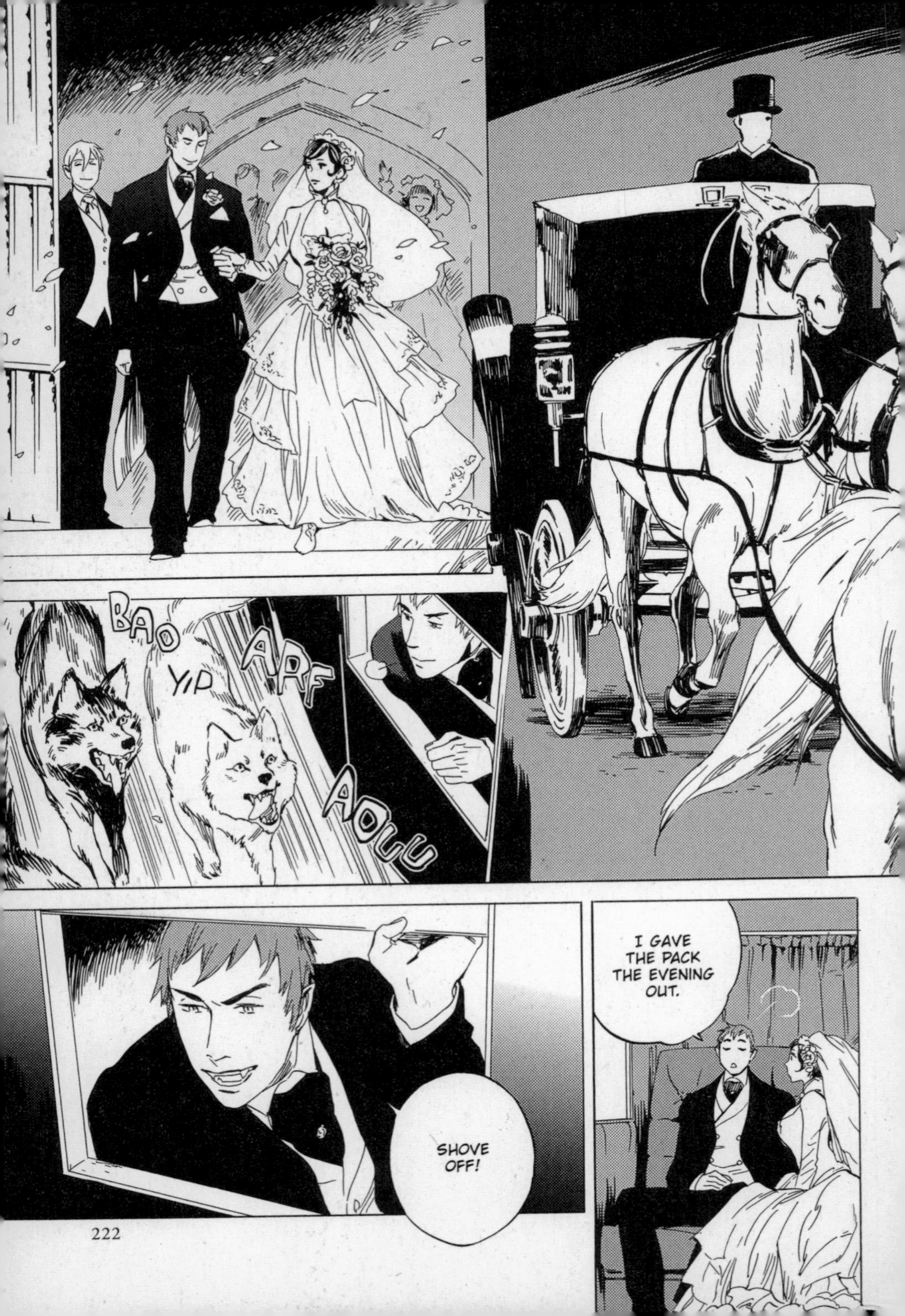
BAO
YIP
ARF
AOUU
SHOVE OFF!
I GAVE THE PACK THE EVENING OUT.

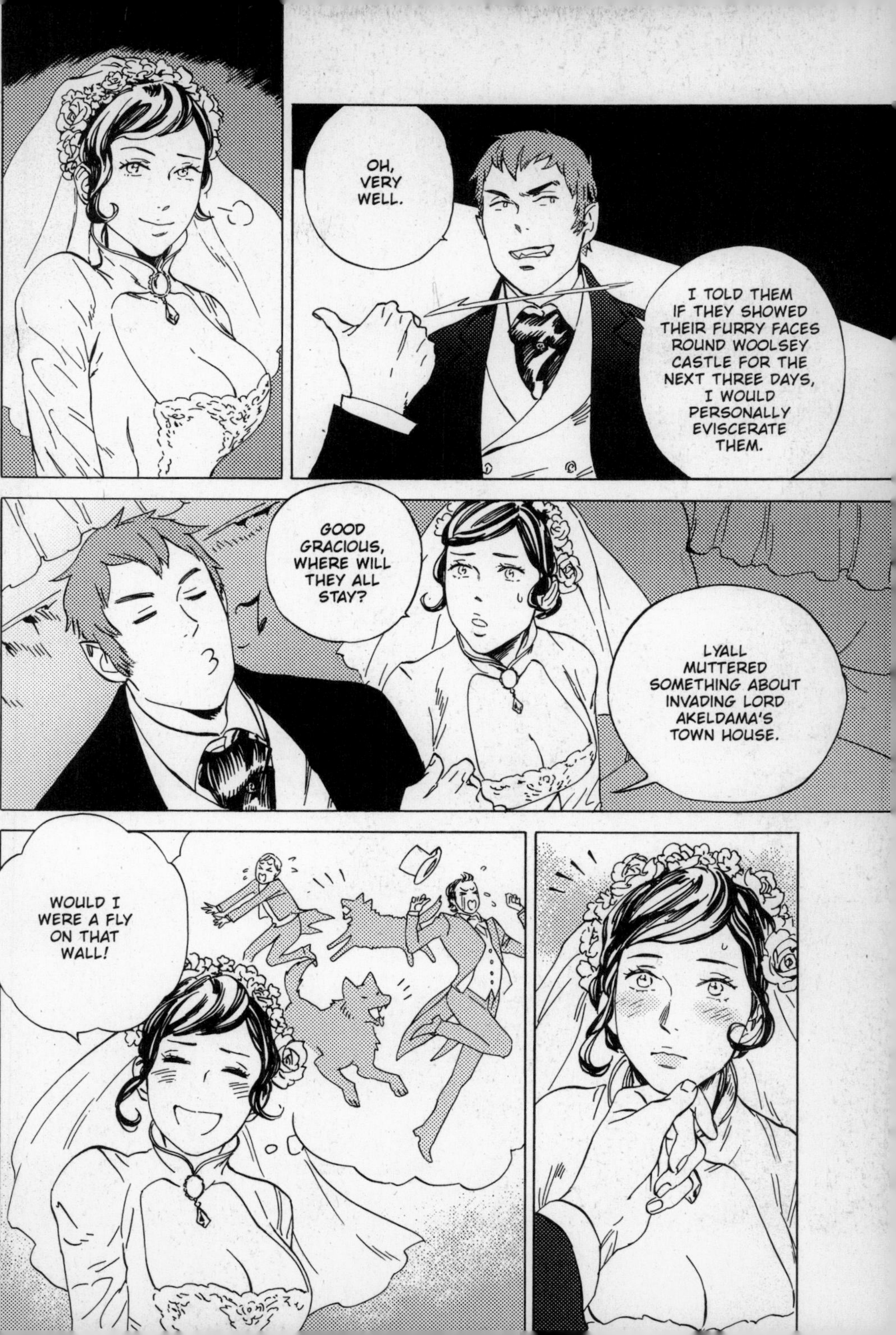
OH, VERY WELL.
I TOLD THEM IF THEY SHOWED THEIR FURRY FACES ROUND WOOLSEY CASTLE FOR THE NEXT THREE DAYS, I WOULD PERSONALLY EVISCERATE THEM.
GOOD GRACIOUS, WHERE WILL THEY ALL STAY?
LYALL MUTTERED SOMETHING ABOUT INVADING LORD AKELDAMA'S TOWN HOUSE.
WOULD I WERE A FLY ON THAT WALL!

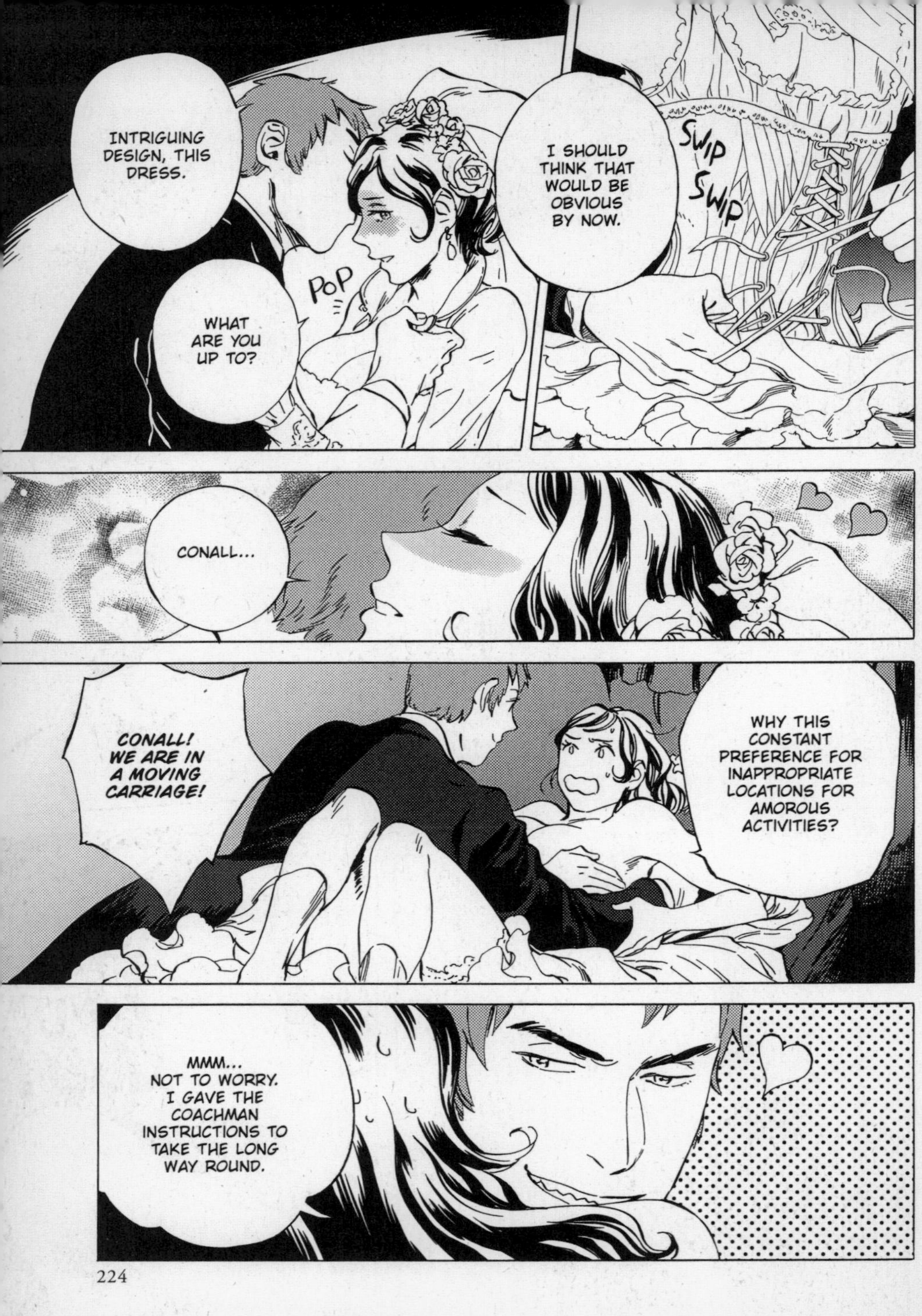
INTRIGUING DESIGN, THIS DRESS.
POP
WHAT ARE YOU UP TO?
I SHOULD THINK THAT WOULD BE OBVIOUS BY NOW.
SWIP SWIP
CONALL...
CONALL! WE ARE IN A MOVING CARRIAGE!
WHY THIS CONSTANT PREFERENCE FOR INAPPROPRIATE LOCATIONS FOR AMOROUS ACTIVITIES?
MMM... NOT TO WORRY. I GAVE THE COACHMAN INSTRUCTIONS TO TAKE THE LONG WAY ROUND.

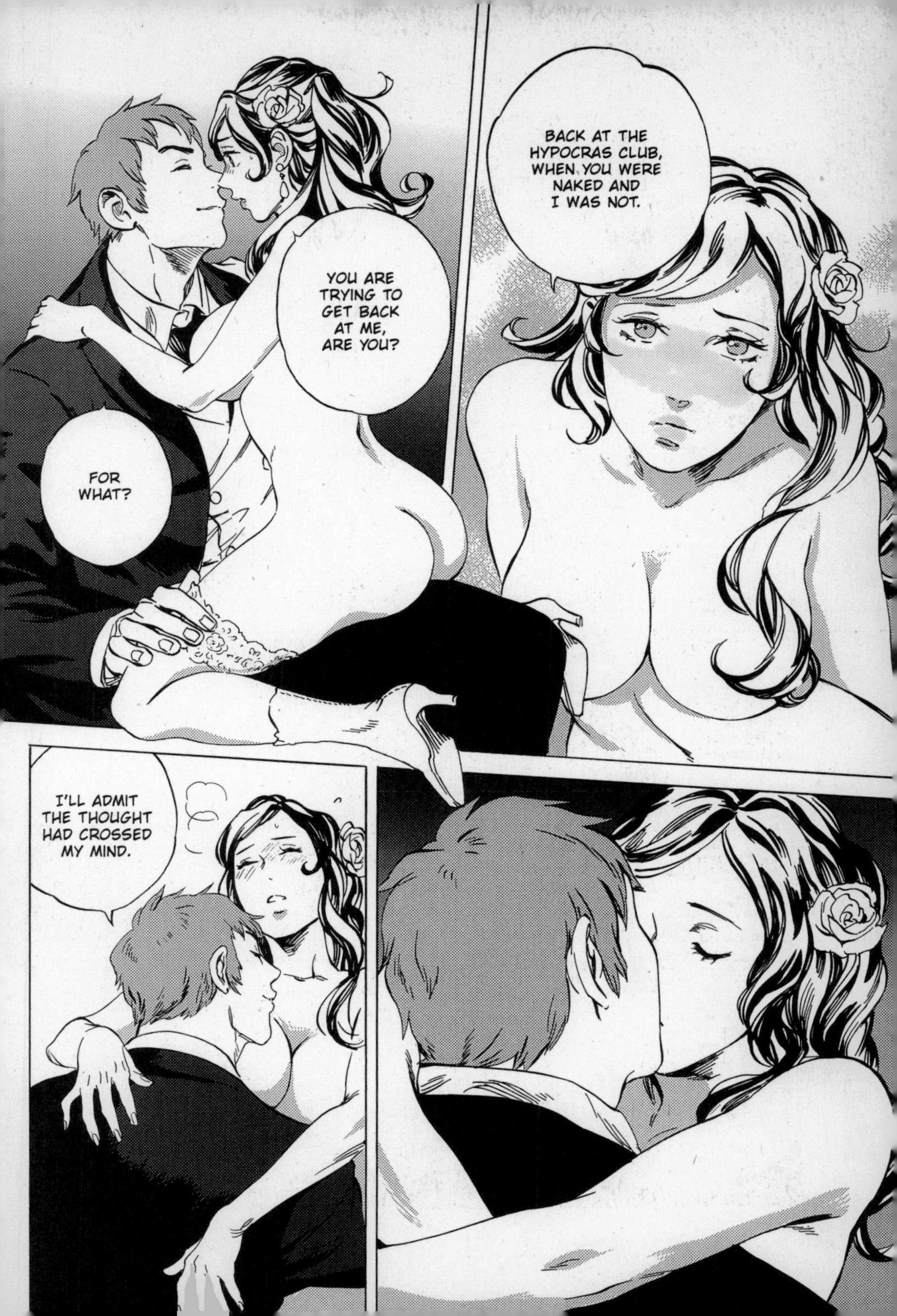
YOU ARE TRYING TO GET BACK AT ME, ARE YOU?
FOR WHAT?
BACK AT THE HYPOCRAS CLUB, WHEN YOU WERE NAKED AND I WAS NOT.
I'LL ADMIT THE THOUGHT HAD CROSSED MY MIND.

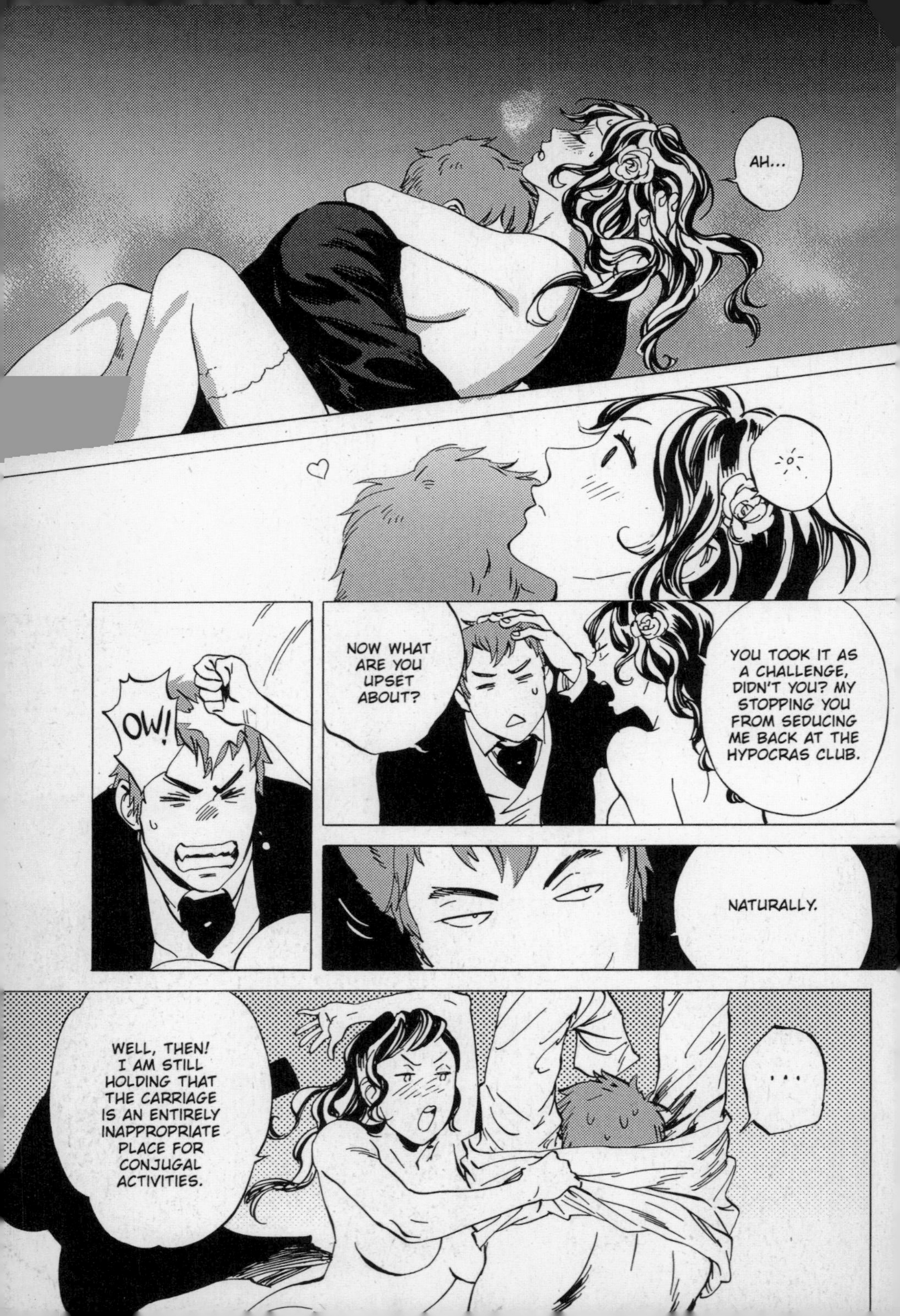
AH...
OW!
NOW WHAT ARE YOU UPSET ABOUT?
YOU TOOK IT AS A CHALLENGE, DIDN'T YOU? MY STOPPING YOU FROM SEDUCING ME BACK AT THE HYPOCRAS CLUB.
NATURALLY.
WELL, THEN! I AM STILL HOLDING THAT THE CARRIAGE IS AN ENTIRELY INAPPROPRIATE PLACE FOR CONJUGAL ACTIVITIES.
...

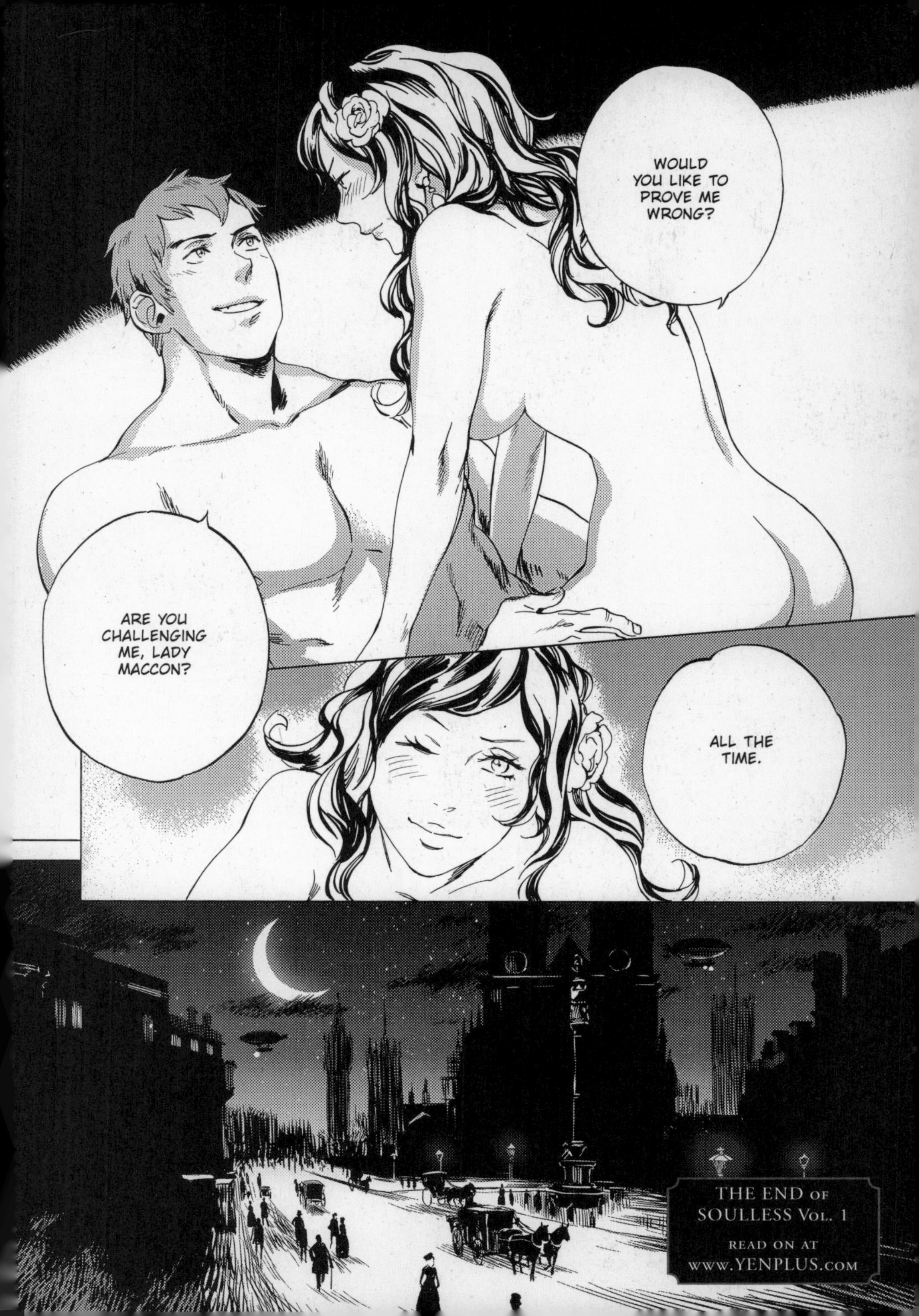
WOULD YOU LIKE TO PROVE ME WRONG?
ARE YOU CHALLENGING ME, LADY MACCON?
ALL THE TIME.
THE END OF SOULLESS VOL. 1
READ ON AT WWW.YENPLUS.COM

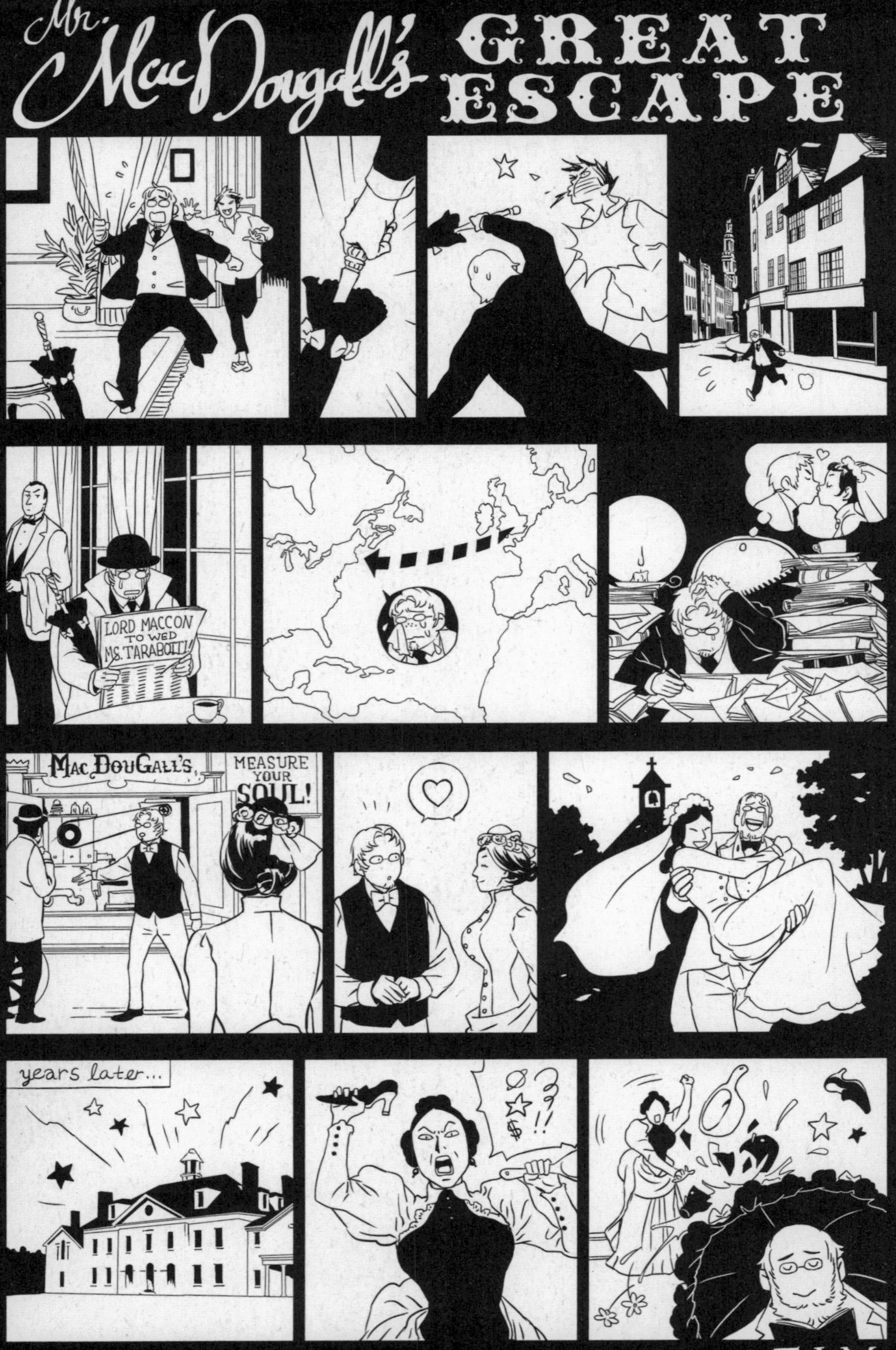
Mr. MacDougall's GREAT ESCAPE
LORD MACCON TO WED MS. TARABOTTI!
MAC DOUGALL'S
MEASURE YOUR SOUL!
years later...
FIN.

SOULLESS: THE MANGA ❶

GAIL CARRIGER
REM

Art and Adaptation: REM

Lettering: JuYoun Lee

SOULLESS: THE MANGA, Vol.1 © 2012 by Tofa Borregaard

Illustrations © Hachette Book Group, Inc.

Yen Press
Hachette Book Group
237 Park Avenue, New York, NY 10017

www.HachetteBookGroup.com
www.YenPress.com

Yen Press is an imprint of Hachette Book Group, Inc. The Yen Press name and logo are trademarks of Hachette Book Group, Inc.

First Yen Press Edition: March 2012

ISBN: 978-0-316-18201-0

10 9 8 7 6 5 4 3

BVG

Printed in the United States of America